Praise for Becky Ward

'Sizzlingly funny and sexy.'
Heat Magazine

'Feel-good and funny!'
Bella Magazine

'Steamy, heart-warming and well-paced . . . the perfect
holiday read.'
The Daily Express

'Heart-warming, unpredictable and filled with passion,
this is the perfect summer read.'
Notebook

'I lived vicariously through this book throughout my
entire read. It was perfect!'
Reader Review, 5 stars

'A feel-good and steamy read with lots of funny
moments.'
Reader Review, 5 stars

'Lots of drama and steamy scenes. This was so good I
stayed up late to finish reading.'
Reader Review, 5 stars

Becky Ward has worked in magazine publishing for over twenty years on titles including *OK!*, *New* and the *Daily Express* supplements. She's had hundreds of travel features, show and restaurant reviews published.

She wrote her first book – a choose-your-own-adventure – at the age of ten and more recently self-published an illustrated children's book to raise money for charity. *Playing the Field* is her second published adult novel following *The Dance Deception*.

Playing the Field

BECKY WARD

avon.

Published by AVON
A division of HarperCollinsPublishers
1 London Bridge Street
London SE1 9GF

www.harpercollins.co.uk

HarperCollinsPublishers
Macken House
39/40 Mayor Street Upper
Dublin 1
D01 C9W8

A Paperback Original 2024
2
First published in Great Britain by HarperCollinsPublishers 2024

A catalogue copy of this book is available from the British Library.

ISBN: 978-0-00-869755-6

Typeset in Sabon Lt Pro by HarperCollins*Publishers* India

Printed and bound in the UK using 100%
Renewable Electricity at CPI Group (UK) Ltd

MIX
Paper | Supporting
responsible forestry
FSC™ C007454

This book contains FSC™ certified paper and other controlled sources to ensure responsible forest management.

For more information visit: www.harpercollins.co.uk/green

Prologue

Strike out!

Millford City striker Ben Pryce's footballing future is hanging in the balance following an altercation with a fan earlier today.

The 22-year-old, who was on target to be the top goal scorer in the Premier League after his hat trick against Barcombe last Saturday, was sent off the pitch sixteen minutes before the end of City's clash against Hamcott Park after a heated exchange with one of the away team's supporters.

It's not yet known what sparked the incident, but the Hamcott fan is thought to have made derogatory comments as Pryce lined up the corner kick that could have propelled Millford City to yet another victory. Pryce was immediately shown the red card and left the pitch to boos from the visitors' stand.

Although there has been no further comment from the Millford camp, a source tells us Pryce is now facing a six-match suspension and a hefty fine for poor conduct. This means he will miss Millford City's three remaining matches, giving rival strikers Harry Fuller and Frank Headingly, from Walthorp Town and East Hedgely respectively, the chance to overtake his 26-goal tally.

He will also be forced to sit on the bench for the first three games of the next season, which, after his recent spout of bad behaviour on the pitch, raises big questions about his future at the club he's played for since he was 19.

'If they can get decent results without him in these upcoming games, they might start wondering if they can do without him,' pundit Owen Smith warned on Channel Six's *Top Goals*. 'For a club looking to streamline its spending, they've got to be looking at their more expensive players and thinking about who they can afford to lose. And when you have a highly paid player like Ben who isn't even on the pitch, making that cut might seem like a no-brainer.'

Hamcott Park has been facing its own financial woes, with the current owners close to finalising a deal that will see their home ground sold to property developers and the club relocated to cheaper premises more than 60 miles away. Chairman Karl Steadman has been accused of treating it as a business primarily and only a football club after that, but the Hamcott Park fans' desperate pleas for a last-minute change of heart have gone unheard.

Pryce has been one of Millford City's star players since he joined the club three years ago, helping to keep them well away from the relegation zone for three consecutive seasons thanks to his impressive goal tally. But only time will tell whether we see him back in the squad or if his career there has reached its final whistle.

1

'I know it's been on the cards for months, but I still can't believe it's actually come to this,' my dad says, his voice heavy with defeat as he sits at our kitchen table, staring at the message on the screen of his mobile phone. I can count the number of times I've seen him this despondent on one hand – and right now is one of the worst.

But I know why he's so downhearted – because I've been sent the same message. Thanks to a combination of greed and poor management, our beloved football club has ignored the protests of all its fans and confirmed it will be relocating to a stadium sixty-three miles away. Which means many of the fans who, like him, have loyally supported the club through good times and bad for most of their lives will no longer be able to go to the home matches.

And the fact that this devastating news has come on the back of a humiliating defeat yesterday to a team that didn't even have all eleven players after their striker was sent off – for assaulting a fan of all things! – makes it an even more bitter pill to swallow.

'After everything we did,' Dad sighs.

We attended every consultation, replied to every email designed to make us feel like our voices matter, even stood through a whole match with our backs to the action, wearing T-shirts with 'Keep Hamcott Park in Hamcott' on the back, but to no avail. The eleventh-hour U-turn we were all praying for never came. The final confirmation has just been posted on the club website and emailed to fans.

'I don't mind doing the drive,' I tell him, trying to find a way to make things better. 'I know it will mean not having a beer in the pub beforehand and probably getting stuck in rush hour traffic on the way home, but we can still go. Lots of people can't. In some ways we're the lucky ones.'

But we both know it won't be the same. Not without the shouty bloke two rows in front who thinks he knows more about the offside rule than the referee. Or the old guy in front of him, who shuffles in on walking sticks every Saturday and promptly falls asleep, often only waking up in time to see the last ten minutes of the match. It will mean our club's fans will make up a smaller proportion of the crowd than the away fans even at our so-called home matches. It will be like every game is an away game.

'Bob and Marge will no doubt be happy to squeeze into my back seat,' I say to Dad, still trying to find a silver lining. They're the couple who've sat next to us for the last twenty years, ever since the very first game Dad took me and my sister Cassie to when we were four and six – old enough to properly appreciate it. Thinking about all those happy afternoons at Hamcott Park now, I can't even begin to imagine the roar of the fans not being a regular fixture in my life.

And there's another reason why this is such a blow. When I was eleven, my sister thirteen, my mum left my dad, leaving us all heartbroken. At that age it was so hard to understand why she would want to go and live on her own in a tiny village in rural Cornwall and not stay in the hustle and bustle of Hamcott. The truth is, she found Dad's love of dinner parties and socialising exhausting and desperately craved a more peaceful existence.

Cassie and I could have gone with her, but we chose to stay with Dad. Neither of us wanted to change schools, lose our friends or live in the middle of nowhere. We'd see Mum in the holidays and she promised to call us every day. Dad, meanwhile, put on a brave face and tried to keep our lives as normal as possible, and a big part of that was making sure we still went to see Hamcott Park as a family every Saturday.

It was good for me and Cassie, but I think it was even more important for Dad. Bob and Marge, among others, rallied round to help him bring up his two headstrong teenage daughters. They became like an aunt and uncle to me and Cassie, and having their support meant everything to Dad. Still does, in fact. So I know he'll be fretting that things won't be the same any more, even if Cassie and I are grown-ups now.

I look around the spacious rustic kitchen that was the main reason Dad insisted he and Mum bought this house, where I still live with him. How many Saturday afternoons after a home match have an assortment of people found their way back here, knowing Dad will have something tasty ready to heat up and share while the latest game is discussed at length? And then I think of our pre-match hangout, The Fox, where a crowd of Hamcott fans congregate for a pub lunch and a pint every other week. Will it now lose all that business?

Dad frowns at the kitchen cupboards behind me, disappointment rolling off him in waves. I hate seeing the wind sucked out of his sails like this. He's one of those people who never wants anyone to see him having a down day, but today there's just no hiding it.

But Dad being Dad, I should have known he wouldn't let this keep him down for long. We've never been a family to just roll over and give up. So just as I'm about to remind him we fought as hard as we could to prevent this from happening, he slaps the table and pushes himself to his feet, his chair scraping back across the mottled tiles. 'This isn't the end of this,' he says, his voice full of determination.

And I nod. 'There are still two more home matches before the season wraps. We can still make the most of them.'

He turns his gaze to me and says, 'That's not what I mean.' And it's almost like I can see the fire light up again behind his eyes. 'Footballers come and go – we all know that,' he says. 'We've seen countless players move on to other clubs or go out with an injury over the years. But the one thing that has never changed in this club is its heart. So all we really need to do is to let these players go, but keep that heart pumping.'

'What are you talking about, Dad?'

'We'll let them go.' His eyes are positively sparkling now. 'And we'll start a brand new club. One that's run for the fans, like it used to be. Like it should be.'

It's my turn to frown. 'We, as in us? Me and you?'

He nods vigorously. 'And Cassie. You've got a business degree. You can look after the money side of things. Your sister's a coach. She can train the players.'

I stare at him in disbelief – he can't seriously be suggesting this. My sister coaches a group of eleven- and twelve-year-olds on Saturday afternoons and I haven't even finished my degree yet. My final exams are still two months away. Plus I'd been planning to spend a couple of months loafing around Europe with my boyfriend before looking for my first job, and Cassie is busy doing up her new house with her fiancé.

Dad may have some managerial experience, but it's certainly not in a sporting environment – he helps run a local coach and minibus hire company. In short, we might know how to support a football team, but we're in no position to start a new one.

But because I don't want to burst Dad's bubble, I humour him when he requests I grab my laptop, so we can start making a list of the things we'd need to make this happen. 'Players, kit, a manager, a team name,' he says, counting them off on his fingers.

And a spark of excitement bubbles up deep inside me, because football is such a massive part of our lives that it's hard to imagine what Saturdays might look like without it. I've had posters of my favourite players up on my wall since I was in primary school and, if I'm honest, my decision to go to a London university was only partly so I could live at home and save on rent – I also wanted to be close enough to Hamcott Park that I could still go to all our home matches.

It's quickly followed by a reality check, though, when

the list expands to include a training schedule, pitch, referees . . . There's no way Dad can start up a whole new football club from scratch with absolutely zero experience beyond playing for his university team thirty years ago, with only me and my sister to support him. I don't know what briefly made me think he could. Especially when he's proposing to have it up and running in time for the new season at the start of August. It's mid-April. That would give us less than four months.

But it turns out I underestimate all three of us that day. Although I don't know it then, that's the day Crawford United is born.

2

Dad's first move is to meet with Bob and a few other Hamcott Park fans at The Fox to put the idea of a new club to them – and the support for it is unanimous. They all know we'll have to start at the very bottom of the football pyramid, going from crowds of thousands to probably one or two hundred, with amateur players rather than pros and grounds that are more likely to have hay bales than stands, a coffee shack if you're lucky. But foolishly or otherwise, they all share the belief that with a lot of hard work and determination Dad, Cassie and I can build a new club that will eventually make its way up through the ranks. Every team had to start somewhere, right?

Before last orders have been called, Dad has declared himself the new club's acting manager and his plan is underway.

Things move unexpectedly quickly after that. As assistant manager I'm tasked with designing and printing off hundreds of flyers that we can hand out at the last two home games to any Hamcott fans who aren't boycotting them, to alert them to our plan and let them know how they can help. Namely through donations. It's a shame we can't put the word out on the Hamcott Park fan site, but aside from not having access to it, they're not about to let us try to lure their supporters away to a new club.

Not lacking in confidence, my sister is fully on board with the idea of coaching the players, once we find them. She did a five-day Football Association Introduction to Coaching course before teaching her Saturday Kickers club and she's adamant she can make the transition to teaching older players at a higher level. She's sport-obsessed and teaches PE in a local school, so she's convinced she has both the physical fitness and authority she'll need for the job. I can't help thinking she'll be amazing.

When it comes to approaching our local County Football Association to get approval for the new team, Dad is more than happy to be the one to get the ball rolling. Between us we also produce a more comprehensive list of running costs. There'll be nets and balls and an FA-approved first-aid kit to buy, we'll need liability and injury insurance for the players, there'll be travel expenses for away games . . .

For the next few days, a new book on football management or setting up a new business arrives from Amazon almost daily – which makes a change from the Alasdair Frowley thrillers Dad is usually ploughing his way through – and Dad throws himself into his research, spending every spare moment poring over the pages of his growing library. I can't help but be swept along by his enthusiasm. A lot of what I've learned on my business studies course will come in useful, but increasingly I find myself pushing my university work aside and reading about team building and match strategy instead.

Had Mum still been around, the unruly tower of books taking over the living room would have driven her crazy, along with the number of people popping round to see where they can help out with the club set-up, but Dad just leaves the back door unlocked so Cassie, Bob, Marge and a few others can come and go as they please.

Bob and Marge's son Adam, who's training to be a web designer, volunteers to pull together a website – no bells and whistles, just setting out the basic ambitions for the club, with details of how to get in touch and pledge support. Marge sets about compiling a list of local schools and sports centres that have pitches we might be able to use for training. I collate a list of rival teams we can approach to discuss the possibility of a ground share.

The nearest ground, the home of Redmarsh Rovers, would be our top choice as it's the easiest to get to from Hamcott – although with a capacity of four thousand, it might be beyond our means. Southmoor also has potential and I'll be contacting every other ground that isn't prohibitively far away too. But Redmarsh is the one we really want.

Meanwhile, Cassie starts trying to find us some players. A couple of the kids she coaches have older brothers who might fit the bill. She also puts notices out on local Facebook groups, spends a few evenings hanging out by the five-a-side pitches in the local park and persuades some of the gyms in our area to put an ad up in their reception areas – anything to spread the word.

'Let's hold player trials on the first weekend after Hamcott's last home game,' Dad suggests at our first official kitchen table meeting, even though we don't know whether our new club application will even be approved yet. We've all decided to optimistically work on the assumption that it will be, which means we can't waste any time if we're going to be ready for the start of the new season.

'We can do it at the West Street Rec,' Cassie suggests. 'It's never that busy there.'

'Good plan.' He adds it to his notes. 'Any updates on the financial side, Lily?'

As well as producing the flyers, I'm learning everything I can about fundraising. While we're all happy to pitch in and do whatever we can to help establish the team, we all know money will have to change hands down the line. We still don't have an entirely accurate idea of how much. So much of it will come down to the cost of the ground-share lease – and our newly learned negotiation skills.

'We're not eligible for a Sport England grant, sadly, but I'm setting up a GoFundMe page for anyone who wants to make a donation to help us get up and running. I'm still reading up on how best to attract investments from local businesses.'

'Keep up the good work,' Dad says.

I don't want to put a dampener on proceedings by sharing the alarming statistic I've discovered that more than three thousand fledgling football clubs have folded in the last fifteen years and it's almost always down to money. I just tell myself it doesn't mean we'll be one of them.

Then we move on to what I think is everyone's favourite moment in this whirlwind of a first week – it's time to select our new club's official kit colour, logo and team name. Bob, Marge and Adam have joined us to help brainstorm ideas. I can't wait to see what everyone comes up with.

Dad puts three bowls in the middle of the table marked with the three categories and gives everyone a pen and some scraps of paper so we can write down all our ideas and put them in the corresponding bowls. We'll put it to a vote at the end. He then dishes up a giant pan of spaghetti Bolognese and pours everyone a hefty glass of red wine.

'And remember, the more suggestions the merrier,' he says, with a beaming smile. I'll never get tired of seeing how happy nights like this make him.

The Bolognese is devoured in virtual silence, punctuated only by the sound of forks hitting china and pens tapping and scribbling. And it's not long before the plates and cutlery have been cleared away ready for the big reveal.

'First up, it's the club name,' Dad announces, rifling through the slips of paper in the bottom of the bowl. 'There looks to be around thirty suggestions, so in no particular order . . . Mike Crawford United.' He shoots us all a withering look. 'We are *not* naming the club after me. That would make me look like a right pillock.'

'I think it's a nice idea,' Marge says. I suspect it's one of hers.

'Absolutely not,' Dad says, starting a reject pile then picking up another slip of paper. But he's even less enamoured of the next proposal. 'Magic Mike's Merry

Men? Come on, you lot, these are meant to be serious. Who put that in there?'

Adam raises a sheepish hand.

'It's very flattering,' Dad concedes. 'But I don't think anyone . . .'

'If we drop the Mike part, I think Crawford United has a certain ring to it,' Bob interrupts. Which gets the rest of us thinking. A quick search on my phone and I confirm it doesn't already exist elsewhere.

'I actually don't mind it,' Cassie says.

'It works for me,' Marge chips in.

Dad rolls his eyes and moves the paper into a maybe pile with a sigh. 'Okay, fine, but let's see what else we've got before anyone gets too excited.'

It turns out there are three other Mike-related names, but Dad won't be swayed from adding these ones to the reject pile. I'd be willing to bet he's a tiny bit embarrassed, even if he appreciates the sentiment.

Hamcott appears in the majority of other suggestions – there's Hamcott United, Hamcott Rangers, plus a Wanderers, a Warriors and a Hamcott Blues. Dad adds them to the maybe pile, but even though two of them came from me, I didn't propose either with confidence. Because as nice as this nod to our neighbourhood would be, I wouldn't want us to ever be confused with our predecessors.

The final two submissions are inspired by our street name – Queens Avenue United – and the name of the local recreation ground, West Street Park FC. Both join the other maybes.

'Okay, time to vote,' Dad says, and he starts reading from the top of the pile.

Cassie puts her hand up for West Street Park. As it's where the player tryouts will be held, she says, it will have some historic meaning. Dad raises his for the Hamcott Blues – until Bob points out that Hamcott Park play in blue, so that could get confusing. It's not until Dad reads out Crawford United that the rest of us shoot our hands into the air.

'That's decided then,' Marge says triumphantly, leaving Dad momentarily speechless.

'Are you sure it doesn't feel too self-indulgent?' he asks eventually.

'I think it's the perfect nod to the founders of the club,' she says. 'All three of you.'

Dad turns to Cassie, the only other person who voted for something different, but she smiles and says, 'It's already grown on me.'

'Crawford United,' Dad says, like he's trying it out for size. 'Crawford United . . .'

'To Crawford United!' Bob bellows, holding his glass aloft. 'Long may it last and successful may it be!'

And finally, Dad laughs and clinks his glass against Bob's. 'Okay, okay, you lot win. It looks like we've got ourselves a club name.'

'There's only one Mikey Crawford,' Marge sings quietly.

'Oh, stop it,' Dad says, turning pink.

Next up, it's the kit colour, and our proposals range from lime and navy stripes to orange and burgundy. It's only my proposal of straight purple that throws in a curveball.

'Just purple?' Dad says. 'Whose suggestion was this?'

I raise my hand.

'Any particular reason?' he asks.

I shrug. 'It's my favourite colour.'

Dad runs his hand over his stubble while he contemplates it. Then he nods and says, 'I can picture it with white shorts. A kind of Cadbury purple. What do the rest of you think?'

'I'm on board.' Cassie is first to respond. 'It's nice and a bit different.'

'I like it too,' Marge says.

Another vote follows, at the end of which purple has a clear lead. I drum my feet on the floor under the table.

'We're a bit short on logo ideas,' Dad says, peering into the final bowl. 'There are only five pieces of paper.'

He scoops them up in one hand. 'We have a standard shield, I think this one is meant to be a foot kicking a ball, this one just says goalposts, we've got a fork—'

'It's a trident,' Marge corrects. 'To represent the three founding members again.'

'I think Manchester United might have something to say about that,' Adam points out.

Dad nods his agreement and adds that one to the 'no' pile. Then he squints at the last piece of paper in his hand. 'Well, we definitely don't have any artists among us, but last but not least, I think we have an owl.'

'It's a phoenix,' Bob corrects. 'You know, because we're rising from the ashes.'

Cassie, Marge, Adam and I shoot our hands up into the air before Dad can even start the vote.

'I think that's unanimous,' Bob says.

'Provided we get someone else to draw it,' Dad says, laughing.

And that's all the important decisions out of the way, so Dad thanks everyone for their contributions.

'I'm so grateful to have you all here on this journey with me,' he says warmly. 'We're now another step closer to making this happen.'

3

Unsurprisingly there isn't the same level of positivity in the air at Hamcott Park's penultimate home game of the season. In fact I'd go so far as to say the atmosphere is borderline funereal. The fans who haven't already given up on the club – which is probably around half of them – are engulfed in a fog of gloom. I think everyone is emotionally exhausted from the weeks of praying for a reversal of fate and the realisation, finally, that nothing can stop the relocation.

But for me, Dad, Cassie, Bob and Marge there is this new hope – hope that we're on the way to achieving something really special. And we're ready to share that hope, so we skip our pre-match lunch at The Fox and instead spread out along the road leading up to the ground so we can hand out flyers to anyone who will take one, briefly explaining our plan and letting them know how they can support us.

I never let the smile leave my face, even when one fan asks, 'You really believe in this?'

'I do.' I beam. 'We're working really hard and all the signs are positive so far.'

This just gets a 'hm' in response, but I refuse to let it dampen my spirits.

'Tell all your friends,' I call after him.

At least he stuffs the piece of paper in his pocket and doesn't toss it away.

By the time I meet the others in the stand, ready to watch the match in the half-empty stadium, I've got through about a third of my flyers. I pass a little bundle to the person on the end of each row and ask them to take one and pass the rest along. I don't know far they'll get before someone just bungs the rest under their seat. In hindsight, I wish I'd put 'win a season ticket' across the top instead of 'Hamcott: the new era' – it might have got people's attention more effectively. I make a mental note to do that ahead of the last home game. It's all a learning curve.

The crowd celebration is lacklustre when Hamcott Park scrape their way to a win. Everyone knows it's not going to change anything. Then Dad, Cassie, Bob, Marge and I race down to the exit with our remaining flyers and try to persuade as many of the departing fans as possible to give our pamphlet a glance. I'm not ashamed to admit we even fish a few discarded sheets out of the top of a rubbish bin and hand them back out too.

'You did make sure the email address works,' Dad checks for probably the twentieth time after the last of the fans have departed.

'It works,' I assure him. 'People can get in touch.'

He takes a deep breath and exhales heavily, seeming momentarily unsure what to do now our whirlwind of an afternoon has ended.

'Come on, let's go and get a pint,' Bob suggests. 'I think we've earned it.'

Marge nods. 'I'm parched. We did good today, Mikey.'

A screwed-up flyer chooses that exact moment to blow past our feet and continue on its way up the street. All four of us watch it go. We knew a number of them would get ditched by people who haven't even glanced at them, but it's hard not to feel a little disheartened by it.

'People just need a bit of time to mull it over, that's all,' Cassie says quietly.

'Some of them thought I was downright bonkers,' Marge admits.

'That was nothing to do with the flyers though, was it, love?' Bob teases, which lightens the mood again.

We turn towards The Fox and slip into our usual routine of analysing the match we've just seen – who played well, who we think should be benched, who we'd like the club to buy if it had unlimited funds.

'I hear Ben Pryce might be out of contract soon,' Marge says.

'Too controversial,' Bob replies. 'I think a lot of clubs will steer clear of him after his suspension, even if he is one of the best strikers in the Premier League. They won't want to risk their reputations.'

'And it's not like he wasn't creating waves even before that,' I point out. 'He must have been carded, what, four times this season for overreacting after a foul. And not even when it was him being fouled. It must drive his teammates mad.'

'Then he'll probably be cheap,' Marge says. 'But it's not going to kill his career. If Cantona managed to come back from that karate kick all those years ago, I can't see any team blacklisting Pryce, even if he won't talk about what happened at the Hamcott game. Everyone deserves a second chance.'

'True, plus it's not like Lionel Messi's about to come knocking at our door,' Dad says.

'I still think we'd be better off with someone like Kyle Robertson,' Cassie insists.

'He couldn't dribble his way out of our backyard!' Marge snorts.

And so it goes on.

When we arrive at The Fox, the landlord, Olly, greets us warmly and agrees to leave our last few remaining leaflets in a pile on the bar.

'I'm a bit busy now, but I look forward to hearing more about this,' he says, which puts a smile on Dad's face.

And it gets even broader when one of the regulars – who I've seen here on match days before, but don't know his name – tugs on Dad's sleeve from where he's sitting and asks, 'Hey, Mike, what's this I'm hearing about a new club you're starting up?'

The man, who introduces himself as Barbour, hangs on every word of Dad's animated description of Crawford United, and halfway through he calls out to the surrounding tables, 'Here, you lot should be listening to this. Hey, Olly, turn the music down a minute, would you? Mike here is trying to talk.'

Olly obliges and more heads turn Dad's way. Soon he's addressing the whole pub and I spot a few people retrieving our flyer from their pocket and giving it a closer look. And Dad sells our idea brilliantly considering it's his first public speech since his wedding with Mum twenty-five years ago. I want to give him a hug, but I'm holding both our pints so he'll have to make do with an encouraging smile instead.

'So that's our plan,' Dad concludes. 'We hope some of you will see it through with us and, er, thanks for listening.'

Barbour, who seems to have some influence, stands up and kicks off a round of applause, which is swiftly taken up by his friends and spreads outwards till the whole pub is clapping. Dad gives an awkward little bow – so Dad – and Barbour shouts to Olly, 'Get Mike here a pint on me.'

Then he turns to Dad and holds out a crisp fifty-pound note. 'I'd like to make the first donation.'

'Oh!' Dad is clearly not sure what do with it. I quickly step in and ask Barbour if he wouldn't mind going through the official GoFundMe page instead, to make it easier for us to keep records, and Barbour pulls his phone out straight away.

I think the whole pub watches as he types in the details, then he shows me the screen and holds his hand out for us to shake. A round of cheers ensues as my clearly choked-up dad manages to thank him and tell him, 'You've really made my day.'

'Sounds like you need this,' Olly says, passing him a fresh pint. 'And good on you for what you're trying to do here. I don't think it will go unappreciated. Maybe hang back a bit after closing, if you're still here that is. I think you and I should have a chat, see if I can't help in some way.'

I don't think Dad stops checking his watch for the next five hours.

Cassie heads off quite early to have dinner with her

fiancé, but my best friend from university, Phoebs, joins the rest of us briefly, glammed up in a silver minidress and with her hair in perfect ringlets. Her only interest in football is to see whether she thinks any of the supporters are hot enough to date, so once she's concluded she doesn't fancy anyone, she makes her excuses and slips away to join her friends who are going clubbing. I'll catch up with her properly at one of our lectures next week.

Even less interested in football chat is my boyfriend Greg, so we never meet up the night after I've been to a home game. The Fox on a match day is probably his worst nightmare. But it's never been an issue in the six months we've been together. He sees his mates on the nights when I'm here and we always catch up the next morning.

Tomorrow, though, there's more Crawford financing I want to work through, so I've postponed our get-together – and he did have a bit of a moan about that. While he'd never discourage me from doing something that makes me happy, he's not exactly brimming with enthusiasm about there being even more football in my life.

Not wanting to be groggy in the morning, I leave The Fox before closing time, while Dad joins Barbour's table and waits till Olly is free to chat. But I'm not asleep when I eventually hear his key in the door, so I pad down to the kitchen in my slippers and pyjamas to find out what Olly had to say.

Dad has a serious case of the hiccups and is holding on to the back of a chair.

'Are you smashed?' I try not to laugh. It's usually me trying to hide how tipsy I am after a big night out. I think

I might be getting an insight into what it's like to be a parent.

'They made me do shots,' Dad explains, hiccupping again. 'To celebrate our new sponsorship deal.'

I stare at him in astonishment. 'Our sponsorship deal?'

He nods then squeezes his eyes shut – I think it made his head spin. When he's recovered, with just the occasional bit of slurring he manages to tell me that Olly is keen to become the official fan pub of the new team, even though Dad has explained we don't know yet where our new ground will be or how many supporters we'll have.

I guess he's set to lose a significant amount of business when Hamcott Park relocates. Until the flats being built on Hamcott's soon-to-be defunct ground are inhabited, his profits are sure to suffer.

'So what he's proposing,' Dad says, 'alongside a Crawford United after-party at The Fox every Saturday, is his pub name and logo on our team shirts and some advertising space on our website and in return he'll shell out for all the players' kits, including any reserve players as well.'

'Oh my God, that's bloody amazing!' I run round the table and throw my arms round him. We couldn't have asked for a better ending to the day.

4

The momentum keeps building after that and a series of breakthroughs follow in quick succession. First, we receive an email from someone who wants to enquire about season tickets, which I excitedly tell Dad, Cassie, Bob and Marge about at our next kitchen table meeting.

'I didn't even know if that would be a thing at this level of football,' Dad confesses.

'It would certainly help with our bank balance.' I tap my pen on the pad in front of me. 'What do you think we could reasonably ask of people?'

'I don't suppose we can ask anything till we've actually got some players and our FA approval,' Dad says. 'Let's give it some more thought then we can put it to a vote further down the line.'

I tick it off the agenda and we move on to the next item – Dad also has some big news to share, courtesy of the coach hire company where he works.

'I thought I might be for the chop when the owner called me into a private meeting. He usually just leaves me to it and we stay out of each other's hair. But it was quite the opposite – after everything I've done for the company, he wants to throw his support behind Crawford United, so he's offered us a complimentary coach to ferry our team to away games and said he'll make sure there's always something spare. I practically bit his arm off!'

If it were possible to burst with pride, I think Dad would be exploding.

'Of course there's an expectation of a mention or two on our website,' he adds. 'But I think we can all live with that.'

'A hundred per cent, that's amazing,' Cassie gushes.

'It'll save us loads,' I agree. 'Please say thank you from all of us. Though I'm sure you already have.'

We move on to the final item on tonight's schedule. And it's more good news from me.

'I've had an email from a reporter at the *Hamcott Herald*. She's somehow got wind of our story and wants to interview me, Cassie and Dad for this Saturday's paper.'

'She must have picked up one of your flyers,' Marge speculates. 'This could really help us let more people know about the player trials and the crowdfunding. Have you already said yes?'

I nod. 'I just need to let her know when.'

It'll certainly make a change from all the Ben Pryce stories that are still dominating the sports headlines thanks to his stubborn silence over the fan incident at the Millford–Hamcott game. The more he refuses to discuss it, the more the speculation keeps growing. What makes a professional athlete lose control to the extent that he risks his whole career over it? Will he get dropped by Millford City for bringing them into disrepute? The conjecture goes on and on. But it's time to move on to a more positive story – our story.

'She's happy to come here to do it, and says we can either supply our own photos or she'll take a couple while she's here,' I explain. I've already got one in mind. It's from Cassie's engagement party and people always comment on how alike we look in it. The hairstyles are different – Dad's is short with the odd fleck of grey among the brown; Cassie's is long, straight and impossibly glossy; mine stops at my chin in a wavy bob – but we have the same blue eyes, oversized smiles and rosy cheeks.

'Does tomorrow suit everyone?' Dad asks. There are nods all round. 'Then I'll pick up some better biscuits on the way home from work. We want to make a good impression.'

The reporter, Helen, laughs when I tell her Dad did this. 'It's much appreciated,' she says as she takes a seat at the kitchen table the following evening, dropping her rucksack on the floor beside her after she's extracted a notepad and her phone. Me, Dad and Cassie are in our usual spots, as if we've never been away.

'I've been run off my feet all day,' Helen tells us, sweeping her hair off her face. She sighs as it flops straight back into the same position. 'Literally all I've eaten is half a sandwich.'

'Then let me put something better in the air fryer,' Dad says. 'I've got a chicken that needs roasting. It'll be ready by the time we've finished chatting. Unless you're vegetarian?'

'I'm not, but there's no need to go to any trouble,' Helen assures him.

'We've all got to eat,' Dad insists. 'There's some cold pasta and salad in the fridge. It won't take me long to throw it all together.'

Helen catches my eye and smiles. 'Is he always like this?'

I laugh. 'He is – he's a feeder. But in a good way.'

'Then thank you, that sounds amazing. And in the meantime, thank you all for agreeing to chat to me. Do you mind if I record our conversation? Just so I don't forget anything.'

'Not at all,' Dad says, and soon we're filling Helen in on what we've achieved so far and what we're hoping to achieve on the long road ahead.

Helen, it turns out, is a big fan of an underdog story and is already rooting for us to succeed. Not only does she want to run this initial piece, she says she'd like to do some follow-ups and asks if we'd be happy for her to come along to watch the player trials too.

'Absolutely,' Cassie says. 'I mean, they're just in the park so we can't actually stop you, but it would be a pleasure to have you there. There might be one or two fans watching from the sidelines too.'

Barbour has already told Dad he'd like to be there.

'Perfect. Then hopefully I can collect some good quotes,' Helen says with a smile. 'I've been trying to get hold of Alasdair Frowley for a comment too – the author, do you know him?'

'Do we?' I roll my eyes. 'Dad is probably keeping him in business. He's bought every single book. He loves a good crime thriller. He even queued up outside our local bookshop when the last one came out.'

'Did you know Frowley was a long-time Hamcott Park fan?' Helen asks. 'When I was doing my research I stumbled across a tweet he wrote a few weeks back about how the managers are ripping the soul out of the community he used to live in by relocating the club. I think it would make a really nice piece to hear his thoughts on the emergence of Crawford United.'

'I had no idea,' Dad exclaims. 'Not that I ever look at social media, but his books are all set in LA.'

'That's where he lives now,' Helen explains. 'But he was in Hamcott as a teenager and apparently never stopped following Hamcott Park. His agent told me he's shut away on some kind of writing retreat at the moment so he's incommunicado, but I can let you know if I ever get hold of him.'

'Yes please.' Dad nods enthusiastically. 'I think I like him even more now. Maybe I'll even get to meet him one day.'

I don't point out that our budget is unlikely to stretch to a trip to Los Angeles.

Helen wraps up our chat just before the air fryer pings, telling us she thinks our story will make a charming read. Tucking her notepad and phone away, she thanks us for making her life so easy and promises anything we say over dinner will be off the record, but we pretty much stay on the topic of football anyway. She's an East Hedgely fan, having been introduced to them by her high-school boyfriend, but admits she mostly only has time to catch their highlights on *Top Goals* since joining the *Herald*.

'Not that I'm complaining,' she adds. 'I love my job.'

Graciously turning down Dad's offer of raspberry crumble and ice cream for dessert, she thanks us for being such great hosts, but explains that she wants to get her piece transcribed so she can get it uploaded first thing. After we've waved her off and are back at the table with loaded pudding bowls in front of us, we all agree that it went as smoothly as a first brush with the media possibly could have.

'Shall we round off the night with an episode of *Dying Days*?' Dad suggests.

It's the TV series based on Alasdair Frowley's books, about a tough female homicide detective trying to make her mark in a male-dominated police department in downtown LA. It started a few weeks ago so I don't know why we haven't watched it before, given Dad's such a Frowley fan, but he's always been more of a book reader than a TV watcher.

It's Mum who loves a good crime drama on telly, so inevitably my thoughts drift to her as Cassie and I make ourselves comfortable on either side of Dad on the sofa. It's hard not to miss her when it feels like this would have been her perfect end to an evening.

I make a mental note to ask her if she's been watching the show next time we chat on Zoom. Given how much she's rooting for me and Cassie to prove our capabilities at Crawford United, I think she'll like the way the actress, Angela Paramore, captures the detective's determination.

Dad, Cassie and I congregate at the kitchen table yet again the following evening, with Bob and Marge back this time, and the first topic of conversation is Helen's article. It talks of fighting back against the big guns and is full of hope, admiration and community spirit, and Marge declares that it feels like a virtual cuddle.

'We just need to see if it has any impact now,' Dad says.

'I don't think you need to worry about that,' I reassure him. 'Traffic to our website has more than doubled today, and a couple more donations have trickled in. We're a long way off our target but they're all steps in the right direction.'

And yet another piece of the puzzle has fallen into place off the back of Helen's feature – we've finally found a training ground! Most of the local schools and sports centres Marge contacted were too concerned about their grass getting churned up to agree to let our team practise there.

'But today Upper Hamcott Academy called me back with a change of heart and I don't think that's a coincidence,' Marge says. 'They've decided the presence of our players might inspire their already sporty students to push themselves even harder and have offered us ninety minutes of pitch time on Tuesday and Thursday evenings.'

'Lock that down,' Dad advises, reaching across the table to high-five her. 'That's a massive win.'

'So we've now got a kit, a coach, a name, a fan pub, a website, a training ground and a friendly face in the press,' I summarise – and all this has happened in a little under two weeks. 'I know we've still got a lot of money to find, but I think we can allow ourselves a little pat on the back.'

'Yeah, at this rate we'll have our team in the Premier League by 2025,' Bob says.

'Steady on, Bob.' Dad laughs. 'We've got bit more work to do before that happens.'

But I think all three of us are starting to feel like we're on a roll and that nothing can stop us now.

5

Of course with so much of my time being taken up by Crawford United there are other areas of my life that are suffering – namely my studies and my boyfriend Greg. After two weeks of me prioritising Crawford over him, Greg is understandably a little fed up. Not only have I hardly seen him, but when we do get together, the new football club is all I want to talk about, even though I know he finds it boring.

He wants us to crack on with planning our summer travels, which are less than eight weeks away, and fails to hide his frustration when I reluctantly admit the link he sent me to a feature about national parks in Croatia is still sitting unopened in my inbox. 'Are you going to leave me to sort out everything?' he asks rather snippily.

'We can look at it now,' I promise, because it's not like I don't enjoy holiday planning. It's just that with all the craziness of Crawford United, I haven't had time to think about it.

Appeased, he starts talking me through his latest research and how he thinks the coastal towns of Montenegro should make it on to our itinerary. And listening to how enthusiastic he is – this trip has been Greg's post-university dream since Freshers Week – reminds me how excited I've been about spending the whole summer with him. He's one of life's good guys and I'm lucky to have met him.

But it also makes me face up to the fact that my priorities have shifted. The thought of disappearing for two months just when Crawford United's first season is about to begin suddenly feels like terrible timing. After all the hard work I've put in, I'd hate to miss out on any of the club's key moments. So as I'm listening, I find myself wondering if he'd be happy shortening our extended vacation to just a couple of weeks in Greece. Or if I should join him just for part of the adventure after all and spend the rest of my time here.

Of course there's still the possibility Crawford won't get its FA approval, in which case it's premature to even be worrying about this. But I still end the evening in a dilemma. I'm reluctant to tell Greg I'm having doubts about our big adventure – I hate letting people down – but I don't want to string him along either. I need to give it some serious thought over the next few days, and accept that I might have a very difficult decision to make at the end of it.

What I also do in the following days is turn my attention back to my textbooks, which have sat largely untouched since I started work on the new football club. With my university lectures now finished, I'm into the month of private study before my final exams and I am definitely not as up to speed on everything as I'd like to be.

'Do you think you should put the Crawford planning on hold for just a couple of weeks?' Cassie asks when I confess I'm feeling underprepared.

'We're on a tight schedule,' I remind her.

'You don't want to finish up without a degree again though,' she says, referring to the law course I ended up quitting after two years when I realised it was making me so stressed I wasn't even enjoying student life any more.

I worked at a bank for a year while I reassessed my ambitions, and eventually went back to university to do business studies in the hope of finding a job somewhere more entrepreneurial at the end of it. And I've been so much happier – I've loved both the course content and all the people I've met across the three years, especially Phoebs. I've never felt like a mature student around her – we hit it off despite the difference in our ages.

Dad's been amazingly generous throughout – letting me live at home rent-free, allowing me to have friends over whenever I want to and even hiring a cleaner to avoid rows about the hoovering. But Cassie's right, it's time to put my university days behind me, so I need to knuckle down and start revising properly.

That's not to say I don't do anything Crawford-related though. I still make time to design a second – better! – set of flyers, fill the Twitter account I've created with all the details of our player trials, and respond to the handful of membership enquiries that come in on the team email.

I speak to four rival clubs about ground-share opportunities too, and with that comes the first real blow we've suffered since the very beginning. Three of the prospects say they'll mull it over, do some calculations and get back to me, but the fourth – Redmarsh Rovers – comes back with a straight no. I might have had some reservations about its cost, but it doesn't stop me feeling disappointed.

'They're not as cash-strapped as some of the others so they wouldn't even consider it,' I explain to Dad and Cassie when I deliver the news. 'They refused on the grounds of potential fan clash.'

I watch Dad's shoulders slump and Cassie drops her head into her hands.

'I really had my heart set on Redmarsh,' Dad says, sighing heavily. 'I had it all perfectly mapped out in my head.'

'I guess our luck had to run out sooner or later,' Cassie mutters through her fingers.

'At least the other three are still considering it.' I do my best to sound optimistic.

'What if they all say no?' Cassie asks, her voice wavering.

'Don't even think it.' Dad shakes his head. 'We've come this far; it can't all have been for nothing.'

But by the time we hit Hamcott Park's last ever home game at the end of the week – the last game of the season – one of the others has dropped out of the running and there are just two possibilities left.

'Worst case scenario, we grovel to the academy to let us fit as many fans as possible round the edge of the pitch there,' Dad says. 'But let's not forget our second favourite option is still on the table, so let's just carry on with today as we originally planned, cross our fingers and really, really hope Southmoor says yes.'

This time, Barbour and his friends have volunteered to help us hand out flyers, and it soon becomes clear that word about Crawford United has started to spread. We're no longer met with scepticism and suspicion – now there are words of encouragement and enthusiastic handshakes, which makes us more hopeful that Crawford will win enough of a following to ensure its success.

Helen catches up with me and Dad before we head into the ground, to get a couple of new quotes for the *Herald*, this time solely about next week's tryouts.

'What kind of players are you hoping to attract?' she asks.

'We'll be delighted if we hear from anyone with previous league experience,' Dad replies. 'But to be honest, we just want to find eleven lads who can kick a ball at this stage. Of course, if anyone from the Premier League fancies a change of pace, we won't turn them away.'

'Let's hope one of them is a reader of the *Hamcott Herald*.' Helen laughs. 'So remind me again what players need to do if they want to take part.'

'Just turn up on the day, then be willing and able to keep turning up – that's all we can ask for really. Belief, enthusiasm and dedication. If we start with that, we can build everything else up from there.'

'Thank you, Mike. That's all I need for now. I look forward to seeing what happens next Saturday. I hope you still manage to enjoy the game today.'

But it's hard to say if we do or not. Although it ends in a three-one win, it's still something of an anticlimax. Hamcott will finish, as they always do, around the middle of the table, but as we're no longer invested in their future, that's not a reason to celebrate. And I don't think anyone can pretend there isn't still a slight sting of disappointment that this is the last Hamcott game we'll ever go to, no matter how excited we are about the emergence of Crawford United.

The mood is jubilant back at The Fox, though. For those who have already declared their interest in Crawford – namely Barbour and his crew – today was more about closure than anything else, saying goodbye to an era long enjoyed but accepting that all good things come to an end. Anyone who still hasn't heard about the new club yet is quickly brought up to speed. By closing time, it's the only thing being talked about.

A quick look at my phone tells me Crawford's Instagram followers have crept up to just over three hundred, which is yet another reason to celebrate. If we can promise to bring a couple of hundred supporters to each home game, we're far more likely to secure a good ground-share deal.

'Helen's piece is already up on the *Herald* website,' I tell Dad, scrolling through it and having a quick read. 'It looks like she spoke to someone at Hamcott Park about us after she spoke to you.'

'Go on,' he says.

'She asked if they're concerned about losing fans to Crawford United and their publicity guy, Chris Parker, said, "We have no reason to feel threatened by Mike

Crawford's plans. Even if he does manage to find some decent players and get this club off the ground, it's not like any of our loyal supporters are about to drop Hamcott Park to start watching amateur matches in the Combined Counties League.

'"I wish Crawford luck, but with all due respect, it's hard enough running a club when you're as established as Hamcott Park. It's not something you can just decide to do one day and make happen the next. So no, we don't see this changing anything for Hamcott Park. What happens eight leagues below us is of no consequence to the future of our club."'

'Arrogant prick,' Dad mutters.

'Dad!'

'Sorry, love. I mean he might be right, but when you look at what's going on right here, right now, the excitement, the camaraderie . . .'

'The overflowing box of Hamcott football shirts and scarves,' I add, pointing to the collection Olly has started with a view to donating it to a charity.

'I hope Chris Parker ends up eating his words,' Dad says defiantly.

There are a couple of other messages on my phone that need my attention. Phoebs has accused me of ghosting her now we're not seeing each other in lectures any more and, in fairness, I did promise we'd get together for regular study days but have yet to organise anything. I know she won't really be annoyed – that's not the way she is – so I suggest meeting up tomorrow daytime. And she replies straight away, saying she'll pop round at lunchtime.

It means not seeing Greg until the evening, which

he might not be too impressed about – he proposed meeting for brunch and going on from there in his last message to me – but he knows I need to revise and I'll get more done with Phoebs than if I study round his, because she won't distract me with conversations about our travels.

It occurs to me then that I'm subconsciously putting off talking to him, because I know, having had more time to think about it this week, that my heart is more invested in Crawford United than our summer plans. I know I want to give its creation my best shot and I can't do that if I'm hundreds of miles away drinking cappuccinos in a sunny plaza in Italy.

I sigh as I accept, finally, that I no longer seem to be on the same page as Greg. If we ever were, that is. If I really delve into it, Greg has never had the slightest interest in the existence of a new football club – he's that guy who you couldn't even pay to watch *Top Goals*. And I think he'd probably be happier with a girlfriend who isn't unavailable every other Saturday.

So perhaps the time has come for us to have an honest chat about our future. Because although I think he's an amazing guy and we get on brilliantly, the truth is, I'm not in love with him. And I'm not sure he'd say he was in love with me either. We do like each other of course – we wouldn't have spent so much time together if we didn't – but I'd be willing to bet I'm not the only one who's wondered if we might drift apart once we no longer have university bonding us together.

When I text him to apologise for not getting back to him sooner and request that we meet a little later in the day, he replies with an apology of his own and says he's decided to head down to see his parents for the rest of the week, so could we postpone until Friday.

'*Absolutely,*' I reply, with a light sense of relief. Then I tell him – and it's still partly true – that I look forward to seeing him then.

6

Straight away Greg seems different when I slide into the seat opposite him at the pub where we've arranged to meet – distant somehow, his voice flatter and quieter than usual when he says hello. But I don't know if that's because I've started to mentally detach myself from him this past week or if it's because I'm late – he's already halfway through his pint.

'Is everything okay?' I ask, hoping, given that he's just come back from seeing his family, that he hasn't had any bad news from home.

There's an awkward moment where he seems to look at everything else around him but me – his hands, the bar, the ceiling, the glass of wine he's bought me – until he finally blurts out, 'I've booked myself a flight to Naples. Just for me. I was drunk when I did it and I thought I might regret it when I sobered up, but now it's done I think it might be what I want. I'm really sorry. I know I should have spoken you first. It's just, I just—'

'I haven't been around?' I finish for him, and he seems to relax having not had to say it himself.

'I don't want to sound bitter or like I'm complaining. I know you've had a lot on your plate. But that's given me a lot of time to think – about the trip, about us – and I just started thinking that I'm not sure it's such a great idea any more. It's not because I've stopped liking you, I still think you're great, it's just that life seems to be taking us on different paths. And I guess what I'm saying is, because of that I think it might be time for us to maybe think about going our separate ways.'

He looks at me then and I can tell from the way he's holding his breath how uncomfortable he must have felt saying this. I'll admit it's taken me a bit by surprise – I thought it was going to have to come from me – but I'm not about to leave him suffering when I've been feeling the same way.

'I'm sorry too,' I tell him, feeling sadder than I expected to now it's come to this, even if I do think it's the right decision. 'You've been so patient with me and I know I haven't been very fair to you while I've been so preoccupied. But I have to agree. I think setting this football club up has made me realise we've got very different lives ahead of us. It makes me happy. I want you to be happy too. And I don't think being a football widower is the way to make that happen for you.'

He laughs lightly then. 'It's definitely not. So does that mean you're okay with this? You agree we should quit while we're ahead and move on with our lives?'

I force a smile on to my face and nod my head. 'I am and I do.'

Because although I'm sure there'll be times when I'll miss him, I also know I won't be sobbing into my pillow every night because it's over.

His shoulders drop as the tension leaves them. 'I had a feeling you might be thinking along the same lines, but I was still slightly worried in case I'd got it wrong.'

It's my turn to laugh softly. 'On the contrary – it turns out you know me pretty well.'

'Well you might not believe this, but I would still like to hear how you get on with all the football stuff, if you want to stay in touch, that is. I know you think I don't care, but I do genuinely want it to go well.'

'I can do that,' I agree with a smile. 'And if you want to, you can send me pictures of all the sandy beaches and plates of fresh seafood I'll be missing out on throughout the summer. If you want to make me jealous, that is.'

'I think it's more likely to be bunk beds in youth hostels and two-euro plates of pasta, but yes I can do that too,' he says.

There's a moment of silence then, in which I think we both reflect on what could have been. But it passes quickly.

'It's been a pleasure dating you, Lily Crawford,' Greg says, visibly more at ease now. 'You'll make someone a very lucky man one day.'

'I hope you find your person too.' And I really do mean it. 'You might even snare yourself a gorgeous Italian girlfriend and end up staying there.'

He laughs properly this time. 'It's kind of you to have such faith in my pulling power, but I think I'm just going to do me for the next couple of months. There's plenty of time to think about everything else when I get back.'

I'm about to tell him he doesn't need to worry about upsetting me – I think he's probably just saying this because he doesn't want me to think he might get together with someone else on the trip I was meant to be on with him – but we're interrupted by my phone, vibrating loudly on the wooden table as it rings. 'Dad' flashes up on the screen.

I push it to one side and tell Greg I can call back later. Sometimes Dad's timing can be terrible. But no sooner has it stopped ringing than it starts up again.

'You'd better get it,' Greg says. 'It might be important.'

'It's fine,' I insist. 'It's probably just something he's remembered to tell me about the player tryouts tomorrow. I'm sure it'll keep.'

But then a message flashes up on the screen, in capital letters, saying, 'URGENT FAMILY MEETING. GET HERE WHEN YOU CAN.'

'Looks like he really does need to speak to you,' Greg observes. 'It's okay, Lily. You should go. If you feel like you want to talk to me about us again later, you can call me, any time, I don't mind.'

The right thing to do feels like staying here and making sure Greg and I both leave the pub feeling absolutely okay about everything we've decided, but Dad would not use the word 'urgent' lightly. And I'm distracted again when a message from Cassie pops up on the screen. 'I'm just watching telly, I can nip round. Lils, are you close to home?'

I can be there in thirty minutes, twenty-five if I'm lucky with the Tube.

'Come on.' Greg scrapes his chair back as he stands up and takes the decision out of my hands. 'Let's drink up and get out of here.'

He downs the remainder of his pint and twirls his hand to indicate I should do the same with my wine. Then we

46

head out on to the street and there's an awkward pause because neither of us really knows how to say goodbye now we're no longer a couple. But then Greg mutters 'oh, fuck it' and pulls me into a hug that we stay in for a long time before he finally kisses me on the cheek and says, 'Good luck with everything, Lil.'

Then he makes me laugh one last time by shooing me in the direction of the station and saying, 'Now go! Go find out what the latest score is.'

It's not his best pun, but I love that he tried.

Back at the house, Cassie leaps out of her chair and says 'thank goodness' the second I walk into the kitchen. She comes round the table and gives me a hug. 'Dad's been driving me mad.'

I look at him over her shoulder. He's beaming at me so broadly it's bordering on maniacal.

'He's been jiggling around like one of my Year Twos when they need a wee in class, but he wouldn't tell me why till you got here,' Cassie says, sounding frustrated.

'You do look a bit crazy, Dad,' I tell him.

'That's because I'm excited,' he says, giving me a hug of his own once Cassie has released me.

'So can you spill the beans please, now Lily's here?' my sister asks. 'Have we won the lottery or not?'

'Kind of,' Dad teases.

'Are you kidding?' Cassie exclaims. 'Am I finally going to be able to pay someone else to finish off the work on my house rather than having to do it all myself?'

'Not exactly,' Dad says. 'But I think you'll still be happy.'

'Is it Crawford-related?' I ask.

'Yes,' he says, grinning so widely it must be making his cheeks hurt.

'Come on, Dad, put us out of our misery,' Cassie groans.

'Okay, okay. Well, as you know, Redmarsh Rovers were quite hasty in their decision not to ground share with us.'

I grip the back of the chair I'm standing behind, anticipation quickly building. Is he about to tell us one of the remaining two has been in touch while I've been out – to finally offer us a deal?

Let it be Southmoor, I silently pray. They're easily the next best option, and once we know where we're playing, we can put our season tickets on sale.

But Dad's still talking about Redmarsh Rovers when he says, 'It seems they've had a rethink and concluded they might in fact be able to benefit from all the press and social media attention we've been getting. So they've reversed their original decision and are now willing to deal.'

Cassie punches the air in delight. 'Oh, Dad, this is awesome!'

But there's something in the way he glances at me that makes me hesitate. I think I can guess what he's going to say next – the rent is not going to be cheap.

'Can we afford it?' I ask.

'It's a big commitment financially,' he admits. 'I've got some savings, but they were meant to be for me to pass on to you two for when I'm no longer around. The hope, obviously, is that we'd make it all back, but there's no guarantee. So I wanted to see how comfortable or otherwise you both feel with the risk.'

I don't think either of us wants to think about when he might not be here any more.

'I'll also look into loan options or, failing that, I'm not too far off being eligible for an equity release from my pension, so one way or another I can cover the cost,' Dad says. 'For the first year at least. But I didn't want to agree to anything without running it by both of you first.'

It's a lot for him to take on board, but I know how much this club already means to him now the feeling of being part of something that Hamcott Park used to give him has gone. So I throw the question back at him. 'Are *you* comfortable with it?'

'It'll be the biggest gamble I've ever taken, but I still feel in my heart like I'd regret it if I gave up on all of this now.'

'Then you have my blessing,' I tell him.

'Mine too,' Cassie agrees.

His smile is back immediately. 'Then I officially declare this a celebration.'

7

I'm not sure any of us sleep particularly well that night after the excitement of Dad's news. I wake up in the early hours and can't stop thinking about the money. We will make some from ticket sales and we've received a few more donations in the crowdfund, but I can't help wishing there was a bit more in the pot already to give us at least a modicum of security. I know I said I was okay with it yesterday but I don't want Dad to have to eat into his pension if we can possibly avoid it.

I wonder if Olly will let us hold a fundraising event in the garden at The Fox. It's got to be worth asking. If we can organise a raffle and a few other payable activities, it might take the pressure off Dad just a little bit. Maybe Helen could put something in the *Herald* to help us advertise it. The idea starts to grow on me.

Dad and Cassie share my enthusiasm when I suggest it to them over breakfast. It's a brief reprieve from the apprehension we're all feeling about the player tryouts today. We have no idea what to expect – hopefully enough candidates will turn up for us to put together a full squad, but who knows what kind of skill level they'll display.

'We just need eleven half-decent players,' Cassie reminds us, drumming her hand restlessly on the kitchen table while Dad makes a hearty fry-up to see us through the day. 'Some subs would obviously be ideal, but we can make a start if we just get eleven.'

'We've *got* to get eleven,' Dad says, flapping a tea towel to dispel the acrid smoke that's started rising from the toaster. I know he's stressing about it because I've never seen him burn toast before. He extracts two charred black squares and chucks them in the bin. 'Open the window for a minute, would you, love? Breakfast is going to be slightly delayed.'

We still end up heading to the park two full hours before the advertised start time, though. There's only so much anxious pacing round a kitchen a person can do.

Cassie has borrowed cones, balls and a whistle from the school that's behind her Saturday soccer classes. A few of the kids will be joining us too, having volunteered to retrieve any runaway balls while Cassie is putting the prospective players through a series of exercises to judge their ability. Dad, Bob, Marge and I will be watching closely too, so we can all share our opinions at the end.

Meanwhile, I'm armed with my laptop and a folding table and chair, so I can note down names, ages, contact details and footballing experience when the candidates first arrive. That we didn't set up an online form and get people to register themselves now seems like a massive oversight, not just in the time it would have saved, but because we would also have known how many we were expecting. But it's too late to worry about it now.

An hour before we're due to kick things off, our first prospect arrives. He introduces himself as Bailey Pryce, with a y, and apologises profusely for being so early. 'I just wanted to make sure I didn't miss out,' he explains. 'But don't mind me, I'll just do some warming up over at the side.'

We all try not to stare too obviously, which is hard when there's not much else to look at yet. He's athletic, that much is obvious, but he's so slightly built he doesn't look like a footballer – not helped by the fact that he has such enviable eyelashes he almost looks like a cartoon version of his own face. I remind myself we were never likely to hit the jackpot with our first contender, but we've still got plenty of time.

Barbour is next to arrive, but not because he wants to join the team. He's brought his wife and kids along and sets them up on a picnic blanket close enough to watch the action but far enough away so as not to get in Cassie's way. He salutes by way of greeting and I laugh and wave back. Luckily we've got decent enough weather for it. It's a balmy nineteen degrees thanks to a largely cloudless sky. We couldn't have asked for better, really.

Barbour is soon joined by a few other families, most of them the parents of the kids who'll be helping Cassie out. And I notice a few of the Hamcott Park fans who've shown an interest in Crawford United down at The Fox have started arriving too. Once a small crowd has formed, a number of curious dog walkers and passers-by also stop to see what's going on.

By this point I've registered twelve prospective players and have started to feel less anxious about the day ahead. Even if no one else comes, we've got enough players to start a team, although we might have our work cut out training the one or two who look like they probably wouldn't last a full ninety minutes on the pitch.

Cassie splits them into two groups of six, having decided it's the optimum number for her to be able to assess each member individually while also seeing how they work in a team, and while they're warming up another eight hopefuls arrive. She starts assigning each player a number and giving them approximate waiting times. I can tell she's in her element – she's always loved being in charge.

But the arrivals don't stop there. The closer we get to the advertised start time, the more candidates join the back of the line, until it's trailing right across the park. When we start hearing talk of traffic backing up on the high street and a desperate hunt for parking spaces, Dad shows the first signs of panic. There are suddenly close to a hundred people in the line – we did not see this coming at all.

Marge is quickly despatched back to our house to grab Dad's laptop and another camping chair, so we can speed up the registration process. She also has the bright idea of taking a short video of each player saying their name, to help us remember who everyone is. I rope one of the Saturday kids' mums into doing this with my phone.

One side of our cordoned-off area quickly turns into an unofficial holding zone, where all those waiting to try out can watch the proceedings until it's their turn. More spectators station themselves around the rest of the perimeter, and a couple of savvy teenagers take the opportunity to make a few pounds by setting up a table selling soft drinks and snacks.

It's gratifying to see Helen from the *Herald* making her way through the bystanders, taking photos and gathering soundbites, but it's an effort to hide my surprise when a photographer from one of the nationals turns up with a camera that wouldn't look out of place at a World Cup game. I'm suddenly glad I'm having a good hair day.

'Phil.' He holds out his hand for me to shake. 'Helen gave me a little heads up – I hope you don't mind. We go way back, to journalism college, so we tip each other off about a good story every now and then. And this sounded like one not to miss.'

'It's a pleasure to have you here,' I manage to reply, wide-eyed.

'Am I okay to set myself up just by the sideline here?' Phil asks.

'Knock yourself out,' I tell him, as Marge turns to me and mouths 'holy shit'. She touches her fingers against mine in a discreet high five. If ever we needed more validation, this is it.

Another drinks table springs up by the park entrance and the afternoon takes on the feel of a village fete. All that's missing is the bouncy castle and the craft stalls. But in among it, the very serious business of finding a football team is not forgotten. Thankfully my sister is unflappable, even when we have so many players waiting to try out that we fear the park might close before we get through them all.

After each set of six has had their assessment, Cassie tells me the key observations she wants me to add to each player's notes, covering speed, stamina, passing accuracy and goal-scoring ability. And we get the full range, from twenty-year-old Craig who trained at Arsenal's youth academy in his early teens, all the way down to Tony, thirty-eight, who may have dreamed of being a footballer since he was twelve, but has never got further than playing FIFA on his PlayStation before today.

In hindsight we should have been a lot more specific about the required experience in our calls for candidates, but we'll chalk that up as another lesson learned. And Cassie, bless her, treats everyone with the same level of respect and gratitude for coming, whether they excel on the pitch or not, and offers kind words to anyone who struggles under the pressure. I'm so proud of how she handles it all.

It's almost dark by the time we wrap things up, feeling exhilarated but exhausted. We've been going for close to eleven hours and seen a little over two hundred players. The passers-by have long since moved on, but our devoted supporters, led by Barbour, have stayed with us to the very end, and a cheer goes up when we wave off the last group of hopefuls.

'So when will you decide who's made the cut?' asks Helen, who has stuck around too, having declared herself an official fan of Crawford after seeing how we've handled ourselves in the face of an unexpectedly challenging day – and, if I'm honest, after one or two beers.

'We've got a lot of notes to go through,' Dad replies, expertly avoiding the question like the pro he isn't. 'But we'll make an announcement as soon as we're ready.'

Despite the long day, Phil from the nationals is still here as well, which I suspect has a lot to do with Helen. 'I ended up taking quite a lot of video,' he says, 'so if you want any of it to look back over, I'd be happy to send it to you, provided you promise not to sell it or upload it.'

'Lily C at Crawford United dot com,' I say quickly. 'And that would be greatly appreciated.'

Dad's in such a good mood after the fantastic turnout today I'm surprised he doesn't invite them back to ours for drinks. Marge, Bob, Adam and Barbour join us for congratulatory bottles of beer round the kitchen table though.

'I think we can safely call today a success,' Dad says, taking a swig.

Inevitably we start throwing our opinions around about which players we thought showed the most promise, until Dad's eyelids are drooping so heavily he almost dozes off in his chair.

'Sorry, I think the poor sleep last night might be catching up with me,' he admits, stifling a yawn.

'I'll call us an Uber,' Marge says. 'There are a lot of decisions to make tomorrow. You need to be fresh for it.'

I wave everyone off while Dad heads straight for his duvet, and once I'm tucked up in my own bed, I instinctively reach for my phone to text Greg and tell him what a whirlwind of a day it's been – until I remember that's not what we do any more. So I message Phoebs instead, telling her how amazing it feels to have so many players to choose from and how I can't wait to pick our top eleven.

While I'm waiting for her to respond, I scroll through the headlines on my phone. Ben Pryce is trending again, even though he's still suspended from Millford City. This time it's because he's been spotted with a new love interest on his arm – although I hardly see how this counts as news given that he seems to date someone new virtually every week.

Phoebs' reply pops up on my screen while I'm reading. *'OMG we're going to be WAGs,'* she's written. *'I can't wait to meet the team.'*

I can't help smiling. *'I'm not doing this to sort your love life out,'* I tell her.

She sends the heart-eyes emoji. *'If that's what you want to think. But I reckon the world is ready for a new Victoria Beckham.'*

I can't tell if she genuinely thinks this could happen with a player from the lowest league.

'They'll be concentrating on their football. And you should be focused on your revision,' I remind her.

'Ha, back at ya,' she writes. *'First exam in two weeks.'*

'I'm on top of it,' I write, even though we both know this isn't entirely true, and this time she sends me a 'nice try' gif.

I silently vow to pull my socks up once and for all. But of course my good intentions fly straight out of the window the second the player selection gets underway.

8

Our original plan had been to let everyone know whether they've made it on to the team before the end of the weekend. But that was before we knew we'd have a couple of hundred candidates to review. By the time we've whittled the number down to a more manageable level, it's already late on Sunday night.

'We need another tryout day,' Cassie says, skimming through the names still in the running on my laptop. 'We can't afford to rush this – we need to get it right.'

I agree. We've been through all our notes, watched the video clips sent over by Phil, discussed everyone at length, and we've still got more than thirty players on our potentials list. It's a privileged position to be in, given that we didn't know if we'd attract any decent players at all.

'Shall we say same place, same time, next Saturday?' I suggest. 'I'll send an email out. I want to make sure all those who are left can definitely commit to our Tuesday and Thursday training schedule too – and the match days and the post-match fan interaction at The Fox.'

'Thanks, Lil,' Dad says. 'You might want to remind them we won't be able to pay them either. I know we've already said it, but I don't want anyone to pull out down the line because they didn't realise what they were signing up for.'

'And perhaps mention that they'll be expected to launder their own kits and bring their own refreshments,' Cassie adds. 'I don't think that will put anyone off but we want to be completely transparent.'

'Noted.' I add it to the list.

'I'd like to handle the rejection emails myself, if that's okay,' she says. And I know this is because she'll want to give everyone a personalised response, even if it takes her hours. After her own frustrating experience of not hearing back from some of the teaching positions she interviewed for, she won't want anyone else to feel that undervalued.

Something else occurs to me. 'What do we do if some of them can't make it on Saturday?'

'Let's cross that bridge when we come to it,' Dad replies. 'Put the email out, let's see what responses we get and we can go from there.'

Happily there's only one player who isn't able to make the second session – Jacob Cox, who has a family wedding that day – although annoyingly he was one of our favourites.

'Is he off the list then?' I ask Dad and Cassie. We've said we'll be strict about timekeeping and attendance once the club is up and running, but this is a different situation. He didn't know he'd be needed this weekend.

'I think we can see wait and see how Saturday goes,' Dad says. 'Tell him he'll hear our final decision a week on Monday, along with everyone else.'

Which seems like the fairest solution, under the circumstances.

When the other thirty-four players assemble in the park for round two of our tryouts, we don't quite recapture the festive feel of the previous weekend. A handful of fans still turn up to watch the proceedings, including Barbour and Helen, but thanks to the heavy grey sky and biting breeze, no one who doesn't have a vested interest in the club is shivering on the sidelines to see who makes the final cut.

Dad and I thank them for coming and supporting us, while Cassie explains to the players how the session is going to work. She wants to simulate a match, so they'll be playing against each other in teams of eleven in blocks of forty-five minutes – but there'll be no restriction on substitutions so she can make sure everyone has some time on the pitch.

'I'm going to start you in the position I think you're best suited to, based on what I've seen so far, but I'll be switching things up as we go along, as I get to see more of how you perform during a match and who you gel with. Try to work together, even though you're competing, because what we're trying to create here, remember, is a team. Best of luck to all of you.'

With no personal details for me to record this time, they get stuck straight in, with the first set of twenty-two players taking their places on the pitch and the rest watching from the sidelines. Dad takes on the role of referee, while Bob, Marge, Barbour and Adam act as linespeople, but we all keep a close eye on the players. I take notes and record sections on my phone to help guide our discussions later.

There's quite a lot of stopping and starting as Cassie manipulates the team, but the players all seem to ramp up their efforts now there's a very real chance they'll bag a place in the squad, and by the end of another long afternoon, I think we all have a clearer picture of who we want in our final selection. Now we just have to see if we agree with each other.

After we've praised the players for the effort they've put in and promised we'll be in touch imminently, we head back to Dad's and take our usual places round the kitchen table. Dad makes sure everyone has a beer and a bowl of crisps in front of them before turning his attention to the easel he's set up in one corner, which I recognise from when Cassie and I were into painting as kids. He must have had it stashed away in the attic for years.

He props an artist's pad on top and quickly draws a box diagram of a four-four-two formation, then adds a Post-it Note bearing the name of each prospective player in the position where we think they were strongest. It leaves us with eight strikers, fourteen midfielders, ten defenders and two goalies.

'It shouldn't be too hard to pick the goalkeeper then,' he says, laughing.

For the most part, we find ourselves in easy agreement about the other positions too. There are nine players who stood out to all of us, so a lot of the Post-its are discarded quite quickly. It's the left striker and right fullback that cause us the most difficulty. In the former case, our two favourites are barely separable. In the latter, four of us are keen on Jacob, even though he wasn't at the second tryouts, but Bob and Barbour think it's too risky to offer him the place.

'He might have impressed us at the first session, but so did everyone else here,' Barbour points out. 'And at least we've had a chance to see how all the others work together.'

'He did come out much higher than the others in my first assessment though,' Cassie argues. 'I think that's worth remembering.'

'I don't suppose there's any way we can get another look at him before we make our final decision?' Bob questions.

I shake my head. 'Not if we're letting everyone know whether they've been successful tomorrow.'

'We've got enough candidates to recruit a full set of eleven reserves,' Marge points out. 'So if we pick him and he doesn't turn out to be up to the task then we could always switch things up later.'

'Agreed,' Dad says. 'So while I understand the reservations, I'm comfortable with giving Jacob the opportunity to prove himself in our first team. And we'll just make sure we pick our reserves carefully.'

'Fair enough,' Barbour says, and Bob also nods his acceptance, so Dad moves Jacob's Post-it into the corresponding box on the chart and we turn our attention to the last position to be filled. Craig Campbell and Billy Holt are the two strikers we've narrowed it down to.

'Before we get into it, there's something I should probably mention,' I tell them.

'What's that?' Dad asks.

'I had an email from Craig's dad William this morning.'

'I know William Campbell,' Barbour says. 'Lives in one of those fancy mansions up on the hill. Fingers in a lot of pies.'

'Well, it seems he wants to stick a finger in this one too,' I explain. 'I wasn't sure whether to bring this up, but according to his email, he strongly disapproves of his son's current career and is willing to do whatever it takes to get him on to our football team. So he's offering a significant investment in the club to help persuade us to make that happen.'

'How much?' Dad asks.

'Ten grand.'

I watch his eyebrows fly up his forehead, in much the same way mine did when I first read the message, and Marge sucks in a deep breath. Cassie sits back in her chair and whistles.

'I can't even tell you how much I wanted to give him our bank details,' I admit, because a sum this size would comfortably cover the deposit for our ground share and mean there was a lot less of a burden on Dad. 'But we'd be no better than Hamcott Park if we start letting money influence our decisions and we'd be crucified by the press if they found out we'd accepted a bribe.'

'It's bloody tempting though,' Marge agrees.

'Ten grand,' Bob repeats. 'There's a lot we could do with that.'

'I know it would take the pressure off our finances,' Dad says, 'but aside from the ethical question, we wouldn't want to feel indebted to him. If Campbell is trying to pressure us into bringing his son on board now, how do you think it will go if we ever want to sub him off, or if there's a player he takes a disliking to?'

'That's true,' Marge concedes. She shakes her head and sighs. 'He must really hate Craig's job.'

'He's a life model,' I tell them. 'I think his dad's exact

words were: "He gets his kit off at hen parties and lets people draw his penis." He reckons half of Hamcott have probably seen his son naked.'

Marge's eyes go wide. 'I didn't even know that was a job.'

'I did write in my notes that he's a bit on the cocky side,' Cassie says.

When we've stopped laughing, Dad suggests we forget about both the money and Craig's anatomy and take a vote to select our eleventh player.

'Based on performance alone,' he says, 'raise your hand if you think we should offer the last spot to Billy.'

No one moves.

'So we're all agreed on Craig anyway?' Dad checks.

'He is pretty nifty with the ball,' Cassie says.

'Then, ladies and gentlemen, it looks as if Crawford United has passed another milestone and we've got ourselves a team.'

9

With Dad and Cassie back at work on Monday, it falls to me to contact the successful candidates – and for the most part it's an absolute joy. My video calls are met with excitement, gratitude and delight, even when I'm honest with them about the fact that we haven't got everything else in place just yet. Regardless, every one of the players is thrilled to be part of this little bit of footballing history we're trying to create.

My favourite conversation is with Jacob, who's probably the happiest of all to be chosen after missing the second tryouts. At seventeen, he'll be the youngest player on the team, but what he lacks in experience I'm confident he makes up for in raw talent.

He's a natural sportsman and currently plays something different almost every night of the week, but Dad, Cassie and I believe if he focuses just on football he'll get even better at it – and really quickly. We'll be firm about him still devoting time to his education though. While Crawford might be a good talking point on his future CV, getting his A levels is more likely to get him a job.

My least favourite conversation is with Craig, who flirts outrageously with me while I'm trying to establish his size so Olly can get the team kit ordered in time for the start of the season. Here is a man who has the confidence of the aesthetically gifted and I realise I'm going to have to establish very clear boundaries if I want him to treat me like a member of the management team and not someone he's just met at speed dating.

Before I can even check if his existing commitments will be compatible with our proposed summer training schedule, he's offered me a free life drawing session so I can see how he 'performs' off the pitch. Then he gives me way more detail than I need to know about the time he had a bucket of cold water thrown over him because he started to get an erection during a session.

I'm sure the intention is to get me thinking about him naked, but I refuse to be drawn in. He may be broad-shouldered and square-jawed, with undeniably alluring caramel-coloured eyes, but I have no interest in mixing business with pleasure.

'Just talk to me about the timing,' I say firmly.

'I usually work on Saturdays, but it won't be a problem,' he says. 'My dad's minted so I can easily knock it on the head. He hates me modelling anyway and I don't need the money.'

I politely suggest he refrains from bragging about this to the rest of the team. I'm curious though. I can't help wondering, when it comes to playing for Crawford, what's in it for him?

'To show Arsenal what they're missing,' he replies. And I nod, as if I agree, but I can't imagine Arsenal will be paying any attention to what's going on at Crawford United.

Wanting to wrap things up, I grit my teeth and tell him I look forward to having him at the first training session on Tuesday, to which he winks and says he's looking forward to seeing *me*. I don't react, I just end the call. I'm not about to let him – or any of the other players for that matter – unnerve me. Not that anyone else tries.

With each of the other calls I learn a little more about the new additions to our team. As I'll be writing player profiles for our website, I ask a bit about their backgrounds and their interests, and I find it fascinating how different their lives are outside their love of football.

Jamie Green, our nineteen-year-old striker who will play alongside Craig, left school at sixteen with five GCSEs and now works on home renovations with his dad. His determination to learn everything so he can eventually set up his own business shows a maturity and work ethic that I hope will inspire his teammates to also want to be the best they can be.

In centre midfield we have our fiery Italian Nico Alessi, who is now a chef but played for his university team in Rome before his family relocated to London, along with Bailey Pryce, who works in IT. Yes, that's the Bailey who I thought looked like the most unlikely footballer due to his petiteness, but stick a ball in front of him and a transformation takes place. He's so fast, so light on his feet and so in control – and he modestly puts that down to just playing in his back garden with his older brother. I can't help thinking it's a shame his brother didn't come and try out, too.

Our left and right wingers are Adio Adesina and

Aaron Chapman. Adio is a banker and Aaron works at a gym. At twenty-nine, Aaron is our oldest player, but he's been five-a-side obsessed forever and showed moments of brilliance during the tryouts. Adio played at a youth academy for two years, until his parents persuaded him to choose a more stable career. He doesn't appear to have forgotten any of the skills he learned, though, and on top of that he seems dependable, likely to turn up on time and capable of keeping the others grounded.

In defence, we have Jacob, Thomas Miller, who's between jobs, Levi Jones, who coaches tennis in the local parks to keep himself active and outdoors – his two favourite things – and Scott Sutherland, who set up his own company at the age of just sixteen selling fishing equipment online and is making a good living out of it.

Thomas has a melodic Irish lilt that I could listen to all day – I can't imagine anyone not falling in love with it. Or him, for that matter. At the tryouts we all noticed how considerate he was towards the other players on the pitch and how his smile rarely leaves his face. I've secretly nicknamed him The Caretaker because I'm already convinced he'll be the one who'll diffuse any tension on the pitch, check on any injured players that go to ground and sweet-talk the referee if anyone steps out of line. He's a solid wall of muscle who looks as if he might be better suited to rugby, but he has an absolute heart of gold. He'll make a great team captain.

And last but not least there's our goalie, Elliot Simmons – six foot six and so self-assured I don't think he'd be fazed even if an eighty-tonne elephant was charging full pelt down the pitch at him. Like Adio, he briefly played at a youth academy, but at that age he struggled with the competitiveness. He works 'in insurance' now, but never stopped wondering what might have been and he couldn't be happier about the opportunity we've dropped into his lap.

And that's our team – this jumble of players who don't even know each other's names yet. I look at all the notes I've made during the calls and can't help feeling immensely proud. Crawford United is now a living, breathing entity. And boy does that feel great.

10

Just thirty-three hours later, Dad and I watch from the sidelines as Cassie kicks off our first ever full training session. Straight away she makes it very clear she's the boss as she addresses the players fanned out in a semicircle in front of her, despite most of them towering over her.

'You're not always going to agree with my methods. Some of you have been to the top academies in the country and might think you know better than me. But you're not there now, you're here, and I expect the same respect from you that you'd give a coach at Manchester United. Understood?'

She doesn't make it obvious she's directing it at anyone in particular, but as both of us have now had a taste of Craig's flirty comments, I'm fairly sure this is mostly intended for him.

The players, who are dressed in a mishmash of sports gear, from Jacob's Arsenal shirt – which must be galling for Craig – to Elliot's black running vest, all nod in agreement.

'Good, then let's get warmed up and after that we'll

work our way through short passes, long passes and set pieces. We'll do some body conditioning work at the end, but I expect each of you to take responsibility for your own physical fitness. Over the next couple of sessions I'll be drawing up an individual programme for each of you to work on in your own time, at the gym if you have access to one, at home if you don't. We're already close to the end of May, which means we've got about seventy-five days to prepare before the first game of the season. Let's make them all count.'

I make a mental note to approach the local gyms about potential player discounts – then nearly jump out of my skin as Dad's phone starts shrilling in his hand. Cassie shoots an unimpressed look our way, and he raises a hand in apology before excusing himself to take the call.

'And one more thing,' Cassie says sternly, turning back to the players. 'Absolutely no phones at training. Your penalty is laps. We'll start with two now. Let's go!'

As they head off round the perimeter, I double-check mine's on silent. I'm going to be filming a lot of the session, so there's an exception to the phone rule for me. But I don't want to interrupt Cassie's flow again.

Dad is still not back by the time she has warmed the players up and started them on shadowing practice. I didn't think anything would take him away from watching the session today so it must be serious. But I put it out of my mind so I can stay focused on filming the nominated followers trying to stay within a metre of their leaders.

I'm so absorbed that I don't look up when someone moves in beside me and says, 'They don't look too shabby.' It's not Dad's voice, but we did tell Barbour and a few of our other supporters that they were welcome to come and watch, thinking it might help the team get used to playing in front of spectators. It's not Barbour either, though – it's not a voice I'm familiar with.

'If she can just get them to stop trying to outdo each other, like they're still at the tryouts, and get them to work together as a team . . .' the man continues, which instantly gets my back up. It's Cassie's first adult training session and I won't hear a bad word said about it.

'And what makes you such an expert?' I snap, spinning round to face him. And I don't know if you've ever experienced the sensation where it feels like all your hair follicles have been sprayed with deep freeze, but that's how my body reacts when I realise it's not, as I'm expecting, an opinionated former Hamcott Park fan or even one of the academy staff standing next to me and sharing their unwanted point of view. It's disgraced Millford City footballer Ben Pryce. Here. At Upper Hamcott Academy. At least I think it is.

He has a cap pulled down low over his face, so I peer a little harder. Yes, it's definitely him. On a second glance, there's no mistaking those dusty blonde curls or his tall, lean body. But what on earth is he doing here?

A smirk tugs at the corner of his lips as he tells me he may have had a bit of experience of training with a football team and I'm momentarily lost for words. I should probably mention at this point that Ben could be a catwalk model if he wasn't a footballer. He's impossibly good-looking – even more so than in the photos I've seen of him online and in the papers. No wonder he gets pictured with a different girl every other week.

'You're probably wondering what I'm doing here,' he

adds, as if he can read my mind. 'My brother's on your team, but I'm guessing he probably hasn't told you that. He'd hate anyone to think he got his place because of who he is, not what he can do.'

Of course. Bailey Pryce, with a y. It never occurred to me they have the same surname.

'He told me spectators are welcome,' Ben continues, 'and I've got a fair bit of time on my hands at the moment, so I thought I'd swing by to see how he's getting on. Unless he was wrong about the spectator part, that is?'

'Not at all, and thank you for your observations,' I finally manage, hoping he can't tell how rattled I am, even if my cheeks are clearly on fire. 'But it's day one, so we're not expecting the team to be perfect yet.'

'Can you tell me anything about them as individuals?' he asks. 'You know, from what you've seen so far.'

And a small part of me wants to say it's none of his business, but another part of me wants to carry on talking so I've got an excuse to sneak another look at him. Plus it's not like I've got anything bad to say about anyone, so what harm could it do?

'Well, we've got Jamie over there – he's been chasing balls around since before he could walk. He'll be playing up front,' I tell him, resisting the urge to fan my face. I don't want to draw attention to how flushed it is. 'And Nico, in the green top there, is such a ball of energy. He's unbelievably competitive, but we think that will fire the others up when we get to playing matches.'

Ben nods and waits for me to continue, so I plough on, inexplicably feeling the need to prove to him that I'm well acquainted with all our players, even if it's not entirely true yet.

'Aaron, on the left there, he's used to playing five-a-side, so we need to work on his fitness a bit. And I'd say we've got some work to do with Scott on his confidence, but overall we're very happy with our choices. We have faith in everybody on the team.'

'Including my brother?'

'Absolutely.' But then I hesitate.

'Tell me,' Ben says, and I debate how honest to be. In the end I decide to go with the truth.

'It's nothing to do with his ball skills – that's clearly something that runs in the family. But I do worry that when he comes up against some of the bigger opponents in a tackle, they're going to send him flying. He's fast enough to be able to dodge the majority, but when they see what a threat he is in the midfield there's always the risk the opposition might start targeting him.'

Ben nods again, but doesn't agree or disagree. Instead he changes the subject entirely and asks, 'So how do you think your coach is going to cope surrounded by all that testosterone?'

Which instantly makes me bristle as it occurs to me that this bad boy of football, with a somewhat shady reputation with the ladies, might really just be here because his brother's told him there's a hot female coach. Well, he'll be disappointed if that's the case. Cassie would never leave her fiancé, no matter how tempting the proposition might be.

'You don't need to worry about her,' I reply tersely. 'She's no wallflower.'

'Oh, I don't doubt it.' He holds his hands up to mollify me. 'But I was wondering, all the same, if perhaps I could offer her some assistance.'

'Because you're a man, so you think you know better than her?' I snap, still on the defensive.

'Because three years in the Premier League has taught me a few things,' he counters. 'And I'd be happy to share what I know with the team.'

I eye him suspiciously, with no idea what to make of him. I still want to put this down to arrogance, and yet it doesn't come across that way. 'Why?' I ask sharply.

'Why don't we discuss that over a drink?' he suggests, so casually I think I must have misheard him.

'A drink,' I repeat, ignoring the fluttering sensation this sets off in my stomach. 'With you?'

He chuckles. 'You're not scared it would tarnish your reputation, are you?'

Well yes, of course I am. I'm not about to join his list of conquests.

'Pity,' he says. 'I didn't have you figured for a wallflower either.'

'I'm not!' I protest, increasingly flummoxed by this turn in the conversation. 'But I'd rather be tackled by Roy Keane than be seen out with you!'

'Roy sends his apologies but he's got other plans this evening,' he fires back, with an infuriating grin. 'So I guess I'll have to do.'

'I've got other plans as well. I've got lots of . . . lots of important things to do.' Not that I can think of a single one of them all of a sudden. It annoys me that I sound so flustered. What the hell is wrong with me?

'More important than talking about football with someone who knows a fair bit about it over a pint and a bowl of chips?' he asks, his tone mock incredulous.

My mind goes completely blank under the gaze he's

now directing at me and I can't think of a single comeback. He pretends to thumb through an invisible dictionary. 'Let me just check that definition of wallflower. Oh yes. Shies away from opportunities . . .'

'Fine,' I snap. I suppose I might as well hear what he has to say. 'But you're buying.'

He turns back to face the pitch with a smile still on his face, while my brain screams at me, *What just happened?* Did Ben Pryce, Premier League footballer, occasional sports brand promoter, full-time lothario, really just suggest we go for a drink – and I agreed?

'I don't want my dad to know,' I blurt out, glancing back at where he's still pacing in the distance. Whatever's going on, he's got enough on his mind this evening without me throwing this into the mix. I already know he wouldn't approve.

'Fine with me,' Ben says. 'I'll wait for you in my car round the corner when the session wraps up. I'm used to sneaking off without people seeing.'

And then, without another word, he heads back towards the exit, leaving my mind in a whirl as I force myself to keep my eyes on the Crawford players and not look over my shoulder and watch him go. It wouldn't surprise me if someone were to tell me I'd imagined the whole thing, particularly as it seems like everyone else was too busy to have even noticed him.

Dad reappears not long after that and I finally get to find out what was more important than watching Cassie put the team through their paces.

'It was the financial adviser I've been waiting to hear back from,' he explains. 'To talk about loan options. Not the greatest timing, eh?'

'What was the verdict?' I ask.

'There are a few different ones to consider. I need to go over it all carefully. Not tonight though. Right now I just want to watch the rest of this then grab a pint at The Fox, if you fancy it?'

'I'm sorry, Dad. I told Phoebs I'd nip round there to run through some course notes,' I fib, although I'm already thinking that might be a better idea than going for this drink with Ben. Now he's not in front of me, I can think more clearly. Yes, he's hot – and yes it would probably be an interesting conversation – but I don't think he's the kind of person I should be associating myself with. Not when he's mostly known for having a combative nature and womanising – which, if they knew what I'd agreed to, Dad and Cassie would be the first to remind me.

'No problem. Your revision's more important,' Dad says. 'I'll see if Cassie's interested, and if not I think Barbour said he was heading over.'

We mostly chat about the players after that, until it's time to thank them all for their hard work at the end of a spirited first session. Cassie's cheeks are flushed and I can tell she's pleased with how it went – her eyes are positively glowing.

We take our time saying goodbye to everyone. We want to make sure they all know how much we appreciate them putting their faith in us and committing to being here. I'm conscious that with it taking so long, it's unlikely Ben will still be waiting for me but, to be honest, I'm okay with that. If he hasn't hung around, it saves me from having to put my reservations about him aside so I can find out whether he has any useful advice regarding the team.

Cassie turns down Dad's invitation to The Fox because

she wants to catch up with her fiancé, so after a quick discussion about the evening – the general consensus being that it was a success – Dad heads in that direction alone.

'You head off too,' Cassie says. 'It'll only take me two minutes to load up the car.'

'Are you sure?'

'It'll help bring me back down to earth a bit,' she insists.

So I leave the academy in the opposite direction to Dad, having decided to forget about the drink with Ben. It was a stupid thing to agree to anyway. But while I'm halfway through texting Phoebs to see if I can pop by – I know she's just at home studying – a set of headlights flashes me twice and I realise it's Ben letting me know which car he's in.

11

I'm momentarily frozen with indecision – because I suspect Ben's real motive for asking me to go for a drink with him is to boost his already inflated ego. But despite that, it's hard not to feel flattered on some level that he's waited for me.

I haven't forgotten that tingle I got from the way he looked at me earlier either – but I'd be willing to bet it's the same look he gives every girl he talks to, which would explain why he ends up with so many of them. He probably practises it in the mirror.

So no, I tell myself, I won't go for this drink, even if his intention was also to talk about football. He's clearly used to everything going the way he wants it to and I'm not about to reinforce that for him. Too polite to leave him hanging though, I walk over to his open window to let him know I've changed my mind.

'I thought I'd been stood up,' he says with a warm smile as I approach.

'There's been a change of plan.'

'You want to take your car instead?' he surmises.

I'm not sure it even occurs to him that I might have decided not to go. He probably doesn't get turned down very often, if ever.

'I don't mind driving, honestly,' he adds. 'The pub I was thinking of is only ten minutes from here. It's really quiet – I think you'll like it. No one will bother us there.'

Ignoring my irritation at the presumption that he has any idea what I might like, I can't help replying, 'Is that where you take all the girls?'

He laughs. 'On the contrary, most of them want the whole world to know they're going on a date with me.'

Which pulls me off my high horse and makes me feel a bit sorry for him. I guess it goes with the territory when he's usually out with models and reality stars, but it must be hard never knowing if someone wants to date you because of who you are rather than how much publicity you can bring them. Not that this would have been a date, of course.

'I thought it would be a good choice given that you don't seem to want anyone to see us together,' Ben says as he reaches across and pushes open the passenger door. He looks at me expectantly. 'So are you coming?'

It feels too awkward to say no now the door's hanging open, so with a sigh I tell myself just one drink will be tolerable. I can put my misgivings on hold so long as I think of it as something I'm doing for the possible benefit of the team. At least if the pub is as empty as he says it will be, I don't have to worry about getting spotted by anyone.

I fire off a quick text to Phoebs as he pulls away from

the kerb, to let her know Dad thinks I'm at hers. *'Just in case he asks how our revision night went next time you're round,'* I type.

'OMG are you shagging one of the players already?' she writes back. *'Unbelievable. You haven't even introduced me to them yet.'*

This makes me laugh. *'Nooo, nothing like that. I'll explain later, okay?'*

'This better be good,' she replies.

I know she'll think it's worth missing another study night for.

'Everything okay?' Ben asks. 'Something to do with the change of plan?'

'Just my best friend jumping to the wrong conclusion as always,' I tell him. And then, for reasons I can't explain – perhaps because I still can't quite believe I'm on my way to a pub with a Premier League footballer for a casual chat about our mutual love of the game – I'm hit by a sudden attack of honesty. 'She thought I must be hooking up with someone from the team.'

'Would you?' he asks.

'No! That would be so inappropriate.'

'You've come out with me.'

'You're not part of Crawford. And we're not about to hook up.'

'I'll ring ahead and cancel the candles.' I whip my head round to look at him, but he's grinning. 'I'm just kidding. But I could be part of Crawford . . . if you let me help coach the team. I meant what I said before, you know – I've got plenty of time on my hands.'

I study his face while he's concentrating on the road and try to picture what it would be like to have him at training every week. From a purely aesthetic perspective, I can't say I'd find it too hard to get used to. There is the slight matter of why he's not currently playing at Millford to be considered though.

'I can suggest it to the others, but I don't know what they'll say,' I tell him. They're well aware of his reputation, so I can hardly imagine them welcoming him with open arms.

Ben doesn't seem to have any such qualms though. 'I think they'll say, "See you on Thursday,"' he replies with a self-assuredness it's hard not be drawn to.

He eventually pulls up in front of a small pub on a residential street that looks like it used to be someone's front room. Inside, there's a row of men sitting on stools in front of the bar and I'd say their average age is well over sixty. They don't seem remotely interested in his arrival, which, I guess, is exactly why Ben comes here. It certainly isn't for the decor. The walls don't appear to have been painted for several decades. There's a lot of burgundy. It's not what I was expecting.

'They don't play music so it doesn't appeal to anyone else under the age of thirty,' Ben explains. 'But the beer's good and the landlady's a friend of my dad's – and you can always get a seat.' He nods towards the two empty tables on either side of the room.

'All right, Ben, pint of the usual?' the landlady asks from behind the bar. When he gives her the thumbs up, she adds, 'And for you, love?'

'I'll take the same,' I confirm.

This gets a nod of approval. 'I'll bring 'em over. You choose yourselves a spot.'

'Don't say I don't take you to all the best places,'

Ben jokes as he holds out a rickety chair for me, which wobbles ominously when I sit on it. 'Oh, and maybe don't go to the loo until you get home, unless you're desperate. They're a bit—' He crinkles his nose up.

'Oi, I heard that,' the landlady interrupts as she puts our drinks down on the table. 'You might be used to all that fancy stuff now, but don't ever forget where you came from.'

'As if you'd let me.' Ben grins up at her. 'And anyway, you know I love it here really.'

She huffs and walks away.

'So, where were we?' Ben asks, turning back to face me.

And despite my scepticism about him, we fall into a surprisingly easy conversation about Crawford United and how much he admires what we're doing and how happy he is that Bailey has finally got a break.

'He's such a good footballer; he just never pushed himself as hard as I did. He used to worry he wouldn't be able to handle the pressure of always needing to win. But now he's watched me having some shockers and seen that I've survived it, he's more comfortable with the idea of just rolling with the breaks. Although of course it's always much better when you win.'

He asks how I got into football – Dad's doing, of course – and reveals why he did. 'It was that or learning guitar to impress the girls. And I'm shit at guitar,' he admits.

It's while I'm laughing at this that I realise I'm actually enjoying his company and struggling to reconcile the person I'm sitting opposite with the one who's essentially on suspension for an act of aggression. I know this is a

83

very different environment to the noise and adrenaline of a football pitch, but he seems so laid-back. It's hard to imagine him getting angry about anything.

He surprises me again when I ask him what he does when he's not playing football. I thought he might say something like playing golf or video games, but he tells me he's just finished a degree in computer science.

Noticing the rise in my eyebrows, he asks, 'Did you have me down as a high school dropout?'

'Not at all. It just seems like a lot to take on alongside a football career. Although I wouldn't have been at all surprised if you'd told me you were expelled for flirting with the teachers.'

He laughs. 'I did have to do my degree remotely. I couldn't have all the professors swooning in my lectures. You know what it's like.'

I'm not sure if he means literally. If he does, it's a very nice compliment.

'I got a two-one,' he adds. 'Not just a pretty face. But in all seriousness, I worked hard for it. I know the football isn't going to last forever and I didn't want to get to the end of it without a plan B.'

'Oh God.' I clap my hand up to my face.

'What?' He sounds alarmed.

'After all the things they've said about you in the papers, I didn't realise your deepest, darkest secret would be that you're *sensible*.'

He cracks up at this. 'It's not something I've ever been accused of. But I'm not the loose cannon they've made me out to be either. They create their own reality when they don't know all the facts, so you can't believe everything you read.'

84

'That must be hard.' I certainly hope it never happens to anyone at Crawford.

'The people who count know I'm not a bad person. I fucked up for sure, but I had my reasons. It certainly won't happen again. I'm just going to have to ask you to trust me on that.'

There's a pause then, while I contemplate it, until I realise I'm probably looking at him a little too intensely. He really does have a very nice face and I need to stop staring at it. He doesn't seem fazed, though – I imagine he's used to it.

'So do you want to stay for one more?' he asks, nodding his head towards my nearly empty glass.

And I find that I do. He's such easy company I could chat to him for hours. But I haven't completely forgotten that I came here specifically to talk about Crawford United, so I request just a half this time and tell him it's so I can remember all the good advice he's about to pass on to me.

'Now who's the sensible one?' he says with a grin.

But I flip this back at him when he orders himself a sparkling water, even if it is because he's driving. He tells me he doesn't usually drink at all during football season – it's only during the summer break that he occasionally indulges.

We end up staying till closing time, the minutes slipping away as we talk about match strategy, team bonding and training regimes. By the time the final bell rings and Ben excuses himself to brave the bathroom before we leave, I've come round to thinking that he could indeed be quite handy to have at Crawford's training sessions.

The landlady comes over to collect our empties and tells me, with a conspiratorial wink, that she's never known Ben to bring a girl here before. This takes me by surprise, but I don't really know what to make of it. Should I feel privileged that he's shown me a bit of what I suspect might the real him away from the glare of the Premier League? Insulted that he didn't think I was worthy of a swankier venue? Or should I not be reading anything into it? There may have been some flirty banter throughout the evening, but I think that's just the way Ben is.

If tonight was about persuading me there's more to him than the temperamental attention-seeker he's been described as in the press recently, then he's done a good job of it. But my main takeaway is what I think he could bring to Crawford United – if Dad and Cassie will let him.

12

'No way,' my sister says emphatically when I bring up Ben's offer of help at the kitchen table meeting the following evening. 'I'm perfectly capable of knocking those boys into shape myself. I don't need some hotheaded yob muscling in and trying to prove he's better at it than me. Guys like Ben Pryce always feel like they know everything.'

'It's not like that at all,' I assure her. 'I had a good chat with him and he isn't out to tread on anyone's toes. You know I wouldn't even be suggesting this if I thought he was. He's just willing to share his knowledge and I think we'd be crazy not to even entertain the idea. It's not like opportunities like this will come knocking every day.'

'You do have to wonder what's in it for him,' Bob says.

'Absolutely nothing, apart from maybe getting to spend a bit more time than usual with his brother. He just wants to help, he believes in what we're doing, and as he's got three years' experience of Premier League football, I really think we should take advantage of it.'

87

'Help by imparting his bad habits on our players?' Cassie hasn't stopped scowling. 'He's slated on *Top Goals* every other week for some kind of blow-up on the pitch. And let's not even get started on his off-pitch activities.'

'For the record, I don't think he's the hot-headed yob you think he is,' I assure her. 'Impulsive, yes. Maybe even a little rash. But he's not out of control.'

'You spoke to him for, like, five minutes,' she huffs. I'm not about to correct her. 'I still say we don't need his kind of help. I've got my training plan set out. I know what I'm doing. I'm happy with everything the way it is.'

'Dad?' I turn to him, hoping he can see this more objectively.

'I'm not sure.' He's frowning at the table. 'I can see both sides of the argument. Not to take anything away from you, Cassie – we all know you're doing and will continue to do a brilliant job. But if Pryce is volunteering to give us an insight into how they train at the very top level of football, and he's offering it for free . . .'

'We could at least invite him down for a couple of sessions to see what he can bring,' I suggest. 'You don't have to like him, Cassie, but it's got to be worth putting up with him for a couple of hours if it means we all get to learn something.'

Dad and Cassie exchange a look. She must know, deep down, that what I'm saying makes sense.

'There's one other thing to consider before we decide,' Marge says, and we all look her way. 'I just thought it was worth mentioning that we've had nothing but positive press since we started this. Isn't there a risk we might undo that if people find out we've brought him in? We don't want to look like we're condoning poor conduct by teaming up with someone with a reputation like his.'

'Another valid point,' Dad agrees, rubbing his chin. 'We do need to weigh up what we might gain from his presence against what we could potentially lose. It's a really tough call – and it could go either way.'

'But they do say no publicity is bad publicity,' Barbour points out. 'If him coming here gets Crawford more exposure, which might result in more fans, that can surely only be a good thing.'

'Okay, let's put it to a vote,' Dad says. 'Raise your hands if you're in favour of accepting Pryce's assistance.'

Barbour and I put our hands up. Bob is hesitant and Marge admits she's on the fence. Eventually she decides to side with me and Barbour, while Bob is more inclined to agree with Cassie. It's down to Dad, who drums his fingers on the table for a while longer.

'Could you cope if we got him down just the once?' he asks Cassie. 'We're so early in our schedule it probably wouldn't throw your plans too far out of kilter.'

She closes her eyes and sighs. 'I hate it when you two gang up on me.'

Neither Dad nor I say anything. It's a line she always trots out when she doesn't get her own way and she knows it too. So after she's had a few seconds to sulk she adds, 'I'm not happy about it, but as long as I'm still head coach, I'll do my best to suck it up.'

'Of course you are,' Dad says. 'He'd be there purely for consulting purposes. I think I'm going to take a punt and say we should go for it.' He raises his hand off the table. 'So with four votes to two, we'll invite Pryce to join us for the session tomorrow evening.'

'And hope we don't end up regretting it,' Cassie says.

'I'll pass the message on through Bailey,' I tell them, not about to admit I've already got Ben's number in my phone – when he dropped me off yesterday he insisted I take it.

Then we turn our attention to the other items on the agenda, and Marge tells us the players' kits have all been ordered now. 'And Adam's working up a template for the season tickets, so that's all in good shape.'

'Fantastic,' Dad says.

'And I've spoken to Olly about a fundraising day at The Fox,' I tell them. 'He's keen and says we can do it on the last Saturday in June, which gives us just over a month to prepare for it. So we can start putting our heads together and coming up with ideas for that, too.'

'A cake competition!' Marge proposes. 'I'll be the judge. I've always fancied myself as the next Mary Berry.'

'We should get all the players involved,' Bob suggests. 'Get them doing car washes or something. And I agree that we should have prizes up for grabs to entice people to come.'

'Maybe some football challenges,' Barbour says. 'Beat the keeper, that kind of thing.'

'All great ideas,' Dad says, nodding his head. 'Let's keep adding to the list and we can pick our favourites nearer the time. Now before we finish up, does anyone else have any other matters they need to raise?'

He looks round at us all shaking our heads.

'Then before we close the meeting, I just have a couple of things I'd like to share, although how I've managed to keep them to myself until now I'll never know. So I'll just give myself a little drumroll by way of introduction.' He strums his hands against the edge of the table, enjoying the curious looks on all our faces, before announcing, 'Ladies and gentlemen of the unofficial Crawford management team, it is with the greatest pleasure that I'm now able to confirm, that from the first week of August, on a twelve-month agreement with an option to extend, we'll be starting our new ground share with the Redmarsh Rovers!'

Cassie and I both squeal. I'll get back to worrying about recouping the costs later.

'Wait!' Dad holds a hand up, leaving us both frozen halfway out of our seats.

'There's more,' he explains. 'Because this exciting piece of news brings me to the very last piece of our jigsaw . . . and I'm beyond delighted to also be able to tell you that, as of today, Crawford United is now officially affiliated to both the London and Surrey football associations – and we've been granted our place in the Combined Counties League!'

The commotion that follows sends drinks flying across the table and chairs crashing to the floor as we all leap up in celebration. There are tears, laughter, high fives, hugs, dancing and a heady combination of shock and ecstasy. We've done it! We've bloody done it! Fully established – and all in a little under six weeks.

'Adam's going to be so gutted he wasn't here for this,' Bob says, his arms still round Marge and Dad's shoulders.

'It is his wife's birthday,' Marge reminds him.

'I don't think that would have stopped him if he'd known,' Bob says, laughing.

'I can't believe you didn't tell us straight away,' I say to Dad.

'And miss out on this moment?' We survey the carnage around us. 'Okay so I might need a new rug and a couple of new pint glasses, but it was worth it for that reaction. I actually wish I'd recorded it so I could watch it again.'

'We could reset the scene and try to recreate it,' I suggest, thinking it would make a good reel for our Instagram page as well.

But Dad laughs and shakes his head. 'I'm not sure my heart could take it.'

'It's going to be so good telling the team,' Cassie says dreamily. 'Although we should probably wait till after we've finished tomorrow's session. They'll be distracted enough having Pryce there without throwing this at them as well.'

'Why don't we organise some kind of celebratory get-together over the weekend, hold off from putting anything online yet and break the news to them then?' I suggest. 'Ben does think the team will play a lot more cohesively if they get to know each other better.'

I realise my mistake as soon as the words have left my mouth and I catch Cassie eyeing me suspiciously. I can only hope it's because she thinks this is Ben trying to push his own ideas on us and not because she's clocked I used his first name. But luckily Dad takes this idea and runs with it before she can ask me about it.

'We could set up a game of rounders in the park,' he suggests. 'Or some other kind of game.'

'Drinking games?' Barbour suggests.

'If they're up for it, why not?' Dad says. 'It will help us build bonds with them too. I want every one of us, players and management, to feel like one big family.'

'Uh-oh, Dad's about to get sentimental,' Cassie warns.

He rolls his eyes. 'You can mock, but that's how I feel. This wouldn't be happening without all of us working together, and I'm so appreciative of how you've all pitched in. You've given up so much of your time and—'

'Dad!' Cassie exclaims. 'Don't kill the mood!'

'I'm just trying to say thank you,' he protests.

'And we get it, but let's stick with the upbeat vibes.'

'Fine,' he concedes. 'But let me just raise a glass to all the legends sitting round this table. Whatever comes next, we should never lose sight of what we've achieved.'

13

Ben arrives early for the training session on Thursday evening. He wants to talk to Cassie before the players arrive, to assure her he isn't trying to suggest he can do a better job than her. When I called him last night to tell him he'd got the green light to join us, I was honest with him about her reservations. And I can tell she's still got her defences up from the way she folds her arms across her chest.

I don't know how I feel as I watch him walking across the pitch towards us, his muscular body more obvious today under a tight orange T-shirt. Conflicted, I suppose would be the best way to put it. I can't pretend it's not very distracting when he flashes his gigantic smile at me, and after our chat on Tuesday evening I am more curious about him. He really wasn't what I was expecting when it was just the two of us, but I remind myself that tonight he's just here to be part of the team.

'Ladies,' he says by way of greeting, then to Cassie, 'I'm genuinely honoured to be here.'

'And we're happy to have you,' I say quickly, when it

becomes evident Cassie isn't going to respond. I nudge her in the side and she glares at me.

'Perhaps you'd like to start by telling Cassie your thoughts on what you saw of the Tuesday session,' I suggest to Ben.

'Sure.' He turns his grin her way. 'When we train at Millford, they start us off with stretches, lateral lunges, high kicks, short bursts of running, then we go into game play, and it looked like you had that spot on. I wasn't there to see the whole thing, but Lily tells me you finished off with penalty practice, which is nice because everyone feels good when they score or save a goal, so it means everyone has the opportunity to go home on a high.'

'Anything you might switch up?' I ask, while Cassie maintains her stubborn silence.

'Just that it was all quite serious, and while you want everyone to stay focused and work hard and be the best they can be, in these early days it's just as important to work on building team spirit and making sure the players have that real sense of a group effort, so you don't have anyone trying to stand out at the expense of the rest of the team.'

'Is there anything you'd suggest?'

'At Millford they do these little initiations when someone new joins, like everyone doing a performance of their favourite song or a party trick or whatever, anything that gets the rest of the players either laughing or joining in. I did find it helped break the ice for me when I first joined.'

I tell him about our plan to hold a rounders game on Saturday.

'That's exactly the kind of thing,' he says. 'Honestly,

so much of it is about developing that team mentality. If you haven't got that, you'll really struggle to succeed.'

'Is Bailey okay about you being here?' Cassie asks, the first words she's said to him.

I follow her eyeline and see Bailey making his way towards us, with Levi and Scott not far behind him.

'Yeah, he knows I'm here to help, not to try and steal the limelight,' Ben assures her. 'And he's more than used to me giving him footballing tips.'

She nods curtly and I'm glad he doesn't seem too put out by her standoffishness. It's no worse than I expected and at least I had the chance to warn him.

I turn to welcome the trio of players, and I swear Scott and Levi pull themselves up to their fullest height as I introduce them to Ben, which convinces me we made the right choice bringing him here. Even if all his presence does is make each of our players step up a gear, it was worth pushing Cassie to agree to it.

Elliot, Jacob and Adio are next to arrive and they jostle each other like excited schoolkids when they first clock Ben. There's no denying he comes with kudos, despite his suspension. He's one of the top goal scorers in the Premier League this year. He's achieved what they barely dare dream of.

Of all the players, it's only Craig who doesn't react enthusiastically. Instead he regards Ben with a cool expression, back stiff, as if he sees him as a threat. Ben either doesn't notice or doesn't care. I imagine he's come up against this kind of machismo plenty of times during his career. But as he's taller than Craig – and in fact all the players except Elliot – Craig will have to look up to him physically, even if he doesn't metaphorically.

Bob and Dad arrive just in time for the warm-up, having stopped off to pick up some agility training rings and hurdles for Cassie from the sports superstore just outside Hamcott. Both thankfully hide any scepticism they might still be harbouring as they shake Ben's hand and welcome him.

Barbour and his two sons put in an appearance not long after that. His youngest, Nathan, is apparently desperate to meet Ben, so he can tell his friends at school, and Barbour has brought folding chairs so they can sit and watch the team training and say hello at the end.

Ben encourages Cassie to run the session just like she did on Tuesday, proposing that while she organises the players, he'll move among them and flag up anything he thinks they could be doing better. And from this set-up, Adio gets to learn how he can make his crosses more accurate and Nico gets some tips on how to best avoid injury from a wayward tackle.

From where I'm standing, Ben appears to slot in as if he was always meant to be there. I think even Cassie starts thawing towards him when she sees the positive effect he's having.

But the real turning point comes after a misjudged ball from Ben himself flies straight towards Barbour and his sons, catching Nathan smack bang on the side of the head. It almost knocks him off his chair.

As Cassie and I race over to check on him, out of the corner of my eye I notice Ben sprinting in completely the opposite direction – towards the exit – at full pelt, and my heart sinks. Just when he was starting to look like an asset for our team, he turns out to be nothing but a coward. I feel slightly sick at the thought of how hard I fought to have him here and how easily I was taken in by him.

But seconds later he reappears at the gate and comes hurtling towards us until he's kneeling in front of Nathan, who is thankfully shaken but not hurt. He ignores the furious glare Barbour is throwing his way and apologises to Nathan, who nods solemnly when Ben asks if he thinks he's going to be okay.

'Do you know what makes me feel better when I'm hurting?' he asks, to which Nathan shakes his head.

'Haribo,' Ben says, producing a packet from his pocket, which makes the little boy's eyes light up. 'I always keep some in my car for moments like these,' he explains.

And I think all our hearts melt a little when Nathan shyly accepts the bag of sweets from him. It does make me feel guilty for jumping to the wrong conclusion so quickly.

'And do you know what else I think might help you feel better?' Ben says, beckoning for me to pass him the offending ball. He retrieves a marker pen from his other pocket and scribbles his signature in big letters across the surface.

'This is for you,' he tells Nathan, whose eyes are now wide. 'You can tell all your friends at school about the time you got splatted by Ben Pryce from Millford City. That sound like fun?'

Nathan nods furiously and looks up at his dad, who by this point is thankfully looking less like he wants to murder Ben.

'Say thank you,' Barbour says.

'Thank you,' Nathan repeats dutifully.

Ben gets back to his feet and ruffles Nathan's hair. 'All

right, then we should probably get back to training. Turns out even I need to work on my passes. I'll buy you a new ball,' he promises Cassie as they turn back to where the rest of the team are waiting.

'I should hope so,' she says. But there's a lightness in her voice that wasn't there previously.

'Maybe he's not such a bad fella after all,' Barbour says to me, looking down at Nathan, who's now chewing a gummy bear and clutching the ball in his lap.

'Maybe not,' I agree, back to wondering if there's more to him than people give him credit for. And when the session wraps up, Barbour even shakes Ben's hand.

'So, same time and place next week?' Ben asks Cassie as he helps stack up the cones. I watch her body freeze. This was, of course, sold to her as a one-off.

'Give us two minutes for a quick confab, would you?' Dad says, beckoning me over to join them.

'Sure,' Ben says affably. 'I'll just wait over there with the kids.'

The three of us huddle together and Dad asks what we thought of the session.

'I thought the players looked quite uplifted,' I tell them. 'There was just something a bit extra from them today.'

Dad nods. 'I agree. And most of them seem pretty keen to have Pryce back again. So what do we tell him?'

We both turn to face Cassie, who sighs then admits she did find it easier having two coaches on the pitch. 'It didn't feel like he was trying to take over,' she concedes.

'Do we know how long he'll be around for?' Dad asks me.

'At least the next few weeks, I guess. I imagine he'll be called back to Millford at some point, but we could ask him to stick around until then.'

'All those in agreement?' Dad says.

I look over to where he's kicking a ball back and forth with Barbour's boys, all three of them grinning their heads off. It overrides any last doubts. I raise my hand.

'I can't quite believe I'm saying this, but it's a yes from me too,' Cassie says.

Dad nods again. 'That's three yeses then. Let's go over and break it to him.'

Ben turns his grin our way as we approach, like he already knows what we're going to say.

'As long as you know we can't pay you,' Dad starts.

'I just want to help,' Ben assures him.

'And it won't cause any problems with Millford?' Dad checks.

'They won't even know I'm here.'

'With twenty-two excitable young players and an occasional fan dropping by to watch? It'll be on social media in no time,' Dad says.

'It'll be fine,' Ben insists. 'My lot are always on at me to try and create a bit of positive publicity, so I can't see them complaining. Not that that's why I'm here, of course.'

'Nevertheless, perhaps you and I should put our heads together and come up with a press release that we can run by your PR team,' I suggest. 'To make sure we're the ones in control of the narrative.'

'Now?' he asks, with a playful look in his eyes.

Did I intend to hint at that? Even if I didn't, I'm not

100

against the idea now he's suggested it. It'll give me another chance to try and suss him out.

'We just need to get everyone out of here so the academy can lock up but yes, after that, let's hang back and have a quick chat about it,' I tell him.

This time, Ben suggests going to a little family-run Italian restaurant, another ten-minute drive from the academy.

'How come you know all these great local places?' I ask him as we're shown to our table.

'I'm always down here in the summer, visiting Bailey and our parents. I've actually got a place over by Redmarsh, for when I'm not up north with Millford. I don't get to spend a lot of time in it, but I assume I'll live in it properly one day.'

'You're not a secret Rovers fan, are you?' I ask.

'Fulham. My dad bought me their strip when I was about seven and that was that. My manager at Millford would lose his mind if he knew. They beat us at our last meeting. I didn't know whether to be happy or sad.'

'Does your brother support them too?'

'He does, but my parents follow Millford City now. I've told them they don't need to feel obliged to, but they always get tickets when we're down here playing the London teams. I guess they'll be following Crawford now too – to keep things fair with Bailey. How about your mum – will she come to the matches or is she not into it?'

I swallow back the discomfort I always feel when I first tell someone about my family set-up. 'She lives too far away. She moved to Cornwall when I was little.'

'Oh I'm sorry.' He instinctively moves his hand

101

towards mine, but stops just before he touches me. 'Do you still see her?'

'When I can. We text each other all the time, and her and Dad still speak now and again. We're kind of used to it now, but we do still miss having her here. I'm glad Dad's always had Hamcott Park – and now Crawford United – to keep him busy.'

We're interrupted by a waiter arriving to fill our water glasses and take our order. I haven't even looked at the menu yet, so I have a quick read.

'Let me know if there's anything you'd like to share,' Ben says.

'That would be pretty much everything on the starters list,' I tell him. 'And I haven't even got to the mains yet.'

'We could order one of each and eat tapas-style,' he suggests.

'What he said,' I tell the waiter, handing my menu back without another glimpse.

When we're alone again Ben asks, 'So back on the subject of Crawford, how do you think the session went this evening?'

'Aside from the part where you nearly murdered a four-year-old?' I tease.

He winces. 'Not my finest moment. It's probably best not to put that in your press release.'

'I'm very happy considering it was only the second get-together. Of course there are a couple of niggles – Nico can't be giving the ball away so often, and those silly little slip-ups from Levi will put so much pressure on Elliot – but then I have to remind myself to keep my expectations in check. Of course they're not going to be as good as Hamcott Park's players – at least not yet.'

'You'll get them there – just give it time. I think Jamie and Craig are showing a lot of promise up front for two players who are only in their first week on the team. I can see them being a really strong double threat once they get used to each other's rhythm.'

'Strong enough to be a threat to you?'

He laughs. 'Let's not get carried away.'

'Getting back to the press release for a minute, I'm thinking we should focus on how you're selflessly giving up your free time to help out a little-known local community team,' I suggest. 'That shouldn't give Millford anything to grumble about.'

He smiles. 'I reckon they'll love it. Like I said earlier, they've been thinking about ways to give the media something more positive to say about me before I get back to playing matches, to keep the sponsors happy. When it comes to protecting their brands they prefer us to be squeaky clean.'

'You could always use this as your opportunity to address what went on at that Hamcott game, while you've got something constructive to offset it against. I'm no expert, but you never know, it might stop the papers raking over it again and again.'

'Much as I'd like that, I can't really go into it. It's just . . .' He sounds uncharacteristically flustered. 'I'm sorry, it's complicated.'

I study his face, wondering if I really want to know what provoked him that day.

Quickly recovering his composure, he adds, 'Anyway, it's not like the papers didn't paint me in a bad light before this – even if, in my opinion, I'm no worse than anyone else in the league. But the best thing I've learned since I started at Millford is not to worry too much about what other people think of me. Someone will always have an opinion – that's just football – but you can drive yourself crazy if you take it all to heart. I couldn't do what I do if I was constantly stressing about it. Although in case it's not obvious, I do care what you think.'

And there it is again, another casual comment dropped into the conversation that takes me by surprise. He holds my gaze as I process the fact that he's basically just admitted he wants me to like him. It's hard not to, of course, when he's so friendly and engaging. But there's liking and there's *liking*, and I'm still not entirely sure which this is.

Our waiter comes back and starts spreading our mishmash of dishes across the table, describing each one in such painstaking detail that by the time he's finished, the moment has passed. But that doesn't stop a small part of me thinking that perhaps I want Ben to like me too. There's just something about him that makes me want to spend more time with him.

With that in mind I ask him, as we walk to the car after the meal, if he'd like to join us for the rounders day on Saturday. It feels rude not to invite him when he's now going to be seeing the team so frequently.

His face lights up all over again as he tells me he'd be delighted. And when we pull up in my street – not right outside the house in case Dad is still up and happens to see – my heart does a little dance when he fires me one last oversized grin and says, 'I'll see you on Saturday.'

14

With all twenty-two Crawford players present, plus Dad, Cassie, Bob and me (Marge declares herself the bag guardian), we end up in a thirteen-on-thirteen rounders battle. Ben is joining us later, once he's completed his weekly Millford check-in – where his coach calls to check up on his diet and exercise from the last seven days and sets a new programme for the following week to make sure he's still fit when he returns to the squad.

Perhaps due to his height, Elliot proves to be a demon bowler, but almost all the players have excellent hand–eye coordination and can run like lightning, so the scores quickly rack up. To begin with at least. On Bob's suggestion, a table of vodka shots is set up at fourth base for anyone who makes it round, so the chances of them doing so again are significantly reduced.

As now seems to be the way, our mini fan club of Barbour's family, Helen from the *Herald* and a handful of others come to watch. Phoebs joins us as well, having decided her revision can wait for a few hours after I told her I'd spent a second evening with Ben.

The conversation went something like this:

'That's it, I'm coming down there, before there's nobody left.'

'I'm not planning on working my way through all of them!'

'I know that, I just mean I want to get in there before anyone else decides to. I don't want to miss out on all the fun.'

I warned her I don't know which, if any of them, are single. But she came back with: 'Leave that to me. I'll soon find out.'

And it's not long before she's mingling with all the players after Bailey, the top run-scorer of the afternoon, declares himself too tipsy to continue with the rounders. Phoebs immediately volunteers to jump in – and starts flirting with Craig as she stands in front of him in the batting square.

'He's definitely in the running,' she tells me, when she makes it to first base where I'm fielding. 'You didn't tell me how hot he is when you said he likes getting his kit off.'

'For work,' I remind her.

'We'll see,' she says with a grin.

Jason is next to withdraw from the game, followed by Scott then Dad, after Bob decides that penalty drinks should also be awarded to anyone who is caught out or who hits the ball further than the back fielder. Barbour steps in to fill one of the gaps and at one point even Nathan has the bat in his hand. But luckily he doesn't manage to connect with the ball – no one wants to give vodka shots to a four-year-old.

By mid-afternoon, it's fair to say the majority of our

players are looking the worse for wear. Time, then, to call it quits on the rounders and bring everyone back together for our second game – a modified life-size version of *Cranium* that Dad and I invented yesterday, with a circle of cones rather than a board for the teams to work their way around.

Our four categories are karaoke, dance move, act it out and animal alliterations, and we've drawn a coloured football on each cone to show which is which. When a team lands on a blue ball, one of the members has to sing a song and the first person, out of everyone, to identify it and shout out the name of the artist gets to move their team on one cone. For a yellow ball, the entire team has to perform a dance move, and Marge gets to judge whether it's good or not, and consequently whether the team gets to advance one cone or move back two.

Green signifies speed charades, where the team has just twenty seconds for one of its members to use another as a puppet to mime whatever film or TV show is on the card that's handed to them. If the remaining two guess it, on they go to the next cone. And in the final category – red, my favourite – the team member who's selected to play must come up with an animal and an adjective that start with the same letter, for instance an elegant elephant, then do an impression of it so the others can try to guess what it is, a correct guess again moving the team one cone forward.

We have six teams of four, including Bob and Marge this time, with Cassie sitting out so she can hand out the activity cards and me so I can film some of the silliness that follows. And it starts straight away with Levi's team landing an animal alliteration and Jacob choosing to act out a sexy squirrel. As he floofs his pretend tail and nibbles coquettishly on an invisible nut, his teammates get the giggles so badly they can't even speak.

'Don't guess anything, just make him keep doing it,' Levi gasps through tears of laughter. 'You are never going to live this down, Jacob. This is going straight on TikTok.'

Jacob rolls his eyes then lays it on even thicker, wiggling his tail and mock stroking tufty ears.

'Oh God, make it stop, it's giving me the creeps,' Elliot snorts. 'It's a squirrel, right? A seductive squirrel? I mean, I want to say a somewhat disturbing squirrel but I don't think that's how it works.'

'A sexy squirrel,' Jacob corrects, 'but that's close enough. And when my TikTok followers double, you'll be wishing you'd done it yourself. I might just put a new one up every day.'

It probably isn't his worst idea if he wants to grow his following.

Phoebs, who is quick to stand in on Craig's team when Adio has to dash off for a toilet break, just as speedily volunteers to be the puppet when Craig is tasked with acting out a movie. He raises her arms up in front of her, thumbs up, forefingers pointing forward, then moves in behind her and jiggles her arms up and down to make it look like she's shooting guns.

'Shooter?' Bailey suggests, to which Craig shakes his head. 'Then can you narrow it down a bit?'

Craig reaches round Phoebs and makes rings with his fingers and thumbs in front of her eyes.

'Binoculars?' Bailey asks with a frown.

'Glasses,' Scott guesses.

Craig nods then moves Phoebs' hands down to waist

height, revs her wrists and swings her body like she's riding a motorbike before moving her back into the shooting arms position.

'Five seconds,' Cassie calls out.

'Oh jeez,' Bailey mutters, just as Scott shouts, 'I've got it! It's the *Terminator*.'

Craig punches the air then holds his hands up to Phoebs for a double high five. And I can't help laughing as she shamelessly ignores them and goes in for a hug instead. Her ballsiness is one of the reasons I love her. Once he's recovered from his surprise, Craig puts his arms round her and hugs her back.

While all this is going on, Dad gets a barbecue going and the game comes to a natural end at the point where the smell of homemade burgers cooking becomes too good to ignore. It's time to flop on to the grass with a loaded paper plate and a can of beer, and that's where Ben finds us, chatting and laughing. It gives me butterflies when he makes a beeline straight for me.

'Have I missed all the fun?' he asks, as I shuffle to the side so he can sit between me and Bailey. 'You're looking a bit bleary-eyed there, bro.'

'Cassie and Lily don't mess around on the drinking games,' Bailey says. 'I can't remember the last time I felt this giddy at this time of day.'

'I'm not going to have to escort you home and tuck you up in bed, am I?' Ben asks. He turns to me and shields his mouth as if he's about to tell me a secret, but says, loud enough for Bailey to hear, 'It wouldn't be the first time.'

'That's fair. He does look out for me,' Bailey agrees. 'Remember that time you brought me home in a shopping trolley?'

'He couldn't walk,' Ben explains, laughing at the memory. 'What were you, fifteen or something?'

'About that. It was the first time I'd ever had alcohol.'

'He was round his mate's house and I got this barely comprehensible voice message asking if I could come to the rescue. I tried to piggyback him home initially, but must have decided he was too heavy. So I broke a trolley free from outside the Morrisons and got him back that way. Mum and Dad were so annoyed they made us offer to pay for the damage the next day. We were let off though, luckily.'

'And he's been getting me out of trouble ever since then,' Bailey says.

Ben nods to confirm this. 'You're good today though, yeah?'

'Absolutely,' Bailey agrees. 'But I'm glad we don't do this at every training session.'

The afternoon gradually winds down once all the food is finished. I think everyone's too stuffed to do any more running around – and I suspect a couple of hangovers might already be kicking in. When Elliot stands up and admits he's ready to call it a day, there are calls of 'lightweight' before two of the reserve team players also say they need to head off. One has a birthday do to get to, the other a demanding two-year-old.

Dad calls for everyone's attention and thanks us for really throwing ourselves into it today. 'It's been a pleasure for me to get to know each of you a little bit better and I hope you all feel the same way. Before you go, I have some news to share that I think will be the perfect way to round off the afternoon. I know you must have been wondering what's going on with our league

110

application and the ground share, and I want to thank you all for your patience . . .'

'Have you got them?' Craig interrupts, sitting up straighter.

The other players who were reclined on their elbows also push themselves upright, poised for Dad's answer, but before he says anything, I think they've already guessed from his face. No one smiles that broadly if they're about to about to crush someone's dreams.

'That will be a yes!' Dad declares.

Which sparks a similar scene to the one in our kitchen, with half the team rolling on to their backs and kicking their arms and legs in the air, and the rest leaping to their feet and tearing round each other in circles before pulling Dad into a bouncing group hug while their cheers ring out across the park. It's the photo that Helen ends up using on the *Herald* website when she breaks the news to the rest of Hamcott.

'This is the best Saturday ever,' Jacob says, beaming.

'Out of interest, by a show of hands, can I see how many of you would be able to make this a regular Saturday meet-up over the summer?' Cassie asks. 'I'm not suggesting we play rounders every week, we'd just have a fun, relaxed session to bolster our other training. Maybe two till five, to get us in the right kind of routine before we start match days.'

Scott is first to reply. 'I'm down for that.'

It's followed by a chorus of 'me too's.

'Let's make it official then,' Cassie says. 'Two till five every Saturday. We'll work on a few things but we'll keep it light. Thanks, guys. You're the best.'

Bit by bit everyone starts drifting off after that, and

I have good reason to be one of them. My first exam is on Tuesday – I can't believe how quickly it's come round – and I need to cram some last-minute study in. I can't help feeling disappointed, though. I'd assumed Ben and I would sneak off somewhere first after our last two liaisons, but although I think I detect an inquisitive narrowing of his eyes as we're saying goodbye, he doesn't suggest it.

I walk out of the park with Phoebs, the ache in my stomach making me realise how much I'd been looking forward to more time with just him. Phoebs, meanwhile, excitedly tells me she's decided, now she's met all the players, that it's Craig she wants to get together with.

'You don't want to pick someone nicer?' I can't help asking. 'You know he's been a bit over-friendly with me and Cassie and he can come across like he thinks he's superior to his teammates.'

'I'm not planning on marrying him.' She laughs. 'Seriously, who'd want to lumber themselves with a footballer? All those girls flinging themselves at them every weekend. No thank you.'

She stops in her tracks. 'Wait a minute. When you told me Ben had grown on you, you didn't mean you'd actually consider dating him, did you?'

I'm about to protest, but the words don't come. I know I was hesitant to even go for one drink with him initially, but that was before I'd got to know him a bit. Now, for the few weeks he's here in Hamcott, I'd be happy to spend more time in his company.

'Oh no, no, no.' Phoebs shakes her head emphatically. 'You don't date the Ben Pryces of this world. He'll break your heart faster than you can say offside.'

'It doesn't matter anyway.' I shrug. 'If he wanted to, I'd be with him now.'

And it's at that exact moment that his name pops up on my ringing mobile phone, instantly making my heart race.

'Speak of the devil?' Phoebs asks as I lift the phone to my ear and nod my head.

'Can you talk?' he says after my tentative hello. 'It was a bit tricky before, under the watchful eye of your dad.'

I feel my shoulders relaxing. So that's why he didn't say anything earlier. 'Yes, I can talk. Where are you now?'

'I stayed in the park. I was hoping you might want to come back.'

'Er, yeah, I could do that. Are you in the same spot?'

'On one of the benches. I've checked – no one else is still around.'

I watch Phoebs roll her eyes as I tell him I can be there in five minutes.

'Am I crazy?' I ask her once I've disconnected the call.

'Yes, but when did that ever stop you?' she says with a smile. 'Go and have some fun, but just be cautious. Remember Craig's not the only one with a few red flags to his name.'

15

'Hi again,' Ben says, standing up to greet me as I approach. 'So have you got any energy left after this afternoon?'

There's a bag by his feet that he didn't have earlier. 'What have you got in mind?' I ask. I assume it's something to do with whatever is inside.

'I had a few bits stashed in the car that I thought might come in handy as it's such a beautiful evening.' He rummages around in the holdall. 'I've got a frisbee, pétanque balls, some table tennis bats . . .'

I smile at him. 'Sounds like we've got ourselves a triathlon. Loser buys dinner; winner gets to choose where?'

He laughs. 'Deal. I hear the Ledbury's summer menu is pretty special. I look forward to finding out.'

'In your dreams!' I grab the frisbee and fling it high into the air. 'It'll be the tasting menu at Gordon Ramsay, I think you'll find,' I call out as he goes tearing after it.

He leaps athletically off the ground and catches it mid-flight, then sends it wheeling back my way. 'Or maybe the Latymer in Bagshot,' he shouts.

'The Fat Duck!' I holler, as I send it on its way again.

We keep this up until he draws a blank on his turn, pausing too long before offering up a tentative 'McDonald's'.

'Am I allowed to say that?' he asks, wincing because he already knows the answer.

'No way! I think what you're allowed to say is that this is one–nil to me.'

'Fair enough.' He walks back towards me and chucks the frisbee back in the bag, holding his other hand out for me to shake. I notice how warm and strong it feels wrapped around mine and I think we both hold on for slightly longer than we need to.

When he finally lets go, he says, 'We'd better go and see if we can get on a table tennis table, so I can even things out.'

'I'm not saying anything,' I reply smugly. I've been playing since I was tall enough to see over the edge of the table. I'm confident of another win. We might not even need the pétanque.

I'm in for a surprise though. It quickly becomes clear Ben is on another level to me. I might have knocked around in the park with friends on and off for most of my life, but he admits afterwards that he played for his borough when he was a teenager. So while I manage to give him a reasonable run for his money, there's no question of me taking a game off him.

'I make that one all,' he says, eyes sparkling as he comes round the table for another handshake.

I give him a playful shove. 'I can't believe you let me think I was in with a chance.'

'You'll always be in with a chance,' he says, holding my gaze.

And any residual resolve not to be charmed by him melts away as I feel a sudden urge to kiss him. I know I probably shouldn't want to – it can only end badly – but being around him just makes me feel so light and happy.

It's Ben who snaps us out of the moment again. 'It looks like it's all down to the pétanque. Good job I've got my throwing arm warmed up already.'

I've never played before, but I'm not about to admit it. There's no need to boost his confidence any further. I know I need to get my balls as close as possible to the marker, but if there's a knack, I'm not aware of it. I just hope the throw-and-pray method is effective.

We toss a coin to decide who's going to set the marker – and he wins. But he doesn't toss it too far away, either because he's being generous or because he wants to make it easier for himself. He invites me to throw first and I misjudge it completely, lobbing my ball about three feet further than I need to.

'Hard luck,' he says, before pitching his first ball to within a few inches of the target. He grins at me, clearly impressed with his effort. 'I think I'm getting hungry. You're up.'

Determined not to let him win, I try to calculate exactly how much I need to rein in my next throw, but I probably should have just trusted my instincts instead of overthinking it. My ball comes up a good two feet short this time.

'Ooh, scallops wrapped in pancetta for the starter I reckon,' Ben says, licking his lips then pulling off another near-perfect throw.

I'm not deterred. For my third and final attempt I take a deep breath, let my shoulder drop and bend my knees

116

so I can use my whole body to direct the ball. And it works! Not only does it land within striking distance of the marker but it rolls right up to it until they're touching.

'I take my steak medium rare,' I fire back at Ben.

He laughs merrily at this. 'You know I thrive under pressure, right?'

'Sweet potato wedges, hold the fries,' I reply.

But he jammily throws his last ball so well it knocks the marker away from my ball and towards his. But is it far enough? We both run over to check.

'We might have to call it a draw,' he says, looking down at the final scatter pattern.

I'm about to suggest we play to the best of three when he says, 'How about we park it there and go and grab something to eat? All that food talk has made me hungry. To be continued?'

I can't say I need another meal after Dad's burgers, but I don't want the afternoon to end yet, so I tell him that suits me. As for the suggestion that we're going to do this again at some point, I'm secretly delighted, even if there are myriad reasons why I shouldn't be.

On the way to the car, Ben says he's got some steak back at his place that he can chuck on the barbecue if I do fancy steak and chips – and if I don't mind two barbecues in the same day. And my first thought is: *Back to his? We all know what that means.*

But even though he's probably used this line a hundred times before, I find I want to go anyway. After all, everyone's got a history, and it's not like I haven't started thinking about getting more intimately acquainted with him myself. So I tell him I'd love to see his house in Redmarsh.

It's hard not to feel intimidated when we pull into the driveway. When he said he had a place there, what he really meant was on the road lined with mansions that leads from Redmarsh into Surrey. Not that Dad's house is small, but Ben's makes it look like a cottage. It must have at least six bedrooms.

I listen to our shoes crunching on the gravel as we approach the front door of the huge white building, half expecting a butler to open it and welcome us. But Ben produces a key.

'Welcome,' he says, holding the door open.

There's a chandelier hanging in the huge white hallway, and a row of trainers lined up along one wall. 'I never got round to buying a shoe rack,' he explains.

I follow him into the open-plan lounge and kitchen, which is another sea of white, from the marble worktops to the eight-seater sofa. I don't know what I expected but it certainly wasn't this. 'You like the minimal look then?'

He laughs. 'The joys of not spending much time in your own home. I haven't had time to put my stamp on it. I'm at a bit of a loss on where to start, if I'm honest. When I bought it I never really thought about all the extras.'

That's when I notice the pool in the garden, with loungers on one side, a cluster of pot plants off to one corner and a covered dining area at the other end. I walk over to the bifold doors for a closer look. 'I think this counts as a pretty good extra.'

He laughs again. 'That part I did put some thought into. I'll give you a quick tour of the rest of the house then we can get out there and get the barbecue going.'

A home gym occupies most of the rest of the ground floor. It has every machine you could think of – and floor-to-ceiling windows looking out over the garden. Upstairs there are just the four bedrooms, rather than six, but four bathrooms too. They're all decked out in white as well and three look like they've never been slept in.

'It's a bit over the top,' Ben says, sounding almost embarrassed. But I don't think he should apologise for being successful.

'It's not ridiculous, it's just . . .' I try to think of the right word to describe it. 'It's just so *clean*.'

'Exactly the look I was going for. Come on, let's get back downstairs and enjoy the best bit.'

It's only when I follow him out on to the terrace that I spot the outdoor table tennis set up at the bottom of the garden. 'Yeah, sorry about that – I probably should have said,' he apologises.

'I'll get you back,' I assure him. 'Maybe next time we'll do Scrabble, Boggle and Articulate.'

He grins. 'You're on.'

With the barbecue warming up and a tray of chips in the oven, we settle on the pool loungers to soak up the early evening sun. The surface of the water glistens in the beams of orange light as we chat about everything that happened before Ben got to the park.

'It looks so inviting,' I think aloud.

'You're welcome to jump in for a quick dip before dinner.'

'I haven't got anything to swim in,' I point out.

He gestures at the garden perimeter with both hands. 'No one's looking. You could just go in in your underwear.'

I'm about to laugh this off, till he adds, 'I'm up for it, if you are . . .'

I'm still in a playful mood after our fun in the park,

but I hesitate, wondering if this is a challenge too far. It's one thing getting competitive over a game of frisbee and quite another seeing who'd be quicker at taking half their clothes off.

Part of me thinks it's too much of a leap when all we've done so far is flirt with each other. But there's something about Ben's devil-may-care approach to life that makes me want to throw caution to the wind too and not think about the consequences till afterwards.

So I decide to stop worrying about whether it's a good idea or not. It's not like there's a huge difference between underwear and a bikini anyway – and I'm pretty sure I'm wearing knickers with no holes in. I take a deep breath, curl my fingers under the hem of my T-shirt and tell him, 'What the hell? Let's do it.'

'Last one in's cleaning the dishes,' he shouts, before I'm even midway through pulling my top up over my head. I wriggle free of it just in time to see him launching himself off the side of the pool and diving in fully clothed. As he surfaces with a grin I can't help hoping his phone isn't in his pocket – that's the kind of idiotic thing I do when I'm trying to impress someone.

'Are you always so competitive?' I ask him, laughing.

He puts a finger on his chin and looks to the sky, as if he's considering it. 'I believe so, yes. That's what happens when you grow up with a brother you're quite close to in age.'

'Does that mean you're going to want a swimming race now?'

He watches me step out of my shorts. 'I think I'm happy enough with today's wins,' he says, sounding very much like me in my underwear might be one of them.

I sashay towards him with an exaggerated hip swing, hamming it up to let him think I might want to be his prize. But just when his grin has got so wide it's taken over half his face, I launch myself into the air, wrap my arms round my knees and cannonball into the water, sending a wave crashing over him.

He's laughing his head off and wiping the splashes out of his eyes when I come up for air. 'I hope you know I'll get you back for that.'

'Oh yes, and I look forward to it.'

'You really aren't like anyone else I've met,' he says, shaking his head and chuckling again.

I'm about to joke that he, on the other hand, is the same as every other super fit athlete I've ever found myself semi-naked in a swimming pool with – I don't know how I always manage it – when he leans towards me and plants a kiss on my lips. But he pulls away just as quickly, apologising and telling me he couldn't resist.

As I drink in every inch of his beautiful face bobbing in front of me, I can't say I feel sorry at all. In fact I wish he hadn't stopped. So it's music to my ears when he adds, cheekily, 'Well, you know, sorry not sorry.'

All our goofing around is suddenly forgotten and we can't take our eyes off each other as the tension sizzles between us. I paddle closer, till our noses are almost touching, and he reaches for my hand beneath the water.

This is it, I'm really doing this, I think as I lace my fingers between his and close the last of the gap between us. And when I press my mouth back against his, I can feel his lips curling up into a smile.

Our tongues touch softly at first, gently exploring. But

121

soon our mouths are crushing together more hungrily, which is quite a challenge while we're treading water, so we swim towards the shallow end, stopping as soon as we can both put our feet on the bottom.

He draws me towards him and snakes his arms round my waist as he kisses me again. I run my hands over his muscular arms, feel his solid back through his soaking T-shirt then slide my arms up round his neck. A flare of heat rushes through me as our bodies press together despite the cool water on my skin.

When he moves his hands to the tops of my thighs and lifts my legs up, curling them round his waist, it feels like the sexiest move anyone has ever pulled on me. Resting my back against the side of the pool, he trails his fingers along my thighs as our mouths meet again.

By the time his hands have found their way back to my waist, I'm willing them to keep moving upwards, all the way to my breasts. But there's a sudden screeching sound from inside the house and Ben quickly untangles us. 'That's the smoke alarm,' he explains.

He apologises as he hauls himself effortlessly out of the pool, water cascading off his sodden clothes. 'Such bad timing, but I don't want the house to catch fire.'

Which I can hardly argue with, even if I'm gutted that we've had to stop kissing.

I watch him jog to the back door, where he pauses to strip his shorts and T-shirt off before disappearing inside, no doubt to stop them dripping all over his parquet floor. It gives me a glorious glimpse of his smooth, toned body and sends my mind off on a little journey about what else we might get up to in the pool when he comes back. My body fizzes at the thought of it.

But when he still hasn't returned a few minutes later, I climb out – using the steps; I doubt I could push myself up at the side as gracefully as Ben did – to go and find out why.

Ben has a towel wrapped round his waist and is flapping another one at the smoke rising from a charred pile of scraps in the top of his pedal bin.

'Slight incident with the chips,' he says, holding the towel out towards me. 'Sorry, this was meant to be for you.'

'So I can take over the flapping?'

He shakes his head, laughing. 'You might have to try not to distract me while the next batch is in.'

I flash him my most seductive smile and take a step towards him. 'I don't know if I can guarantee that.'

He reaches for his phone. 'Hold that thought please. I'm setting an alarm this time.' Then he draws me back towards him.

We don't stop kissing till the buzzer rings, initially in the middle of the kitchen then back outside on one of the loungers, the last of the evening sun drying any residual dampness on our skin. Now I've stopped trying to tell myself I shouldn't be doing this, I don't seem to be able to get enough of him. Whenever his hands brush against my breasts or my buttocks it makes my whole body sing.

It's so tempting to ignore it when his phone starts bleeping but, not wanting a repeat of earlier, he runs back indoors and emerges with the steaks for the barbecue and a bowl of perfectly golden chips, plus a fleece blanket to throw over us as the temperature drops.

We trade stories about the best steaks we've ever eaten while he's cooking the meat. 'No pressure then,' he says, laughing. And when he sets up a speaker so we can have some background music, we discover we like lots of the same bands and chat about which ones we've been to see.

After we've eaten, we recline side by side on one of the loungers, my head against his chest, both his arms around me.

'I reckon I could fall asleep out here,' he says drowsily.

'Am I boring you?' I ask, mock offended.

'Not at all. I'm just really comfortable around you. I think I could get used to it.'

I turn my face up towards his, thinking – but not saying it in case it sounds too cheesy – that it does feel like we fit. Even though we live in different worlds and we've known each other for less than a week, right here, at this moment, it feels like it's meant to be.

But his next words slam the brakes on that line of thinking. 'I suppose I should start thinking about getting you home in a minute. I don't want to keep you too long when you've got to crack on with your studies.'

I want to insist it's fine, I can catch up tomorrow, but he's already shifting his weight beneath me. And it is the smart choice, so I sit up and reach for my shorts and T-shirt, which are still on the floor by the lounger where I discarded them. As much as I don't want to rush back to my books, I know the longer I stay here, the harder it's going to be to leave.

16

Phoebs is brimming with a confidence I wish I shared when we meet for a coffee ahead of our first exam on Tuesday. I've barely left my bedroom for two days, reading pages and pages of notes on corporate ethics and responsibilities, but all too frequently my thoughts have drifted to Ben – how it felt to have his arms round me, how my heart swelled when he said he could get used to it, how I might be in danger of falling for him.

But there's a nagging doubt about him in my mind as well, because he's notorious for the number of girls he's hooked up with and yet he didn't even try to sleep with me. I know we kissed, and I don't doubt he enjoyed it, but I can't help wondering if he cut the evening short because he decided he didn't feel that way about me after all.

'It doesn't make sense, though, because he video-called me yesterday to let me know he was thinking about me and sent me a good luck text this morning, saying he couldn't wait to see me at training later,' I tell Phoebs.

'Maybe he was worried it might make things awkward

now you're sort of working together,' she says. 'You'll just have to see how he is with you this evening. But I did warn you not to let yourself get carried away with this.'

If I was sensible, I'd skip the training completely just for this week and next. I've got two more exams on Thursday, then one each on Wednesday and Friday next week. But I'm determined to always be there for the team – it's not just because I want to see Ben.

'I really don't feel very prepared for today,' I admit to Phoebs.

Also squeezed in around my revision there was the Crawford United team blog to write and our new season ticket offer to promote, after we decided to sell £100 tickets to the first one hundred purchasers before increasing the price to the £200 we hope fans might be willing to pay.

But in the end it's not that I don't know the answers to the questions that trips me up in the exam, it's more that I don't plan my time properly – which is so unlike me. So I fail to get a few key points down on paper before the bell rings to signify our time is up.

'Thank goodness that's over,' Phoebs says, linking her arm through mine as we walk out of the exam hall. 'One down, four to go. How do you think you did?'

'As well as I could have, not as well as I might?'

'Yeah, that sounds about right. I think I've done okay though. I managed to answer everything. So I was thinking, I might reward myself by taking this evening off and coming to Crawford's training session with you. Then I can help you try to suss out where you stand with Ben . . . and, you know, just casually remind Craig I exist.'

'I'm sure he hasn't forgotten. But yes, please do come.

126

I'd appreciate your take on things. I was going to tell Dad I'm going to yours afterwards though, to cover up sneaking off with Ben again. Will that still fit in with your plans for Craig?'

'I just want to say hi. I'll still be able to cover for you. I could even drop you over at his house after if it makes it easier. Then I'll get to check out this lush pad of his. From the outside, that is. I'm not about to invite myself in and get in the way of your love life.'

'That would be amazing. Thanks, Phoebs.'

We treat ourselves to a plate of tacos at Hamcott's best Mexican café before we head to the academy – a mini celebration for getting our first exam out of the way – but we make sure we're at the training session well before the players so Phoebs can try to engage Craig in a bit of banter before it begins.

It's hard greeting Ben with a handshake when all I really want to do is kiss him. Even his hand feels different in mine today, reminding me of the feel of it touching my body. I have to force myself to let go after telling him it's good to have him with us again.

I have to be careful not to focus on him too much in the videos I take of the session too, for Cassie to review later. But I'll admit I do zoom in on his face a couple of times while the camera is off. He's more attractive than ever when he's absorbed in the sport he loves probably more than anything else in the world.

It's Phoebs who first notices I'm not the only one pointing a lens in his direction. She nods her head towards the entrance gate. 'Have you seen what's going on back there?'

I turn to see a couple of photographers tracking Ben's

movements with their cameras. It was always a possibility, I suppose, once the news was out that he's here. I hand Phoebs my phone. 'Here, carry on filming the players, would you? I'm just going to alert Dad, Cassie and Ben.'

Cassie tells the team to grab a quick drink break when she sees me beckoning them over.

'You have more experience of this than any of us, so how do you want to play it?' I ask Ben.

'Just let them get on with it. When they see I'm genuinely here to help and that there's no big story behind it, they'll lose interest and go away. I'm not about to engage with them, but I wouldn't try to prevent them from filming either. In my experience, the harder you try to stop them, the greater lengths they'll go to, to find another way.'

Dad nods. 'Lily, why don't you and I head over there and just answer any questions they might have about Crawford. Hopefully that will be enough to keep them happy. Ben, you and Cassie can crack on with the session.'

'On it,' she replies.

And the photographers do, thankfully, seem happy when Dad greets them warmly and agrees to answer a few questions, telling them he's delighted to know Crawford will be making the headlines again, while flashing his most disarming smile. I think the homemade biscuits he offers them go some way to ensuring we keep them onside.

He politely declines to bring Ben over to join us and even manages to sound quite protective of him. 'Ben is busy with the team and won't be making a statement today. But what I can tell you is that he's a local lad who just wants to give back to the place where he's from. We're aware of his past but what we see before us is a young man who's made mistakes and is trying his best to redeem himself.'

Satisfied with this soundbite they eventually leave us to it, which is a huge relief to me. Their renewed interest in Ben could have made it hard for me to meet him in secret, if they'd decided to start following him around. But I guess they know from when the fan incident first happened that they're unlikely to get him to talk about it.

When we wrap up the session, Phoebs gets straight in with Craig for more of a chat, while Cassie, Dad and I work our way round thanking the other players. It takes longer now we're getting to know each other better. There's more familiarity so there's more to talk about.

Eventually I find myself in front of Ben and I'm amazed no one can tell how attracted I am to him. He winks when he says he'll see me again soon and I can't help but smile knowing just how soon it will be.

Phoebs confesses, once we're in her car, that she's swapped numbers with Craig now. 'But he more or less told me he doesn't want a girlfriend while he's focusing on the team.'

'Well it's good for me to know he's taking Crawford so seriously, but I'm guessing that isn't what you wanted to hear?'

'Oh no, I told him that's just fine with me. I'm perfectly happy with no-strings sex while I've still got exams to do. And after that, there'll be a job to find, so it's not like I haven't got my own stuff to deal with.'

'So did you arrange a hook-up?'

'Not yet, but I'm pretty sure we're building up to it. I can be patient. Up to a point, that is.'

She lets out a low whistle when we pull up outside

Ben's house. 'I think I might have changed my mind. I do want to come and see inside.'

'I'll send you some photos,' I promise her, laughing. 'I've got little enough time with him this evening as it is.'

She pulls away as I walk up the driveway, and when Ben opens the door, inviting food smells waft out from the kitchen.

'I wasn't sure if you'd be hungry so I've started making a Thai curry,' he explains, after a quick – much quicker than I was expecting – peck on the cheek.

Doubt creeps back in as I follow him into the kitchen. I can't help wondering, when he turns his attention straight back to the pans on the stove, if he's making himself busy to avoid kissing me properly or even talking about what happened the other night. I know it's ridiculous when not so long ago I was worried he just wanted to sleep with me – now I'm worried he doesn't!

As the TV's on in the background we end up discussing things we've watched recently while he's busy cooking. He never puts *Top Goals* on because it feels too much like work, but he says he could imagine getting sucked into *Dying Days* after I've described it to him.

Then the conversation drifts back to Crawford United and I mention Phoebs' newfound interest in Craig. 'I'm hoping she doesn't distract him too much,' I admit. 'Especially once we start playing matches.'

'I actually think I'm more focused when I'm in a relationship,' Ben tells me. 'On the rare occasions when I've had someone I care about watching me play, I've been even more determined to win.'

'And there I was thinking you were just out to impress *all* the ladies.'

I'm laughing when I say it, but he turns round and frowns. 'Is that what you think of me?'

His creased forehead makes me hesitate. 'Well yes, if I believe what I read in the papers.'

'I thought we'd talked about the nonsense that gets printed about me.'

'Only in the footballing sense.'

He sighs. 'Some of the girls they picture me with are people I've never even spoken to who've just asked for a photo, but life's too short to waste my time trying to correct all the stories. A few have been genuine dates, but others were set-ups by Millford's PR team. I think their hope is that one day I'll like one of them enough to get more settled. But they've never asked me what *I* might be looking for in a relationship.'

'What are you looking for?'

'Someone who I get on really well with,' he says. 'Not someone who's just motivated by money and sex. Someone whose ambition isn't just "being famous", who's interesting and funny and passionate about what they do.'

I'm just about to say this doesn't sound like too much to ask for when he adds, 'Someone like you, I guess.'

My heart flutters as our eyes meet. It doesn't sound like he thinks the other night was a mistake, but until I'm a hundred per cent sure I'm still hesitant to admit he's ticking a lot of my boxes too. Deciding there's only way to find out, I tell him I definitely don't care about the money or fame. 'But the sex . . .'

There. I've put it out there. I hold my breath as he reaches behind him and puts the spoon that was in his hand down on the counter.

'Remember what happened last time you distracted me while I was cooking?' he asks, a smile creeping on to his lips.

I smile back at him, feeling bolder now. 'Don't curries taste better if you leave them to simmer?'

He takes a step towards me. 'Are you trying to lead me astray?'

I tilt my head up towards his, a challenge in my eyes. 'I might be.'

We're inches apart now. 'What happened to wanting a Roy Keane tackle more than to be seen with me?' he asks.

'No one has to know,' I remind him.

He tucks his hand behind my neck and brushes his lips against mine in a way that makes my insides go gooey.

'I was trying to be good,' he murmurs, reaching behind him again to turn off the hot plates. 'And go about this the right way.'

I wrap my arms round his waist. 'Didn't we do being good on Saturday?'

His smile gets even wider and I finally get the kiss I wanted.

This time there are no kitchen emergencies to interrupt us and I do get to feel his hands on every part of my body. He caresses my buttocks through my playsuit and gradually trails his fingers up to my breasts. I can't stop a soft moan escaping from my lips as he gives a light squeeze that hardens my nipples. Pressing against him, I can feel him stirring in his shorts and it's a thrill to finally feel confident that he's as into me as I am him.

At some point we move to the sofa, where he tips me back against the cushions and lowers himself onto me. He nuzzles my neck as I curl my legs around his, then finds my mouth with his again as I slip my hands under his T-shirt.

I don't know how much time passes like that, but I feel like I could kiss him forever. And when he shifts his weight to the side of me to free one of his hands up, he makes me smile mid-kiss as he starts caressing my breasts again.

'You like that,' he whispers. I nod my head, *oh yes*.

And I like it even more when he discovers my playsuit is loose enough at the top for him to be able to push the material to one side, exposing my bra. He circles my nipple through the lace with his thumb, then pushes that aside too and cranes his neck to take my nipple in his mouth, rolling his tongue around it and sucking gently.

My body tingles as I watch, and the tingles intensify as he lets his hand drift down to my waistband, where it lingers tantalisingly. I reach down and guide it lower, and he starts a slow, circling massage that makes me so aroused I can't help but push my hips towards his.

He explores the bottom of my playsuit but realises there isn't an easy way to get underneath, and for a moment I think he's just going to stop what he's doing, but in the time it takes me to think, *Please keep going*, he's sat up, drawn me upright and is helping me wriggle free of it.

With only my bra still in place, he pushes me gently back against the cushions and spreads my knees wider so he can bring his head down between them. My body trembles as his tongue strokes against me and I push my hands into his hair, my breath growing ragged as he teases my clit.

'That feels so good,' I murmur breathlessly as I teeter

on the edge. When he pushes a finger inside me, my body arches in ecstasy.

'Are you ready?' he whispers against my skin.

A frantic nod. My God am I ready.

He moves his tongue back to my clit and flutters faster than ever, seeking out my G-spot as he pushes another finger deep inside me. My grip tightens on the sofa as he takes me closer and closer to orgasm until suddenly I lose control, my body jerking and juddering as it tears through me.

He doesn't withdraw his hand or mouth though, stretching out my climax until I have to beg him to stop. 'Please, I can't take any more,' I finally manage to gasp, feeling light-headed and panting heavily. I don't think I've ever orgasmed as hard as this.

For a moment I can't even think straight and I look at him in bewilderment. I had no idea my body could feel this way.

'Are you okay there?' he asks, with a devilish grin.

I shake my head. 'I'm not sure. I think you might have broken me.'

He leaps athletically to his feet. 'I'll get you some water.'

I still haven't moved when he comes back with two filled glasses.

He hands me one and I finally prop myself upright as he sits back down next to me. Neither of us can stop smiling. I still can't believe how good he made that feel.

'Looks like it got pretty late,' he says eventually, nodding at the dusky sky outside the window.

'Time really does fly when you're having fun,' I agree.

'I'm glad you enjoyed it. I enjoyed watching you come.'

'Even my screwed-up come face?'

This makes him laugh. 'I thought it was sexy. And you haven't got a look at mine yet.'

'I've nearly recovered,' I tell him.

He smiles. 'That wasn't a hint. It'll keep till next time. I don't want to rush any of this. So I was wondering, rather than another short evening together on Thursday after training, how would you feel about spending the whole day with me on Friday? I know you've got more exams next week so I understand if you can't. I just thought it might be nice to have more time together, but that's me being selfish.'

'I'd love to,' I say quickly before he talks himself back out of it. 'I'll need a day to regroup after the back-to-back exams on Thursday. I very much doubt I'll be productive if I throw myself straight back into it.'

'Then how about we meet mid-morning and head out somewhere? I'll think of something good, to give you a proper break from all the stress.'

I tell him that sounds lovely. A whole day with Ben! The thought of six hours in a stuffy exam hall suddenly seems a lot more tolerable now I've got that to look forward to at the end of it.

17

I really have to fight with myself not to get to Ben's too early ahead of our grand day out. While he will have been busy in his gym since the crack of dawn, I've shaved my legs, painted my nails, plucked my eyebrows, styled my hair, worked my way through multiple outfits before settling on jeans and still had time to pace round my room for over an hour. I can't wait to get round there.

It's not that I've forgotten his questionable pitchside behaviour or the fact that he's only in Hamcott temporarily, but I've decided not to dwell on it and just enjoy it for what it is, happy now in the knowledge that the attraction is mutual and that, although I might be the latest addition to his list, from what he's said that list is nowhere near as long as everyone imagines it to be.

Yesterday's exams – effective leadership and managing change in the morning, data analytics and financial decision-making in the afternoon – were predictably tough, and afterwards Phoebs and I went back to the Mexican, having decided it should be our wind-down routine on all our exam days.

While we were waiting for our tacos I admitted I was worried about my grades, but she was full of reassurance. 'I know you want to get a first, but it doesn't matter if you don't score a hundred per cent – a degree's a degree.'

Then she confessed she hadn't been studying quite as hard as I thought she had either – after she dropped me at Ben's on Tuesday she decided to invite herself to Craig's. 'Then I kind of didn't leave till the morning,' she said, grinning as she told me she'd already planned his next post-training warm-down.

I might not be Craig's number-one fan, but if this makes her even half as happy as I feel about seeing Ben then I can keep my opinions to myself.

Ben is fresh out of the shower and bouncing with energy when I get to his, only seven minutes ahead of our agreed meeting time. He still smells of soap as he pulls me towards him for a kiss.

'Do you fancy going for a drive today?' he asks.

'Sure, where to?'

'Down to the coast? I've not had a chance to take my little roadster out for a spin yet this year, and I reckon we could get away with putting the top down today, if you don't mind a bit of wind and noise, that is.'

'I think I can manage.'

'Great.' He pulls a bulging bag from the fridge and admits he's already made a picnic. 'I'll find a jumper you can borrow too. Your legs will be warm enough in those jeans, but your T-shirt probably won't cut it.'

He digs out a pair of socks too, in case I want to slip them on instead of the gold strappy sandals I'm wearing.

The car is a pale blue 1950s Mercedes convertible, which looks as good as new despite its vintage. 'I love her – she's got so much more character than that modern box you usually see me driving,' Ben says proudly. 'Your hair might get a bit messed up and it does make conversation a little limited, but I hope you'll agree it's worth it.'

I nod, feeling excited. 'Let's do it.'

It only occurs to me as we speed away from his house that I didn't ask exactly where we're going. It could be anywhere between Bournemouth and Broadstairs, but luckily I like surprises, so I decide to just wait and see. As the shops and houses of Hamcott are replaced by the fields and forests of the Surrey countryside, it feels like we're setting off on an adventure that could take us anywhere.

Ben reaches across and squeezes my leg periodically to check I'm okay, but I think the grin I can't wipe off my face tells him I'm loving every minute.

We eventually arrive in Deal on the Kent coast and Ben finds a parking spot on a road right next to the sea. He retrieves the picnic from the boot and we wander across the pebbles to a stretch of beach where there are just two other couples making the most of the sunshine.

'This'll do,' he says, unfurling a blanket and spreading it over the stones. 'We shouldn't get bothered by anyone here.'

He doesn't want me to have to deal with any unwanted intrusions, which he says are more likely now his name's been back in the press, even if it is for positive reasons this time.

'They usually just want me to sign something or pose for a selfie, but it can still feel quite invasive when you're not used to it,' he tells me.

He starts pulling pots from the cool bag and laying them out on the rug.

'Are we expecting friends?' I ask, my eyes widening.

He looks down at the spread and laughs. 'I have gone a bit overboard, haven't I? I wanted to make sure I covered all the bases so there'd definitely be something you wanted to eat.'

'I eat everything!'

'I should have just asked you. But we can chuck whatever's left back in the cool bag. It's good for twenty-four hours so it won't go to waste. We can always have the leftovers for dinner.'

Which is fine by me – the assortment of salads and cold pasta dishes looks amazing.

There's a half bottle of wine too, but despite how organised the rest of the picnic is, Ben has forgotten to bring cups. 'How do you feel about swigging wine out of a bottle?' he asks.

I can't help laughing. 'My favourite way to enjoy a chilled rosé.'

He hands me a plastic plate. 'At least I remembered forks.'

While we eat, we watch two paddleboarders wobbling unsteadily on their boards until they both fall into the sea. They're giggling as they scramble back up, only to topple over again almost immediately.

'Ever tried that?' Ben asks.

'Only on a very flat lake, which must be a lot easier because I didn't fall off once.'

'It's more fun when you've got a few waves to contend with. Next time we come to the coast, I'll chuck my boards in the car – you can see for yourself.'

Next time. The words send a shiver of excitement through me. Against the odds, could this actually turn into something lasting?

'Yet again I'm wishing I'd worn my bikini,' I admit, after we've packed away the excess food. It's far warmer than the forecast suggested, not that I knew we were coming to the coast.

Ben looks from me to the water then back to me with a mischievous gleam in his eye.

'There was no one around last time,' I remind him, 'if that's what you're thinking.'

'They won't be able to tell from over there whether you're wearing a bra or a bikini,' he says. 'Unless you've gone commando. But I assume not – that would not be comfortable under jeans.'

'I haven't, but I'm not sure my knickers won't be seethrough.' They're pale blue and unsurprisingly I've never worn them when they're wet.

'I'm not sure my boxer elastic is up to the task, either, but I'm willing to risk it,' he says.

It's enough to have me pulling my T-shirt up over my head. I will crack up if they end up floating down round his ankles.

'Is this becoming our thing?' I ask as we scramble out of our jeans.

'There are worse things that could be our thing,' he points out. So true.

'And I presume it's another race into the water?' I check.

'If you insist.' Said with his usual grin.

But no sooner has he taken off across the shingle than he stops and turns back to me with a pained expression on his face. 'Bloody hell, I'd forgotten how brutal these stones are on your feet. Let me give you a piggyback. We'll call this one a draw.'

I don't feel very sexy jiggling up and down against his back as he starts off across the beach again, but it's a really sweet thing for him to do for me.

As Ben's toes hit the water, he shudders and says, 'I hope you're ready for this.'

'Is it cold?' A silly question – it's not the Med.

'I'd like to say refreshing but I'm going to shoot for ball-numbing,' he warns.

'Maybe I'll just head back and wait with our stuff on the beach.'

But he doesn't release me – he's already thigh-deep, the chilly water creeping up over my ankles. 'On three?' he asks.

'Oh boy.' I take a deep breath.

'One, two . . .'

I shriek as he plunges us both into the waves.

Once the shock has subsided, it's not as bad as he made it out to be. And when he wraps his arms around me I forget about the cold altogether. We kiss for a long time, tasting the salt on each other's lips, and I forget about the other people on the beach too.

Once he's established that his boxers will in fact stay in place, he shows off with handstands under the water. It's only when we head back up the beach after a lazy swim that we remember we don't have towels with us, so we stretch out on the pebbles to dry off, enjoying the warmth of the stones against our skin.

'Could you see yourself ever properly dating a footballer?' Ben asks, rolling on to his side to face me.

141

I turn my head towards him. 'With all those lonely Saturdays and score-related mood swings?' I don't know why these are the first things that pop into my head, rather than thinking about why he might be asking.

'I know it's not ideal with all the weekends away and the strict regimes to contend with. And there's the odd story in the media, but you do get used to ignoring them pretty quickly and it's not like I'm on the same scale as David Beckham. On the flipside there's the long summer break, the days off after match days and we don't train round the clock twenty-four-seven. There is time for all the fun stuff as well,' he says.

And the penny finally drops when I see how earnestly he's looking at me. 'Are you saying you want me to be your girlfriend?'

'I want you to know I'm not just messing around. I know we haven't known each other long, but I really like you, Lily. So what do you reckon? Do you think you could put up with all my madness on a more official basis?'

All thoughts of this just being a summer fling fly out of my head. 'Well I do very much like all the fun stuff,' I tell him.

He mini punches the air and whispers, 'I think that's a yes.'

I wriggle closer to him. 'It's a definite yes.'

He leans in to kiss me. 'Does this mean I no longer have to keep my distance from you at the academy?' he asks. 'It's so hard trying to make out like I don't fancy the pants off you.'

But I still think we should stay under the radar and I tell him as much. Some people – Dad and Cassie specifically –

might not be so cool with it, and I don't want anyone else on the team to think I'm unprofessional. So Ben promises to behave himself and not give anything away.

Once we're dry, we put our clothes back on and go for a stroll, hand in hand, along the coastal path, and I ask Ben which of the houses he'd want to live in if he didn't have the Whitehouse, my nickname for his Redmarsh mansion. He picks a modern detached structure with a mostly glass front and a huge south-facing terrace on the first floor, giving a perfect view of the sea.

'I'd choose that one for the balcony alone,' he explains. 'Imagine having a coffee there in the morning, a glass of wine to watch the sunset.'

'For the six weeks when it's warm enough.'

He laughs. 'There'd be eight or nine at least. It doesn't make me want to move abroad though. The weather might be better but I like the fact that I can pop home from Millford whenever I have time to. I couldn't do that if I played for a club overseas.'

'It's not something I've ever seriously considered either. I do love holidays, but I didn't even move to a different city for university. I'm pretty sure I'd get homesick.'

'How much do you reckon a place like that would cost?' he asks, still looking at the terrace. 'It must be a lot – I suspect even I'd need a lottery win.'

'Let's buy a EuroMillions ticket, pick half the numbers each and split the winnings,' I suggest. 'You can buy this place. I'll cover Crawford's running costs for the next ten years.'

'You're on,' he says with a grin. 'Next shop we see.'

At the end of the long stretch of houses, we find a pub with tables and benches set out on the beach. We stop for a pint of orange and lemonade each – him because he's driving and me because I'm already feeling giddy from the earlier wine and the fact that I'm now officially dating him.

I look around at the other customers. 'Everyone seems so relaxed here. They all look so happy.'

'Maybe we need a dog,' he says, pointing out there's one at almost every table.

'I'd love one. It's always been my retirement plan.'

'Mine too, when life gets a bit more settled. I draw the line at matching anoraks, though,' he says, nodding towards a couple with his and hers red cagoules. 'Even when we're seventy.'

I laugh, because I can't believe he's even joking about us being old together. 'I think it's sweet. But they were probably just on a two-for-one offer.'

'It's still a no,' he says. 'No matter how in love you might be.'

And I roll my eyes, but his use of the L word doesn't escape me.

18

Back at the house that evening, I look up the lottery results while Ben grills some lamb chops to go with our leftovers.

'Ooh.'

This makes him look up. 'Have we won?'

'Two pounds seventy,' I confirm.

He laughs. 'You'd better cancel that anorak order.'

'And the deposit on that place by the sea. I should probably step up the Crawford fundraiser planning too. We've only got a couple more weeks.'

'Let me know if I there's anything I can do,' he says. 'I'd love to help.'

While he's clearing up after we've eaten, he asks if I want to take a shower to wash the sea salt off my skin. 'I probably should have offered before serving up, but you know what I'm like once I start thinking about my stomach.'

'Why don't you come in with me? To make up for it,' I suggest.

He walks over and scoops me up in his arms. 'Just try and stop me.'

145

Somehow he manages to carry me up the stairs without falling over, my legs curled round his waist, kissing me all the way. He sets me down in the master bathroom, which has a huge walk-in shower, pulls his T-shirt up over his head then turns his attention to mine, pushing my arms into the air so he can lift it clear and drop it on the floor with his.

'Are we going in in our underwear again?' I ask as he turns on the water. Which makes him pause for a moment while he studies my bra.

'It's very pretty, but not this time.' He reaches behind me to release the clasp, his eyes lingering on my breasts as I shake my arms free of the straps.

He bends his head lower and brings his mouth to my nipples, teasing one then the other with his tongue. I feel the fire starting up between my legs and when he straightens up to kiss me again I can see the erection in his jeans.

He tugs at his buttons and pushes the material down to his ankles, stroking himself for a second as he steps clear before reaching again for me. I brush his hand to the side so I can undo my own buttons, but my jeans are too tight to easily step out of, so he lifts me up onto the sink edge and raises my legs so he can pull them free.

There's a moment of hesitation during which I think we both contemplate having sex right there on the sink, but then he lifts me back to the floor and leads me into the shower, where jets of hot water spray us from all sides as well as above, reminding me of a fancy spa with even fancier facilities.

We take our time rubbing shower gel all over each other, his hands sweeping foam along my arms, across my back, down over my bum, then back to my breasts, where he focuses for a deliciously long time. I run my hands across his torso, his powerful biceps, feel the tautness in his backside and marvel at the rock-hard muscles in his thighs.

His erection nudges against me as he kisses me hungrily, and when he reaches down between us, bringing his fingers to my clit, each stroke sends an electric current to every one of my nerve endings. A gasp escapes from my lips as he pushes a finger inside me and I have to cling on to him for fear of my legs giving way beneath me.

He backs me gently against the wall to help me balance before adding another finger, bending to take my breasts in his mouth again, sucking and flicking my nipples with his tongue. There isn't a single inch of my body that doesn't feel alive from the sensations he's creating.

And suddenly I want more. I want to feel him deeper inside me. So I draw him back up to kissing height and after one more seductive meeting of our lips, I slide my mouth round to his ear and whisper, 'Make love to me.'

A smile creeps on to his lips as I withdraw his hands from my body and beckon for him to follow me over to the sink, where I lean over, looking back at him over my shoulder with an inviting wiggle of my hips.

As he pulls on a condom, I wipe the condensation from the mirror with my hand so I can see his reflection. He moves in behind me, spreads my legs a little wider and has one last play with my clit before he places a hand on each of my buttocks and guides himself inside me, making my whole body shudder as he presses himself against me.

His gaze stays down for a moment, a look of pure concentration on his face as he slides in and out agonisingly slowly. I close my eyes, savouring the sensuality of it, then meet his gaze in the mirror again when his thrusts take on more urgency.

It's not long till we're both breathing heavily, my body writhing as he pulses against me. I think it's fair to say neither of us wants the exhilaration to end, but there's also a desperate need for release.

Just as I think we're both seconds from coming, he withdraws, grabs my hand and pulls me into his bedroom, tumbling us both on to the bed and rolling on top of me.

'I want to see you properly,' he says huskily as he moves quickly back inside me, pushing in deep and fast and never taking his eyes off me.

'I'm going to come,' I moan softly, biting down on my bottom lip. Then my head tilts back and my mouth falls open as I start bucking uncontrollably. He starts juddering moments later, not stopping till he collapses, panting, on top of me.

As he kisses my neck and buries his face in my hair, I can feel his heart pounding wildly in his chest. My own heart feels like it's been blown wide open. If I thought I might be able to keep a handle on my feelings, I realise that's no longer the case. I am wholly and irreversibly smitten with Ben.

19

Hard as it is to force myself to be sensible after that realisation, a whole week passes before I get to be alone with Ben again. Although we see each other at Crawford United's Saturday social and the two midweek training sessions, we reluctantly agree not to sneak off together afterwards until my last two exams are done and dusted. I desperately need to do some last-minute cramming.

We FaceTime each other daily though, which alleviates any fears I might have had about him backing off now I've slept with him, and we make plans for a romantic night at his house on Friday that he promises will feel even more special after the seven-day wait.

Wednesday's paper on strategic human resources management doesn't cause me too much trouble, but my confidence dips again come Friday morning. As global communication in the digital age is a fairly new module for the university, there aren't many past papers kicking around, which makes it far harder to predict which questions might come up. But I try not to fret about it and just focus on how good it will be to be reunited with Ben afterwards.

He texts me while I'm on my way to knock for Phoebs so we can walk to the examination hall together. *'How do you feel about an evening out on the town tonight instead of coming to mine? Get our glad rags on and properly celebrate the end of your exams?'*

'Where are you thinking?' I type back, thinking perhaps I should actually do something special to mark my last day of being a student and that I'll still be able to have him to myself back at his place afterwards.

'I'll surprise you. My treat. Can you be ready for seven?' he writes.

'Of course.' My exam will be over by five, so I'll even have time for a quick drink at the Mexican with Phoebs before I go home to get ready – holding the tacos this time as I'm sure Ben's plan will involve food.

He tells me he'll message me again later to check the coast is clear before he comes to collect me and wishes me luck in the meantime. I debate whether I should just come clean to Dad about our relationship, but I'm pretty sure he'll say I'm being foolish and I don't want anyone to burst my bubble yet.

By the time I'm sitting at a desk in the exam hall, waiting for the invigilator to say we can turn our papers over, my stomach is twisting at the thought of the three hours ahead. And it really does turn out to be my worst nightmare. Of the six questions we have to answer, only one relates to a subject I went over this morning, and another two are about things our course barely touched on, which hardly seems fair.

I glance across at Phoebs on the desk alongside mine

and she mouths 'what the fuck?' at me. It doesn't make me feel any better. If she's thinking that, even with all the work she's been putting in, I don't see how I'm going to stand a chance of doing well. I turn back to my paper and scribble down anything I can think of that might be deemed relevant.

'That was a stinker,' Phoebs complains afterwards, when we're sipping mango margaritas at the Mexican. 'I wanted to end today on a high but I'm really pissed off. Who even came up with those questions? There are so many other things they could have asked us.'

'I'm holding on to the fact that we both thought economics was a disaster last year, but we both passed that,' I admit.

'I guess we'll find out in six weeks,' she huffs. That's when the results come out. 'At least Craig can take my mind off it later. I'm going to nip round to his when you go off to meet Ben.'

'You're seeing quite a lot of him, for someone you're not in a relationship with,' I point out.

'The sex is fun.' She shrugs. 'But I'm only twenty-one. I don't need to find someone who's boyfriend material yet.'

As we toast the end of our university adventures, she asks if I've thought any more about what I'm going to do next. She's applied for six jobs already and can't wait to get a foot on the career ladder.

I'm glad to have a bit of breathing space before I have to look for paid work. Dad is happy to support me while I'm ploughing my time into Crawford United, my latest task being to finalise all the player contracts. It might not be doing anything for my bank balance, but I do think having this experience on my CV will ultimately make me more employable than a lot of graduates.

'Do you reckon you'll end up working at one of the big football clubs?' Phoebs asks. 'Now you've started out along that path.'

'Maybe, but my real dream would be for Crawford's ticket sales to generate enough revenue for me to stay working there. As a paid employee, I mean.'

She clearly thinks this is madness. 'Surely it would be more interesting to be somewhere like Arsenal, where there's more of a challenge. Bigger budgets, tougher decisions. Craig said he'd go back at the drop of a hat.'

She realises she probably shouldn't have said this as soon as it's out of her mouth. 'Not that he isn't loyal to Crawford,' she adds hurriedly, seeing how unimpressed I am. 'He's really grateful to be playing for you. All I'm saying is, at some point some of your players will probably start thinking about career progression and earning potential – I just think you should keep that in mind for yourself as well.'

I don't know why this hits such a nerve. Probably because Crawford is only just finding its feet so I don't want to already be thinking about the possibility of our players using it as a stepping stone to get into a better squad.

'Maybe let us at least get a season under our belts before you have all our players leaving and me managing a club a hundred times Crawford's size,' I suggest.

She cringes. 'I'm sorry, I didn't mean to be offensive. I know Crawford means a lot to you – and to your dad. I was just . . . no, let's talk about something else. Tell me more about your big night out with Ben this evening.

You said it was somewhere fancy. Have you got an outfit planned?'

I admit I haven't got a clue what to wear. Something tells me Ben would say I looked gorgeous even if I turned up in the hoodie and leggings I'm in now, but I want it to be something that makes me feel sexy. As we finish our drinks, Phoebs gives me her top three suggestions from what she's seen in my wardrobe, then we say our goodbyes so I can head home and decide on my favourite.

What I end up in is a midnight blue Grecian-style minidress I bought a couple of years ago to wear to one of my cousin's weddings, with gold hoop earrings and my trusty gold sandals for that extra bit of glamour. And Ben does shower me with compliments – sort of – when I climb into the taxi he picks me up in.

He kisses me and tells me he had no idea I could scrub up so well, but he's laughing as he says it and I tell him, as I mock punch him on the arm, that he could have made more effort himself. In reality he looks gorgeous in a slim-fitting black shirt tucked into smart grey trousers with white trainers on his feet.

'So where are we headed?' I ask.

'Chelsea,' he replies, but he doesn't elaborate. He takes my hand and asks how I got on with the exam today and I admit it didn't go brilliantly. But I know he's right when he says there's nothing to be gained by worrying about it now. I can't turn the clock back so I might as well forget about it and just enjoy myself.

It's only when we pull up outside Gordon Ramsay that he tells me this is where we'll be spending the evening. 'So I hope you're hungry,' he says, his grin expanding.

'Are you serious?' My eyes are wide. First of all, I thought places like this usually have a three-month waiting list. But more than that I can't believe he's remembered from our frisbee game that this was my number-one request.

'But you didn't lose the triathlon,' is all I can think of to say.

'No matter. I quite fancied checking it out myself and I managed to get us in on a cancellation.' He squeezes my hand. 'I'm looking forward to it. I've read only good things.'

The dining area feels sophisticated without being stuffy – white tablecloths, simple table settings, low-key decor. It's not as grand as I thought it might be, but perhaps that's because they don't want anything to outdo the food, which is exquisitely presented and filled with flavour. From the lobster ravioli in a perfect circle of foamy sauce and topped with edible petals to the neatly stacked tower of sweetness in the pecan praline parfait, every dish is delicious, not to mention photogenic.

I tell Ben I'm going to have to get Dad to up his game. While he often comes up with a tasty new creation, it invariably looks like it was just dropped onto the plate.

'Maybe he needs a lady in his life – someone he wants to impress,' Ben says.

'Dad?' I can't imagine it. He's been single since Mum left.

Unless he hasn't, and I'm not the only one who's been keeping my love life to myself. It is possible that on some of the nights when he said he was meeting his football buddies, he was actually on a date. But no, I can't imagine it and I'm sure he would have told me. 'I think the only long-term relationship he's interested in right now is with Crawford United.'

Ben laughs. 'No shame in that. As you know, it does require a lot of time and dedication.'

I tell him about my conversation with Phoebs earlier and her suggestion that I perhaps could do better. 'She seemed to think I should be more ambitious.'

'More ambitious than setting up your own football club from scratch?'

'She was talking about me getting a job with a Premier League team – you know, where the pay might be better. But I really want to see it through with Crawford, even if it fails.'

He reaches across the table and threads his fingers through mine. 'You only get so many chances to follow your dreams so I don't think you should worry about what Phoebs said. And besides, Crawford's not going to fail with you, Mike and Cassie behind it – because the three of you won't let it.'

It warms my heart to know he has such faith in us.

'Of course if you did ever decide you want to do something different, and I say this purely selfishly, I could always check if there were any vacancies at Millford City,' he says.

'So you can see me every day?'

I'm only half serious when I say it, but he grins and says, 'I think I could get used to it.'

I've been trying not to think too much about what might happen when he goes back to Millford, whether this could work with him based up there and me down here. But I'm not ready to delve into that minefield just yet.

In the taxi home at the end of the night he confesses that while he loved every course of the meal, he still feels hungry. I guess that's what happens when you burn through as many calories as he must do with the amount of training he still does every day.

But despite talk of rustling up a midnight snack, it's quickly forgotten when we get back to his. With a week of pent-up desire boiling over in both of us, there are other things on our minds and a good few hours pass before we get any sleep.

20

Because he's so disciplined, Ben is still in the gym at seven o'clock the next morning. He leaves me tucked up under the covers, thinking I might drift off again, but when I'm still awake an hour later I give up and get up, deciding I might as well join him.

I've thrown on one of his T-shirts, though it's more like a dress on me. 'I hope you don't mind.'

He looks me up and down and grins. 'Absolutely not. It's one of my favourites but I like it even more on you.'

I climb up on to the exercise bike and start a steady pedal while he works his upper body with chest presses. But not wanting to be too distracting, I leave him to it after a half-hour cycle and head outside for a dip in the pool. As a little treat to help push him through the rest of his workout, I strip down to nothing before jumping into the water naked, knowing he can see me through the gym's massive windows. As I sink under the surface I can picture the smile creeping over his lips.

If he wasn't so serious about his fitness, he'd probably race out and join me, but we can come back to that later, after today's team-building meet-up in the park. For now, I do a few lengths, then shower, dress and head home to Dad's, to change into something more appropriate for an afternoon with Crawford United.

There's good news waiting at home, so much so that I don't think Dad notices I'm still wearing the same dress I went out in. He proudly spins his laptop round to show me the club's bank balance, which is now standing at over £10,000.

'We've just sold our one hundredth season ticket,' he says proudly. 'This has made me a very happy man. That's a hundred people who now believe in our team.'

'That's incredible.' I do a quick calculation in my head to see how much debt this still leaves us with. We've still got a way to go but at least we're making progress.

'Some of the clubs we'll be playing only pull in that many fans after being established for years,' Dad says. 'They'll be very pleased to see our lot turn up and double the earnings they make on match day food and drinks. It should mean we get a warm welcome at the majority of places.'

'It's meant to be a pretty friendly league anyway,' I remind him. 'I can't wait to get started on the competitive matches. That's when this is going to start feeling really real.'

'Forty-nine days and counting,' he says, smiling. It feels like forever and yet no time at all.

Back up in my room, I change into leggings and a running vest, then I gather up my revision notes from yesterday and add them to the rest of my exam prep. I'm not entirely sure what to do with the thick wedge of paper now I don't have any more facts to memorise. I don't want to just throw all my hard work away, but will I realistically ever read any of it again? I end up stuffing it in a box and sliding it under my bed.

Ben texts me while I'm tidying up. *'Fancy another spin in the Mercedes later?'*

'Of course,' I write back immediately. *'Where to this time?'*

'There's a really nice restaurant about an hour away.'

'Sounds good. I'll wear something warm this time.'

'Just wear your normal clothes. I'll lend you extras for the journey.'

Same gold sandals it is then, plus my favourite jeans. All I need to do now is choose a top to go with them. I start rifling through my wardrobe to see what I feel sexiest in.

By the time I rejoin Dad in the kitchen, he's finished putting together a list of team-building games for this afternoon's session with our players. Cassie's going to be late, as it's her Saturday Kickers club's annual friendly tournament, so he's stepped in to help with the planning. As we walk to the park, he tells me what he's got in mind – and luckily his ideas go down a treat.

To kick things off, he gives the players a list of ten exercises. Number one is a burpee, number two is a crouch back to standing, three is a high knee jump, four is to turn in a circle on the spot . . . you get the picture. As he explains what each number is, he gets everyone to do the corresponding action, but they only get one run-through of it. Then he lines everyone up and calls out numbers at random and anyone he catches not doing the right exercise for its assigned number is eliminated.

The game is over really quickly – ten is a lot to remember. After Dad's called out just three Elliot is the only one still standing, and that's only because the others went wrong before he'd even reacted.

'We'll go again,' Dad says. 'And this time you'll do it in teams. If one of you goes out, you're all out, okay? So split yourselves into six teams of four – Ben and Lily, you can join in and make up the numbers – and let's see if you can do any better this time.'

The answer's no. This time Elliot wipes my team out on the first command, quickly followed by Levi, Adio, Ben and Bailey, leaving only Nico's team standing.

'Again,' Dad says. 'And this time try to think of a way to beat the system.'

As I already know the secret, I don't say anything, to give the others a chance to figure it out for themselves. And it's Bailey who first works out that if each team member only memorises a couple of actions rather than everyone trying to remember everything, those people can lead the rest of their team through the right moves.

The other teams catch on not long after Bailey starts winning every round, and by the end of it all twenty-two players, plus Ben and me, are getting it right every time.

Dad applauds us. 'Well done, guys. Hopefully this has shown you how much more effective it is when you work together, but how each one of you has an important role in the team.'

Next up is an adult version of hot potato. This time we have four groups of six, and each group is given two balls. Starting in a small ring, the two players with the balls must throw them to another team member and each time a catch is made, that person has to take one step backwards and widen the circle. It's the only time we're allowed to move our feet.

'If a ball is dropped, it goes out of play,' Dad explains. 'So once you've dropped both, your circle is frozen. The winning team will have the biggest circle at the end of one minute, so spread out and give yourselves plenty of room.'

Bailey joins myself, Elliot, Aaron and two of the reserve players.

'Do we have a plan?' Elliot asks.

'To beat my brother,' Bailey replies, just loud enough for Ben to hear.

I look over to see Ben mouthing 'not a chance', accompanied by a self-assured grin.

Dad starts a timer and it's quickly apparent that the hardest thing this time is making sure the two balls don't hit each other in the middle. Two teams are frozen instantly when a clash throws both balls in directions that make them impossible to catch. It leaves only my team and Ben's in the running.

'We need a system,' Bailey says, his voice full of urgency.

Aaron suggests calling out 'go' each time we have a ball safely in our hands so the other one can be tossed. I notice Ben's team have the same idea.

When Dad blows his whistle it's impossible to say whose circle is bigger. He tries counting how many strides it takes for him to get from one side of each circle to the other, but concludes he can't do this with any level of accuracy. So he declares it a draw and suggests we move on to version B.

'What were we supposed to learn this time?' Jacob asks.

'To never drop the ball,' Dad replies with a grin.

For the next version, we'll be kicking rather than throwing the ball, so we need it to land as close as possible to our team members' feet. If no one can reach the ball, it goes out of play, which is not so difficult for a footballer, but is much more of a challenge for me. This time, it's fair to say Ben's team – he's got Jamie and Craig with him too – make a significantly bigger circle than the rest of us.

'Hard luck, bro,' he says, clapping Bailey on the shoulder.

'It's not over yet,' Bailey reminds him.

Cassie arrives in time for the final challenge, but signals to Dad to just carry on with things. He sets down two cones around thirty metres apart and tells us two teams will compete at a time in this game, owing to the number of footballs needed. He moves my team and Ben's to the starting line and gives us five balls each. On Dad's whistle, we're to balance one ball between the chests and backs of each team member, then all six of us must try to reach the other cone without dropping a ball.

If one drops, the whole team must go back to the beginning. No hands are allowed once our balls are in place. I look over at Ben and he winks at me. Game on, I know he's thinking.

It's harder than you might think – and even harder once Elliot and I get the giggles. Because he's so tall, the ball between us is nearer his bum than his back, so after a few false starts, we have a quick reshuffle to put him at the back, me at the front and everyone else in height order between.

Ben's team have already made good progress thanks to their coordinated march, with Levi calling out 'left, right, left, right' to keep them all in perfect timing.

'We've just got to go for it now,' Bailey says. 'Elliot, you drive us from the back and the rest of us will just have to make sure we keep up with him.'

It does prove effective, and Elliot propels us over the finish line just a few steps ahead of Ben's team.

'I knew you had to be better at something,' Ben teases his brother.

'Being balanced?' Bailey quips back.

Ben makes an 'ooh' shape with his mouth. 'I walked into that one,' he says, laughing.

While Dad lines up the next two heats, I grab my phone so I can film them. I think it's nice to show our fans that the team has a fun side as well on our social media.

Cassie takes back over from Dad after that and leads the team through some more football-specific challenges. All in all it's a brilliant session and it's so gratifying to see the smiles on everyone's faces at the end of it.

Dad and I are both on a high as we walk back to the house, though for me this is as much to do with what I know is coming next as the fun that's been had already. I'll be heading over to Ben's just as soon as I've got changed and I can't wait to see what our next evening together brings.

21

I team my jeans with a white blouse, tied at the midriff to show off my waist. It's not the most practical open-top car attire but it'll be fine underneath the jumper Ben lends me.

He whisks me off to a vineyard in the South Downs, which is surrounded by rolling hills as far as the eye can see, and we manage to bag a spot out on the restaurant terrace so we can soak up the scenery while we eat. He orders me a glass of the house bubbles, a sparkling water for him.

'They've started hiring out a couple of cottages here recently so people don't have to drive after dinner,' he tells me. 'They were fully booked this evening but if the food turns out to be as good as I think it will be, maybe we could come back and stay over another time.'

Which, of course, sounds good to me. 'I'm definitely up for a couple of mini breaks in the UK now I'm not doing my big European trip any more. And it's so beautiful here I'd happily do another visit.'

'It's not quite the national parks of Croatia, but it is

pretty special,' he agrees. 'Remind me where else you were due to go on your trip?'

'Italy for sure, and Montenegro was on the list. Some of the Greek islands, too – the smaller ones that aren't so touristy. I'd still like to get to all of them one day, but maybe just not all on the same holiday.' It makes me think about Greg for the first time in weeks. Wherever he is, I hope he's as happy as I am. 'What about you, what's on your bucket list?'

'Oh you know, a villa in Tahiti, an African safari, a dive boat to the Galapagos.'

I laugh. 'No harm in dreaming big.'

'It's never hurt me before. I'll start ticking them off once the football dries up, provided I can find someone who wants to do it all with me.'

'I think I might be free.'

'I'll put the business class flights on standby,' he says, grinning.

I feign disappointment. 'No private jet?'

He claps his hand to his head. 'Oh, so you *are* just like the other girls. And there I was thinking you were different.'

'I'm not averse to lounging around on a sundeck in one of those villas over the sea. It just might take me until you retire before I can afford it, assuming you've got at least another ten years in the Premier League and I'm not still working at Crawford for free.'

'More than ten I hope,' he says, laughing. 'And by then I'm sure Crawford will be paying you back for all the effort you've put in. There's so much love for it already, and your players are all so proud to be part of the story.'

165

'With the possible exception of Craig,' I point out, 'who seems to think he should be playing for the big bucks and fighting off lucrative advertising deals.'

'It sounds like he hasn't let go of his past,' Ben observes. 'It would be sad if he let what happened at Arsenal stop him from enjoying this experience. Maybe I should tell him it's bloody weird some of the stuff you get asked to promote anyway – he might start thinking of Crawford as a blessing.'

'What was your weirdest?' I ask.

'It has to be the anti-ageing hair-loss shampoo, given that I'm only twenty-two.' He points at his mop of curls. 'I don't think anyone is going to believe using that led to this. I've turned down a few burger and pizza promotions too. I don't want to encourage people to eat rubbish. And speaking of eating, shall we order? That chicken dish that just went past smelt amazing.'

I look back down at my menu. 'That's what I had my eye on, too. That, or the lamb sounds really tasty.'

'That was my first choice, till I smelt the chicken.'

In the end we decide to share both, and they are equally delicious. Generous, too, so at the point where I can't eat another bite, I suggest getting a takeaway box for what I haven't finished.

'Just slide it over,' Ben says.

I laugh and push my plate towards him. 'There goes my breakfast.'

His eyebrows rise – until he realises I'm just messing.

'Never joke about food,' he warns. 'I can't guarantee your safety.'

I smile coquettishly. 'Might you kidnap me and take me back to your lair to have your wicked way with me?'

His fork stops midway to his mouth. 'And definitely never joke about that. We might not even make it as far as my lair if you put ideas like that in my head. There are plenty of secluded spots between here and home.'

I lean in and whisper, 'I think we should find one of them.'

He doesn't need asking twice. Ten minutes later we've paid up and we're on our way.

We're still gigging about what we got up to when we walk back through his front door just as dusk is setting in. There was a walking trail entrance just a short drive from the vineyard, his hand locked with mine as we followed the path into the woods. After a quick check for ramblers and dog walkers who might be making the most of the evening sun, we made out in a clearing, leaning up against a tree, the sounds of birds all around us, our hair fluttering gently in the breeze.

On the way back to the car I could still feel the imprint of tree bark in my back as we brushed bits of foliage off our clothes. We stopped off to pick up ice cream and felt like everyone in the supermarket must be able to tell what we'd been doing.

'I think we might have found our new thing,' Ben says, when we're curled up on his sofa sharing a Häagen-Dazs. 'Although I'm still a fan of jumping into water in our underwear too.'

'Well, we did say we'd go back there one day,' I remind him.

He tells me he'll check when there's next availability.

22

With my exams out of the way, we see each other every day for the following fortnight. While Ben's training in the mornings, I make sure Crawford's accounts and membership register are up to date, liaise with the other clubs in the league about the match schedule for the upcoming season and look into setting up a couple of friendly games over the next month so we don't end up playing our first competitive match having never faced another team.

Ben and I fall into a pattern of lazy afternoons by the pool, with sunny evenings spent walking hand in hand on Box Hill, driving down to the coast with Ben's paddleboards or cuddled up on his sofa in front of a movie – although the latter invariably ends up with us kissing till we realise we've missed a good number of the key scenes.

We play the board game triathlon I suggested, which I win, and another three-part tournament involving shuffleboard, bowling and darts, which I don't. He treats me to a chef-prepared fairy-lit dinner in his back garden for my victory. I buy him fish and chips in a newspaper to celebrate his. In my defence, the Ledbury was fully booked.

When we lie in bed with our arms wrapped round each other, it seems impossible that we've only known each other for a matter of weeks. I've never before felt so in tune with someone, who seems to think like I do and wants to do all the same things. I know, in normal relationship terms, this is more like how things might be six months or even a year in, but with the clock ticking till Ben goes back up north, there's been a natural acceleration. And now it's hard to imagine ever not wanting to be with him.

By now Dad has worked out I've got a new man in my life, from the number of nights I'm spending away from home, but he's never been a prier so he doesn't bring it up. It amazes me he hasn't sussed out it's Ben, even if we do try to be professional at training. But both he and Cassie are so absorbed in the players, I don't think either of them notice how my cheeks glow whenever I'm standing near Ben.

There's only one moment when we almost give the game away and that's on the Saturday before the fundraiser, when Dad's latest idea for building the bonds between the players involves heading to a golf club out of town for a game of footgolf, which is essentially like crazy golf but played with footballs on a much larger course with bigger holes.

On arrival, he tells us to split up into nine teams of three – with all the players plus himself and Cassie, Barbour, Ben and me making up the numbers. Bob and Marge are at a family party they felt they couldn't miss. The game is simple – the teams take it in turns to hoof their ball towards the green and the aim is to get it in each of the nine holes with the lowest number of kicks.

I team up with Ben and Bailey, and when it's our turn, being gentlemen, they insist I go first – and Ben falls about laughing when I chip the ball straight into the rough.

'What was that?' he half splutters, half squeaks.

'Don't be mean! I'm not a footballer!' I give him a playful shove.

He can't stop chuckling. 'Yes, but you have *seen* a ball being kicked before?'

Bailey rolls his eyes at his brother. 'Just ignore him – we can still rescue this,' he says to me.

'I'm sorry,' Ben says, instinctively reaching for my hand and only dropping it when he remembers someone might see.

'I don't know why you two don't just be open about it,' Bailey says. 'No one's going to be bothered.'

'I'm not sure my dad's quite ready to be okay with it,' I admit.

'Lily, Bailey, Ben, you're up,' Dad shouts at that exact moment.

We look up to see the other teams have advanced a fair way up the field. Which has probably saved us from having to answer some awkward questions about the hand-holding.

'Coming!' Bailey shouts back before flicking the ball, as promised, out of the long grass and a decent distance in the direction I'd originally intended to kick it in. We're still a bit behind the others but as Ben will take our next shot, we'll soon be back in the running.

And things do level out over the next few holes. Thanks to the uneven ground and unruly tufts of grass, everyone has at least one misfire. Which is less frustrating for me than the actual players – having only ever kicked a ball around as a kid, I didn't expect to be good at it.

Dad keeps track of the scores, so he can do a grand reveal in the bar afterwards, and to my surprise my team doesn't come last. It's Elliot, Bob and Caspian from the reserves who bring up the rear and their penalty is to pay for the first round.

'Thanks, lads,' Dad says, ignoring their groans. 'Much appreciated.'

'Are we hitting the driving range next?' Elliot asks, nodding his head towards the line of bays outside the bar window. 'Give me a chance to redeem myself.'

Several hopeful faces turn Dad's way – mine included.

But when Dad checks with the reception desk, they're fully booked. 'So it's back to plan A, a couple of beers then we'll head back to Hamcott. Let's just enjoy one of our last opportunities to have a pressure-free Saturday. The first game of the season is creeping up on us, so after next week's fundraiser, it'll be football all the way. It's time to get serious.'

'We'd better get another round in then,' Aaron says, which is met with a chorus of cheers.

I get a cab home afterwards with Cassie and Dad, who's in a particularly jovial mood. 'You know, as much as I might have doubted Ben in the beginning, I have to hand it to him for recommending us to build up the team not just with football. I think these last few weekends have made a real difference. It feels like the lads are more than teammates now – they're proper friends.'

'Which can only be a good thing,' Cassie agrees. 'It's going to get significantly tougher from this point forwards, so they're going to need that strong foundation. Especially when Ben's no longer here to help them see how important it is.'

I wonder if now is the time to confess that we're dating, while they're both feeling so positive towards him. But the reminder that he won't be in Hamcott forever makes me think twice about it. Ben and I haven't discussed what will happen when he goes back to Millford so, much as I don't want to admit it to myself, there's always the possibility I won't even need to come clean.

His ears must be burning, because my phone pings with an incoming text from him, to tell me he's got an idea for an evening adventure.

'That your mystery man?' Dad asks. 'We promise not to bite if you let us meet him.'

But I'm already back to thinking I'll cross that bridge later, and only once I know whether Ben is going to be in my life for as long as I want him to be.

Ben's adventure involves another drive to the South Downs. He doesn't tell me where we're going till we pull up at a golf club high up in the hills, which has a driving range alongside its swanky clubhouse that faces out over a lush green valley.

'I saw the look on your face when your dad said the bays were full earlier, so I thought you might like to come and have a little hit,' he explains.

'This is stunning.' I look out at the hillside surrounding us. 'It's such an amazing spot for it.'

'You're welcome to share my clubs,' he offers, 'or we can borrow a set from inside. Mine are designed specifically for my height, so you might find them a bit awkward.'

'Is now a good time to mention the reason I looked disappointed earlier is because I've never actually hit a golf ball before?'

'Are you kidding? I thought . . .'

'I've played mini golf and I do like that, but I haven't ever tried the real thing.'

'Then I'm even happier I brought you here. What a great place to start. And this is far more satisfying than mini golf once you get the hang of it. I'm not sure how good a teacher I'll be but I can tell you some of the things my coach told me, to get you started.'

'Your coach? Is this going to be another thing you're a secret expert at then?'

'I wouldn't say I'm a pro, but I do have a respectable handicap.'

I roll my eyes. 'Come on then. You'd better show me how's it done.'

And he drives his first ball so far I can barely see where it's gone, until it plops into the lake at the bottom of the valley.

I have a go after that, to see if I have any natural talent before he starts trying to guide me. I don't. I miss the ball completely on my first two attempts and move it only an inch on the third and only then because it's rolled off the tee.

I'm suddenly grateful we've got the place to ourselves. Despite the beautiful surroundings, there's no one else using the range, either because it's dinner time or because we're in the middle of nowhere. With only four tee-off spots, people might not want to drive all the way out here without the guarantee of a space being free.

Ben manages to control his giggles as I swing and miss

a fourth time, just about. But that's largely down to the fact that he moves in behind me after that, placing his hands on top of mine so he can show me what to do. With his arms wrapped around me I think we both start thinking about other things beside golf, so a lot of kissing happens in between working on my swing.

'Is this how you got taught?' I ask.

'Not exactly. My coach was a middle-aged man,' he says, laughing. Then he releases me and backs away so I can take another shot. 'Not because I don't trust you, but I do quite like my teeth.'

'I've got this,' I assure him, determined to pull off a shot that will impress him.

But although I do connect with the ball, the momentum of the club makes me spin right round till I'm facing him instead of the valley. He stifles a snigger, then apologises, but his eyes are brimming with amusement. When my next try hits the fake grass rather than the tee, he snorts as he tries not to laugh and I get the giggles myself from watching his reddening face trying to hold it in.

'You look like you're trying to murder a seal,' he gasps, which sets us both off even more.

'You're the one who taught me!' I'm clutching my stomach now.

'I know, and I can only say I'm sorry. I did say I might not make the best teacher.'

'If you hadn't kept distracting me . . .'

'I can't help it. You're very distracting.'

I turn away from him and line my club up again, taking a deep breath and mentally willing the ball to behave for me. I'm going to do this, I am *not* going to let it beat me.

And thankfully – at last! – I manage to send it sailing down the hill for the first and only time.

'Oh thank God,' Ben gasps. 'That was killing me.'

'I was just waiting for my moment,' I tell him. 'And now I've had it, I might just stop so I can go out on a high. And so you can make it up to me for taking the piss out of me.'

'I'm sorry, I couldn't help myself. There's a really nice gastro-pub up the road. Do you fancy that? My treat?'

I pretend I'm still offended. 'That'll do for starters. Let's see what else you can come up with while we're eating.'

'What about a romantic night away after the fundraiser next weekend?'

I'd been thinking more along the lines of what we could do back at his place later, but if that mini break back at the vineyard is what he's suggesting, I'm a hundred per cent there for it.

23

It's my turn to have a giggle at his expense the following Friday, the evening before the fundraiser, when I propose we both make an entry for Marge's cake competition. We pick up all the ingredients we might need and lay everything out on his kitchen counter. He's chosen to do a Crawford shirt, while I'm planning to recreate a football pitch.

My past baking experience mostly involves cornflake cakes, while Ben admits the only thing he's ever baked is a potato. But when we look at a how-to video on YouTube, it doesn't look too taxing.

With music on in the background, we sing along and dance around the kitchen while cracking eggs and sending flour flying all over the place. Ben has definitely got rhythm – thanks to a brief dalliance with breakdancing as a teenager, he tells me – but it would be fair to say he probably wouldn't have been asked to join the choir, so I'm already taking the mickey out of him by the time our cake tins are in the oven.

'Face of an angel, voice like a rusty nail scratching down a window,' he admits.

'Maybe next time you advertise something, it should be noise-cancelling earbuds,' I tease.

'So I can block out your sarcasm?'

I can't help laughing. 'Touché.' At least what he lacks in melody he makes up for in wit.

He winks at me before we turn our attention back to the carnage we've created on the countertop. There are utensils, discarded eggshells and gloops of cake mix everywhere.

'We've made such a mess!'

He points at the jars of food colouring sitting to one side, waiting to be added to our icing. 'And the fun hasn't even started yet. Let's get this lot in the dishwasher, ready for round two.'

When the oven timer pings I think it's a surprise to both of us that our rectangle sponges both look to have turned golden and risen perfectly.

'I was expecting to have to nip back to the supermarket and buy a ready-made cake base,' Ben confesses.

'It smells so nice, I could eat it just like this.'

He proposes we have a slice when it's cooled down and he's cut out his shirt sleeves.

We pass the time out on the terrace with a bottle of wine, reclined on the loungers and talking about everything from our expectations for tomorrow's event to our favourite sweets as kids – fizzy cola bottles for him, Smarties for me – as well as whether Ben should take singing lessons.

'I think I'm beyond help on that front. Football was definitely the right choice for me.'

'To be fair, you probably wouldn't have ended up in a boy band.'

He laughs. 'Not even busking in an Underground station.'

'I would have chucked you a quid.'

We've finished the wine by the time the cakes are cool enough to ice. I'm not sure it helps Ben with cutting his base into a shirt shape.

'It'll be more obvious once the colour's on,' he says, not sounding overly convinced.

I mix up my butter icing and add enough food colouring to make it bright green, then smear it over my sponge, using a fork to rough up the top to make it look grass-like. They didn't have any purple colouring at the shop, so Ben mixes red and blue with icing sugar and water to try to recreate the Crawford indigo.

'Is that after a few too many hot washes?' I mock, looking at the plum-coloured concoction in the bottom of the bowl.

'I see what you're saying, but it's going to look fine once the writing is on,' he insists.

We arm ourselves with piping bags filled with white icing and it quickly becomes apparent that the lines of a football pitch are much easier to draw than the words on a football shirt. While mine are not perfect, you can tell what they're meant to be. His letters not only smudge in the not-yet-dried purple undercoat, but he runs out of space when he's only written Crawfo. I'm not sure which of us is laughing harder when he reluctantly admits it could have gone better.

'I think I might have a solution,' I tell him when I've finally caught my breath enough to speak. 'Just run a line up there and you can turn the o into a d. Then it's kind of an abbreviation.'

178

He takes my advice then says, 'I know it's probable insanity but I kind of want to put the logo underneath.'

'Are you sure?'

'It can't make it worse.'

But he's quite wrong about that. His phoenix has me clutching my sides again. 'It looks like a snowman!'

'All right, Picasso. It's an artistic interpretation. Let's see how your ball and goals turn out before you get too cocky.'

I'm making the ball out of marzipan then coating it with white icing and using the blue food colouring to paint on the pattern. The goals I make by piping a grid of icing on to a sheet of baking paper, curling it slightly then sticking it in the freezer. I have no idea if it will work but if it doesn't it will at least give Ben some ammunition to get me back with.

When we finally stand the finished cakes side by side – I don't know if my goalposts will last overnight but for now they're standing up – Ben folds his arms, purses his lips and glances at me. 'Can I give myself nine out of ten for effort?'

I slide my arm round his waist and grin up at him. 'We could just pretend someone's kid made it.'

'But then who would collect the prize when it wins?'

'I hate to break this to you, but it's not going to win.'

'But Marge is judging and she loves an underdog.'

'Tell you what, between you and me, whichever one gets eaten first tomorrow can be our personal winner.'

'Are we allowed to buy slices of our own cake?'

'No.'

'Bribe some of the team to buy slices?'

'No!'

He reluctantly agrees that we'll leave who wins to fate.

I tell him I'm going to post a picture of mine in the Crawford United fan forum. 'If they see how low I've set the bar, it might inspire other people to reach for their aprons.'

But when I reach for my phone and pull up the site, there's a nasty surprise waiting. Ben watches the colour drain from my face as I follow a link that's been shared to an opinion piece in the sports section of one of the national papers. It basically debates whether the club is taking the opportunity it's been given seriously, in light of the video clips I've shared online from the foot golf, rounders day and park games. It ends with the suggestion that we might be better at drinking than we are at football – and that's aimed at both the managers and the players.

'This is so unfair.' I turn to Ben, who's moved in beside me so he can read it over my shoulder. 'I was just trying to make us more relatable when I posted those reels.'

'Try not to take it to heart – it's just one person's opinion,' he soothes.

But when he reaches across and scrolls down to the comments, his brow furrows as the first one turns out to be a snarky remark about us teaching our players the wrong sport and the next suggests we might have been better off starting a brewery rather than a football club.

My frustration boils over. 'They've literally ignored all the hard work everyone has poured into making this happen and made us look really unprofessional. This could really screw us over at the fundraiser tomorrow. Who's going to come and donate if they think we're just doing this to amuse ourselves?'

'People will come – a lot of them won't even see this. And of those who do, don't forget there's every chance they'll react the same way you and I have and dismiss it as rubbish.'

He's right of course, but it still troubles me. I'm annoyed with myself for not realising this might provoke a backlash. In future I won't be so naïve. 'I just want tomorrow to go well. It's our chance to really promote Crawford and to celebrate it.'

'Just focus on how good it's going to feel when the season starts and you prove this guy wrong,' Ben advises.

But his article keeps me awake long into the night. I can only hope tomorrow demonstrates how committed we are to making the club a success.

24

I'm a ball of nerves when everyone assembles at The Fox early the next morning. There's a lot to do to get the pub ready before we throw the gates open at eleven, and the whole team – minus Cassie, who's teaching her Saturday group, and Craig, the only player who hasn't shown up yet – is pitching in.

Levi and Scott blow up balloons and fix them to the fences around the garden. Marge is in charge of organising the tables for the cake competition and the raffle prizes. Bob is assembling the homemade tombola he's fashioned out of an empty five-litre water bottle. It's a hive of activity and I run round like a headless chicken trying to oversee everything. I want it all to be perfect.

'Do you think we need to put the marquees up or do you think we'll get away with it?' Olly asks, glancing up at the sky. It's mostly blue, with a smattering of cloud, but the Met Office website says there's a chance of rain mid-afternoon.

'Why don't we just do a couple? One to go over the

cakes, just in case, and one for people to shelter under if we do get a shower. Or if they get too hot,' I suggest.

Olly nods and calls Adio over to help him, and I get back to attaching bunting to the front edges of the tables – in the team colour purple, of course.

Dad and Elliot are out in the car park setting up a portable goal on a square of artificial grass that Olly keeps stashed away for the occasional times when the pub hosts a wedding party. Visitors will be invited to see for themselves what it's like trying to score from the penalty spot against our goalie. I suspect Elliot's going to have a busy day.

Ben will, too, I reckon. Bob has created a picture frame out of scraps of wood and hung it from a tree in the corner of the garden, so fans can get a framed photo of themselves with a Premier League footballer – or any of the Crawford players who are not busy elsewhere.

Craig, Adio, Nico and Aaron will be walking around with coin buckets, as we're operating a pay-what-you-can entry system. We don't want anyone to be excluded from the day by the cost, but the hope is that our supporters will give more generously than we maybe would have requested. Bailey, meanwhile, is our official photographer and will be taking pictures throughout the day for us to post on social media – although I'm hesitant now to post anything that isn't strictly football-related.

Thomas and Jacob – as well as Phoebs, who's also helping out – will be serving drinks with Olly behind the bar. Based on the number of customers Olly typically serves on a Saturday afternoon, we're anticipating a minimum crowd of around a hundred and fifty. Plus the kids from Cassie's Saturday Kickers club and their families, and anyone else who's curious to see what's going on.

When Craig finally makes an appearance, I head straight over to berate him for leaving everyone else to do all the work. So much for being a team player. I don't know why Phoebs wants to spend her time with him. But before I have a chance to open my mouth, he shows me the contents of the giant bags he's carrying and I'm faced with five phoenix-shaped piñatas, coloured purple, which he admits he had custom-made especially.

'I had to wait in for the delivery,' he explains with an apologetic smile. 'I thought some of the kids might enjoy giving them a good whack to get the sweets out.'

I shake my head and sigh. I can hardly stay angry with him now, can I? 'That's really thoughtful, thank you. Why don't you take the picture frame down off that tree and hang them up there? The frame can go elsewhere, or Ben can just carry it around with him, it's not too heavy.'

His smile grows wider, no doubt at the thought of making Ben's life a little harder. But then I follow his line of vision and see Phoebs wiggling her fingers and mouthing 'hi' at him. So maybe I'm judging him unfairly. But there's no time to dwell on it; there's more bunting to put up.

A sudden blast of noise from the speakers Olly has strung up around the garden makes me – and probably everyone else – jump half out of my skin. Olly pops his head out of the pub door and shouts, 'Sorry! I was just testing the volume and I think the knob must be on backwards. I thought that was going to be too quiet.'

184

'The boys over at Fulham probably heard it,' Bob says. 'And they're playing up in Manchester today!'

'Yeah, let's aim for creating some atmosphere, not bursting eardrums,' I suggest.

'On it,' Olly shouts, disappearing back inside.

I follow him in, so I can pin some bunting to the shelf above the bar.

'Need me to hold the back of the chair?' Craig offers. I hadn't realised he'd also come inside.

I stare at him and ask him straight out what's going on with him today. First the piñatas and now this? Helpful – or generous for that matter – are not words I typically associate with him.

He shrugs. 'Phoebs wants you to like me if we're going to go on double dates.'

I have to fight to keep my expression neutral but my whole body goes rigid. No one is supposed to know about me and Ben, especially no one from the team. I'm going to kill her – this is the last thing I need right now – so my voice is cool when I tell him I didn't know he and Phoebs were officially dating.

'More like kind of seeing each other,' he says. 'She doesn't want anything serious.'

And yet she's proposing hanging out with me and Ben as a cosy foursome? It sounds to me like she's more invested in him than she's been admitting.

'So I was thinking,' Craig continues, oblivious to my concerns about my secret getting out, 'that as well as supervising the kids with the piñatas today, maybe I could contribute to the auction too.'

'How so?' I manage to ask, still recovering from the shock of Phoebe's indiscretion. I don't doubt Craig would fancy himself as a charismatic auctioneer, but that's Dad's role and I know he's excited about it, so I'm not about to let Craig take over from him.

'Well, I'm sure people will bid for the training session with Ben, but what if we offered up a life drawing afternoon with me as well?' he suggests. 'It's not like I don't have the time and I reckon someone would shell out for it. I was making £250 a sitting before and that's when I wasn't even on a football team.'

Feeling guilty for misjudging him again – unless this is just an attempt to try and outdo Ben – I tell him every contribution is welcome.

But just when I think we're moving on to safer ground, he circles back and says, 'So how long have you and Ben been a thing?'

'We're not discussing that.' I cut him short, glancing furtively around the bar to make sure no one else is in hearing range. 'And I'd appreciate it if you didn't discuss it with anyone else either. It's not up for debate.'

We may have been working on making the players also feel like our friends, but there have to be boundaries. Clearly I'll need to remind Phoebs of this, too.

'As you prefer,' Craig says, just as Marge ambles over to join us. I seize the opportunity to put an end to the conversation. 'Marge! You wouldn't mind taking over from Craig for a moment, would you? I'm assigning him to water duty.'

'Oh yes, this looks way easier.' She nudges him out of the way. 'Do you know where to find the cups?'

He shakes his head, so she directs him to a stack of beakers in a bag behind the bar. 'Tap water to the top then pop them on the end of the counter. Thanks, love,' she says, then to me, when he's out of earshot, 'Not still trying to get in your knickers, is he?'

'Marge! He's dating my best friend. No, I just wanted to talk to you about the cakes,' I fib. 'I heard you telling Olly there was some kind of disaster?'

'Only that some of my muffin balls have got stuck together. The icing wasn't quite set when I popped them in the box. It's not a problem though – I'll just sell those ones as duos for double the money.'

Bless her, she spent the better part of yesterday baking, just in case no one else brought in an entry and we ended up with nothing to sell on our cake stand. With mine, Ben and her efforts, at least the table isn't empty. Time will tell if the prize of a Crawford season ticket encouraged anyone else to attempt cake decorating.

By 10.45 a.m., all our preparations are complete and we're ready to welcome the first arrivals. My stomach twists with anxiety as the official start time comes and goes, and Dad drums his fingers on the bar impatiently. I must check my watch at least every twenty seconds. I have to keep reminding myself it's still early.

It's just before midday when the first visitor finally appears and it's such a relief I almost burst into tears. Thankfully, they're followed by plenty more in quick succession. At last our fundraiser is happening.

The younger kids drag their parents straight to Elliot's goal, while a couple of teenage girls make a beeline for Ben, phone cameras at the ready. When Cassie arrives, she finds me chatting to Marge at the cake stand. She apologises for not having changed out of her sports kit. 'I didn't want to get here any later. Most of my students are coming down with their parents and I wanted to make sure I was here before them.'

'Don't worry – there isn't a dress code,' Marge says kindly, even if she is wearing the most glamorous outfit I've ever seen her in. I'm used to seeing her in jeans and a sweater for the footie – often with a winter coat. Today she's in a floral tea dress with a matching cardy, albeit still with trainers on her feet.

'Whoa!' Bob exclaims. 'Is that what I think it is?'

He's looking over our shoulders at a close to full-size replica of the FA Cup advancing slowly towards us on a cake tray.

Marge lets out a slow whistle. 'That makes our contributions look rather amateur.'

'Tell me where you want it – it weighs a bloody tonne,' comes a voice from behind the cake.

'Barbour?' I'd recognise that raspy tone anywhere.

'Yeah, but before you get excited I'm just the courier. My wife's parking the car up then she can take all the credit.'

Tempting as it is to swipe a bit of the icing off the side as he follows Marge over to the cake table, I manage to resist for fear of sending the whole thing toppling over. It will be enough of a shame having to slice it up when the time comes.

'It's a cup cake, geddit?' he says, once it's been safely deposited.

'It's amazing.' Marge beams, looking delighted that her cake table has suddenly improved so dramatically. 'It must have taken ages.'

'She even missed Coronation Street.' Bob sounds very proud of this.

'And we're all very grateful,' Marge tells him.

By one o'clock, the fundraiser is in full swing. The FA Cup cake has been joined by a boot, three more football shirts and a scarf all iced in the colours of Crawford United. There's also a far superior football pitch – my goals have collapsed on to my cake by this point – and a face that I suspect is supposed to be Dad's. Olly announces over the Tannoy that the judging will take place in just a few moments – we need to get it done early so we can start selling slices. Or whole cakes if anyone is keen.

Needless to say, Barbour's wife is declared the winner. She gives a little bow and tells us how she made discs of sponge and held them together with butter icing to get the height, then covered the whole structure with gold frosting for the finished effect.

'A deserved winner, I think you'll agree,' Marge says to the crowd gathered in front of her table as Mrs Barbour grins from ear to ear.

'You'd better award the prize to the second place winner though,' she says. 'We've already got our season tickets.'

'Who baked the scarf?' Marge asks.

Another delighted baker steps forward and everyone applauds as Marge hands her the ticket.

'Now let's get some photos of these bad boys and get them chopped up,' Bob says, 'so we can see if they taste as good as they look. Make mine a slice of the scarf though. I've had thirty years of the missus's cooking.'

'Two pounds a slice and remember it's for a good cause,' Marge reminds everyone as she starts handing out paper plates.

I let the assembled crowd know that the pub quiz will be kicking off next. 'Inside the pub in ten minutes, teams of six, leave your phones in your pockets please.'

Then I move on to check on the boys queueing up to take part in the keepy-uppy contest on the other side of the car park. Jamie is recording names and scores, and the winner will be announced at the end of the day and gifted a ball signed by the whole team.

'Twenty-three is the number to beat so far,' he informs me. 'If you want to have a go.'

I politely decline on the grounds that I need to keep schmoozing. There's no need to show myself up in front of anyone today.

Back in the bar, I have just enough time to ask Phoebs how the raffle ticket sales are going before she's swamped by people wanting to get a drink before the quiz starts.

'Make it two for a quid for anyone buying four drinks or more,' I tell her, before turning to the next customer. I can help out here for ten minutes until the rush dies down.

I don't stay for the quiz though – I helped compile it so I know all the answers. Plus with Dad, Cassie and at least half the visitors now preoccupied inside, it's a good opportunity to grab a few minutes with Ben.

Bin bag in hand, he's gathering up discarded paper cups and plates and I want to hug him for taking on the one job that nobody else on the team volunteered to do. But for now just my hand rested on his arm will have to do. 'Thanks for doing this. I really appreciate it.'

'How do you think it's all going?' he asks, and we both turn our gaze towards the giant see-through bin where Adio and co are depositing their coins any time their collecting buckets get heavy. It's not even a quarter full, but it's a big old bin, so there's no telling exactly how much is in it.

We debated whether to have it on display, or if that would be too tempting for thieves. In the end, we decided it was more likely to inspire people than attract any wrong'uns. Plus it's not like anyone could grab it and jog up the street with it – it's way too heavy.

'There's still a steady stream of people arriving and there's a collection bucket beside Elliot's goal that hasn't been added to the pot yet, so there's still time to get closer to our target.' Which is a black line Cassie has drawn halfway up the bin with the word 'goal' written above it. 'I know we probably won't make a fortune, but if people go online afterwards and buy a season ticket, or even a match ticket, we'll still be in a better place financially than we've ever been.'

'You're doing a grand job,' Ben assures me with a grin. 'I want to kiss you.'

I smile up at him. 'I want to kiss you too.'

We both look around us. There are too many people nearby.

'Meet me behind the cake tent in two minutes?' he suggests.

I laugh. 'Like horny teenagers?'

His grin widens. 'I hope so.' And it's all I can do not to break into a run.

With his arms wrapped around me and his lips meeting mine, I think I relax for the first time all day. I hadn't registered how stressed I've been trying to make sure everything is going to plan. I melt into his embrace, savouring the brief reprieve.

We're mid-clinch when Olly announces over the Tannoy that the pub quiz prize has been taken by the Johnsons – one of the families from Cassie's Kickers club. Each member of the team will be presented with a Crawford season ticket, giving us another handful of fans to add to our slowly growing following. I'm gradually allowing myself to be optimistic that we will end up with quite a few more, given how many people have come here to compete for the chance to win.

I freeze when I hear my sister's voice in the cake tent with Marge. 'Have you seen Lily? I reckon we're probably at peak attendance round about now so it's a good time to get the auction underway.'

'I did see her head round back with the rubbish with Ben,' Marge replies, shattering my illusion that we'd sneaked away unnoticed. Then something else I hadn't noticed comes to light – there's a flap in the back of the cake tent that allows both Cassie and Marge to poke their heads through, leaving Ben and I frozen in each other's arms, well and truly busted.

25

For a second my insides turn to ice. This was not supposed to happen. Not at all, but definitely not like this. I scan their faces to see how they'll react and Marge seems uncharacteristically lost for words, a silent 'oh' forming on her lips. Cassie, on the other hand, looks like she has plenty to say.

'We can talk about this later,' I quickly tell her, releasing Ben and ushering him away. 'The event is the most important thing right now so let's just try to stay focused on it.'

'I'll get back to work,' Ben says, winking at me before scooping up his bin bag and heading back out into the melee.

I step through the tent flap to join Cassie and Marge, who finally finds her tongue and says, 'Are you sure this is a good idea?'

'No,' I admit. 'But he's funny and thoughtful and all the things the press don't make him out to be, and I want to enjoy it for as long as I can.'

'I genuinely had no idea,' she says, shaking her head.

'I had my suspicions,' Cassie admits, but from the frown on her face I'd say she's far from impressed by it. 'Even if you hadn't started disappearing off to see a mystery man just after Ben arrived on the scene, the matching his-and-hers cakes were a bit of a giveaway.'

This hadn't actually occurred to me. So does that mean we've accidentally outed ourselves to everyone? Even Dad? But surely he would have mentioned it, and I didn't get the impression from Craig earlier that anyone else on the team had guessed.

'Why didn't you say anything?' I ask Cassie.

'What am I supposed to say? That I think you're making a huge mistake? I know he's been generous with the time he's invested in Crawford, but let's not forget why he's got so much free time in the first place.'

'I promise you, he's not a bad person once you get beyond his public image.'

She folds her arms in front of her chest, still not convinced. 'Hasn't he dated every wannabe WAG from here to Scotland? You're not one of those girls, Lily. I don't know why you'd want to be.'

'You're right, I'm not, and that's why this is different. It's not about being seen together – we genuinely like each other. We really click. He makes me happy.'

'She does look happy,' Marge points out.

'But for how long?' Cassie sighs. 'It's not that I'm trying to rain on your parade, sis. I just don't want you to get hurt.'

'And I have considered that possibility. But I can't just never take a risk on anything in case it doesn't work out. If that's how I lived, there'd be no Crawford United.' I put a reassuring hand on her arm. 'He's treating me nicely and I enjoy his company. So let's just leave it at that and get back to enjoying the day, shall we?'

'It does look like the auction's about to begin,' Marge says, nodding her head towards the makeshift platform where Dad is taking his place.

'We'd better get out there then,' I say firmly, leading the way.

Olly's voice booms out over the Tannoy, asking all the prospective bidders to make their way to the stage. 'And don't forget all the proceeds are going to Crawford United, so bid as generously as you can, please.'

Dad can't stop grinning as I step up on to the stage beside him – for him, this is the highlight of the day. My role is to help him keep track of who's bidding, and Cassie joins us after Dad has announced that the first lot on offer is a personal training session with her, starting at the bargain amount of thirty pounds.

'We haven't got an official system so just stick your hand up or shout out if you want to make a bid,' he tells the crowd.

Ben gets the ball rolling with a ten-pound increase, even before Cassie's fiancé has had a chance to jump in. I know it's his way of encouraging other people to get involved and sure enough it precipitates nine more bids, taking the total to eighty-one pounds. It's one of Cassie's twelve-year-old students who makes the final offer. Dad frowns in his direction, and I know he'll be thinking he should have specified an age limit. But the boy shouts out, 'Don't worry, I've just got a louder voice than my mum. She's paying.'

'As long as she knows she is,' Cassie warns.

There's a thumbs up from the woman standing next to

him and Dad breathes a sigh of relief. He wants this to go smoothly, not come unstuck with the very first bid.

'Thank you, Mrs Jennings,' Cassie calls out. 'Come and see me afterwards and we'll talk about a date.'

She jumps down off the stage and Levi and Scott step up to join me and Dad in her place. They're offering their car-washing services to the highest bidder, as suggested by Bob. Dad kicks things off once again at thirty pounds and this time the final amount creeps up to an incredibly generous hundred and twenty-five. It seems a lot for a car wash until Dad says to the winner, 'Do you want to tell them how many cars you've got or shall I?'

It turns out he's a colleague of Dad's, with a penchant for classic Minis. He has seven in total. 'At least they're small,' he says jovially. But when he sees the looks of horror on the two lads' faces, he adds, 'But only three of them are dirty.'

The third lot is Craig and his life-modelling afternoon. There's a collective 'ooh' as he struts up on to the stage, flaps his T-shirt to flash his abs, flexes his biceps then poses majestically with his hands on his hips and his chin up high. I look over at Phoebs and she's laughing her head off. I wonder if he's noticed, but somehow I think his ego would remain unscathed regardless.

Marge makes the first bid, and throws a few more into the mix as the price starts climbing, to keep it moving steadily upwards. At least I'm assuming that's why and not because she wants to win. But she needn't have worried. There's a fierce to and fro between two other women, neither of whom we know, and the sale eventually closes out at two hundred and thirty pounds.

'Oh thank God,' the winner exclaims. 'My original

plan for my stepdaughter's hen party fell through – this has saved my life.'

'Then I'm happy I bowed out,' her rival gracefully concedes.

And this brings Dad to the final lot. 'Last, but not least, up for grabs is a three-hour practice session with a bona fide Premier League footballer. Not to take anything away from the Phoenixes of course.'

A hand shoots up in the crowd before Dad has even announced the starting price. 'A hundred pounds,' comes the accompanying cry.

Dad laughs. 'Looks like we've got ourselves an opener.'

The bidding climbs in bigger increments this time, right up to £400. But just when Dad is about to declare the winner, there's a new shout from among the crowd. 'Five thousand pounds.'

The speed at which everyone's heads spin round to see who has spoken is enough to give them all whiplash. People start moving aside so the bidder can make himself known. Like me, I suspect they're probably thinking it's either a crazed superfan or someone pulling a prank.

'Fuck's sake, Dad,' Craig mutters when he realises it's his father William. 'How many times do I have to tell you not to embarrass me?'

'And how many times do I have to tell you I want this club to work out for you. So just let me help make that happen. And if you get to learn something while I'm at it then I can only see that as a bonus.'

There's an uncomfortable moment where they stand glaring at each other, until Craig eventually says, 'Fine, whatever, it's your money.'

'Yes it is,' William says firmly. 'And this is how I

choose to spend it. Mike, I'll grab the details off you and do you a transfer, unless anyone else wants to make a higher offer?'

You could hear a pin drop. I think Dad is in shock and everyone else is afraid that the slightest sound might be interpreted as a counter bid.

'Congratulations, Mr Campbell,' I say quickly, to break the tension. 'Lot four, three hours with Premier League footballer Ben Pryce, is yours for five thousand pounds.' I get goose bumps saying the amount out loud. 'Crawford United is incredibly grateful. To everyone here, in fact. We'd like to thank you all for your generosity today. It means the world to us.'

I look at Dad, but as he doesn't seem to have recovered yet, I continue. 'And that concludes our auction, but please stick around and come and chat to us and the team. There's still cake to be eaten, the raffle to draw and a keep-up target to beat.'

All of which keeps us busy till Olly rings for last orders and we're all dead on our feet.

26

It takes four of the lads to heave the money bin into the back of Dad's car at the end of the event. The crowd has dispersed, the Crawford players have all mucked in with the final tidy-up so Olly won't struggle to get the pub open again in time for Sunday lunch, and we've all treated ourselves to a celebratory beer. Dad wants to start counting the collected coins straight away, to see how we did, but I convince him it'll be better done tomorrow. It's not going to be a quick job.

When we do finally tot it all up, we've raised – including William's donation – over eight thousand pounds. And in the days that follow, we see the hoped-for spike in season ticket sales. By the following weekend, we've sold close to two hundred in total, which means we can now pay off a large chunk of Dad's loan for the ground share. We're all understandably delighted. Dad has no doubt that we can meet the remaining amount through ticket sales throughout the season. We only need to attract around fifty extra spectators per match to cover his initial outlay.

There's more to celebrate too, which I share with Dad, Cassie, Bob, Marge and Barbour at our Friday night kitchen table meeting.

'I've finally secured our first friendly match,' I announce proudly.

It hasn't been easy. A lot of the other clubs have either got games booked in already or have given their players time off over the summer and can't scrape together a team.

'It's against Mayfield North on the last weekend of July. At their ground, obviously.'

We don't have access to ours yet, which is another reason it's been harder for me to get anything organised.

Dad fist-pumps the air. 'That's great news, Lily. It will be so good for the lads to get a real game under their belts.'

'It'll probably be tough – Mayfield finished fourth last season – but it will hopefully make the debut match of the season seem less daunting. I don't know that we'll persuade many fans to come and watch though, what with it being at the furthest club from Hamcott and on a Wednesday evening.'

'We could set up a car-share scheme on our website,' Marge suggests. 'People could offer up their spare seats for a contribution towards petrol.'

'That's a great idea,' Dad says. 'Can you ask Adam to build something into the website for that? A kind of noticeboard-type thing, so they can organise it among themselves? We've got enough to do already without adding the coordination of that.'

'Will we be able to get a team coach for it?' Bob asks. 'Because if so, let's not forget there'll be a few empty seats on there as well.'

'Another excellent idea.' Dad says, nodding. 'And it won't be a problem borrowing a coach on a Wednesday evening. It's not a high-demand time slot. And we'll only need, what, twenty-five seats for us and the players, so we can offer up the rest on a first-come, first-served basis. Hopefully there'll be a few supporters who don't mind getting to the game a couple of hours early if it means they get to travel with the team.'

I make a note to add an announcement to the website and follow it up with an email alert.

'We could make that a regular offer,' I point out. 'And pick thirty people at random to get a free ride to each away game.'

'Would that work for the journey home, though?' Cassie asks. 'We don't want the players having to wait around for any stragglers after the matches, but if we drove off without someone we'd get slaughtered on social media.'

'True,' Dad says. 'Maybe we should keep it a bit smaller on the real match days and make it more of a treat. The lucky five perhaps. Let's use this friendly as a trial and see how it goes. We won't mention the longer-term intention until we've seen how it pans out.'

'So just to recap, that's in a little over three weeks?' Cassie checks.

I nod my head.

'Then we'll go straight into drills followed by match practice tomorrow,' she says. 'I want to make absolutely sure the lads are prepared for it.'

Before we all meet in the park the next day, I get a weekend bag ready. Ben is whisking me off for the romantic night away he promised me straight after

Crawford's not-so-social Saturday meet. All he's told me is that it's not at the vineyard, that it's in fact two nights not one, and that I'll need trainers and a jumper in case it's cool in the evenings. I can't wait to find out where we're going.

I pack my bikini, just in case. As well as my sandals, three changes of clothes and enough underwear for half a week. It's so unlike me to be this indecisive but I want to make sure I've covered all the bases. I'll pop back after the football to collect it all while Ben goes home for a shower before I meet him at his.

'I did tell you it was only for two nights?' he teases when he sees the wheely bag I've ended up filling.

'It's hard to pack when you don't know where you're going.' I think this justifies it.

He pretends to buckle under the weight as he hoists it into his boot. 'Have you got bricks in there?'

I wince and shake my head. 'It's just shoes and toiletries. I did think I was better at travelling light.'

'You'd have needed a shipping container for your European trip,' he says, laughing. 'At least you won't have to carry this anywhere though. There might be a bit of uneven ground at the other end, but I think you'll manage it.'

I'm even more intrigued now. I know we can't be going too far away because he's told me we'll arrive in time for dinner. But somewhere with rough ground within a two- or three-hour radius? It could be anywhere. Camber Sands or Hastings or somewhere else by the sea? But he reckons it's somewhere I won't have been to before. Oxford or Cambridge perhaps? But I'm not sure I've ever mentioned that I haven't visited either, and they don't exactly scream rough terrain. Plus the warm jumper recommendation suggests it will be somewhere breezy – a boat trip maybe?

'Have you chartered a yacht?' I ask him, once we're on the road.

'I have not. I'd rather do that when we go *away* away, with nicer weather and a flatter sea.'

I can't help smiling at the when, not if.

'A barge then?' I remember Phoebs doing a river cruise with her ex once and saying it was romantic.

'Not that, either,' Ben replies with a grin. 'You'll just have to wait and see.'

'And you said the drive will take how long?'

'I didn't.' He laughs. 'But don't worry, there are emergency snacks in the glove box, if you get hungry.'

I flip the catch and discover a multipack of Smarties inside, which makes my heart swell. He remembered! I reach across and give his thigh an appreciative squeeze. 'Did you know the UK is the only place where the orange ones are flavoured? And that the blue ones are coloured with sea algae?'

'I did not know either of those things, but I think I've just worked out what your *Mastermind* specialist subject would be.'

'I can also tell you that when they were first invented the brown ones were coffee-flavoured and that the boxes used to have letters inside the lids. I think I'm done after that though. How about you, what would your specialist subject be?'

'It should probably be something like Premier League goal scorers between 2018 and 2023, but realistically it would have to be something easier, like Oasis lyrics.'

203

'Do you know them all? Let me test you . . .'

After three failed attempts, he admits it's not so easy when you can't hear the tune.

I can't help laughing. 'I hope you're better at the general knowledge round.'

We decide to find out by searching for quizzes on my phone to entertain us for the rest of the journey. And by the time Ben pulls on to a dirt track at the end of a winding country lane in the heart of Dorset, we've concluded we know about as much as each other.

'This is it,' he announces, even though we appear to be in the middle of nowhere. The last farmhouse we passed was a good mile or two back. There's a little wooden signpost pointing into the trees though, with *Shepherd's Hut* etched into the bark, so I finally know where we'll be spending the next two nights.

Ben parks up and carries my case the rest of the way down the track, with his own bag slung over his shoulder, and on the other side of the trees we find a stilted wooden hut in a fenced well-kept garden with uninterrupted views of the lush countryside. There's an outdoor hot tub, an ornate bistro set and a firepit surrounded by a curved bench, with a glowing pile of logs filling the air with the sweet smell of wood smoke.

'Nice touch,' Ben says approvingly. 'And it's actually bigger than I expected from the pictures online.'

I'm already heading for the steps, eager to see the inside. Behind the wide double doors that can be opened right out is a kitchenette brightly painted in cream and oxford blue, with a matching sleeping area at one end of the hut and a shower room at the other. On the counter there's a welcome basket filled with breakfast essentials and a bottle of red wine. A decent one, which Ben admits he preordered before we arrived.

'And if I'm not mistaken . . .' He reaches down to open the fridge and there's champagne and a platter of nibbles inside – cold meat, cheese, olives, focaccia, sundried tomatoes, hummus and nuts. 'Yep, I think that's everything we need for tonight.'

He turns back to face me and I slide my arms round his waist. 'Thank you for this, Ben. I love it.'

He grins. 'So what do you reckon, quick bite to eat first or straight into the hot tub, before it gets dark?'

'We should eat.' If I can feel my stomach rumbling then I know he must be ravenous. 'We can stargaze in the hot tub later.'

'Excellent choice,' he says, grinning. 'I was hoping you'd say that.'

We carry the platter to the outside table so we can dine al fresco. With no noise from the road and not another soul around, I don't think there could be a more tranquil setting.

Ben pours the champagne and holds his glass up to mine. 'To fun times in the wilderness,' he says. And I repeat it back to him because I'm pretty sure I know what kind of fun we're going to be having.

The temperature gradually drops while we're eating and chatting, so we're more than ready to climb into the hot tub by the time the champagne is finished. Ben grabs the fluffy white towels from inside the hut while I slide the cover off the tub, releasing pillows of steam.

'I'm glad I brought my bikini with me for once. I think it's going to get plenty of use.'

'I was hoping you might have forgotten it,' Ben replies, a mischievous glint in his eyes.

All thoughts of changing into it vanish instantly.

We undress quickly, shivering slightly in the crisp night air before we swing our legs over the side of the tub and lower ourselves into the soft bubbles. Ben draws me close, kissing me as the steam swirls around us and playing with my nipples, which have hardened in the breeze.

It's only by accident that we discover the bubbles can be made more ferocious, when his arm brushes against a sensor neither of us had noticed. We laugh as the first splashes of water hit our faces, but with it getting in our ears and going up our noses, it becomes a lot harder to kiss. We concentrate on touching each other instead and by the time the cycle has finished and the bubbles have mellowed again, my body is aching for more than just his hands against my skin.

As if he can read my mind, he lifts me out on to the side of the tub, pushes my knees to the sides and moves his head between my legs. Then all I can think about is the feel of his tongue on that sweet, sweet spot and it's no longer the cool air that's making me shiver. I arch my back and sigh as he pushes a finger inside me, the tremors quickly intensifying.

I don't know if it's because it's so relaxing here in our own little bubble or because I'm feeling really loved up this evening, but quite suddenly I start to climax, my mouth falling open and my stomach muscles tensing as I'm overcome with the pleasure.

Ben quickly replaces his tongue with his other hand so he can look up and watch me, pulsing his fingers against my clit till I'm gasping. It's only when it starts feeling so ticklish that it makes me want to giggle that I grip his wrist, meet his eye and shake my head.

'You want me to stop?'

I nod. 'Just for a minute. I think I need to come back up for air.'

Smiling, he draws me back into the water. 'That was a quick one,' he says, kissing my lips, my cheeks, my neck.

'That's the effect you have on me,' I murmur as I reach for him under the water. Then it's his turn to perch on the side of the tub and have his breathing made ragged.

Afterwards, we sit in the bubbles with our bodies entwined as the sky darkens above us.

'We probably should have saved the champagne,' he says, stroking my back absently.

'Is it weird that I'm more in the mood for a beer? I know it's not as romantic, but I could quite happily sip a pale ale right now while we look at the stars.'

'A girl after my own heart, and your wish is my command.' A quick dash to the hut and he returns with two freshly cracked-open bottles.

We shift positions so I'm sitting between his legs with my back against his chest, his free arm loosely round my waist. Then we put the bubbles back on maximum speed and stare up at the night sky – both admitting the plough is the only constellation we recognise – until our drinks are empty and our skin has started to prickle from the chlorine.

'I guess it's bedtime,' Ben says after we've showered off, because there's nowhere to sit inside the hut except the snug sleeping area. But of course with us both being naked and in such romantic surroundings, it's not long before our bodies are intertwined beneath the sheets.

This time there's a tantalisingly slow build-up to my orgasm that makes it even more consuming, and Ben admits after he's climaxed that it was one of his strongest ever. I think we're both still wearing satisfied smiles as we cuddle up together and drift off to sleep.

27

The next morning Ben pulls two exercise mats out from under the bed and asks if I want to join him for a stretch in the rising sun. We roll them out in the garden and I watch him fold himself into positions that don't look like they ought to be possible – he's been practising yoga for years. I do my best versions alongside him.

After breakfast we head off for a long walk through the countryside, eventually circling back to the cosy country pub we spotted right at the beginning to grab some lunch. Then we spend the afternoon playing cards in front of our hut, with me mostly winning up to the point when I suggest the loser should shed an item of clothing after each game. Ben's luck suddenly takes a turn for the better and I accuse him of hustling. But it's not long before we're both semi-naked and the cards are discarded pretty quickly after that.

We barbecue steaks for our dinner, which we have with the red wine. Then we sit by the firepit, Ben's arm round my shoulder, my head resting on his, listening to the sound of the logs crackling in the flames.

I reach for his other hand and thread my fingers between his. 'This has flown by so fast. I can't believe we'll be back in Hamcott tomorrow.'

'I may have another little something in mind for the weekend after next,' he confesses. 'To celebrate your exam results, if you're up for it. You did say you get them that week, didn't you?'

He's right, but I've been trying not to think about it – that last paper still fills me with a sense of foreboding. 'Is it another glamping trip?' I ask, looking up at him.

'Something different.' But he doesn't say what.

'So I'm not getting any clues this time either?'

I don't mind, though, when he shakes his head. I'm getting used to our secret adventures and he hasn't had a bad idea yet.

'You know you don't have to keep spoiling me like this, don't you? I mean I love it, obviously, but I'd want to be with you even if we were just round at yours watching telly.'

'I know and that's why I want to do it. You never expect it and you always appreciate it. Plus I love seeing you smile. It makes you even more beautiful.'

My cheeks flush at the compliment and I nestle my head back on his shoulder, feeling happy and lucky and like I never want this to end. And it suddenly feels like the perfect time to confess something that I've been keeping from him, even though it's been on my mind with increasing frequency.

I say it into the flames, scared to watch his reaction in case it's not what I'm hoping for. 'I think I'm falling in love with you, Ben.'

I hold my breath, heart pounding as I worry that it's

too much too soon. But he tucks a finger under my chin and turns my face towards his. 'I've been falling for you since the first day I met you,' he says, making a gazillion fireworks explode all around me.

We stare at each other for a moment then we both burst out laughing.

'I'm so relieved we've got that out of the way,' Ben says.

'It was kind of nerve-racking,' I agree. 'I hadn't planned to say it first.'

'I almost said something last night but I didn't want it to look like it was just because of the sex – not that it isn't a bit because of the sex. But it's so much more than that. You're just so easy to be around. It feels, I don't know, like we were meant for each other or something.' Then he checks himself. 'Sorry, that sounded so corny.'

'It's okay. I feel exactly the same way.'

His expression turns serious for a moment. 'This isn't going to be easy, you know. Conversations are starting to happen about my return date to Millford, but I didn't want to say.'

'Is it imminent?'

'Nothing's agreed yet, but it will be sometime in the next few weeks. They'll want me to have a decent amount of training time with my teammates before they put me back out on the pitch.'

'But we'll still be able to see each other?'

'On Sundays we'll definitely be able to meet in person, but I'm usually stuck in a hotel wherever we're playing on the Friday night before a match, even for home games, and the team always travel back together afterwards. But I'll be able to get down to Hamcott late on Saturday or

211

first thing Sunday – or you can come up to me. I'd have to head back Sunday evening. There's always a post-match analysis on a Monday first thing.'

It's hard not to feel like the odds are stacked against us. 'It's going to be tough going to that from all this.'

'I know, and I wouldn't blame you if you decided it was too much to deal with. FaceTime can make up for some of it, but I know it's not the same. I'd never ask you to miss Crawford training, but if you ever felt you could skip it on a Tuesday, you could stay up at mine a bit longer. I could get my apartment set up so you could work from there at the start of the week. I know that's asking a lot though, and I don't want it to sound like I think my life is more important. All I know is, when I go back, I don't want it to be the end of this.'

'I don't want that either.'

'Then we'll find a way to make it work,' he promises. 'I'll make sure of it.'

28

I do my best not to let the thought of him leaving ruin the precious time we have left after that, but it's never too far from my mind. As we're already into July, the new football season starts in just five weeks. By now I'm used to seeing him every day, so it's going to feel utterly heart-wrenching when he goes away. But at no point do I ever regret having met him. Not when I think he just might be my soulmate.

On the Saturday between our two mini breaks, I arrange a night out in central London to thank him for both the glamping and whatever he's planned for the following weekend. It's my chance to surprise him for a change.

Figuring his ideal evening would include a bit of romance, good food and some kind of challenge, I book a floating hot tub in the Canary Wharf waterways to kick things off – a throwback to our stay in Dorset. After that there'll be a steak dinner and we'll round off at a bar that has computerised clay pigeon shooting. I think that covers all the bases.

'So where to?' Ben asks when he meets me at the Tube station, showered and refreshed after Crawford's Saturday training session.

'East,' I reply cryptically. It seems only fair that I take a leaf out of his book and don't give away more than that till we get there.

He eyes the backpack I'm holding, but that won't give him any clues. The bottle of wine inside is wrapped up in two towels – and he has no idea I sneaked a pair of his swimming shorts into my bag the last time I was at his house.

I notice a couple of people looking at him on the journey, but no one tries to talk to him so it might just be because he's so insanely handsome rather than because they recognise him. Ben either doesn't notice the stares or is used to ignoring them.

When we change on to the Jubilee Line, he starts trying to guess what I've planned for the evening. 'Is it a band at the O2?'

I shake my head. 'They don't allow backpacks in there.'

'Please tell me you're not taking me shopping in Stratford.'

'We're definitely not trawling round shops on a Saturday night.'

'Thank goodness for that. Okay, last guess – are we doing that walk over the top of the O2? I've always liked the look of that.'

I tell him we're getting off at the next stop, and when he sees that puts us in Canary Wharf, he knows he's guessed wrong again.

As we pull into the station I'm hit by a sudden wave of doubt. When I told him I'd planned a surprise for him, he said he trusted me to pick something good. But what if he has an aversion to guns or thinks the hot tub experience is naff? Climbing the O2 didn't even occur to me, so maybe I was wrong to assume that because I've loved all his surprises, mine would go down just as well.

My fears are short-lived though. When we arrive at the hot tub hiring hut, he starts laughing. 'Ah brilliant, I've seen people doing this on Instagram.'

I finally show him what I've got stashed in my bag and he tells me I've thought of everything – although we find out during the safety briefing that whoever drives the hot tub isn't allowed to drink any alcohol.

'I'm happy to abstain if you're okay with me doing the steering,' he says.

There's a dressing room where we can get changed and lockers for our bags. On the boat there's a dry box for our valuables and an ice box for our drinks. I buy some sparkling water from the venue so there's something for Ben, and so I can cool down when I need to – for some reason I didn't expect the hot tub water to be quite so hot.

After a quick chug round the practice area – it doesn't take Ben long to get the hang of it – we set off, cruising between the towering buildings and raising our glasses to the other tubs we pass. Each one has a different vibe. There's a raucous hen party cackling at anything and everything, other couples enjoying cosy date nights, and a group of lads on a floating barbecue, who try to give us sausages to apologise for nearly crashing into us, then almost tumble overboard when they realise they've just made chipolata jokes to Ben Pryce. I'm not convinced they're abiding by the sober driver rule.

Ben's still laughing about it when we're back in the changing room afterwards. 'I'll be amazed if they all make it back to base dry. That was really fun, thank you.'

'That's not the end,' I tell him. 'There are two more things planned.'

'Is one of them food-related?'

'Of course, then there's an after-dinner activity.'

'And is that what I hope it will be?'

I laugh. 'I think you're thinking of the after *activity* activity.'

'I can't deny it. So what's on tonight's menu?' He catches me smirking. 'To eat, I mean. Have you got somewhere specific in mind or are we just going to see where we can get a table?'

'I've booked a steak place. I was thinking a sirloin and a nice glass of red.'

His smile widens. 'It's like you know me or something.'

Bailey calls him while we're on the way to the restaurant.

'Do you mind if I get this quickly?'

'Not at all – go ahead.'

'He's been working through some stuff,' Ben explains afterwards. 'So I always try to be there. He's fine, though. He's just been talking to our mum and she's decided to do a family roast tomorrow lunchtime. We're both invited – she's keen to meet you. What do you reckon?'

It only seems fair given how many times he's met Dad and Cassie, even if the circumstances aren't exactly the same.

'I should probably warn you though, I haven't taken anyone round since I've been up in Millford,' he adds.

I'm not sure if this makes me feel special or terrified. 'No pressure then!'

'It's nothing to worry about – they're all really easy-going,' he assures me. 'The only one to watch out for a bit is my nan. She's lovely too, but she's very nosy.'

'Am I meeting the whole Pryce clan?'

He grins sheepishly. 'Is that okay? I promise I'll jump in if Nan asks too many questions.'

I tell him it's fine. Luckily, I've never been too intimidated by the prospect of meeting my boyfriends' parents.

By the time we've finished our meal, Ben admits the wine, which we've drunk fairly quickly, has gone to his head. And I'm half a bottle ahead of him after the hot tub, so I'm even more tipsy.

'I hope whatever's next doesn't require a lot of dexterity,' he says. 'I'm not sure I could drive a hot tub in a straight line after this.'

'How about firing a gun?'

'Is that a serious question?'

I tell him where we're headed and he laughs. 'That's a lot less concerning.'

'Have you done it before?'

'Never, so it's another great choice. I'm feeling quite spoilt. It feels like my birthday.'

It's a short walk to the venue, and when we get there we're shown to a booth and given a brief explanation of how everything works. The first thing that strikes me is how heavy the gun is, and the host explains it's a real gun, just not real bullets. There are sensors that will figure out where we're pointing the barrel.

She shows us how to reload, tells us which of the five

217

games are most suitable for beginners and explains the system for ordering drinks.

'Would you say a cocktail improves your aim?' Ben asks her.

'An espresso martini maybe, but I'll leave you to be the judge of that,' she says.

It's hard to tell if the cocktails have any effect or if we just us get the hang of it as we work our way through the games. While my accuracy averages a meagre eleven per cent in the first game, it's more than doubled by game three.

Ben doesn't do much better. He has a slight advantage in that his hands are bigger so he can reach the reload button more easily, but he's just as perplexed by the speed of the 'pigeons', so there are only a few points separating us as we enter the fourth game – and I'm in the lead.

With everything to play for, I think we both get a little more competitive, which might explain why we both do really well in this round, despite it being harder than the previous three. At the end of it, I've just about clung on to my advantage, but Ben could easily overtake me in the remaining few minutes. He's up first in what will be the fifth and final game, and there's a danger I might not get another turn as the clock ticks down towards the end of our time slot.

'Hurry up,' I mutter as we wait for the screen to load. Ben's already in position, ready and waiting.

'Go, go, go,' I shout as the first pigeon appears and in his haste he tracks, shoots and misses. But as he's used to refocusing after a misfire, he just slows down for the next one and smashes eight of the remaining discs. He's looking more than a little pleased with himself as he passes the gun back to me. It has left my score trailing and we're now into the last thirty seconds.

With nothing to lose, I scatter bullets at will as soon as my turn begins, and my score creeps back up until I need just one more five-point pigeon to steal a victory.

'No!' His arms fly up in disbelief as I hit it at the exact second the screen freezes. 'You lucky devil.'

I can't resist a celebratory dance, which he pretends to be annoyed about until he relents and congratulates me. 'It just goes to show, quantity over quality can be very effective,' he says mock begrudgingly.

'Let's leave that theory in this room though,' I suggest. And he laughs – he knows exactly what I mean.

'So are you ready to head home now?' I ask, now he's got me thinking about the quality time I want to spend with him. He nods with an enthusiasm that tells me the next activity is one we're both going to win.

29

While Ben's in the gym the following morning, I allow myself a lie-in. His parents live close enough to his house for us to be able to walk there, so there's no great rush to get out of bed ahead of our lunch date.

Their house, while not quite on the scale of Ben's, is still impressively big, with red-brick walls and large bay windows. When we arrive, his nan Tilda is trying to make herself useful in the kitchen, but is mostly just getting under his mum Helen's feet.

'Get this woman out of here, would you?' Helen says good-humouredly. 'She's driving me crazy. Welcome to the madhouse, Lily. I'll say hello properly when I've got these last bits in the oven, but for now, shoo, the lot of you, or lunch won't be ready till teatime.'

Tilda tilts her face up so Ben can kiss her on the cheek. 'Finally someone who appreciates me,' she huffs. 'Let's get you both a drink and then we can get out of grumpy chops' hair and you can tell me all about yourself, Lily, and whether this one's been behaving like a gentleman.'

'Just a water for me, please,' Ben says.

Tilda sighs. 'You footballers. Lily, will you join me in a prosecco?'

'Go on then.' I'm not sure she'd take no for an answer even if I didn't think I could benefit from a bit of Dutch courage.

'Where's Grandpa?' Ben asks.

'Pottering about in the garden with your dad.' Tilda points out the window. 'They're debating whether to cut down that bloody awful tree. It might shelter you from your neighbours but it does block out all the sunlight. At the very least it needs a good trim.'

Ben frowns. 'They're not thinking of doing it themselves, are they?'

'Of course they are. Your grandad won't pay someone else to do something he thinks he can do himself for free.'

'I'll pay for it,' Ben offers. 'That's got to be better than letting those two up a ladder with a chainsaw.'

'I'll let you talk to them. You know how stubborn your grandpa can be. Or even better, don't talk to them. Just organise to have it done while they're out at the pub one evening. Then I won't have any hospital visits to contend with.'

We head out into the garden so Ben can introduce me.

'Nice to meet you, Lily,' Ben's dad says, holding his hand out to shake mine.

'I see Tilda's got you on the bubbles already,' his grandad observes. 'You want to watch her; she's a fiend. Has been all her life.'

'That's why you married me,' she reminds him, and he laughs and tells her she's right.

'So how does it feel to be seventy, Nan?' Ben asks as

221

we make our way back inside. He explains to me that it was her birthday last week.

'Don't! When you say it out loud it sounds so ancient,' she says. 'I feel exactly the same as I did when I was thirty, give or take the odd creak. You never really get old anywhere other than in your bones.'

'You don't look seventy,' I tell her. She's slim, dressed in skinny jeans, a floral blouse and white pumps, and her white hair is cut into a chin-length bob the same as mine. She could easily pass for fifty.

'You want to know the secret?' she asks. 'Never stop laughing. I've been with that idiot out there for half my lifetime and he still makes me chuckle every single day.'

I look at Ben and he fires me a grin. Laughing is definitely something we do well together. But his expression changes to mortification when his nan adds, 'And good sex. You need plenty of that too. Makes you happy and keeps you fit.'

'Lily doesn't need to hear about your sex life, Nan,' he says quickly. 'Sorry,' he mouths to me.

'Fine, I was only saying. And I appreciated the compliment, thank you, Lily.'

She changes the subject then, much to Ben's relief. 'Ben tells me you're something of a football fanatic, like him and his brother.'

I tell her how Crawford United came into being, how it's been great having Ben's input into the team and how things are about to step up a gear as our friendly match is now only two weeks away.

'It all sounds very exciting,' Tilda says, then she asks me if Ben has been putting as much effort into our relationship. She says the glamping trip sounded like a

222

winner, but that our trip to Bruges next weekend would be more up her street.

'Nan!' Ben bursts out. 'It was meant to be a surprise.'

Her free hand flies up to her mouth. 'Oh God I'm sorry.' She looks at the prosecco in her other hand. 'Maybe I should listen to your grandpa and not start on this stuff so early. Can you pretend you didn't hear that?'

'It's already forgotten,' I assure her, but I think she can tell from the happy smile I direct at Ben that I'm delighted.

Bailey joins us and temporarily becomes the focus of Tilda's scrutiny. And I swell with pride listening to him talk about how well organised Crawford United is already, how the bosses are doing a great job and how excited the players all are about the upcoming season.

'And how's *your* love life?' Tilda asks pointedly.

'You know I don't like talking about it,' he says, which makes her roll her eyes.

'Just tell me when I need to go hat shopping,' she says, which is something of a surprise to me. I don't think I've ever heard him mention a girlfriend, let alone suggest a wedding might be on the horizon. But maybe that's what Ben was talking about yesterday when he said Bailey had a lot on his mind.

The conversation turns back to Crawford United over lunch, so Ben's parents and grandad can hear about it too, but Tilda and Ben don't seem to mind. And staying on the topic of football has the added advantage of keeping Tilda away from asking any further probing questions about anyone's relationship.

Ben and I stay for coffees afterwards, and even though I've mostly been the centre of attention, I still feel like I've had a relaxing time. They couldn't have made me feel more at home really, and I suddenly want Ben to feel the same way around my family. I'm sure Dad would make him feel just as welcome now Ben's had the chance to show him what he's really like. And Cassie's been a lot less concerned about his intentions since I told her about him confessing his feelings round the firepit.

So on the way back to Ben's place, I announce I'm ready to tell my dad about us.

'Are you sure? Doesn't he still think I'm a bit of a neanderthal?' Ben asks.

'I think you've proven him wrong on that front by now. And he trusts my judgement, so he won't be questioning that.'

But life has a way of throwing you under the bus sometimes, so it all comes out before I get to have that conversation with Dad.

30

I'm home in time to have breakfast with Dad on the Monday morning, because there are some Crawford outgoings I need to sign off and I want his approval before he goes to work. While I call up the relevant documents on my laptop, he scrolls through the news on his phone and stumbles across a picture-led splash on Ben.

'Have you seen this?' he asks, turning his phone round. 'He's apparently been spotted floating round Canary Wharf half-naked with a girl and they've suggested he's more interested in adding another notch to his bedpost than getting himself ready for his return to Millford City.'

I silently curse the person who managed to film us without us noticing. This is hardly going to help Dad see Ben in a more positive light.

Time seems to go into slow motion as I watch Dad squint at his phone screen, zoom in on the picture with his fingers and squint a little closer before he looks at me again. 'Is that *you*, Lily? Are you and Ben . . .' He leaves the question unfinished.

I briefly consider insisting it's a doppelganger, but

there's no point when I'd already decided to tell him about us. It might as well be now.

'We are,' I admit, wincing. 'I'm sorry I didn't say anything sooner, but with us kind of working together at Crawford we thought it would be better to keep it to ourselves.'

'Is it serious?' he asks.

I nod. 'I really like him. It feels like I've met the male version of me.'

'Oh, Lily,' he sighs. 'I can't say this is one of your smartest choices. I can see how you'd think he's charismatic – even I can see that – but what about the fact that he's got such a volatile streak? Can you be certain he won't lash out again next time a fan – or anyone else, you even – hits a nerve? I don't want you to have to deal with that kind of thing.'

'He let his temper get the better of him once. Of course it shouldn't have happened, but he's assured me no one knows that more than him. He's adamant it will never happen again. And I believe him – he's not an angry person and he hasn't given me any reason to doubt him.'

There's still concern etched on Dad's face. 'He wouldn't be the first person to make that promise. And you've only known him for a matter of weeks. What about six months down the line, when he's caught back up in his Premier League lifestyle? Have you thought about what happens when he goes back to Millford?'

'We've talked about that and we're both determined to make it work. Yes, it'll be complicated and there'll be a lot of travelling, but we're both prepared to put the effort in. I know it isn't perfect, so I understand why you think I

226

should be cautious, but he makes me happy in a way I've never felt before. And I want a future with him, even if it's not a conventional one.'

Dad sits back in his chair and sighs again. 'I'm just worried you're making your life more difficult than it needs to be. But it sounds like you've made up your mind so I'll do my best to support you, even if I'm not very happy about it.'

I didn't expect him to brim with enthusiasm, but at least there's a glimmer of acceptance.

To my relief, when he sees Ben at training the following evening, he acts like nothing has changed and doesn't start warning Ben he'd better be nice to me or anything equally mortifying. So I start to relax, thinking he's just going to leave me to get on with it. But his support is significantly challenged when another bombshell lands just two days later – on the day I get the results of my degree.

We're back at the kitchen table, at breakfast time again, because the email from university is due before nine and Dad wants to be there when it arrives. There's an untouched slice of toast on the plate in front of me – my stomach is too jittery for me to want to eat it.

It makes us both jump when my inbox pings. I take a deep breath and cross my fingers under the table as I click to open it. 'Okay, here goes.'

Dad leans forward in anticipation as I start reading aloud. 'Strategic HRM . . . pass.' Yes! 'Corporate responsibilities . . . pass.' Huge relief! 'Global communication in the digital age . . . Oh.'

'What?' Dad catches the change in my tone.

'I didn't pass it. I had such a bad feeling about that one. It was absolute hell.'

It doesn't stop me feeling gutted that I didn't manage to scrape through, though.

'Can you retake?' Dad asks.

'We can resit one module. Any more and it might mean repeating the year. Wait!' I stare in horror at the screen. 'I haven't passed effective leadership and managing change either?'

I knew it wouldn't be a brilliant score, but I did not expect to fail. There's panic in my voice now. 'There must be an error. I must have done better than this. I can't sit through the whole year again.'

'Perhaps you should have spent less time thinking about your love life and more time with your books,' Dad comments.

'This really isn't the time for a lecture, Dad. I actually feel quite sick about this.' Especially as Phoebs has just texted me three champagne emojis and a 'woohoo' gif.

I start frantically scanning to the bottom of the email, to find the information relating to resits. 'Oh thank fuck! It says here I can redo up to two modules without repeating.'

It might just be the most relieved I've ever felt – once I've confirmed I've also passed data analytics, that is.

'There's a retake day in August,' I tell Dad, then I reread the date. 'Oh shit!'

This makes Dad jump. 'What now?'

'Please don't do this to me,' I mutter, grabbing my phone, pulling up my calendar and scrolling forward as fast as I can. 'Oh thank God.' I drop it back on the table. 'I thought it was going to clash with Crawford's first league match. It's the day before though. That nearly gave me a heart attack.'

'You and me both,' Dad exclaims. 'That gives you just under a month then, so you'd better knuckle down this time. We can ask Marge to help keep an eye on Crawford United until your diary frees up again, and you'll just have to tell Ben you're too busy to go on dates.'

I'm about to protest, but he adds, 'I know you won't want to step back from the club, but Marge and I can keep everything ticking over. I'll take a bit of time off work and she'll be happy to help.'

He's right – I don't want to give it up, even temporarily, but I do also know it makes sense.

I'm not about to cancel the Bruges trip with Ben though, despite Dad's reaction to me telling him this. He shakes his head despairingly. 'You shouldn't be gallivanting off to Belgium while this is hanging over your head.'

'It's just for one night, and I'll get Ben to download a movie to watch on the Eurostar so I can do some revision on the journey.'

I tell him I'm not prepared to miss the Mayfield North friendly either, after all the work I've put into organising it – nor skip all Crawford's training sessions. While I can't bear the thought of failing again, I will need a few study breaks and I can't sacrifice everything.

Dad can't hide his infuriation – the word 'irresponsible' is mentioned, followed by, 'On your head be it.'

31

Ben is sympathetic when I tell him Bruges isn't going to be quite the celebratory trip we'd anticipated. 'Do you still want to go?' he asks. 'I could always rebook it for a later date.'

I point out it might be the last bit of fun I get to have for a while, so I'm keen for it to still go ahead.

When I speak to Phoebs, she assures me we're not cancelling the graduation piss-up we'd planned either. 'After sitting through three years of lectures together, I'm not doing it without you,' she says. 'I'll just have a cheeky glass of champers with Craig for now and the big party can wait till August, when we've both got some letters after our name.'

Dad manages to bite his tongue when it's time for me to head to Bruges and begrudgingly tells me to enjoy it. I do keep my promise of studying on the way there though. And instead of downloading a film to watch on the train, Ben volunteers to test me from my revision notes, which I happily agree to. It might even help me remember things better if I associate them with him.

By the time we arrive in Belgium, he probably knows more than he'll ever need to about corporate social media strategy.

We check into our hotel – a stylish boutique on the edge of the old town – and take our bags up to our room, which manages to be both modern and ornate at the same time. Peacock blue walls are adorned with gilded frames containing black and white photography of the city, and in the green and white mosaicked bathroom there's an elegant rolltop bath and a shower big enough to fit half a football team in.

'We can have some fun in there,' Ben says, his grin wide.

'I do want to see at least a bit of Bruges,' I say with a laugh. But that's not to say I don't also want to make the most of this gorgeous room.

We do venture out of course, wandering hand in hand through the pretty streets, admiring the architecture and peering in the windows of the many chocolate shops. We share a waffle and a bowl of frites, and stop off at a bar late in the afternoon to sample beer that's served in a test tube, beer with more foam on top than beer and – my favourite – beer that is only brewed on a full moon.

We go for dinner in a candlelit bistro and as we're walking back to the hotel afterwards – taking the longer, more scenic route along the canals to burn off some of the day's excesses – we pass a tiny, dimly lit bar where a band is setting up, and there's one table empty, which feels like it has our name on it.

We head inside thinking we'll just stay for one drink, but once the talented band starts playing its melodic rock set, the little space around us quickly fills up and we realise we were lucky to get seats. Two full hours pass before we eventually decide it's time to call it a night, the tiredness finally catching up with us after our early start this morning.

'That was a real find,' Ben says, putting his arm round my shoulders as we turn towards our hotel again. 'We would never have stumbled across it if we'd stuck to the main tourist streets.'

'It was the perfect end to a magical day.' I slide my arm round his waist and snuggle into him. With each new memory we create I feel even closer to Ben. And when he stops and pulls me into his arms for a kiss, it's the best feeling in the world knowing he feels the same way.

He insists I spend the next morning studying and disappears off to the gym to give me some peace – but he makes sure he's back in plenty of time for us to make the most of that shower, so we're not just glowing from the heat of the water when we check out of our room and hand back our keys.

We leave our bags at the reception desk and head out for an al fresco brunch in the market square, followed by a romantic boat trip along the canal. Then we round off our trip with a private chocolate-making workshop Ben has arranged, and I'm hopeful that when I give Dad the wonky-shaped pralines I come away with at the end, it will stop him grumbling that I should have stayed at home revising.

But instead of making him less annoyed about me going on this trip, what they actually do, unintentionally, is out my relationship with Ben to the rest of Crawford United. It starts when Ben passes his own chocolate creations round at Tuesday night's training – a fact I'm not aware of as it's the first session I skip to focus on the course notes I've dragged back out from under my bed.

With just over a week now till the Mayfield North game, Dad invites the players back to our house after the session so he and Cassie can talk to them about tactics – and I take a break from my books to squeeze into the kitchen with them because I don't want to miss out on everything.

Dad starts by promising he won't keep them long as only eight people have seats. 'Perhaps going forward I'll look at having smaller groups here for tactical training – defenders Tuesday, forwards Thursdays, just for half an hour extra, before any of you start panicking.'

He's done some research on our opponents and, while Cassie passes round Lucozades and waters, he tells us Mayfield North have progressed to the Isthmian league on three separate occasions since they formed in 2002. 'But they've always gone straight back down again, so no matter how good they look on paper, they're not infallible,' he tells the team.

Which is when Elliot spots the confectionery bag that matches Ben's on the counter and says, 'Hey, aren't those the same chocolates Prycey had?' I can almost see the light bulb go on in his mind as he works out the connection. 'So that girl in the hot tub picture . . . Aaron was right when he said it looked like Lily?'

It feels like the whole room comes to a standstill as everyone turns their eyes in my direction. I glance at Ben and he nods, letting me know he's happy for me to spill the beans.

'It doesn't change anything,' I tell the players quickly. 'Our first priority will always be Crawford United.'

'Get in.' Scott cackles. 'No wonder she wouldn't look twice at you, Craig mate.'

Craig rolls his eyes. 'I'm very happy with Phoebs, thank you very much. But maybe if *you* put yourself out there from time to time, you wouldn't have to spend all your nights home alone in your bedroom.'

He winks at Scott, who laughs and concedes it's a fair point, then apologises to me and Dad for being inappropriate in the first place.

Bringing the focus back to the football, Dad highlights where he thinks Mayfield's main weaknesses are, based on the few videos he's found on their fan site, then runs through how Crawford can best take advantage of them. And at the end, he reminds everyone of the kind of behaviour he expects from them on the pitch.

'I don't want to see anyone diving, pretending you're injured if you're not or challenging the ref's decisions. I want you to be proud of your performance, and I want it to stand up to scrutiny.'

He looks round the room to make sure everyone's listening. 'So no dirty tricks and no throwing your toys out of the pram. It's not what we want Crawford to be known for. And that stands for all future matches, not just any friendlies.'

'What if our opponents are doing all that shit?' Scott asks.

'Rise above it,' Dad says. 'Keep your cool and know you're the better man. With the right attitude on Wednesday, I believe we stand a really good chance of winning.'

'I second that,' Ben says, which sparks a murmur of agreement.

Dad wraps things up then, and thanks everyone for this extra bit of their time. 'Get plenty of rest between training sessions over this next week,' he advises. 'And if you haven't already done so, remember to arrange it with your work so you can be here promptly at four next Wednesday for the drive down to Mayfield. I don't want anyone finding out on the day that their boss won't let them leave before six.'

He shakes everyone's hand at the door on their way out, then when it's just Ben and me left he heads up to his room to give us some privacy – although not before reminding me my textbooks are upstairs waiting. As if I could forget.

'So we're fully official,' Ben says when we're alone.

'It looks that way,' I agree, smiling up at him.

'Then you won't mind if I do this.' He leans forward to kiss me. Like I've ever wanted to stop him.

It's the first time it's happened in my own house though, and I'm so glad we no longer have to be sneaky. But we do say goodnight eventually – I think it'll still be a while before Dad's comfortable with a cosy breakfast à trois.

32

On the day of the Mayfield match, I manage to concentrate on my exam prep up until just after lunchtime, when Dad pulls up outside our house in the coach he's brought home from work for the evening. It looks huge and out of place on our residential street.

He's not behind the wheel, I should point out. He does have a coach licence so he can move parts of the fleet around at the company HQ when required, but as a special treat for our first game, we've splashed out on a driver, so Dad can focus on prepping the team rather than road safety.

'Er, where are you going to park it?' I ask from the doorstep as he jumps down from the doorway and turns back to give the driver a thumbs up.

'At the Marks and Spencer,' Dad says with a smile. 'I called them from the office and they've agreed to let us borrow their loading bay. They're not expecting another delivery till after seven and we'll be long gone by then.'

'Should I contact the players and get them to meet us there instead?'

'They can still come here, then anyone who's early can wait indoors. We'll bring the coach back to load up just before we set off. It won't block the road for long. It's probably too risky changing the location anyway – half the fans who are joining us would probably not see the message and end up missing out on their free ride.'

This means there's quite a crowd assembled on our driveway and flowing out on to the street by the time the coach returns, and a few of our neighbours come out of their houses to see what's going on, drawn to the sound of our excited chattering. While Cassie, who's rushed to get here straight from her last lesson at school, does a headcount and ushers everyone on board, I apologise to the neighbours for the disruption, and to the two cars stuck behind us. I promise them it won't be long before we're loaded up and moving.

'Just Craig and Phoebs still to come,' Cassie tells me when I rejoin her. She checks her watch. 'Come on, Craig,' she mutters, drumming her fingers together anxiously. 'Don't let me down today of all days.'

'They'll be here,' I reassure her, although I'll be having a strong word with my poor timekeeper of a friend, who was adamant she wouldn't be late. If Crawford was one of the top flight clubs, Craig would almost certainly be getting fined for this.

Cassie and I stand side by side staring at the coach while we wait. I think we're both having a bit of a hard time believing it's real.

'It's a shame they wouldn't let us spray the club name on the side,' she says.

'I'd say that would be an ask too far.' It gives me an

idea though. 'Back in two,' I promise as I race back into the house.

I emerge with a bundle of A4 paper and take it straight on to the bus, handing a sheet and a felt tip pen to each person sitting on the side nearest the pavement. I dish out instructions and strips of sticky tape and by the time I'm back outside with Cassie, the grin is back on her face. The large, coloured letters being drawn and stuck to the inside of the coach windows eventually spell out Crawford FC. It might look a bit haphazard, and it's a shame all the letters aren't in purple, but at least it's something. And I can get some more professional versions printed up for both sides of the coach ahead of the first game of the league.

It means Cassie is less cross than she might have been when Craig and Phoebs finally run up, full of apologies. She just herds them on board and shouts, 'Okay, let's get going!'

There are whoops all round as the driver pulls away.

Spirits are high on the journey. I'd say our seat-filling fans have a really positive influence, offering encouragement to the players and sharing tales of their favourite past Hamcott Park victories. If there are any nerves ahead of our first ever game against anyone other than ourselves, they're momentarily forgotten. It gives me a good feeling about the evening ahead.

When we get to the Mayfield North ground, Cassie starts prepping the team with a light warm-up while the fans head off to their allocated area in the stands. In the hour leading up to kick-off, a straggle of other supporters arrive, bringing our attendance up to around a hundred and fifty – about half the number of the opposition fans. It's not bad for a first gig.

A few nerves start to show on some of our players as the start time approaches. Levi shifts agitatedly from one foot to the other; Jamie's jaw is visibly clenched. Cassie reminds them today is all about practising together and learning, and does her best to make them forget it's only six weeks since we cobbled them together and started calling them a team.

I desperately want a win for them. It might not mean anything in terms of the league, but the confidence they'd gain would be invaluable. I watch from the sideline as Cassie delivers a final pre-match pep talk. Ben claps each player on the back as they jog out on to the pitch. Then he comes and sits beside me and grips my hand tightly in his.

'Steady on.' I laugh. 'It hasn't even started yet.'

He apologises and rubs the blood back into my fingers. 'I don't know why I feel so anxious for them. I think it's just because I know how much a win would mean to them.'

The first half is a difficult watch, though. Our players may have got used to each other's little foibles during the in-club games we've played, but they don't have that advantage against their opponents, and from as early as ten minutes into the game, the Mayfield number ten gives our defenders the slip and fires in their first goal.

It's gutting, even if it wasn't entirely unexpected, but I'm pleased to see Thomas and Levi respond by patting each other on the shoulder and trying to gee each other back up, rather than getting despondent.

When they fall out of formation again not long afterwards and concede another goal, it's clearly harder for them to shake the disappointment off. Nico fails to hide his frustration, throwing his arms up in the air theatrically. But Thomas has a quiet word and he quickly settles down again.

'Don't get deflated,' I implore them quietly as heads are shaken and eyes are turned up to the sky. 'There's still time to turn it around.'

'Come on, Crawford,' a fan shouts out from behind me.

'You can do it,' another calls.

'Show 'em what you're made of!' Barbour's voice rings out across the pitch.

A cheer goes up from the stand as Nico passes the ball back to Bailey to get the game underway again. And after that our fans continue to cheer every single time a Crawford player makes a successful pass – a heart-warming gesture that does give our players a lift.

Sadly, Craig still can't find a way past the Mayfield defence though, and the opposition score an exasperating two more times before half-time. Lifting our players' spirits during the break is going to be an uphill battle for Cassie.

Dad, Ben and I head over to the team with her and pass on any feedback we think might be useful based on what we've observed so far. Aaron could try taking the ball wider to the left, where we think Mayfield's defence is a bit more hesitant. All of them are guilty of trying to kick the ball straight up to Craig without passing or dribbling it.

I think they all must be feeling that a win is impossible now, but Dad points out, 'If they can score four in one half, so can we.'

And I'd say there is a noticeable improvement in

Crawford's performance in the second half, with two decent – albeit thwarted – attempts on goal and no more conceded. Our fans continue to make as much noise as they can throughout the game, and I'm so grateful to them for making the effort to join us, despite the distance and the fact that it's only a friendly.

We all stand and applaud when the referee blows the final whistle, which I hope goes some way to making our players feel less fed up about losing four–nil. I don't want them to be too hard on themselves over it. It's not the result anyone hoped for, but we can't expect it to all come together immediately.

The journey home is somewhat subdued though, even after Dad reminds the team this is only the beginning. The players either focus on their phones or stare out of the windows and Dad decides to leave them to it for the time being. Ben idly strokes my hair as I lean against his shoulder. After all the time and energy he's invested in Crawford, I know he's as upset for everyone as I am.

When we arrive back in Hamcott, Dad calls for everyone's attention. 'I wanted to give you this time to lick your wounds, but once we get off this coach, I don't want a single one of you to still be thinking of this evening as a crushing defeat,' he says defiantly. 'The full post-match analysis can wait till tomorrow, but for now I want you all to have a think about what we've actually achieved.

'Two months ago, we'd never met. Ten days from now, we play our first league game at our new home ground in front of two hundred fans who have so much faith in us they've shelled out their hard-earned cash on season tickets. That doesn't sound like defeat to me.

'So I want you all to draw a line under today. We all

knew there'd be ups and downs along this road, but no matter what, we will always be the team that came from nowhere and proved that anything is possible if you put your mind to it.'

I don't think I'm the only one who isn't sure whether to applaud.

'Can I say something too?' Ben asks, hauling himself out of his seat.

For a second Dad looks surprised at the interruption, but as Ben is now standing he tells him to go ahead.

'I just wanted to add that I find humour to be a great reliever after days like today,' he says, looking round at everybody. 'It doesn't mean you don't take your games seriously. But when something awful happens, be that missing the penalty that costs your side a game, or hoofing a shot so far over the top of the goal that the ball nearly clears the stadium – both of which have happened to me – you really only have two options. You can either beat yourself up about it or choose to laugh it off, and you don't need me to tell you which is easier to live with. And if your teammates start calling you Hoofs for a little while afterwards, which also happened to me, my best advice is to just take it on the chin.

'You've got to be able to deal with it when things don't go your way. Sometimes you'll feel like you've played the game of your life and you still won't get the result, but you can't let it drag you down or you'll stop enjoying it. Your motivation will go, your enthusiasm will dip and then you'll find it really hard to play at your best again.

'So I guess what I'm saying, in a slightly longwinded way, is just to always try and keep in mind that sometimes it's your day and sometimes it's theirs. The next time you meet it could be you who outplays them. Be hungry for the win, but don't get eaten up by the losses. Because once you develop that mentality, that's when it really is game over.'

It's another heartfelt speech and for a moment I wonder if Dad's going to think Ben was trying to steal his thunder, but Dad in fact breaks into a grin. Then he lightens the mood for everyone by saying, 'Thanks for that, Hoofs. We really appreciate it.'

33

With nine days till my resits, I crank my revision up another gear. While I hate being less involved in the running of Crawford, I want to make sure I get this box ticked off so I can put my student days behind me and turn my attention to whatever lies ahead.

I do still make time to see Ben, but our evenings are much more low-key, spent mostly at his cooking dinner together before I reach for my textbooks while he watches Netflix. He sits on one end of the sofa wearing headphones so as not to disturb me – I sit with my feet in his lap, so he can massage them while I study.

When my eyes get too tired, the TV goes off and he turns his attention to the rest of my body. I can't think of a better way to wind down after hours of poring over my notes. As soon as his lips find mine, all thoughts of social media strategy go out of my mind – temporarily, at least. I think we have sex on the sofa more than anywhere else during this period.

I miss him on the nights when I stay in my own bed, but at least it gives me a night off from Dad moaning that I'm throwing my education away. He doesn't believe I do any work while I'm at Ben's, but the truth is, I probably get more done there than I do at home. There's something about wanting to make sure there's time for our extracurricular activities that makes me very focused.

At mine I get distracted by text messages, trips to the fridge and occasional visits from Phoebs. She does come with the intention of testing me on some of the topics we think will come up in the resits, but inevitably we end up talking about Ben and Craig.

Phoebs is now seeing Craig a few times a week, but she still refuses to call it a relationship. 'The moment we put a label on it, it won't be the same any more. I'm happy as things are,' she insists. 'I like to call it my sixty-two-night stand.'

'Has it really been that long?'

'I'm going for a world record.'

'You might just win it. But wouldn't you prefer to know you're exclusive? That he's not seeing other people when you're not with him?'

'I'm using reverse psychology on him,' she says, waving her hand dismissively. 'By leaving it open, it makes him wonder if *I'm* really into *him*. Then he has to try a little harder to make sure I am.'

I can't help laughing. It's not how I'd want to do things, but it does appear to be working.

'So do you think Ben's going to ask you to move in with him now you're round there most nights?' Phoebs asks.

'If he didn't have to leave soon I think he might.' More and more of my clothes have ended up staying at his place and he hates it whenever we have to say goodbye. 'But once he goes back to Millford he'll only be there himself once or twice a month at most, so I'll be back here for the most part with just the odd night at the Whitehouse.'

I'll miss it, I realise. I feel so relaxed there and associate it with so many good times.

I admit as much to Ben on the last day before my exams. Having decided I can't possibly take in any more information, we're in the garden playing table tennis until he goes off to Crawford's Thursday night training session and I go home for an early night.

'Why don't I give you a set of keys, then you can pop over whenever you want to,' he offers. 'My family use the pool a fair bit when I'm not here but they won't mind. I get it if that would be a bit weird though.'

'It's hard to imagine doing lengths alongside your nan.'

'I was actually going to ask how you felt about staying in a hotel on some of the weekends when we meet up after I head back to Millford. I thought we could maybe find a few places halfway between here and there, so we can meet up a bit earlier than we'd be able to if I was coming back to Hamcott. If you don't mind a bit of a drive, that is.'

'Of course I don't.' I'm keen on anything that will mean spending more time together.

'I did have a quick look and Stratford Upon Avon is more or less in the middle,' he says. 'I think that's meant to be pretty. Or there's a really nice-looking spa hotel just outside Loughborough. We could make a list of all the places we like the look of then just work our way through it.'

'You had me at spa hotel,' I tell him, laughing.

We abandon the table tennis and head for the pool

loungers to make a start on our list, cuddling up together so I can also see Ben's phone as he hunts for interesting places to stay. Although it's a reminder that he's leaving, listening to him plan for our future does take some of the anguish away. We get so absorbed, it almost makes him late for Crawford's training.

I head home for a long, relaxing bath as he races off to the academy. For me, there'll just be a bit of telly then a good night's sleep, and then, all too quickly, retake day is upon me.

As before, I've got one exam in the morning and one in the afternoon, but this time there are students from all the different courses in the hall with me, so I hardly recognise anyone. Our papers are laid out on preassigned desks, and once everyone's seated we'll all have three hours to complete our questions, be they on Shakespeare or nuclear physics.

I wonder if I'm the only person from business studies having to resit and for a moment I'm embarrassed to have found myself in this position. But then I remind myself it doesn't mean I'm not as smart as everyone else on my course – it's just because I let life get in the way.

This time I'm feeling a lot more confident, because I've done all the preparation I possibly could. And sure enough, when the invigilator tells us we can start, a little party popper goes off inside my head once I've flipped over the question sheet. I know exactly what to write on all six of the topics. I won't be failing this paper again.

Three hours later I'm not just satisfied with my efforts, I'm ecstatic. While I'm getting some fresh air before the next exam starts I send a quick text to Ben.

'Pretty sure I've nailed it,' I tell him. *'I couldn't have*

asked for better questions. One down, one to go. I hope the next one goes as smoothly.'

And suddenly I can't wait till the second one is over. I'm so ready to get back to running Crawford United, spending time with the team and going on more adventures with Ben. If this is my last ever day as a student, I'm not in the slightest bit upset about it.

I grab a coffee on my way back to the exam hall, to give me a boost now the earlier adrenaline has subsided. So I'm not sure if it's the caffeine or a bit of nervousness creeping back in that makes me tap my pen impatiently against the side of my leg until we're told we can turn over our papers.

But a quick scan of the questions and my spirits lift. All I need to do is stick to thirty minutes per answer and I should sail through this exam too. The words flow on to the page, and when the professor calls time at the end of the three hours, two thoughts go through my head. One, Phoebs had better get our graduation piss-up rebooked, and two, there is now less than twenty-four hours before the first official match for Crawford United.

Ben is waiting for me outside the exam hall, which I was not expecting, with a huge bunch of flowers in his hand. I burst out laughing. 'What's this for, you soppy git?'

'To celebrate if it went well and to cheer you up if it didn't,' he says, kissing me on the lips. 'But I assume from the smile on your face that this afternoon went without a hitch?'

'I'm leaning heavily towards celebrating,' I tell him.

'That's what I was hoping you'd say. So what do you fancy doing?'

'Is it weird that what I want to do first is go and sit

248

outside the Redmarsh ground for ten minutes to try to get my head out of exam mode and focused on the fact that it's finally time for Crawford's debut match.'

'Totally weird,' he says, laughing as he threads his fingers through mine. 'But I don't mind doing a drive-by if it makes you happy.'

'I think it might make it feel a bit more real after being so detached from it these last few weeks. Then maybe just a glass of bubbly or two afterwards? I want to be fresh for tomorrow, so I don't want to go too crazy.'

'I've got a bottle chilling at home – we can head back and just have a mellow evening. In about twenty-two hours' time, I think you'll find Crawford's debut will feel incredibly real.'

I take a deep, calming breath. I only hope our players are ready for it.

34

The following morning, Dad, Cassie and I set off early for the Redmarsh Rovers stadium – now our stadium too, though I still have to pinch myself to believe it. We want to be there well ahead of kick-off to give us time to familiarise ourselves with it.

We check in with the ground management team, who assure us everything is as it should be, then oversee our players arriving, welcome the Oakhampton manager and players and meet with the referee.

Thankfully even Craig makes it to the locker room well before the time we suggested, and I think he sums up all our first impressions when he looks round at the stark white walls and plain wooden benches and says, 'Glad they did the place up for us.'

Not that we were expecting velvet cushions in our team colours or a welcome banner hanging over the door, but I did think it might be more plush.

The pitch is another story though. The grass is immaculate, with crisp white lines and none of the scuffs that are regular fixtures at the academy. It feels huge compared to what we're used to, but that's just the optical illusion created by the four thousand seats in the stands surrounding it.

It's only when Dad and I have been in the dugout for fifteen minutes, going through our notes while the lads warm up on the pitch with Cassie and Ben, that we realise the match should have started – but the linespeople are nowhere to be seen.

'Something's wrong,' Dad says, checking his watch then casting his eye round the ground. There are a fair few fans in the stands – more than we expected – and others are still arriving and shuffling down the rows to find their seats. He nods in their direction. 'Maybe they're just allowing them a few more minutes.'

'Maybe this is just what happens when a match isn't being televised,' I suggest. Without any previous experience, we have no idea if everything is just a lot more laissez-faire at this level of football.

But even the Oakhampton players stop warming up and start shrugging their shoulders at their coach when the match still isn't underway a full ten minutes after it should be.

'I'll go and find someone who might know what the hold-up is,' I tell Dad.

'Thanks, love,' he says gratefully. 'I'll wait here in case they announce anything.'

Noticing he can't stop jiggling his knee, I hand him a packet of chewing gum before I go. He hates the stuff, but I tell him it might help with the stress. Why else would almost every football manager always be chomping furiously?

'Thanks, love,' he says again, accepting the packet without his eyes leaving the stands.

I hurry off to see what I can find out and when I return, he leaps to his feet. 'Is it bad? Has someone been hurt?'

Ben jogs over to join us, too, concern creasing both their foreheads as they watch my eyes well up with emotion. 'There's a bit of a problem with the turnstiles,' I explain.

'Someone's stuck?' Dad jumps to completely the wrong conclusion.

I shake my head. 'They've never had to deal with the ground being at full capacity before.'

'Full capacity?' Ben repeats.

I finally break into a grin. 'And then some.'

I watch Dad's mouth fall open as I tell them there are so many Crawford fans outside trying to buy tickets that the box office is completely overwhelmed. 'They decided to delay the game while they work through the queue.'

Dad grips my arm. 'Are you serious?'

'They don't even think they're going to be able to get everyone in,' I tell him, a tear finally escaping and rolling down my cheek. 'There's talk of sorting out some kind of livestream, so no one misses out.'

Dad's eyes grow wet too and he turns his face up to the sky. I don't think he wants us to see. Then he turns away from us and fist pumps the air. Twice. 'Yes.' Then louder. 'Yes!'

He's got his grin back by the time he turns to face us again and he thumps his fist against his chest, too choked up to speak. I know, come the end of the match, he'll be trying to find a way to thank every single fan individually.

Ben heads back to the team to share the news. I watch eyebrows rise and heads turn towards the stands in

252

disbelief. I only hope it inspires them and doesn't make them nervous.

We later learn that on top of the three hundred and twenty Oakhampton supporters, more than four thousand former Hamcott Park fans have come to see Crawford United's debut. Which means of the twelve thousand fans Hamcott had in the first place, around a third have come to watch our new club today. And that means they really do want this, this return to the way things used to be, and that makes us even more determined to deliver it for them.

Of course we don't know if they will permanently switch allegiances. I'm sure some will have come purely out of curiosity today. But this is massive – massive enough that we eventually spot a news helicopter circling up in the sky above the ground. And the record-breaking attendance for a new club's debut makes the home page of a national news site before the match has even started.

It finally kicks off over an hour late, which is tough on the players, but the fans don't seem to have any complaints – they're just excited to be here in such a cracking atmosphere. There are frequent shouts of 'Come on, Crawford' and a drummer thumps out a steady beat in between each cheer.

'We're going to need a team anthem,' Cassie observes. 'Have any of us got any song-writing skills?'

When no one puts their hand up, I suggest running a competition on the website and asking the fans to submit their ideas. You never know, one of them might produce something decent.

'It's got to be worth a try,' Dad agrees.

It makes me wonder if we should also have a team

mascot. It's a bit over the top perhaps for a club at our level, but if we're going to attract this many people on a weekly basis it doesn't seem too crazy. Maybe a few of the kids Cassie teaches would be interested in dressing up as a phoenix for half a day. I wonder if any of the mums has any costume-making skills.

After all the drama, it takes a while for the players to settle into the game. The opening minutes are more like tiddlywinks than football as the ball pings from end to end with little in the way of quality passing, but Crawford do find their rhythm eventually.

Sadly it's not before Oakhampton have pulled themselves together though – I guess that's where their previous experience gives them the advantage – and a few minutes before half-time Crawford concede their first goal, an easy touch for Oakhampton after a careless error from Jacob, who instead of making a clearance from the penalty area, scuffs the top of the ball with his boot and sends it straight to the feet of the player he's marking.

He stops dead from the shock, then closes his eyes as he berates himself for his blunder. I'm gutted for him. It's not like Oakhampton have massively outplayed Crawford in the first half, so to end it a goal down feels really unlucky.

I can only offer up a flat smile as Ben squeezes my knee and stands up to join the team's half-time huddle. I hope he and Cassie can restore their confidence before the game resumes. Meanwhile, Dad gets busy with his phone. I don't think he wants to say anything at all at this stage, for fear of jinxing things.

'They've processed it,' Ben tells me when he rejoins us fifteen minutes later, leaving Cassie on the sideline so she can shout instructions to our players. 'They're going to come out fighting.'

And they do put up a good battle for most of the second half, with the midfielders chasing down every ball and Craig getting two shots on target within minutes of each other. But neither has enough power to find its way past the Oakhampton goalie and Craig reels away in frustration both times, cursing as he rakes his fingers through his hair.

I scan the crowd whenever there's a break in the action, still marvelling at how vast it is. I try to gauge the mood. If this were Hamcott Park we were watching, some of the fans would likely be slating their own team. But perhaps because Crawford's so new and the expectation isn't there yet, they just keep urging our players to go for it.

Sadly, though, this half becomes a mirror of the first, with opportunities missed and the opposition slipping through our defence in the closing minutes to score their second goal. It brings three of our players to their knees – with so little time left on the clock, they know there's no coming back from this.

The game dips in energy, with Oakhampton not trying too hard to score a third goal and Crawford not trying too hard to stop them. I think most of our players have run themselves ragged to the point where they're completely out of steam.

Cassie decides to use all five of our substitutions, not because she thinks fresh legs will save us, but to give some of our reserves the chance to say they participated in the team's debut game. They do engineer one last surge forward, but ultimately nothing comes of it.

At the final whistle, I watch Craig's chin dip to his chest. Elliot puts his face in his hands and Nico purses his lips and shakes his head. I imagine, like me, they're feeling the score doesn't fairly reflect all the effort they put in.

The Oakhampton players are not about to let them stay downhearted though. After a quick celebration in front of their fans – no doubt kept short because it's a difficult win to celebrate in the circumstances – they turn back to our players, raise their hands above their heads and applaud them good-naturedly.

It warms my heart watching our lads' heads lift. They poured their hearts and souls into the match today and it's generous of Oakhampton to acknowledge it. Meanwhile, a chant starts up in the stands – one voice at first, then twenty, fifty . . . until all four thousand former Hamcott fans are singing at the tops of their voices. 'We're Crawford till we die, we're Crawford till we die . . .'

This time I can't stop the tears rolling down my cheeks. And when I glance at Dad his cheeks are wet too, though I know he won't want to admit it. We might not be going home victorious, but the support we've had for our players is astounding. Our boys really showed up today. And sooner or later their hard work is going to pay off. I just know it.

35

Luckily, news of the crowd numbers reaches The Fox before we descend upon it. It turns out it was Olly who Dad was messaging in the half-time break, to warn him he might be about to get very, very busy. And in the time it takes for our players to warm down, the ground to empty and for a large number of us to make our way over there, Olly pulls off something of a miracle.

He loads up a couple of tables in the pub garden with canned and bottled beers for anyone who doesn't want to queue inside for a pint on draught, and ropes in some of his regular customers to man the tables and collect the money, telling us they spent almost an hour bringing up stock from the cellar with him. He even gets all the cars cleared out of the car park so it can be used for overspill.

Even then it's a battle to get the drinks served fast enough, but they make it work. And Olly has also batch-cooked every sausage roll he had in his freezer, handing them out free of charge to anyone who's peckish.

Our players manage to put their disappointment to the side as they mingle with the supporters. Dad and Cassie have done a good job of convincing them they played well enough today and that they'll only get better – and that the number of fans who came to watch them should give them a clear indication of the belief people have in the team.

One of my proudest moments of the post-match get-together is when the Oakhampton players arrive – on Dad's invitation – and are warmly welcomed by everybody. They might have beaten us, but they have our fans' respect thanks to their magnanimity. Dad has said from the beginning that his hope is for both our fans and our players to be courteous to the opposition teams, so I know this will make him happy.

In the locker room before today's match, he said to our players, 'I'm aware that you're not getting paid to play at Crawford, so I'm doubly grateful to you all for being here. But I also know that because of this, some of you may move to different clubs in the future, where there is a salary, so my best advice to you is this: stay on everyone's good side today, even if the game goes against you, because those players you're coming up against now, one day you might end up on the same team.'

It's good advice for all areas of life, if you ask me.

Inside the pub, Olly bangs an empty glass on the bar and calls for Dad to give a speech. The colour flushes across his cheeks as the noise of conversation recedes and hundreds of eyes turn towards him. Several people take out their phones and start recording.

'Go on, Mike,' Marge urges. Dad holds up his pint in acknowledgement then begins.

'Firstly, I just want to say the biggest thank you to everyone here for the overwhelming support you've shown Crawford United today – for the atmosphere you created at the match, for the boost you gave our players on the pitch, and of course for your money, which will help secure the future of the club going forward, hopefully for many years.'

This gets a laugh from the crowd.

'When Lily, Cassie and I sat down in our kitchen just three short months ago and cooked up this idea to create a new football team, some of you thought we were mad, some of you thought we had no idea what we were doing – and I'll happily admit, you were all absolutely right. But we never stopped believing a new football club was what Hamcott needs, and when I look around at all of you here with us now, it doesn't just validate that belief, it smashes it right out of the park.'

He waits for the whooping to subside before he continues.

'Oakhampton played a really strong game today, so congratulations to them once again. But our players showed heart and determination and promise, so I want to say thank you to each and every person who plays their part in our team. We know we've still got a lot to learn and we're at the very start of our journey, but it's our mission to improve week on week and to give everyone here a real reason to call yourself a proud Crawford fan.

'You know we can't promise you a win every Saturday, but what we can promise is that we'll never give up trying. So stick with us and let's enjoy this ride together.' He raises his glass again. 'To everyone here and to Crawford United!'

When the cheering has subsided and the hum of conversation has resumed, Dad makes his way back to where Cassie, Ben and I are standing, shaking hands with everyone he passes on the way like the mini celebrity he's fast becoming. I squeeze his arm. 'Proud of you, Dad.'

He clinks his glass against mine. 'Back at ya, kid.'

And I'm suddenly happier than ever about the part I've played in making this happen – and will continue to play, too. Whatever the outcome at the end of the season it will be something to be celebrated, because perhaps even more important than the team itself is the bond we're creating among this newly connected group of people.

The players, bar Jacob who's too young, have all been told their beers are on the house by Olly. While Crawford's rules ask them to refrain from drinking alcohol on Mondays, Wednesdays and Fridays – namely the days before any training or matches – there are no such restrictions on a Saturday night. I'd be willing to bet they lose count of the number of supporters who also offer to buy them drinks.

I notice Thomas, especially, really engaging with the fans, asking about their own sporting endeavours and who their favourite footballer of all time is. Happily, at least two of the younger ones say him.

In another corner Phoebs is chatting to Craig and he's laughing at whatever she just said. I notice his eyes don't drift once – he's completely engaged. Maybe her reverse psychology really is working.

I think everyone stays at the pub longer than they intend to, so I imagine there'll be a few sore heads in the morning, mine included. Not that I've got anything pressing to get up for now my exams are behind me. Ben and I might head to the beach once he's finished his workout and I've had a Crawford handover chat with

Marge. After the stress of the last two days, I could do with some time to relax.

I'm glad the team have such a lively evening for their first post-match get-together, though. Regardless of the result, it has felt like a celebration thanks to the incredible turnout and the air of optimism our newfound supporters seem to share. If this is a sign of things to come, we're in for a memorable season. There may be a long and possibly rocky road ahead of us, but today all that matters is that we're on our way.

36

'It was a great night but I'm never drinking that much after a match again,' I hear Levi telling Elliot as they change into their football boots at the academy the following Tuesday. 'I woke up with breath like a cat's arse.'

'That's disgusting,' Elliot says. 'What were you drinking?'

Levi shrugs. 'Everything, I think, by the end. I really shouldn't have let myself get so carried away.'

'What about if we beat Windham Park next Saturday?'

Levi laughs. 'Then I might be tempted by a Jägerbomb or two.'

Elliot claps him on the shoulder. 'Better get the headache pills stocked up for next Sunday then.'

It's a relief to know the Oakhampton defeat hasn't put them in the mindset where they think they'll never win. Something else is concerning me though – Ben isn't here. He always arrives before the last of the players so he can chat to Cassie about her plans for the session before things get underway, but today she's ready to start and there's still no sign of him.

I check my watch. It's not that she's starting early. She fires a questioning look in my direction and I shrug in response. There's no message on my phone to say he's been held up and I know there isn't much traffic out on the roads.

As Cassie gets the team lined up and ready to begin, I try not to panic, but a creeping sense of dread starts swirling in the pit of my stomach. I try to convince myself he must just have got distracted by something and that he'll be here soon. But instinct tells me that isn't the case.

Cassie tells the players she's intending to step their training up a gear in terms of intensity. 'I want to see you pushing yourselves harder in our upcoming matches,' she says. 'And to make that happen on the pitch it needs to start right here. So let's get started with our warm-up.'

She sends them off for a faster-than-usual sprint round the field. While they're gone she comes over and asks me if I've heard anything yet.

'His phone's going straight to voicemail. I've left a message.'

'Are you okay?' she asks, hearing the wobble in my voice.

'It's not like him.'

She touches my arm. 'There'll be an explanation.' But then the players arrive back at the starting line and she turns her attention back to them.

My phone stays stubbornly silent until the very last minutes of the session, when an apologetic text finally comes through from Ben. I'm almost too scared to read it.

'*So sorry for not replying sooner. I've been caught up on a call,*' it says. '*Do you want to come here after the session? I can't believe I've missed the whole thing. I'll apologise to Cassie later.*'

I read it twice more before I reply. What kind of call could take up so much time? I don't think there are many things that would stop him being here – at least that's what he's always led me to believe – so whoever called him, it must have been something he couldn't miss. And the only thing I can think of that fills that criterion is Millford City.

I tell him I'll be there shortly and pass his apologies on to Cassie before I leave, then try my hardest not to think the worst on the drive over to his house. But when he opens his front door I can tell straight away that something's not right – his smile is too forced and it doesn't reach his eyes.

'What is it?' I ask, gulping back the icy grip of fear.

'Let's get a drink.' He turns away without kissing me, which he's never, ever done before. I push the door closed behind me and follow him into the kitchen, my heart pounding in my chest. Is this where he tells me it's over? Is my heart about to split into pieces?

He turns to face me and his eyes search mine, his brow creased with unfamiliar tension.

'What?' My voice sounds weirdly high-pitched and not like my own.

'I've been recalled,' he says flatly. 'I'm going back up north.'

It hits like a punch, even though we both knew it was coming. Even though we promised each other that when it came we'd deal with it.

'When?' I ask quietly.

'Tomorrow. I still can't play in Millford's next two matches but they want to make sure I'll be ready for when my suspension lifts.'

It takes every ounce of control to keep my face from crumpling.

He turns away and bangs his fist against the work surface. 'It wasn't meant to be this hard.'

I move in behind him and slide my arms round his waist, feeling the need to comfort him despite my own anguish.

'We've talked about this,' I remind him. 'We'll make it work.'

'There's more,' he says, and I wonder if he can feel my body stiffen, pressed against his like this. I back away and pull him back towards me so I can see his face.

'I want you to know this wasn't my idea,' he says, his eyes finding mine. 'The PR team are saying I still have some damage control to do, to coincide with my return to the squad.'

This time I just wait for him to say whatever it is he has to say, so he takes a deep breath and finally gets to the crux of it. 'There's going to be a girl.'

I feel the colour draining from my face. 'What kind of girl?'

'She was on some reality show or other, and now she's apparently one of the nation's sweethearts,' Ben explains. 'The thinking is that if people believe I'm in a relationship with her it will help some of the sponsors forget why I've been off the team. And her agent's thinking is that if they want to get her name in the papers more often, linking her to me is a good way to do it.'

'And what, you're supposed to go out on dates with her? Get photographed with her? Are you supposed to sleep with her?'

'I don't have to sleep with her,' he says quickly.

'But if she's your *girlfriend*?'

'I don't have to sleep with her,' he repeats. 'It's just a set-up by our PR teams. It only has to look like it's a real thing.'

I feel myself getting angry. 'Did you even tell them about me?'

He looks away, which answers that question.

'You must have known how this would make me feel, Ben. I can't believe you'd agree to it.'

'I wasn't given a choice,' he says defensively. 'It's either this or spend the rest of my time at Millford on the bench.'

He sighs again and rubs the back of his neck. 'I'm not ready to hang up my boots yet, Lily – I'm only twenty-two. This is not what I want, but my PR advisor is adamant it will help my public image, and if it's what I have to do to save my career . . . I know it puts you in the shittiest situation, but if there's any chance you and I can still be together – in the background, I guess, till my reputation is deemed sufficiently repaired . . . I'll understand if you just want to walk away, though. I know it's far from ideal.'

'I don't want that,' I whisper. 'But how can we possibly make this work now?'

I get that his career has to come first, of course I do, but it was going to be hard enough dealing with the long distance without adding this to the equation. 'What about me coming up to stay with you? What if we get spotted on our spa trip?'

'I know the logistics are trickier, but we managed to keep it a secret before. We can do it again?' He says it more like a question than a statement. 'Or we can just tell everyone we're really good friends. They know I've been helping out at Crawford so it would be perfectly reasonable for us to still want to meet up.'

'Every weekend?' I shake my head at the impossibility of it.

'It will probably only be for a month or so,' he says, his voice small. 'I know it's an absolutely dickish thing to ask you to be okay with this, but I have to ask you anyway. I don't want to lose you, so could you please, maybe, just roll with it until the dust settles?'

I'm so conflicted my whole body feels like it's shaking. How can I say no to him when he sounds so tortured? And wouldn't I be a fool to throw away what we have over something which, like he says, is only temporary? But the thought of him with this other girl . . . I've never considered myself the jealous type before and yet I can't bear it, even if it is just for show.

We stare at each other, neither knowing what else to say, until a single tear of frustration bursts free and trickles down my cheek.

He reaches across to brush it away, then pulls me into an embrace, but I can't bring myself to put my arms back round him yet so they hang limply by my sides.

'I'm so, so sorry,' he says into my hair. 'I didn't want our last night together to be like this.'

It's not what I want either, so I turn my head up to kiss him, willing my pain to go away. But hard as I try to lose myself in the moment, I can't stop feeling like this is going to ruin everything.

The tears start rolling down my cheeks more readily.

'Please don't,' he whispers. 'I love you, Lily. This isn't where this ends.'

It's the first time he's said it and it hangs in the air between us while a small part of me flares with anger – how can he be saying this now, of all times?

But I finally manage to pull myself together and find some resolve. I love him too. We can't let our relationship fall to pieces over something neither of us wants and which will eventually go away. So I decide there and then I just won't overthink it. I'll enjoy these last few hours we have together then we'll do whatever we can to keep it alive until it can be like this again.

'I love you too, Ben,' I tell him. And this time I do put my arms round him and kiss him like I mean it.

We undress each other slowly after that and our lovemaking is gentle and more heartfelt than it's ever been. Afterwards we sit out on the couch on his terrace, wrapped in dressing gowns, his arm round me as I lean against him.

'Do you really think we'll still be able to meet up secretly?' I ask.

'We'll find a way,' he promises. 'And I'm going to call you every day. I'm not going to suddenly stop wanting to know how you are, what you're up to, how the team's getting on or any of those things.'

It's late when we eventually head inside to bed, but I don't think either of us sleep. I lie nestled into him with my head on his shoulder and my arm draped over his chest. I'm sure he can feel my eyelashes fluttering against his skin every time I blink.

He runs his hand over my arm, massages my shoulder and kisses the top of my head from time to time. Eventually we give up all pretence of sleeping and roll over till we're facing each other. Then we kiss till the sunlight creeps under the curtain.

37

'I might have to fill my boot up with cans of Red Bull,' Ben says over breakfast, referring to the four-hour drive he's got ahead of him.

'Do you have one of those hydration backpacks, with a straw?'

He laughs, but it's a hollower sound than usual. 'That's not a bad shout, but I wouldn't want to get it all sticky.'

'When's your first meet-up with your teammates?' I ask.

'Tomorrow. But they'll be fine. They'll rib me a bit for letting the side down then we'll just crack on. I'm not worried.'

'And your new girlfriend, when does that get announced?' I ask.

'This evening.' He looks away. 'That's why I have to get back today – there's some event I have to be seen at. Then they can coincide breaking the news of our relationship with announcing I'm back on the team. Quite the diversionary tactic,' he says bitterly.

I swallow my surprise. I don't know why I thought it wouldn't happen so quickly.

'I'll probably just fall asleep on her, though,' Ben adds. 'She's not going to get any sparkling conversation out of me when I'm this tired. She'll probably wonder what she's got herself into.'

I can't say I'd be too sad if she decided he was too boring to keep up the façade.

All too soon it's time to say goodbye. Ben holds on to my hand for the longest time on his doorstep, and tells me again that he loves me before he finally releases me. On my drive home, it takes all my strength not to let our new reality overwhelm me.

Ben will call Dad and Cassie later to apologise for not saying goodbye in person. They might be disappointed but they'll understand. I can't say the same for when I explain about his new 'relationship', though. Like me, I think they'll find that harder to get to grips with.

I'll need to choose the right moment for that conversation. It will go much better if I can explain it without sounding upset. For now I'll just throw myself into Crawford business and try to put it out of my mind.

We've sold more season tickets off the back of Saturday's game and there are some requests for interviews that I need to look into following the *Herald*'s piece about the debut match. But for a good while I just stare at my inbox without taking anything in. How am I supposed to get into any kind of rhythm when all I can think about is how much I already miss Ben?

He's promised to call me as soon as he's settled in, and I keep my phone close, checking every few minutes in case I've missed him, even though he won't even be off

271

the motorway yet. Hours later, when I'm certain he must have arrived, I check several times that the volume is set to full and contemplate sending a test text to Phoebs to make sure it's definitely working, but I know it is. Ben will have been swept up in a whirlwind upon getting back to Millford, with 'back to work' meetings to prepare for, friends to catch up with, food to buy and . . . her. He'll call me when he can.

When Dad gets home from work, I finally fill him in on everything, which sends him into full 'I warned you he was trouble' mode. I think he'd been getting used to me and Ben being a couple, but now he's back to thinking it was never a sensible move.

Later in the evening, a knock on my bedroom door interrupts my moping and Phoebs pokes her head through. 'I thought you might need some company. Craig told me about Ben.'

I can't help smiling. He must have let the rest of the team know he's had to leave now. She must have known I'd be devastated.

'Wanna talk about it?' she asks.

'He's only been gone a few hours and I already hate it,' I confess. Then I fill her in on Ben's 'PR campaign', after she's promised not to blab about it to Craig. Thankfully she understands there could be serious repercussions if we don't keep this between ourselves.

'It sounds really tough,' she empathises. 'If there's anything I can do to help you deal with it, just say.'

I thank her and glance down at my laptop. 'I'm just glad I've got Crawford to keep me busy – otherwise I'd probably drive myself insane.'

She props herself up against my pillows at the other

end of my bed. 'Speaking of Crawford, if it ends up being successful – I mean when – do you think you might be able to find a job for me?'

So far her search for employment hasn't amounted to much.

'Wouldn't you rather do something you're interested in?'

'Well yes, but I'm hardly in a position to set up my own business as a party organiser, am I?'

'Why not? People are always having parties.'

'True, but now it's so easy to order everything online, do people still pay for someone else to do all the organising?'

'You should look into it,' I tell her. 'I think you'd be great at it.'

'Can we have a look now?'

'Sure.' I move up the bed to sit beside her, more than happy to have another distraction, and we spend the rest of the evening investigating what's already out there and throwing ideas around about how she could add her own spin.

'Maybe I should put a portfolio together on Instagram and see if it gets any interest,' she says. 'Hasn't your dad got a big birthday coming up?'

It's his fiftieth in September and I don't imagine he'll get round to organising anything more than a nice dinner round our kitchen table. Getting Phoebs to make the occasion more special would be a lovely surprise for him. 'It's in a couple of weeks and I think you should go for it. It could be the start of something really amazing.'

'And when Crawford win the league, maybe I can organise the celebration for that too,' she says. It's kind, but I tell her she might have to wait another season or five before we get to that stage.

'I'll get Craig to step things up a gear,' she promises. 'I'll tell him no more blow jobs until he starts scoring goals.'

This makes me cringe-laugh. It's not how I want to think about him.

'Oh come on, you know we don't sit around at his playing board games,' Phoebs says, rolling her eyes. But that gets me thinking about Ben again. I was blissfully happy the night we played our games triathlon on his terrace. I'd do anything to do that again with him.

I pick up my phone and wake up the screen. Still nothing. Should I call him, to see how he's getting on? I'm not used to feeling needy but I'm desperate to hear his voice.

The phone chooses that exact moment to buzz in my hand, making my body jolt so hard I nearly drop it. It's him! A WhatsApp message rather than a call, but at last, it's him.

'I'll leave you to it,' Phoebs says, kissing my cheek and standing up to leave. 'But call me any time you're finding it hard and I'll be here.'

I thank her for being such a good friend and wait till she's closed the door behind her before I open Ben's message. My heart races with excitement as I wait to read it.

'*Sorry this is so late. It's been a loooong day. I'm only just getting back to the flat and I'm shattered,*' he's written. '*Texting because I doubt I'd make much sense if I called, but I'll speak to you tomorrow. I hope you've had a great day. Love you xx.*'

I read it again. I'd be lying if I said I hadn't been hoping for more. Despite how chatty he usually is, he doesn't even hint at what he's been up to – specifically no mention of this evening's event. But maybe he thinks I don't want to hear about his 'other woman'. To be fair, yesterday I didn't even ask what her name is.

I pull up Google and type 'Ben Pryce' into a news search. Nothing yet. Why didn't I even ask who she was? Perhaps because I knew I'd spend the rest of today looking at pictures of her, possibly even watching the show she was on, and I can't let myself go down that rabbit hole. It won't do me any favours.

But the devil on my shoulder still taunts me. Maybe she was so engaging he didn't even think about me till it got so late. Maybe there's a more sinister reason why he texted rather than called. Maybe he's not beyond temptation while I'm down here and he's up there.

A wave of paranoia takes hold. Am I a fool to believe all his talk about wanting to date a real girl who's happy to talk about football over a nice draught beer in a pub with sticky carpets, when he could have a party lifestyle filled with champagne, VIP enclosures and glamorous TV stars? What if I really was just a convenient summer hook-up for him while he took a break from the endless stream of wannabe WAGS trying to get him to fall in love with them?

But then I bat those jitters away. If any of that were true, he wouldn't have messaged me at all. He could have just ended things before he left if he wanted that other life. He certainly wouldn't have signed off with love and kisses.

'So just stop it,' I tell myself sharply. I might have only known him for a few months but I know he's not that guy. And all this fearing the worst? That's not who I am either.

We're both tired and we'll catch up properly tomorrow. For now I just fire a quick message back to him. *All good. Talk tomorrow. Love you too x.*

38

Ben calls me first thing the next morning – from his car, on the way to Millford's ground – and apologises again for being too exhausted to chat last night, which reassures me that yesterday's uneasiness was unfounded. But I still can hear the hesitation in my voice when I ask how his first day back went.

He tells me he was caught up on a rollercoaster of meetings – a lengthy session with the team psychologist to make sure his temper is under control, a fitness test with the head coach to make sure he's match-ready, then a few hours with the physio, who 'flexed and prodded' every inch of his body to check for any stiffness that might present an injury risk.

'Well, not *every* inch,' he says, laughing. 'There was no stiffness there! But it was non-stop. And now I've got a training morning with my teammates to integrate me back into the squad. It almost feels like I've never been away.'

And I can tell from the animation in his words that he's buzzing to be back.

'But enough about me, tell me about the rest of your day,' he says, which instantly rouses my suspicions about last night again. Why isn't he mentioning it?

'I caught up with Phoebs,' I tell him, deciding to skip the part where I tormented myself for hours waiting to hear from him. 'She's still keeping Craig on his toes, but they both seem happy.'

'Good for him. He needs a strong female influence in his life. As well as you and Cassie, that is. And how would you say the team seemed in general on Tuesday? I forgot to ask what with everything else going on. Are they managing to forget last weekend and look ahead to the next game?'

'I think they've taken on board some of the advice you gave them. I'd say they all seem to be dealing with it.'

'It's nice to know I had a bit of a positive influence before I left.'

We hesitate then. I think we both know it's time to face up to the giant elephant in the room. I take a deep breath and brace myself for whatever's coming. 'So . . . tell me about your date.'

He sighs. 'I'm trying not to think about it too much. I feel really shit about it.'

So that's why he didn't bring it up – he doesn't want to upset me. But as he starts telling me more, I can't help wondering if it's actually me he feels bad about upsetting.

'I don't want to lie to you, she's sweet,' he says, which is so not what I want to hear. 'There's no pretentiousness or sense of entitlement. She just feels really lucky to have all the opportunities that are falling into her lap and she wants to enjoy everything for as long as it might last.'

So she's nice, positive and level-headed. Great. Any unredeeming qualities?

'There's a horrible part, though,' he continues. Oh phew, let me hear it. 'She was told it was me who contacted her management to set up the date after seeing her on TV. She had no idea it came from my PR team. It felt really cheap stringing her along. No one deserves that kind of treatment.'

It does make me feel some level of sympathy towards her.

'What did she say when you told her?' I ask – adding, when he doesn't answer straight away, 'You did tell her, didn't you?'

'How could I?' He sounds exasperated. 'What if she then refused to go along with it? Or worse still, sold her story to the papers and made me look like even more of an arsehole? I couldn't risk it. I hate this position they've put me in, but they've got me completely over a barrel.'

I'm still processing this when he adds, 'I wouldn't have agreed to it if I'd known she wasn't in on it. The only way I can see to get through it now is to be nice enough to her that she wants to stick around, but not so nice that she'll be upset when I end it. If she wasn't so sweet, that would be a lot easier to live with.'

I can't even speak for a moment afterwards. I get that he feels bad for her. *I* feel bad for her. And if he was okay with this it wouldn't say much for him. But if he gallantly wants to protect her feelings, I can't help wondering where that leaves mine.

'When are you next seeing her?' I ask, not sure if I really want him to tell me.

'I'm supposed to be taking her out after the match on Saturday, somewhere where we'll get seen.'

'Then will you and I get together on Sunday?' He will only have been gone for four days by then, but I suddenly feel a desperate need to be with him.

'I'd love to, but I think we might have to hold off for a week,' he says, crushing that fantasy. 'There's still all this reintegration stuff going on. It'll be easier once I'm back in my normal routine. I know it's frustrating, but it's just one more week.'

For the first time I find myself wishing he wasn't a Premier League footballer – that our lives could just be normal, we could see each other whenever we wanted and that there was no grand PR scheme. And this troubles me because if I'm wishing he led a completely different life, does it mean he's in fact not the right person for me? Even though I feel with every fibre in my body that he is.

'I can wait,' I say softly. 'But I miss you.'

'I miss you too. And believe me, I genuinely am aware how much harder this must be for you than it is for me. But the way I'm trying to see it is that if we can get through this, we'll be able to get through anything life throws at us. So please, please keep bearing with me.'

I bury my resentment and tell him I will.

It's not till after he's ended the call that I realise I still haven't even asked him who this girl is. But I find out not long afterwards, when a headline pops up on the news feed on my phone: *Ben Pryce, back to scoring goals – and scoring girls*. My sensible head tells me I shouldn't upset myself by reading it, but I don't take my own advice. I chew my bottom lip anxiously as I click to open it.

When I see the picture of his 'new love' Georgina,

looking stunning in a shimmering dress and towering heels, it sends such a surge of jealousy coursing through me that it feels like I've been speared straight through the heart. Doubts flood straight back into my mind. Why didn't he mention she was so pretty?

'Perhaps he doesn't see it?' Phoebs suggests, when I meet her for lunch, still feeling shellshocked. 'She can't be everyone's cup of tea. Although I have to admit, it's hard to see how she wouldn't be.'

When she realises she's not helping she adds, 'You're just going to have be honest with him and tell him how you feel.'

'What I feel at the moment is that I'm not sure how I'm going to get through the next few weeks if Ben dating Georgina already makes me as stressed as this. It's only been twenty-four hours and I'm already a wreck over it.'

'Then tell him that. And in the meantime, let's find as many distractions as possible to fill the Ben-shaped hole in your life. We can go to the beach, play some tennis in the park, plan our grand post-grad night out. It's only two weeks till your results come out now so we should get something booked in.'

When I still look doubtful she continues, 'And didn't Ben say you could go to his house any time to use his pool? You know I'd love to see it. Although Craig's dad is getting one installed at their place and that'll be ready soon, so if it feels weird being at Ben's without him there, we can just invite ourselves over to the Campbells' instead. Unless it would feel even weirder to have Craig see you in your bikini.'

'It wouldn't feel very appropriate. I try to look professional around the team. I'm kind of dreading seeing them tonight though. They obviously know Ben's gone, but now they're going to think he immediately dropped me for Georgina.'

'And presumably you can't correct them because Ben needs it to look realistic?'

I nod. 'I know I shouldn't worry about what they think, but it is going to be humiliating.'

'Do you want me to come with you this evening, for moral support? I was going to head to Craig's afterwards anyway – now he can give me a lift.'

I nod gratefully. 'I'd really like that, thank you. This all just feels so rubbish after such a summer of highs. I hate feeling like this.'

'Talk to Ben again,' she says firmly. 'He's the cause of all these emotions so he needs to find a way to fix things.'

And I do, over the next couple of days, because I can't stop doing my own head in.

I admit I can't help fretting that he isn't telling Georgina the truth about their set-up because he wants to keep his options open, or wondering if the real reason he isn't coming down on Sunday is so he can stay up there with her. When he promises me neither of these things could be further from the truth, I move on to what Georgina's going to think when he drops her home after their dinner dates and there isn't so much as a goodnight kiss.

She's twenty years old and beautiful, adored by viewers of her show and in demand for interviews and advertising. It probably seems perfectly natural to her that she'd be courted by a Premier League footballer – but she'll be expecting more than just a few decent meals out of it.

'I'll just tell her I'm being a gentleman,' Ben insists. 'Try to look at it this way: if Jake Gyllenhaal turned up on your doorstep, wouldn't you happily go for dinner with him?'

I mumble a reluctant yes.

'But would you sleep with him?'

'Of course not . . . But then he doesn't think he's my boyfriend.'

He sighs. 'I don't know what else I can say, Lily. I just need you to trust me. I don't want this to drive us apart.'

And I stop then, because I don't want that either. I hate that I've started feeling so insecure so quickly and I don't want it to result in me pushing him away.

'Maybe we should just agree not to talk about it any more,' I suggest.

'If that's what it takes to prevent us arguing.'

We agree not to discuss it again until Ben is back down in Hamcott and can properly show me how much I mean to him.

Thankfully I've got Crawford United's first away game tomorrow to stop me brooding about his dinner date with Georgina. I've got all the arrangements to oversee as we head south to play Windham Park, who usually finish in the bottom half of the table and so will hopefully give us less trouble than Oakhampton did. I vow to put Georgina out of my mind for the time being and focus all my energy on the team.

39

This time when Cassie and I stand beside the coach waiting for the players to board, there is much less amateurish lettering spelling out Crawford Utd in the windows. I've poured a good few hours into upgrading our previous hand-drawn efforts, producing computer-generated graphics and even going so far as to get them laminated. And this time there's a purple phoenix at the beginning and a purple team shirt at the end.

'It looks great, sis,' Cassie says, arms folded in front of her as she nods her head approvingly.

Dad pokes his head out of the door of the coach. 'Are you two coming? We're all set in here; we should get going.'

We follow him on to the bus and I instantly feel lifted by the sparky banter toing and froing between the players. They seem just as energised as they were before our debut match and I think that's going to grow and grow as the season progresses.

Dad's driving today, having decided hiring someone else to do it every time is an unnecessary cost. 'Let's do this,' he calls out as he pulls away from the kerb.

But within minutes of turning onto the A road that will take us most of the way to the Windham Park ground, we find ourselves caught up in a traffic jam that stretches as far ahead as the eye can see. There are so many cars in front of us that we can't tell what's causing the hold-up, and we can't reverse back out of it – the cars behind us have already hemmed us in.

'Someone look it up on your mobile, will you?' Dad requests. 'See if there are any news reports. Make sure we're not going to be stuck here all day.'

Cassie shows me the screen on her phone before breaking the worrying news to him: a three car pile-up on the southbound to Winchester is causing tailbacks around junction thirty. Drivers should expect delays of up to three hours. And there we were thinking we'd factored in plenty of time for any complications. Now we're in danger of missing the starting whistle.

'Shit, shit, shit,' Cassie mutters.

'I'll get on the phone to them.' I scroll to the Windham Park number and hit dial.

'I'll check if walking's feasible,' Marge says. 'Looks like it would take an hour and forty – but that would mostly involve walking along the side of this dual carriageway.'

Dad shakes his head. 'We can't do that – it's too dangerous.'

'Not if nobody's moving,' Bob points out, just as we manage to crawl forward another few metres. But then we grind back to a standstill.

It's not long before the drivers up ahead start switching off their engines and getting out to stretch their legs. When one of them comes to knock on the coach door, Dad opens it, thinking it must be a fan wanting to meet the team. But it turns out the man, who looks to be in his seventies, hasn't even noticed my artwork in the windows.

'I don't suppose I could use your toilet, could I?' he asks. 'I'm an old bugger and I don't think I can last however long it's going to take for the road to clear. I'm bloody bursting!'

Elliot stifles a snigger as Cassie moves aside to let him pass. 'And there we were thinking we were famous.'

The man does clock all the matching shirts as he walks along the aisle, though.

'Hang on a minute, are you that new football team? I've seen you in the papers. Are you on your way to a match somewhere?'

'Windham Park,' Thomas tells him. 'You should come and watch us. It's going to be a classic.'

'If I didn't have my granddaughter's birthday party, I absolutely would. I used to love going to the football back in the day.' The man smiles. 'I'll spare you a thought while I'm blowing up balloons. And let's hope we all get to our destinations in good time today.'

'I'm through,' I call out, pointing at my phone and gesturing for some quiet while I explain the situation to my counterpart at Windham. When I'm done I let everyone know, with a sigh of relief, that he's happy to push the start time back for up to an hour and has just requested that we keep him posted on our estimated arrival time.

'So do we stay put and hope things get moving or do we cut our losses now, leave you with the coach and get the rest of us walking?' I ask Dad.

'I think we should wait, now we've got a bit of time,' he replies. 'We don't want everyone's legs to be knackered before we even get to kick-off.'

At that point our elderly guest reappears, thanks us profusely for helping him out and says he hopes karma repays us with a win. I'd be happy enough if it could repay us with a way out of this traffic jam.

Once he's departed, Aaron asks, 'Can we all jump out and get some air? It's pretty stuffy in here.'

'I don't think your insurance covers standing outside your vehicle in the middle of a motorway,' I point out. 'But as it's pretty warm in here, I'm going to say yes, as long as you stay in front of the coach at all times and promise to be vigilant.'

'Watch out for motorbikes,' Dad adds. 'In case anyone's trying to weave their way through this lot. It's a shame I don't work for a moped hire firm. We could all have zipped up the middle in a convoy.'

With all the purple shirts grouped together out on the road, a couple of fans who are stranded ahead of us realise this is the team coach and wander over to say hello. They're delighted to hear the match will be delayed.

'We debated whether to do the away games as well or just stick to the home ones and we were starting to think we'd made the wrong decision,' one says.

To show them how grateful we are for their support and the effort they've made, I offer them free tickets to our next two away games. Hopefully this will get them in the habit. At the very least they go back to their car with smiles on their faces.

We've sold close to seven hundred tickets in advance for this fixture, which may be significantly less than last week's numbers, but is still pretty epic for an away game, given the travel cost and effort needed to get there. Windham has granted us a whopping fifty per cent of its two-thousand-capacity ground for this match – five times the typical allocation for away fans in the Premier League – but as its average attendance is around a thousand it could afford to give us the space, and our ticket sales will give its income a massive boost.

Dad makes every one of our players jump out of their skin when he toots the horn at them and beckons them back onto the bus. 'It looks like we're about to get on the move again,' he explains. 'Things are starting to shift up ahead.'

Sure enough, people are returning to their cars, restarting their engines and the slow crawl towards Windham begins. In the end we arrive only thirty-one minutes after the scheduled start time, but that does mean our players have little time to warm up. And what that means is they don't have their heads in the game for at least the next thirty minutes, conceding a humiliating three goals and barely getting the ball out of their half before half-time.

I know being cooped up in the coach for so long is partly to blame, but it's hard at this point not to wonder if we haven't made mistakes with some of our decisions – in our player selection, perhaps in letting Cassie coach the team, in thinking we could pull this off in such a short time period. It's hard to fathom why exactly it isn't working. I don't think the Windham players are any better than we are. Our lads have worked so hard since our crazy idea came to fruition. They seem motivated. There have, thankfully, been no injuries. And yet here we are again, several goals down to the opposition.

I know Helen will still find some positives to report when she writes it up for the *Herald*, about the number of fans, the atmosphere and the unwavering team spirit, and I'm eternally grateful to have her in our corner. But I don't imagine the social media posts will be so kind. Although our fans have been blessedly non-judgemental so far, I'm not sure how long that will last if we keep getting walked all over like this.

Cassie works doubly hard to fire the players back up with a rousing team chat at half-time. I wonder if, despite her initial reservations, she's actually missing Ben at this moment. I notice Elliot is looking particularly gloomy and make a note to get Cassie to have a private word with him after the match. I don't want him to feel like this is his fault. And I want to know about it if anyone else on the team suggests it is.

If anything it's Bailey whose performance is lacking. He's giving the ball away far too often, which is not like him. Maybe Ben's absence is having an effect on him too. It certainly looks like his mind is elsewhere this afternoon.

Our players don't fare any better in the second half and the score finishes at five–nil, our worst loss yet, leaving us all very conscious that we're going backwards. I'm surprised and very grateful when the fans still give the team a standing ovation. It doesn't lift them enough to put anyone in the mood for another late-night party at The Fox afterwards, but we still head over there to show our faces.

Having managed not to worry about it since I first boarded the coach, thoughts of Ben and Georgina start creeping back into my mind while I'm sipping my beer. Are they enjoying their meal together? Has she already started falling for him? Will he admit his heart isn't in it?

I turn my phone off and bury it in my bag, to stop myself from continuously checking it.

I don't even turn it back on when I eventually crawl under my duvet – if Ben hasn't been in touch yet it will only distress me. Better to get a good night's sleep and try to forget about it for now. After Crawford's defeat, I don't want to feel any more deflated than I do already.

40

There is a message from Ben when I check in the morning, saying he's gutted about Crawford's loss and that he's sorry he couldn't get hold of me. I check when it was sent – 11 p.m. I can't help thinking that's respectable.

When I call him back, I fill him in on the nightmare journey to Windham and he empathises – and laughs – at the appropriate parts of the story. He says he might take the train instead of driving when he comes down next weekend, to avoid a similar fate.

We discuss the game and I mention Bailey wasn't on his usual form. 'Is everything okay with him?'

'He might be letting his new relationship affect his concentration,' Ben speculates. 'It's the first time he's been really serious about someone so it's quite a big deal for him. I can have a word, if you like.'

'It's fine, I'll handle it.' I certainly understand how that feels after meeting Ben.

'If you think it might be useful, I could have another word with all the players,' he offers. 'To remind them to keep looking forward and not dwell on any setbacks.'

'I'm sure they'd appreciate a little morale booster in the team WhatsApp group,' I tell him.

He admits he's feeling a bit frustrated himself after watching Millford City lose yesterday. He's got one more week on the bench after this and can't wait to get back to playing. 'I'm not saying I definitely would have made a difference, but I hate not even being able to try. On the flip side, it does have the advantage of making it easier to see you next weekend.'

We won't be going to a hotel for this visit because there are a few bits he wants to pick up from the Whitehouse. But he should get away from Millford promptly on Saturday, seeing as he won't have to warm down, so we'll have a decent amount of time together. He promises to find somewhere nice for us to go for lunch on Sunday, so we don't spend his entire visit in bed – although we're both keen to make sure there's plenty of that as well.

Not once in the conversation do I ask about how things went with Georgina, and he doesn't bring her up either. But this doesn't, as I worried it might, leave me with hundreds of possible scenarios running through my mind. On the contrary it helps me keep her out of my thoughts, and I end the call no longer feeling quite so bereft.

So that's all I need to do for the time being, I tell myself, just focus on me and Ben. If I do slip and start thinking about her, I bring his Jake Gyllenhaal analogy to mind and force myself to think of her just as his new friend. Because friends do go out for dinner and have a laugh together, and that makes it easier to accept. And this strategy works, more or less, for the whole of the following week, by the end of which I'm beyond excited about being reunited with Ben.

I wake up at the crack of dawn on the day of our home match against Merribridge, feeling as elated as I was on the day Crawford United got its FA approval. Merribridge finished second from the bottom of the table last season, so we've got a really good chance of beating them. And then there'll only be a matter of hours before Ben arrives, so it's shaping up to be a very good day.

Dad's already up too – I can hear him in the kitchen – and when I head downstairs, he asks if I want a cooked breakfast. 'I feel like I'm going to need all the energy I can get today,' he says.

I tell him to hold the hash browns for me, but to pile on everything else.

'Coming right up.' He beams, seemingly sharing my good mood.

Cassie wanders in through the back door a few minutes later. 'Couldn't sleep,' she explains, sliding into the seat opposite me at the table, and shortly afterwards Marge and Bob turn up too, followed, to my surprise, by Thomas and Levi.

'You're very early,' I observe.

'Your dad said we could come,' Thomas explains. 'Because of not working and all that, I'm a bit skint, so Mike said about stopping by here and grabbing something, if I wanted. Then Levi got FOMO and asked if he could join me. I hope that's okay, Mike.'

'Of course,' Dad says. He's so in his element when he's got a full kitchen table. 'Grab another pack of sausages out of the freezer, would you?'

'Yes, boss,' Thomas replies.

'I'll dig you out some cheap nutritious recipes,' Cassie says. 'You need to eat properly all the time, not just today.'

'I could come round and walk you through them if you don't know what you're doing,' Marge offers. 'Maybe I should offer all the team cooking lessons. We don't want anyone getting malnourished.'

'You're such an angel,' Dad says.

'Well it's not like we're one of those fancy clubs where they get all their meals cooked for them,' she points out.

'Except for Craig – his dad's got a chef,' Levi says. Phoebs never told me this.

Dad laughs. 'We'll all invite ourselves round there for brekkie next weekend then.'

The rest of the team arrive throughout the morning until we've got a full house. Craig and Scott head out to the garden to practise keepy-uppies. Aaron and Jacob watch videos with Dad and talk tactics. Cassie gives Jamie's calves a sports massage and Marge talks food with Thomas. Everyone looks relaxed and happy, just how we want them to be before each game.

Advance ticket sales have been strong again this week, close to three thousand, perhaps owing to the reports of people missing out on our first home game. I feel a bit sorry for the Merribridge fans – there are only a hundred of them. It's a small club with a small ground and a small following. Coming up against such a huge crowd will be quite daunting for them – especially as the rest of our tickets sell out throughout the morning.

As it's a home game and Merribridge has a less than perfect track record, I think we're all expecting a win today, so we arrive at the ground full of eager anticipation. And once the match gets underway, I spend much of the first half on the edge of my seat, drumming my feet on the floor with nervous energy as our lads run rings around the visiting team – with the possible exception of Bailey, who still seems a bit off the pace. Dad's just as restless beside me and even resorts to chewing gum again.

I'm amazed we don't score given that we must have at least two-thirds of the possession, but this is still looking hopeful for Crawford. It's the first time we go into the second half without being several goals down. I make a point of congratulating Elliot on his clean sheet during the break. I know it's been tough on him losing our previous three games, and this will hopefully restore his confidence.

'Come on, Crawford,' I call out, as the second half gets off to a flying start with a quick attempt at goal from Craig. The ball clatters against the post and is hastily booted away by a Merribridge defender. Denied again.

Our fans bang their drums and sing their hearts out, but sadly no amount of encouragement seems able to power our boys onto the score sheet. I can almost taste their frustration when the final whistle blows, but Dad gathers everyone round and reminds them today is still something to be celebrated. We might have been held to a nil–nil draw, but that means Crawford United has its first ever league point – we've finally got a foot on the ladder.

'All we need to do now is keep climbing,' he tells them.

I suddenly wish Ben were here to share this moment. I feel like I've just watched my baby taking its first steps, but without its other parent there. At least I can show him some of the highlights on my phone when he gets here later.

I check the Millford City score and see their game also ended in a draw. It feels fated somehow, like our days are in sync with each other. He'll be heading to the station soon and will text me his ETA once he knows which train he's getting. I'll hang out with the team at The Fox while I'm waiting, counting down the minutes till he arrives.

It's another packed-out evening at the pub and the bar area is swamped.

'My new staff haven't quite got used to match days yet,' Olly apologises.

I volunteer to jump behind the bar and help out until the initial rush dies down – partly so I can organise pints for the team and partly so I can thank some of the fans I'll serve for their support – and Olly doesn't complain. But with this, then getting caught up in conversations with both the players and the fans afterwards, it's gone seven before I finally have a chance to look at my phone. Ben should be halfway to Hamcott by now, and from the three missed calls and two voice notes listed on my screen, I'm guessing he's already bored of the journey and impatient to get here.

But when I head outside so I can hear them properly, my heart sinks as soon as I click on the first message. 'Lily, it's Ben. Give me a buzz back when you get this, will you?'

It's not the sound of someone who's about to deliver good news – his voice is loaded with stress.

'No, no, no,' I mutter, holding my breath as I start the second message.

'It's me again. I didn't want to do this on VoiceNote but I can't get hold of you and I don't want to leave you hanging. I can't come down tonight. I'm really sorry. We've been ordered to attend a special team meeting tomorrow morning after Millford's mediocre result today and there's no way I can get out of it. It's the new coach they've brought in. He's got some different ideas about what he thinks commitment should look like. I'm so, so sorry. I was really looking forward to this; I know you were too.

'I'll make it up to you, I promise. Next weekend we're playing down in London so we can sort something out for then. Maybe you can come and join me in the hotel the night before the game? Give me a call back when you get this anyway and we'll figure it out. I hope you're not answering because you're busy celebrating Crawford's first point. I'm made up for you guys and so bummed I'm not there. I miss you. Call me. I'll speak to you later.'

I slump back against the wall, eyes closed, the high I've been on all day evaporating like a puff of smoke. I've been building up to seeing him all week, living for it really, and now there's at least six more days before there's even the possibility of being with him again.

I slam my palm against the bricks in exasperation. I can't believe this new coach has spoilt our plans. Who holds a team meeting on a Sunday? And what does it mean going forward? Is he going to spring meetings on them at short notice like this every weekend?

For a moment I'm tempted to jump on a train up to Millford. If I left now I'd just make the last one. But it would be close to midnight by the time I got there, and if Ben's busy tomorrow anyway . . .

I rage against the unfairness of it all. I was so looking forward to having him back. It was going to be the cherry on the cake after what I'd hoped would be a brilliant day. A tear trickles down my cheek as my body aches with the disappointment. I don't brush it away. I need a few moments to wallow before I go back inside wearing my best poker face.

But before I've got a grip on my emotions, Bailey walks out into the garden, looking all around him as he pulls out a vape. He freezes when he sees me. 'Lily!' It's hastily stuffed back into his pocket as he comes closer. 'Are you okay?'

He sounds so much like his brother it threatens to set me off all over again.

'I'm fine,' I tell him.

'You're clearly not,' he says gently. 'Is it Ben?'

I nod. 'I miss him. I wish he was still here.'

'It must be tricky, especially with the Georgina thing.'

Of all people, I'm not sure it's Ben's brother I should vent about it to, but it all comes spilling out anyway. 'I hate it. I hate that she's the one who's getting to spend time with him and I hate that everyone believes they're genuinely together. It makes me angry because it feels like I'm the one being punished for Ben's behaviour. I wish I could just turn the clock back and make that incident with the fan go away.'

'Don't we all.' Bailey sighs. 'But if it's any consolation, I know he's just trying to make the best of a bad situation. He's under pressure to play the PR game, but he'd much rather be with you than with Georgina. He's actually pretty miserable that the two of you can't spend as much time together.'

'Thank you, Bailey.' It's what I needed to hear. 'And I'm sorry, I shouldn't be offloading my frustration on you.'

He waves my apology away. 'Sometimes you just need to get it off your chest. But honestly, it'll work itself out in the end. You guys are so perfect for each other.'

I inhale deeply, feeling calmer, then switch back into work mode, pointing at the vape poking out of his pocket. 'Meanwhile, you know we're going to have to talk about that.'

'I don't use it often. I've just been a bit stressed lately.'

'Anything you want to share with me?'

'Something I need to work through on my own. But thank you, I appreciate it.'

'Well I'm here if you need me, but you've got to knock it on the head if you're serious about playing for Crawford.'

'Honestly, I can stop,' he assures me. 'It's just temporary.'

'Then I'm willing to pretend I didn't see it on this occasion.'

We agree that when we go back inside, we'll both forget this conversation.

I end up staying until closing time, to keep myself from moping about Ben, so I'm somewhat the worst for wear when I eventually stumble into my bedroom just after midnight. It's only then that I start feeling bad for not even texting him back. He must be wondering what's going on.

He's usually in bed by now, but I decide to chance a call anyway. When he answers I can tell from the bewilderment in his voice that he wasn't awake.

'Hey, babe, everything okay? You get my message?'

'I'm drunk,' I confess. 'I drank a *lot*. I really missed you this evening.'

'I missed you too. Did you have a good night at The Fox?'

'I did. But now I'm . . . I'm quite drunk. My head's in a spin.'

'You probably need some sleep,' he says drowsily. 'It's late.'

'I know. I just didn't want you to think . . .'

'Why don't we talk in the morning?' he suggests. 'When we're both more with it.'

Because I want to talk now, I think, even if tomorrow's more sensible. But what I actually say is, 'Sure. I'm sorry I woke you.'

'Night, babe, love you,' he says quietly, ending the call before I have a chance to say it back.

My heart sinks as I stare at my phone in my hand. I know it's the middle of the night, but I thought he might sound happier to hear from me. Instead, after not seeing each other for ten days, and now with another whole week to wait, it feels like we're starting to drift apart.

41

After a restless night, I wake up cranky. I should be enjoying a leisurely breakfast with Ben on his terrace then heading out somewhere fun together, not nursing the worst hangover I've had in as long as I can remember.

Ben, on the other hand, seems bright as a button when he calls me before I've even emerged from under my duvet. 'Hey, Lils, how's the head this morning? I'm sorry I couldn't talk last night. I couldn't keep my eyes open. It sounded like you had quite the session though.'

'I'd be on the painkillers if I could only reach them,' I confess. So far even the walk to the bathroom cabinet feels like a NASA space mission. 'I don't think I'm going to be doing very much today.'

'We all need a duvet day from time to time,' he says. 'I'd be in there with you if I had my way.' Which would usually bring a smile to my face, thinking about us cuddled up together, but today only reminds me that he's hundreds of miles away.

'What did you do with your evening?' I ask, then

301

instantly wish I hadn't when he tells me he 'ended up seeing Georgie'.

He doesn't elaborate, as per our agreement, but it sends my mind into overdrive. What does he mean by 'end up'? Did she suggest it? Did he? And are they already so familiar with each other that he's started calling her *Georgie*?

'I know it's not what we said, but I think I might need you to tell me about it.'

'There isn't much to tell.' I imagine him shrugging. 'We had a drink at a place called the Alchemist. She had a couple of cocktails; I stuck to the alcohol-free beer.'

'Was it fun?'

'She's easy company – funny. I think you'd like her.'

I doubt that very much. I brace myself for my next question. 'And after the Alchemist?'

'I dropped her home. I had the car.' He's in it now. I can tell from the slight echo. 'I've told her I want to take things slowly after being burned in past relationships.'

Which should make me feel reassured, but instead makes me seethe. He might want me to think he's keeping her at arm's length, but the fact is, he didn't *have* to see her last night; he *chose* to. When he was supposed to be with me.

'And she actually believes that? She didn't ask you in?'

'Well, yeah she asked me, but that doesn't mean . . .'

'She asked,' I interrupt, oddly triumphant, like it proves some kind of point. 'Which means she thinks there's a chance it's going to happen. Which of course she would when you're seeing her every other evening.'

'I'm not seeing her every other evening.' I can tell I've got his back up now. 'I just found myself unexpectedly free on Saturday night and she happened to ask if I wanted to do something. I didn't realise it would be such a big deal.'

'Of course it's a big deal, Ben. Can't you see where this is going?'

'It's not going anywhere. I don't know why you're picking a fight with me.'

'She clearly thinks it is! And I'm supposed to just sit here and be okay with it. Well I'm not. And I can't believe you think I should be.'

He doesn't answer straight away. The only sound is the click of his car indicator and my own heavy breathing.

'I can't get into this now,' he says quietly. 'I've got this meeting.'

But there's no 'let's talk later', I notice, so I practically shout 'fine' down the phone at him before I cut him off. Then I instantly regret it. What the hell am I doing? I'm never usually like this. I blame it on the hangover, even though I know it's not the real culprit.

I type out an apology, then delete it – twice. My stubborn streak tells me this is for him to make right, not me. So I text Phoebs instead. 'Got time for a girl chat?'

'Always,' she replies. 'Am I coming round or are we going out for coffee?'

'Here's probably better. I'm not dressed.'

'Oh dear, this sounds bad. Hang fire, I'll see you in twenty mins.'

I don't do much beyond stare at the ceiling till she arrives. I romantically thought Ben and I would never have an argument, but now I realise how naive that was.

'I feel like I'm pushing him away,' I confess to Phoebs, when she's made herself comfortable on the end of my bed. 'I don't want to ruin it, but it's like I can't help myself.'

'I hardly think you're the one who's ruining anything. He's asking a lot of you; it's little wonder you're stressed out about it.'

'I just don't know how to handle it. If he talks to me about her I hate it. If he doesn't, it feels like he's hiding things.'

'Has he ever hidden anything from you before?'

'No, but we both know he has secrets. His suspension, for example. He never, ever talks about that.'

'I didn't think you were concerned about it.'

'I wasn't, but now I'm questioning everything.'

'You're a good judge of character, Lily. I don't think you would have given Ben the time of day, let alone the whole summer, if you didn't think he was worth it.'

I want to believe her, but I can't help thinking if we fell in love so quickly, couldn't we fall out of it just as fast?

Phoebs thinks we just need to time to adjust to our new set-up. 'And in the meantime, you've got another match to prepare for, and you've got your exam results this week . . .' She sees my eyes go wide. 'Don't tell me you'd forgotten?'

'There's been so much else going on.'

She shakes her head disbelievingly. 'I've already got my outfit planned for our big night out on Tuesday. Results day.'

'I'll be at training,' I point out.

'You can miss one session on the day you finish university.'

'Or we could go out afterwards?'

'Lily Crawford,' she says sternly, 'you've been trying to get your degree for five whole years. We are not postponing the celebration of you finally passing for another minute.'

I roll my eyes. I know she won't back down. 'You're such a bossy cow sometimes.'

She just laughs and moos at me.

But to make sure I don't change my mind, she comes to my house early on results day, so she can be there when I get the email. After that she's insisting we go shopping to find me something sparkly to celebrate in – she doesn't doubt I'm going to pass this time – then we'll come back here and get dressed up before we hit the town.

I end up glad she's here, because Dad is putting me on edge as he fidgets in his seat. They both look at me expectantly from the other side of the table as I open my laptop. 'Effective leadership . . .' I leave them hanging for a few seconds. 'Pass.'

'Yes!' Dad beams.

'Go, girl,' says Phoebs, holding her hand out for a fist bump.

'And global communication . . .'

'You've got this,' Phoebs encourages.

I try to sound as upbeat as I can. 'I smashed it!'

It's not that I'm not happy to be graduating – of course I'm pleased. It's just while they high-five each other before coming round the table for congratulatory hugs with me, what I want to do more than anything is tell Ben, but right now we're barely speaking. Our conversation on Sunday night didn't manage to resolve anything. He's still pissed off that I accused him of encouraging Georgina.

I ended up suggesting we take a few days out to think about things.

I don't know why I did it. I guess I was admitting to myself that I'm not happy. I don't like the insecure, uneasy person I've become while I've tried – and failed – to handle the position I've found myself in. I thought a few days to regroup might help, so I can get back to feeling more like myself. Then I'm hoping we can revert to the fun and flirty chat that's the reason I fell for him.

I resist messaging him while I'm out shopping with Phoebs and while we're doing our hair and make-up, but I finally take the first step towards reconciliation when I drunk-text him from a bar later in the evening, while Phoebs is queuing for drinks.

It's just a short message. '*It turns out I don't like not talking to you.*'

His response is immediate. '*I hate it! Are you free to chat now?*'

'*I'm at my graduation drinks. Phoebs made me do shots. I'm a little slurry.*'

'*You passed? Why didn't you tell me?!*'

'*We weren't speaking,*' I remind him. '*But we are now. And when I see you on Friday we can make up properly.*'

There's a longer pause this time before his three dots start flashing. '*About that,*' his message starts and it's probably just as well I'm quite tipsy. It means my reactions are dulled and I don't fly off the handle when he says, '*Under the new coach there's a ban on wives and girlfriends the night before a game, so I'm not going to be able to sneak you into the hotel.*'

'After the game then?'

'Flying straight back to Millford with the team. I'm not trying to make things even more difficult. What about if I could get you a seat on the same flight?'

'We're away at Feybrook on Saturday. I'd never make it.'

'Sunday then. Somewhere in the middle. One of the nicest hotels on our list. It's probably better that way anyway – less chance of getting spotted.'

I ignore the reminder that we're not allowed to be seen together and tell him, alongside a string of happy-face emojis, that he's got himself a deal.

42

The day before we're due to see each other, Crawford United scrape another draw out of the match against Feybrook. It's a miserable day that starts with Dad, Cassie and I staring out of the kitchen window at rain that hasn't stopped for three days straight. And there I was thinking August was meant to be summer. We can't imagine too many of the fans wanting to travel for an hour to stand around in this for the afternoon, and we're right, we end up with our lowest attendance to date.

As we stand pitchside, huddled under Dad's golf umbrella, it occurs to me that I should have had some team ponchos printed up.

'Let's look into costs and see if we can get some on sale on the website for next time,' Dad says.

By half-time, our players are soaked to the bone. We shelter inside the coach while Dad and Cassie go over a few pointers with them, as the Feybrook ground doesn't have locker rooms. It's really just a pitch with a fence around it. I feel terrible that they don't have a dry kit to change into as they sit wrapped in their towels. I make a note to try and find a way to work this into our budget. At least it's not cold, only wet.

Cassie reminds them to be unselfish with the ball and to make sure they're communicating with each other. Dad praises them for their spirited first half and tells them to keep pushing.

In the second half, Cassie grows concerned about Aaron's ankle, which took a knock during a tackle at Thursday's training session. 'I'm not sure he's being honest with us about how much it's hurting him.'

We watch closely and it does look like he might be trying not to wince whenever he has to change direction.

'I'm bringing him off,' Cassie says. 'I don't want him to do any long-term damage.'

Dad nods. 'Let's start him on some physio tomorrow and have a chat about injury management with the whole team. They need to be open with us if they've got any problems, or we can't help them. Knowing Aaron, he'll think he's letting the side down if he says anything, but they need to know their personal welfare is the most important thing.'

Caspian, the sub, generates a heart-stopping moment when he wins Crawford a penalty close to the final whistle. But Craig can barely see for all the rainwater running into his eyes. At least that's what I tell myself when he scoops the ball straight into the arms of the goalie. Minutes later it's all over.

'Tortoise and hare,' Dad says on the way back to Hamcott afterwards, referring to the fact that we've clawed another point out of this match. 'Let all the other teams race ahead. We're just biding our time and we'll catch up with them eventually.'

While everyone heads home for a hot shower before reconvening at The Fox. I check the Millford City score on my phone and discover Ben's marked his return to the pitch with a cracking header into the goal. He must be delighted. That's one way to prove he hasn't lost his touch.

He'll be in post-match warm-down for a while yet, so I'll call him later to congratulate him. Maybe after I've watched the highlights on *Top Goals*, so I can share in his glee.

After a few drinks with the Crawford players, I make sure I'm home in time for its ten o'clock start, leaving Dad in the pub with the team. The Millford City game is the first one covered, partly because their opponents are currently top of the table, but also because there's a lot of chat around Ben's return to Premier League football.

The presenters discuss how he hasn't let the six-match suspension affect his performance, whether it was appropriate punishment for his behaviour, how he's been rebuilding his reputation through community work – Oh my God! Crawford United gets a fleeting mention on *Top Goals*! Just wait till I tell Dad! – and they end with the suggestion that his new girlfriend Georgina must be the calming influence he needs.

As if that wasn't tough enough to hear, a picture of her flashes up on the screen in the crowd at the match, looking stunning with her blonde hair curling round her shoulders and 'Go, Ben!' emblazoned on her T-shirt. I don't know what's more irritating: that he didn't tell me she was going to be there, or this public declaration of her alliance with him.

And then a second picture flashes up – the one that changes everything. It's on the screen so fleetingly I could almost convince myself I imagined it. But I could see it was a selfie so I call up her Instagram account on my phone and sure enough, there it is. Ben is looking at the camera, not at her, but as she presses her lips against his cheek his smile is as wide as it's ever been.

It doesn't make me cry, as I thought it might, but I do feel pain in every cell of my body. I know I could rationalise it and say he's not kissing her back, or that he's just smiling because he's had a great day back on the pitch, but neither changes the fact that it's her in the picture, not me. And I know in that moment that I need to be out of this situation.

For my own sanity I can't let it eat me up for another day, let alone a few weeks or however long it ends up having to go on for. It reminds me of a quote I once read on Instagram – the drawn-out agony of clinging on hurts far more than the short sharp sting of letting go.

My stomach lurches as I take one last look at the photo. Even knowing how badly I want to be free of the torment, I feel sick at the thought of the conversation I now need to have with Ben. The only way to do it, I conclude, is quickly. So I take a deep breath to psych myself up for it, and dig my nails into my palm to try and stop myself shaking as I listen to his phone ringing.

He's laughing when he answers, pub noises in the background, still high on the day's adrenaline. It doesn't feel like a good time to do this – we should be sharing anecdotes from our respective days – but I need to get it over with.

I feel my heart shattering into a thousand tiny pieces

as each word leaves my mouth. 'I can't do this any more, Ben. I think we should break up.'

There's silence on the other end of the phone while it sinks in.

I decide not to make it about Georgina and instead say, 'It's not that I don't want to be with you – I do. But you've got your life up there, I've got my commitments down here, and I think we just need to quit while we're ahead.'

I explain how I don't want to get into the cycle of cancelled plans and petty arguments that feels inevitable. 'I've got such amazing memories of this summer with you and I don't want to ruin them by ending up feeling bitter.'

'But what about tomorrow?' he asks.

'I think it would be a mistake. It won't do either of us any favours to stir up our feelings. I do wish things could be different – if our lives were at different stages, or if you were nearer . . . but I think it's time to move on and the sooner we accept that the better.'

There's another long pause before he says, 'If you're sure that's what you want then I have to respect it.'

And I waver, because I'm not at all sure it is. But then that image of Georgina pops back into my head and reminds me how worn down I've been feeling by all the anguish and uncertainty.

'I'm gutted about it, but I do believe it's for the best,' I tell him. It will hopefully give us both a chance at happiness in the long run.

'Will we still talk?' he asks.

'I don't think we should, for a while at least.' It kills me to say it, but I know it will be ten times harder to move on if he's still sending me messages every day.

'So this is goodbye then?'

I nod sadly. 'I'm sorry. Goodbye, Ben.'

I end the call before he can say anything that might make me change my mind again. But it doesn't stop me staring at my phone for a long time afterwards, wishing he'd call back and tell me I'm wrong and that he can't live without me. When he doesn't, I eventually come back round to thinking this is the right decision. This is not the life I want for myself, and I need more from a relationship.

It'll be hard trying to find another guy who lights my world up as much as Ben has during our few months together. But I'd rather be with someone less enthralling if it means they're at least present. That's what I'll have to keep telling myself anyway.

43

Despite it being my decision to end things, I sink into a depression after that call. I play the conversation with Ben over and over in my mind and, when I wake up the next morning, my new reality hits me like an eighteen-tonne truck. It's over. There won't be any more conversations with Ben.

I hardly leave my room for three whole days while I question whether I've done the right thing. Should I have held on a little while longer before walking away from the man who might just have been the love of my life? But much as I might want to, I can't escape the fact that it wasn't working.

On top of that, I start fretting about the fact that I'm twenty-four, not earning an income and still living at home with my dad. I know he's told me not to worry while we're still in the throes of establishing Crawford United, but I can't do this forever so I need to start working out what kind of job I want and how to fit Crawford around it.

Assuming there still is a Crawford United by the end of the season. My financial projections are optimistic if I base them on the ticket sales of our first three fixtures. But unless the rain stops and we start winning some games, there will likely be some downward adjustments as all the fair-weather fans lose interest.

Not for the first time, I wonder if Dad, Cassie and I need to switch up the team, swapping in more of the reserves. Caspian will be standing in for Aaron for at least the next three weeks and is blending in pretty seamlessly. Do we bench Bailey as well, till he's back to his best? Craig, to see if Billy Holt should have been our number-one striker after all? But when I bring it up at training on Tuesday evening, Cassie is adamant we already have the strongest players in our starting line-up and that they just need a bit more time.

I've told her and Dad about Ben, so I don't need to explain my red, puffy eyes to them, or why I look like I haven't slept. But it doesn't escape Bailey's notice, perhaps because he's the only other one on the team who doesn't think I broke up with Ben a few weeks ago.

'Don't take this the wrong way but you look terrible,' he says when I call him over while the players are having a drinks break, to check how he's getting on with quitting the vaping. 'And there I was thinking Ben wasn't handling this well,' he adds.

'Is he not?' I can't help asking.

'He's devastated,' Bailey admits. 'Are you sure the two of you can't fix this? It seems so stupid when you clearly both still want to be together.'

'That's not going to happen as long as Georgina's around. But don't worry, we'll both find a way to make our peace with it.'

He offers a sympathetic smile then turns back to where

Cassie is resuming her training drills, without me even having had the chance to ask about his vaping. But at the end of the session he asks for a moment of everyone's time, announcing there's something he wants to share with us all. *His addiction,* I think, based on the way he glances at me. And he's probably going to ask for their help in beating it. Good for him.

'Let's hear it,' Dad encourages.

'So, er, I like to think we've all got to know each other fairly well since we first met a few months ago. For instance, we all know Elliot still hasn't passed his driving test after three attempts and that Scott watches *Love Island* by choice, not just because his girlfriend makes him.'

This gets a laugh. 'Yeah, you big girl's blouse,' Thomas teases.

'But there's something I want to tell you about me, now a certain situation has come to a head.' He rubs the back of his neck as he looks from one team mate to another, and I realise he's nervous. 'The thing is . . .' he takes a big breath. 'Okay, I'm just going to say it. The thing is, I'm gay.'

'Oh thank God,' Jamie exclaims, clutching Elliot's arm as if he'd been about to collapse. 'I thought you were going to say you were leaving us to play for the Rovers.'

Bailey snorts. 'Please! Give me some credit. I'm not disloyal; I just like men. Not you lot, though, before you start freaking out because you think I might have been checking out your dicks in the showers. My type is skinny and nerdy, not beefy and stupid, which you'll see when you meet my new boyfriend.'

'Can he play football?' Craig asks. And now I've

recovered from my surprise, I love that this is anyone's first question.

'Absolutely not. He's a bona fide exercise hater. But he's incredibly funny and he means the world to me, which is why I no longer want to hide him away. I'm not going to lie, I've been agonising over whether to say anything – not because I'm ashamed, but because there's still such a stigma about gay men in football.'

'Not in this club,' Dad assures him, and I don't think I've ever felt prouder of our team as they all vocalise their agreement.

'Thank you,' Bailey says, one hand placed over his heart. 'You have no idea how good it feels to be able to stand here and be proud of being me.'

'I can't believe you think we're all stupid though,' Aaron says, grinning to show he's not really upset about it.

'But beefy,' Craig reminds him, which kicks off a round of competitive bicep flexing that gets everybody laughing.

'Are we allowed to make jokes about playing for the opposition?' Scott asks, now the mood has got lighter.

'Or coming from the offside position.' This is from Nico and gets a round of sniggers, but Bailey takes it with the good humour that's intended.

'You can even joke about who's got the worst tackle,' he says. Then he puts a finger across his lips in a hush sign and whispers, 'It's Aaron,' which makes everyone laugh again.

'Whatever.' Aaron rolls his eyes, but we all know he's just pretending to be offended.

'Shall we go and get a pint then?' Bailey suggests. 'I think I could use one after that.'

I tell them I'll cough up for the first round. It beats another night of moping about Ben.

The team all give Bailey supportive slaps on the back as we turn towards the exit, and because The Fox isn't busy and raucous like on match days, we're all able to sit round one big table together. As we discuss everything from childhood misdemeanours to relationship disasters, I really get that sense of being one big family Dad and I always hoped to achieve, so it ends up being one of my favourite nights at The Fox ever.

I even manage to push Ben out of my mind for a few hours, giving me some much-needed headspace. But it's only a temporary reprieve – he comes crashing back into my life just two days later.

I flounder for a moment when an incoming call from him pops up on my phone screen, because although I miss him like crazy, I do think having no contact will help us heal. It would be lovely if we could find our way to being friends at some point in the future, but right now I'd just spend all my time secretly wanting more from him. And if he got into a real relationship with someone else, especially if that person were Georgina, it would hurt too much to hear about it.

But his call is hard to ignore. If what Bailey said is true and he's struggling with the split as much I have been, I don't want to leave him hanging. So I take a deep breath and click 'connect', my heart rate spiking even though, as it's early in the morning, I'm still lying in bed.

His voice sets off a familiar flutter in my stomach as he opens with, 'I didn't wake you, did I?'

'No. Is everything okay?'

'I'm worried about Bailey. I can't get hold of him. I

take it you haven't looked at this morning's headlines yet? He's only gone and spoken to a reporter. It's getting picked up everywhere.'

I sit up straighter and reach for my laptop on the bedside table, quickly bringing the screen to life. A search for Bailey's name brings up stories ranging from 'Ben Pryce's fight for LGBTQ+ rights' to 'I did it for my brother'.

'I'm scanning,' I tell him, skim-reading to get the gist of the story.

Bailey says he wants to 'set the record straight' about when Ben lashed out at that fan, saying it's high time his brother's reputation stopped getting dragged through the mud. He describes how the fan, an old classmate of Bailey's who had spotted him holding hands with his new partner, was spouting such homophobic poison about him that Ben felt compelled to step in.

It continues, *I know a lot of people will still say he should have ignored it, but it's hard not to see red when someone's badmouthing your family. And if you ask me, he was right to call that person out for the disgusting things he was saying. No one should have to listen to that kind of hate.*

He goes into more detail about how his brother couldn't be more caring or supportive, even willing to let his own career suffer so as not to have to out Bailey, who at that point hadn't felt ready to talk about it openly.

But things have changed now and I want people to stop blaming my brother because he's never been the real villain of this story.

'Is that true?' I ask Ben.

'Yes, and I'm sorry I didn't explain it to you, but

319

Bailey has always kept his private life to himself before, so I didn't feel like it was for me to share. I was trying to be the protective big brother as usual, even though I know he's perfectly capable of looking after himself. I have no idea why he's suddenly decided to talk about it so publicly now.'

I tell him Bailey announced it to the team on Tuesday and seemed relieved to have done so. 'I think he just wants to be able to bring his boyfriend to The Fox and before this maybe he felt like he couldn't.'

'How did the others react when he told them?'

'They just cracked a few jokes then got on with it.'

'Well that's one less thing to worry about. But I'm concerned he might be under siege by the press. Our parents are on holiday this week and he's not answering his phone. And I can't go round and check on him when I'm so far away.'

There's an unspoken question there and I offer to pop over, to put his mind at rest.

'It feels cheeky asking you under the circumstances, but I'd be eternally grateful. And if you could drop me a message afterwards, or get him to call me, that would be amazing.'

'Consider it done,' I tell him, already reaching for the joggers and T-shirt on the top of my yet-to-be-put-away laundry pile as an image of Bailey cowering behind a curtain to hide from a pack of nosy journalists flashes into my head.

But despite Ben's fears, there's not a single reporter camped outside his parents' place. I ring the doorbell anyway. Now I'm here I might as well check everything else is okay.

Bailey doesn't answer on the first two rings, but the door finally flies open just as I'm about to leave. He has a towel knotted round his waist and his hair is sticking up all over the place. 'Lily? What brings you here?'

'Your brother. He's been trying to call you since he saw your story in the papers.'

'Ah,' he says, looking sheepish. 'I probably should have warned him. But I didn't want him to try and talk me out of it. I wanted to get it out there.'

'Who is it?' a voice calls from down the corridor. Deep. Booming. Male.

My cheeks redden instantly. 'You've got company? I'm sorry.'

'It's not a problem. I won't invite you in though, if that's okay. It's the first time I've seen my boyfriend as an openly gay man, and Mum and Dad are away so we've been celebrating rather heavily.'

'You can spare me the details. Just send Ben a text, will you? He thought you might have stopped answering calls because you were being hounded by the press.'

'We've just been a bit busy, that's all, but I promise I'll call him back later.'

I think he's about to head back inside, but then he pauses and says, 'I did it for you as well, you know.'

A frown creases my brow. 'What do you mean?'

'All this stuff with Georgina, it's my fault it had to happen. But Ben won't need to keep it up now everyone can see him for who he really is.'

'Oh, Bailey. You didn't have to do that.'

'Didn't have to, but I wanted to. Seeing how miserable you both were got me thinking about how I'd feel if I were in either of your shoes. It would break my heart if I was forced apart from Jasper. He makes me happy every single day. He's shown me how amazing it feels to be in love. I want you and Ben to be able to have that again.'

I look down, too choked up to speak.

'Just talk to him, will you?' he says. 'If you've got even the slightest chance at happiness, it would be such a shame to waste it.'

I tell him I'll give it some thought as I turn away.

His words don't stop swirling round my head on the drive back to Dad's. Could I get past the hurt of the last few weeks and start over with Ben if he was no longer with Georgina? Or are we too detached now? Is it simply too late? What I conclude is that while I do want to speak to Ben to let him know his brother is fine – because I'd be willing to bet Bailey will be too distracted to do it himself for a while yet – I need more time to work out exactly how I feel about the prospect of a reconciliation before I'm ready for a more emotional conversation.

Ben appears to have other ideas, though. 'I've finished with Georgie,' he blurts out straight after thanking me for looking in on Bailey.

It sends a shiver right through me. 'Already?' It's like he could read his brother's mind.

'I didn't want to mislead her for another minute,' he says. 'You know how much I hated the dishonesty.'

'Did she take it okay?' I don't know why I feel the need to check.

'She was just a bit worried about how it would make her look. But I told her she can frame it however she likes. I'm not concerned if people think it was her who ended it.'

I listen as he takes a deep breath, then he asks the

322

one question I think I'm craving and dreading in equal measure. 'So do you think there's any chance you and I could get back together?' When I don't answer immediately, he adds, 'I know some crappy things have happened, but I miss you, Lily. I miss our banter. I don't want us to not be in each other's lives.'

But still I hesitate, because as much as it's killed me, I've spent days trying to convince myself I'm better off out of this. And while I might once have wished things could be different, can I honestly say being with Ben would make me happy now I have a clearer picture of what our future would look like? Occasional days snatched together when our schedules align, a few weeks of quality time in the summer, but having to survive with just video calls the rest of the time. Would that ever feel like enough?

'Is that a no?' he asks when I've been silent for too long.

I close my eyes and sigh. 'You are, hands down, the most amazing guy I've ever met, Ben. Your sense of humour, your kindness . . .' I laugh softly before I add, 'Your body. But we can't get away from the one thing that's always going to stop this from being perfect – the distance. So we've got to be realistic, no matter how much it hurts. If you were here, it would be a different story, but I just don't know that it could ever work while you're up in Millford.'

'I don't think we should write it off before we've properly tried,' he says. 'We were so determined to keep it going before Georgina became an issue. I still believe we can make a go of it, especially now we won't have to hide it.'

The reminder of how optimistic we both were before he left brings a tear to my eye. It seems impossible that we could get so quickly from there to here, but I'm still not sure there's anything he can say that will change my mind.

'Can we at least keep the conversation open?' he asks. 'Maybe talk about it again when everything's had a chance to settle down?'

And I agree that's the best way to leave things for now, because it wouldn't be so hard to let him go if a small part of me didn't still wish things could be like they were before.

44

I try not to spend all my time thinking about him after that. I need to give myself the space to work out if I feel better off without him. Luckily, there's plenty to keep my mind occupied – there's all the Crawford paperwork to keep on top of, I'm with the team on Tuesdays, Thursdays and Saturdays, and I hang out with Phoebs on the nights when she's not seeing Craig.

I still watch *Top Goals* though, to see how he's doing. He scores a goal just three minutes into his second game and another the week after. I'm pleased for him. What better way to show the Millford fans he's back and he means business.

Crawford United, meanwhile, lose their next home game against Portleigh and suffer yet another defeat when they face Southmoor away, leaving us goal-less now with six matches played. We do our best to keep everyone believing our time will come. It has to, we've worked too hard to watch our dream slip away.

In a bid to give the team an extra boost, I finally get round to running the competition Dad, Cassie and I discussed a few weeks ago, asking our fans to come up with a Crawford team song. And the three of us have a giggle-filled night with Bob, Marge, Barbour and his wife, taking it in turns to try and sing the entries that have been submitted on our website. It confirms what I suspected all along – that football lyrics are a lot harder to write than you might think. Why else would people still be singing the anthem from the 1996 Euros?

We have an impressive sixty-two entries, but by the time we've run through them all, there are only two left on the shortlist. The one we finally select is a sweet little ditty from a fan called Antony Brierly, aged fourteen, which is short, easy to remember and we all agree captures the spirit of the club.

'Ashes to glory, that's Crawford's story, among new friends, we rise again, Hamcott so long, here's our new song, we're all delighted, to be United.'

'I actually really like it,' Dad says, humming the tune again with a smile on his face.

We announce the winner on the website – awarding Antony a family season ticket – and include a cringey video of Dad, Cassie and me singing it, so the fans get to know how it goes. I send it out in our e-newsletter too. Time will tell whether anyone else makes the effort to learn it, but we all really hope it takes off.

Surprisingly it's Georgina who initially starts Ben and me communicating again, after a kiss-and-tell appears online on the day after the Southmoor defeat in which she says she realised there was something wrong with their relationship when it became obvious he was avoiding sleeping with her.

'There I was thinking he must be some kind of sex god

because of all the women he's been with, but it turns out he doesn't even like doing it,' she is quoted as saying.

He sends me the link on WhatsApp. No words, just the link. I presume it's because he wants to prove there was never any intimacy between them.

'*Don't like sex? You?*' I type. Then I delete it, preferring to keep my reply light, and instead I write, '*I guess that's blown your chances with Margot Robbie.*'

'*I hope I can get a refund on my Ken costume,*' he writes back, referencing her role in the *Barbie* movie.

I can't help smiling. '*Maybe see if they've got a Harry Styles you can exchange it for. Everyone loves a bit of Harry.*'

He sends some party-popper emojis. '*Finally, I get to be in the boy band.*'

It's a sweet reminder of all the daft back and forths we used to have and it makes me miss him. Perhaps for the first time it gets me thinking about what I'd gain if we did rekindle our relationship. I don't say as much to him though. I don't want to give him false hope when I still don't really believe it's feasible.

It's me who initiates our next conversation – after an email arrives in my inbox that is either the greatest birthday present I could ever dream up for my dad's fiftieth birthday this week, or a cruel prank someone's decided to play on my family. Even after I've read it three times I'm not still sure which, so I don't know whether to be excited or exasperated by it.

I desperately want another opinion, but I don't want to talk to Dad – or anyone else involved with Crawford for that matter – till I know whether or not it's someone yanking my chain. Phoebs is out too, because I know she

327

wouldn't be able to keep it from Craig. So I use it as an excuse to ring Ben, because I know he'll be able to look at it objectively.

'This is a nice surprise,' he says, when he answers my call.

'I've been sent a weird email,' I announce without preamble. 'Can I read it to you? I need someone else to tell me if it sounds genuine.'

'Okay.' He sounds suspicious – as perhaps he should be. Because the email purports to be from the author Alasdair Frowley and its contents could have a huge impact on the future of Crawford United.

'It starts off very believable,' I tell him. 'Frowley explains that he writes the Inspector Marlowe books and *Dying Days* on Netflix. Then it says, "What you might not know is that I spent some time in Hamcott in my youth and have followed Hamcott Park ever since."' But we did know that because Helen from the *Herald* told us about it.

'He goes on to say he's lost respect for the club since the owners started treating it like a profit-making machine, and that he still holds on to the romantic view that a football club should be the beating heart of a community – which is why he now wants to throw his support behind Crawford United. I'll read you the rest . . .

'"I would have been in touch sooner but I've been shut away on a six-week writing retreat so I'm only just catching up with what's going on in the real world. And I was thrilled when I learned about Crawford United. I had a brief dabble with playing football at this level myself when I was younger – and a lot fitter – so I'm well aware how important these new clubs are to amateur players like me."'

Then comes the exciting bit. '"It was hard enough back then for managers to keep their clubs going, so I can only imagine how tough it is now with the ever-changing regulations and escalating costs. The regulations I have no control over, but the costs are where I can hopefully make a difference.

'"As you can see, life has taken me on a very different path since I was a young lad kicking a ball around on Hamcott Common and I now find myself in the very privileged position of having more money than I know what to do with. I'd like to use some of it to ensure Crawford Football Club keeps going – and, if I'm honest, to stick two fingers up at the owners of Hamcott Park."'

And next comes the reason for my scepticism. '"So I'll be making a significant donation to your crowdfund in the next few days and I wanted to give you a heads up first so you're not alarmed when it drops in. Rest assured it comes with no strings attached. It's a good old-fashioned gift from someone who's been lucky financially and would like to pay it forward."'

It concludes with: '"When I'm next back in Hamcott, after I've finished going over the latest *Dying Days* scripts, I'll be sure to catch a Crawford United game. It would be an honour to meet the founders while I'm there too, should that be convenient. And in the meantime, come on The Phoenixes!"

'So what do you reckon?' I ask Ben, who's stayed silent on the other end of the phone – either because he's as stunned as I was or because he thinks it's nonsense and doesn't want to break it to me. 'Obviously I'd love it to be real, but if Helen could find out Frowley was a Hamcott fan, anyone could, so it could just be the most elaborate wind-up ever written. And it does make me think of that old adage: if it sounds too good to be true, it probably is.'

Ben puffs out a mouthful of air. 'I hope for Crawford's sake it *is* real, but it does sound quite far-fetched. Have you looked at your crowdfund to see if this significant sum is showing up yet?'

'I have and it isn't. But the email does say in the next few days and I've only just received it.'

'Have you tried confirming it via his agent?'

'It's four o'clock in the morning over there at the moment. I keep thinking, though, if this isn't from Frowley, who would send it? Some of Dad's friends must know he's a massive Frowley fan, so this could be someone's idea of a joke for his fiftieth. Or maybe they are going to make a donation but they want to do it anonymously.

'I don't think it's a scam because the sender hasn't requested our bank details for the transfer. And the only other person I can think of is Craig's dad – masquerading as the author in another attempt to future-proof his son's place on the team. But he definitely isn't the type to hide behind an impersonation.'

'I guess all you can do is wait and see,' Ben says. 'And try not to get too excited about what you could do with the money until you know exactly what the deal is.'

I laugh, because he knows me so well. I'm already thinking that if it's as large a sum as is hinted at, I could work up a plan that would make the club sustainable for the next few years, with no loan repayments to cover for the ground share, plus we could start paying the players a nominal sum per match. We could possibly even look at adding a women's team.

And what if I could become a full-time salaried employee? There'd be no more needing to squeeze running Crawford in around another job – which I could probably manage in the short term with a lot of help from Marge, but couldn't sustain indefinitely, unless I resigned myself to having no social life, boyfriend or hobbies.

In other words, if this email is real, it could change everything. But Ben's right – it's still a very big if. He agrees I should sit on it until I know one way or the other.

'So what else has been keeping you busy?' he asks, and I'm sure what he's really asking is whether I've had any further thoughts about me and him.

The truth is, I'm more conflicted than ever, swinging wildly between wishing we could go back to our original plans for getting together on Sundays and never again wanting to deal with the anxiety our long-distance relationship gave me. I think, deep down, that by delaying that conversation, what I've been trying to do is reach a point where it won't hurt so much to say no to him, and yet it feels like we still have unfinished business.

'Phoebs is organising a bash for Dad's birthday,' I answer, to stop the conversation from getting heavy. 'I've got a feeling she's really pushing the boat out for it.'

I explain about her party planning business proposition and how she hopes Dad's do will give her a launch pad.

'Does your dad know?' Ben asks.

'He knows there'll be drinks, but he doesn't know about the balloon arch, fancy canapés and live band. And Phoebs has commissioned Barbour's wife to do another football trophy cake too, this time with Crawford United etched into it.'

'I can't see him going crazy over the balloon arch,' Ben admits, 'but the cake sounds perfect for him.'

'It should be a fun night. We're doing it in a marquee in the garden at The Fox. All the Crawford players are coming. It's a shame you can't be here for it.'

It slips out before I think about what I'm saying and I freeze, breath held, heart thumping in my chest. I hadn't intended to get into this.

'I'd like to be there,' he says quietly.

My voice softens too. 'It's on a Thursday. There's no way.'

'The distance thing,' he says solemnly.

And I nod, even though he can't see me. 'The distance thing.'

'Well, let me know how it goes,' he says, forcing some brightness back into his voice. 'And keep me posted about the mysterious Mr Frowley.'

'Absolutely.' I try to sound just as upbeat. And then, because I don't know how else to end the conversation, I just thank him for letting me waffle on about it.

45

I decide not to contact Frowley's agent in the end, preferring to keep the dream alive for as long as possible before the email is potentially exposed as a fake. If I've heard nothing more by Friday, I'll know either way anyway. But that doesn't stop me from checking the crowdfund account about once an hour, just in case.

It's the morning of Dad's birthday when the money does drop in. I don't know if this is pure coincidence or if Frowley somehow managed to find out about the date. I bet if he trawled through my Facebook posts he'd find a reference to one of Dad's previous birthdays, but would anyone go to that much effort?

I'm not sure how long I stare at the amount on the screen, but it's long enough for my bowl of cereal to become too soggy to enjoy. There are more noughts than I ever could have imagined seeing in our account. How we'll thank Frowley I have no idea.

There's enough to set out a salary for Cassie and Dad as well as me, should they want to leave their jobs. And we can now think seriously about club merchandising, which didn't seem viable in the beginning when we'd only sold a couple of hundred season tickets, but now we know we've got a solid following, it would be great to make scarves and football shirts available to the fans. We want them to be able to wear the official team colours and feel as much a part of the team as we do.

I can't wait to see the players' faces light up when we tell them what this means for their bank balances, and before that to blow the minds of Cassie, Bob, Marge and Barbour, who I know will be as astounded as I am. But before all that, there's the one person I look forward to sharing this momentous news with more than anyone else and that, of course, is Dad.

I shout up the stairs at him. 'Can you come down here a minute please. Something big's happening.'

He walks into the kitchen with shaving foam still covering half his face. 'What is it?'

'Let me start by asking if you could have one thing for your birthday, what would it be?'

'A win for Crawford United?'

'Well, that's kind of what this is.'

I'm shaking with adrenaline as I turn my laptop screen towards him. I watch him crane his neck closer then his hand flies to his mouth, most of the remaining shaving foam ending up on his fingers as his jaw drops open. 'Is that real?'

A Cheshire cat grin takes over my face as I nod and show him Frowley's email. His eyes grow wide in disbelief.

'We'd better send him a season ticket,' he says eventually, which makes me want to hug him. Of course that would be the first thing he thinks of.

'I've compiled a thank you message, but I'll try to set up

a video call as well so we can thank him more personally. Maybe on Sunday, when you and Cassie aren't working, if that fits in with Frowley.'

'Have you told your sister yet?' Dad asks.

'Her phone's always off while she's teaching. But we can fill her in this evening – she's coming here first before the party.'

Dad squints at my laptop again then shakes his head. 'I'm not sure this has really sunk in yet,' he confesses.

'It took me a while to stop thinking it was somebody messing with us, too. But now all I can think about is reworking Crawford United's budgets.'

'Why don't we put our heads together now,' he suggests.

'Is that really how you want to spend your birthday?'

'I could think of worse ways,' he says. 'And it might help me to get my head around this.'

While he finishes shaving, I send my thank you note to Alasdair. It starts by apologising for being so slow to respond and admitting I was initially suspicious about the authenticity of his email, adding that I hope he won't be offended by this.

I express our gratitude and tell him how proud we are of Crawford United, share some of the highs and lows of the team's journey so far and spell out our hopes for the future, which now looks much rosier thanks to his generosity.

I sign off with the suggestion of a video call and say we'd all be delighted to meet him.

I know there won't be an immediate response – it's about one o'clock in the morning in Los Angeles – and to be honest I don't expect to hear back from him this side of the weekend, given how long it took me to reply to him. But while I'm waiting for Dad to finish making himself a cup of coffee, Alasdair's name pops up again in my inbox. I click to open the message and feel the skin prickling all over my body as I read what he's written.

'Er, Dad.' My voice wobbles. 'We might need to get some extra security in for the match against Ashbridge on Saturday.'

Dad frowns. 'Have their fans got a bit of a reputation?'

'It's not that. Alasdair Frowley has already come back to me. He's apparently more embarrassed than I was that I thought his email was a hoax, and says he can see now how he could have gone about this better. So he's flying to London for an impromptu visit, to introduce himself to us properly. And he wants to make sure he catches a game while he's here, so he's arriving tomorrow evening.'

'And coming to the Ashbridge game? So I'm actually going to meet him?' Dad exclaims.

'It looks like your dream is coming true.'

He chuckles softly, eyes sparkling. 'What a birthday this is turning out to be. I don't think security will be a problem though, will it? How many people really know what authors look like?'

'He's not coming alone,' I tell him, still not quite able to believe who's going to be accompanying him. 'Apparently he's having a late-night drink with some of the *Dying Days* cast right now, and when he started talking about his love of soccer, Angela Paramore mentioned she's never been to a match before. So he asked if she wants to rectify that, and she's decided she's going to join him.'

Dad leans back against the kitchen counter and lets out a low whistle. 'Today just keeps on giving. So we now have my favourite author and one of the most famous actresses on both sides of the Atlantic coming to sit with us in our uncomfortable plastic seats for the best part of two hours while our lads face the club that's held the top spot in the league for something like six consecutive years. Do you think we should order in some cushions?'

'I'm not worried about whether their bums go numb!' I exclaim.

'So you think we should put a message out on the website to say we need a few extra volunteer stewards? There's got to be a couple of bruisers among our fans who'd be willing to stand around looking burly in exchange for a free pitchside view of the game.'

'Did you just say *bruisers*?' I roll my eyes. Sometimes Dad stops being a football club manager and is just my dad again. 'I think we might have to hire official event staff on this occasion, for insurance purposes. We need people we can rely on, and we can afford it now, thanks to Alasdair.'

'Good point. Okay, get it booked in. Do you think we should ask them if they want to stay at ours?' he asks.

I assume he means Angela and Alasdair, not the 'bruisers', and I can't help laughing. 'I don't think Cassie's old bedroom is quite going to cut it when they're used to LA mansions and five-star hotels.'

'They'll miss out on my breakfast special.' He sounds affronted.

'I'm sure Claridge's, or wherever it is celebrities stay these days, will put on a decent spread. You can always bring a half-time snack to the game if you feel the need to show off your culinary skills.'

He takes a deep breath and shakes his head again.

'Angela Paramore – who would have thought it? You know, I didn't think I was going to like turning fifty but it turns out I'm really quite enjoying it.' Then he laughs softly to himself. 'I might even treat myself to a haircut.'

By the time Cassie arrives at the house so we can all head to Dad's party together, he has finally got used to the idea that he's going to meet one of his idols and that Crawford United is now one of the most well-funded football clubs in the lower leagues. Once she's got over the fact that we didn't share any of this news with her immediately – 'You were at school!' I protest – Cassie goes through the same series of emotions as Dad and I, from disbelief to gradual acceptance to: 'I don't think I'll ever stop smiling.'

As I watch them bouncing round the kitchen I find myself wishing Ben could have been here. It's a moment I would have loved to share with him. I fire off a quick text to let him know the Frowley saga has panned out even better than I could have hoped for. He replies straight away, saying he's so glad everything is working out for me. But looking at the kisses he's added afterwards, I can't help thinking, *Not everything*.

That evening, Phoebs' party set-up is incredible. She's gone all out with a purple theme, from the balloon arch to the plates for the nibbles. There's a purple welcome cocktail – a mix of champagne, blue curacao and red grenadine, aka a Meet Me At Midnight, she informs me – and the band she's hired kicks off with a rousing rendition of Jimi Hendrix's 'Purple Haze' and ends with an impressive cover of Prince's 'Purple Rain'.

All the players come to wish Dad a happy birthday, as well as Bob, Marge and Adam, Barbour and his family,

Olly – who's left his assistant manager in charge in the main bar – a few other fans we've got to know at The Fox and a handful of Dad's colleagues. Phoebs flits about taking photos, making sure glasses stay full and ensuring the table of party food remains presentable.

There are more balloons above it, along with purple candles – far enough away from the balloons that they won't pop – and two glass jars filled with white and purple fairy lights and two containing purple orchids. If anyone dares upset the ambience with a discarded paper plate or napkin, she sweeps it away and quickly disposes of it.

She's pleased as punch with her efforts when I manage to get her on her own for a minute. 'Look at your dad's face.' She beams. 'He's loving it.'

I glance over to see him surveying the room, eyes bright as he soaks up the scene. Then he's swept back up into a conversation with Bob, Marge and Barbour, who take it in turns to clink their glasses against his.

'It does look amazing,' I tell her. 'I hope you haven't got yourself into debt doing all this.'

She tells me Craig gave her some money to help get her new business off the ground.

'He doesn't even care whether I pay him back or not, but I will once I start making a profit,' she admits. 'He says it's enough that he's making his dad happy by finally showing an interest in investing in a local business. Even if it ends up being the only time he does it. He's been brilliant, to be honest – really encouraging me to build something where I can be my own boss. Without the two of you, I might never have chanced it.'

'Does this mean you're finally going to admit you're in love with him?' I ask.

'God no, he'd probably run a mile if I said the L word to him.'

She laughs, but I notice she automatically seeks him out in the crowd. And as if he can feel her eyes on him, he looks across and winks. I may still think he's a bit on the cocky side, but I have to admit he's grown on me since I've seen how he looks out for Phoebs.

I scan the room, taking in all the happy faces, until I realise I'm subconsciously looking for the one person who to my mind has a bigger smile than everybody. But of course I don't find him, because Ben isn't here.

46

My stomach is in knots on the day of our Ashbridge game, and I don't think I'm alone in that. Dad can't sit still, pacing the corridor outside the locker room while we wait for the last of our players to arrive, and Cassie's just as fidgety, glancing at the wall clock every two or three minutes. After six straight losses, we're in desperate need of a win today. And with Alasdair and Angela here to watch us, it would be a good time for a victory.

We've called the team to the ground earlier than usual because we don't know exactly what time our star guests will arrive and we want to make sure we're all there to greet them. We're also ready to share the news of Alasdair's donation with the players, having calculated what we'll now be able to pay them for the rest of the season. We're hopeful it will give them a much-needed boost.

Dad claps to get everyone's attention once the team is fully assembled. 'Just a couple of club announcements today before we get started. First, as ever, a huge thank you to all of you for everything you put into Crawford

341

United. We haven't got off to the easiest of starts, but I want you all to know my faith in this club is unwavering.

'And that's why it's an absolute privilege for me to be able to tell you that there are no longer any question marks hanging over our longevity. Thanks to an incredible donation from the author Alasdair Frowley this week, I'm now in a position to extend our contract here at Redmarsh to a minimum five-year tenure, which means Crawford United is here to stay.'

There are whoops across the room.

'Way to go,' Levi says with a grin.

'Is that our best result so far?' Jacob asks cheekily.

Dad laughs. 'I think it might well be.'

He holds up his hands for silence again. 'Back to the serious stuff, though. We want you to know this isn't going to change anything in the way we run things. All it means from our side is that Cassie, Lily and I will now be official staff, not just volunteers. My title will officially be manager, Cassie is head coach and Lily is club secretary and treasurer.'

'Do we have to start calling you sir?' Adio asks.

Dad looks horrified. 'Always just Mike if you don't mind.'

'Yes, sir,' Adio says, laughing.

'Thump him, will you, Elliot?' Dad requests, then waits till everyone has settled again before continuing. 'Lily will be looking after the day-to-day running of the club full-time. Cassie and I will be maintaining our other jobs, but all three of us are dedicated to making this club the success it absolutely deserves to be.

'We can't do that on our own though, of course, which is where you lot come in. The time and energy you've each devoted to this club has never gone unappreciated. So it gives me immense pleasure to be able to tell you that going forward there'll be a fixed payment per match, regardless of your position or how long you're on the pitch. And as an extra thank you, we'll be backdating it to the start of the season.'

'Get in!' Thomas punches the air.

'You can give up your paper round now, Jacob,' Craig teases.

'There's more,' Dad calls out, commanding their attention one last time. 'Frowley is coming here to watch the game today, so you'll have the opportunity to meet him. And he's bringing a special guest with him.' When he reveals it's Angela Paramore, it sparks a round of wolf whistles.

'So I want us to really bring our A game this afternoon. Let's show them what we're made of. I *know* we can do better than we have done so far. Now it's time for us to get out there and prove it.'

'We've got this,' Thomas says, his voice full of confidence.

And an equally fired-up Craig adds, 'We're ready for it.'

But there's still no sign of Alasdair and Angela when it's time for the team to start warming up on the pitch, leaving me fearful they've changed their minds about coming and that our players might lose their earlier momentum.

When they eventually arrive mere minutes before the starting whistle, flanked by our last-minute security guards, I'm almost too relieved to speak. They make their way to the seats alongside me and Dad, and Frowley is immediately full of apologies. 'We had such good intentions, but it's not always easy getting through a crowd with Angela.'

Which is no great surprise given how striking she looks in her purple jumpsuit, with her black hair cascading down her back.

'It only takes one person to ask for an autograph and it starts an avalanche,' Frowley explains. 'But your chaps were very efficient at whisking us through once it started looking like we were in danger of missing the kick-off.'

'Or like *they* were,' Dad corrects, making Frowley chuckle.

Dad holds his hand out. 'Mike Crawford.'

'A pleasure,' Frowley says, then reaches across to shake hands with me, before insisting we call him by his first name.

'And Angela,' the actress says. And I notice she's even done her nails purple as she puts her perfectly manicured hand in Dad's then mine. 'I'm so excited to be here. I even learned the offside rule on the flight over to make sure I don't say anything stupid.'

'Eleven hours well spent,' Dad says with a supersized grin.

I'm slightly in awe of the effort she's made when I'm just in a Crawford sweater and jeans, but I stop feeling self-consciousness as soon as she's on her feet shouting encouragement as loudly as the rest of us when Craig and Jamie make it into the penalty box an unprecedented three times in the first twenty minutes. Suddenly we're just two people who want the same thing.

But it's agonising for our strikers. The Ashbridge goalie is probably the best in the league and pulls off a series of frustratingly brilliant saves. Then we have to brace ourselves for their counter-attacks and they push themselves back up the pitch with annoyingly impressive speed. But credit where credit's due – Elliot plays the game of his life. Without him we could easily be five–nil down by half-time.

My adrenaline is pumping as we clap the players off the pitch. If I was someone who bit my fingernails I think they'd be down to the cuticles after the last forty-five minutes. Angela's face is glowing as she asks me if now would be a good time to meet the players. 'Or would that be too distracting? If they've got a strict routine to follow, I don't want to interfere.'

I honestly don't know the right answer. Cassie will be delivering her usual pep talk in the locker room. Will Angela's presence disconcert the team or inspire them? In the end, I decide there's nothing to lose.

Alasdair stays pitchside with Dad, keen to hear more about how we're planning to use his donation, and our security guys head off to find refreshments as the corridor to the locker room is not open to fans. Angela's animated chatter about the match as we walk reminds me of how giddy I used to feel when Dad first started taking me to see Hamcott Park.

'It's so much more dramatic than baseball,' she says. 'You do usually get a good atmosphere in the bigger baseball arenas, but even if it starts off entertaining it just goes on and on – and it's so repetitive. I'd say it's worth seeing once if you haven't seen it before, but I can't imagine devoting every weekend to it like you guys do with your football.

'The last time I went with my boyfriend it lasted more

than five hours. Can you imagine? I could have flown from Los Angeles to New York in the time it took the LA Angels to win. There's no ebb and flow like we've been seeing today. Maybe I should persuade him to start watching LA Galaxy instead. I've never thought about it before, but I could really see myself getting into it.'

We arrive at the locker room and I shout out 'incoming' before pushing open the door, to give everyone inside fair warning. But while I'm expecting to find the players sitting on the benches while Cassie runs through what she wants to see next from them, it only occurs to me when I'm confronted by the sight of eleven bums pointing up towards the ceiling – not as terrible a view as it might sound – that it had been too quiet for Cassie to have been mid-speech.

She registers the alarm on my face as our eyes meet, but when I spin round to tell Angela it's not a good time to meet the players after all, it's too late, she's already followed me in.

'Oh gosh,' she exclaims. 'This is more than I bargained for.'

'We're doing some yoga,' Cassie explains.

'Now?' I ask, incredulously.

'I thought I'd try something different,' she explains. 'Rather than trying to hype everyone up, we're working on grounding ourselves so we can focus better.'

'Oh, that's exactly what I like to do before a big scene,' Angela says. 'It stops me from panicking about whether I'll fluff my lines or not. I highly recommend it.'

The sound of her voice has the nearest players scrambling to their feet. I watch Scott and Jacob smoothing down their tops and sweeping their hands through their hair. I don't think I've ever seen Levi smile so broadly.

'I love you in *Dying Days*,' he gushes, thumping his chest. 'Big fan.'

'Playing it cool as always,' Craig mutters, rolling his eyes.

Angela laughs. 'It's always lovely to hear. I hope you'll all forgive the intrusion today. I've got such a fascination with what goes on behind the scenes. I think it comes from being on TV and knowing how different the reality is to what you get to see on screen.'

'It's not usually like this,' Craig tells her.

'But if it helps you guys be even more awesome, then it's got to be worth it, right?'

'Exactly, so how about you get back into position,' Cassie says, her voice commanding. 'Hands to the floor, buns back in the air please. Two more minutes of downward dog then we'll have just enough time for dancer pose, then tree.'

She catches my eye again and winks at me as the players drop back on to all fours. Angela smiles approvingly and says, 'That's how to boss it.'

'I'm just going to film a bit of this for the fan site,' I tell them, and Angela asks if I'd like her to join in with the team for it.

'I don't imagine the floor is particularly clean.'

'Hands can be washed,' she says brightly, 'and there's no harm in letting people see my fun side every now and again.'

The resulting footage later becomes our most-watched reel.

Hamstrings stretched, Cassie gets everyone into dancer

pose to work on their thighs. While Angela is perfectly poised, with one leg raised up behind her, the same can't be said for Jacob or Elliot, who wobble precariously next to her. It gives Elliot the giggles, which sets everyone else off. It makes me optimistic that Cassie may be onto something here. The team definitely seem to be leaving the stress of the match behind them.

'Last up, tree,' Cassie instructs. And this time Angela makes her way round the room while everyone's balancing, telling each player how privileged she feels to meet them. It's so humble, given that she's the star, and I think they all fall a little bit in love with her.

Back out on the pitch, our fans have another surprise in store for us. As the lads fire themselves back up with a few short sprints, the crowd launches into a rendition of our new team song. It makes my heart swell. The sound of four thousand voices echoing round the ground in support of our players will never grow old.

'Come on, boys,' I whisper under my breath, crossing my fingers in my lap as the referee blows the whistle and the second half gets underway. They so deserve a break. Please let it be today.

But it's a fraught first ten minutes for our team as Ashbridge waste no time piling on the pressure. They quickly close in on anyone who gets the ball in midfield until it's back in their possession. Twice they break away from our defenders and race towards the goal, and we only get away with their first surge forward thanks to a poorly taken header. The second onslaught is even more gut-wrenching as the ball skims the top of the net with mere inches to spare.

'It's giving me palpitations,' Angela admits and I think we all share that sentiment.

Our fans step their chanting up a notch and the team song rings out round the stadium. Spurred on by their support, Nico manages to keep hold of the ball long enough to reach the thirty-yard mark, but it's almost like he's so surprised to find himself there that he doesn't know what to do next and Ashbridge take full advantage of his hesitation, leaving Crawford on the back foot yet again.

Some solid teamwork from Thomas and Jacob puts things back in our favour, and this time Bailey weaves his way through the opposition with a timely display of the skill for which we selected him in the first place.

'That's my boy,' I murmur. 'You can do it.'

But when he passes the ball wide to Adio, instead of running with it Adio decides to fire a wild ball down the pitch in the hope it'll be picked up by Craig.

I think everyone watching feels their heart sink, believing he should have just kept hold of it as both Craig and the Ashbridge defenders tear after it. But it's the seventy-seventh minute, legs are starting to get tired and it turns out Craig just has the edge.

The Crawford fans leap to their feet, hollering 'come on' at him as he gets to the ball first.

'Keep your cool now, don't rush it,' I murmur, on the edge of my seat as his teammates scramble up the pitch to help him.

But Craig isn't waiting. He deftly switches the ball to his right foot and pelts it towards the goal when he's still some distance away, and for a second you could hear a pin drop as four thousand fans hold their breath.

We follow its arc with our eyes, willing it – for once – to go in, and there's a horror second in which we all hear the clink of metal that tells us he's hit the post yet again. But just as disappointment is about to send everyone slumping back into their seats, the ball ricochets awkwardly, slips through the goalkeeper's fingers and drops into the back of the net. I can't even describe the euphoria or the volume of the cheering as Craig slides across the grass on his knees in celebration.

I get goose bumps at the sight of all the dancing, hugging and even tears in the stands, while the rest of the team pile on top of Craig on the pitch. We've done it! We have finally broken the dry spell that's plagued Crawford United since the beginning of the season and scored our first ever goal. I'd say it's just about the happiest I've ever been.

There's an agonising wait for the clock to tick down after that. The fightback from Ashbridge is relentless, with no less than three shots on target, and I can feel the tension throughout my whole body, my hands balled into fists, my knees squeezed together, my jaw clenched. But Thomas and Levi defend as if their lives depend on it, and Elliot makes the save of the match, flinging himself into the path of the ball in the closing minutes as if he's trying to save a family member from a flying bullet.

I don't think I've ever been more relieved than when I hear the three long whistles from the referee to signal the end of the game. As the crowd erupts, Dad, Cassie and I race out on to the pitch, throwing our arms round the players who haven't sunk to their knees as if they've just won the FA Cup. It's been such a long time coming. It is *such* a relief. And to have won against the top team in the league only makes the victory sweeter.

If Ashbridge are in any way put out by our over-the-top celebration, they don't show it. They were here too once upon a time, so they know how much it means. When Dad and I have finally calmed down a bit, their managers congratulate us on a brilliantly played game and wish us well for the rest of the season.

Back in the dugout, Angela and Alasdair are equally full of praise, but I'm lost for words. 'I just . . . I can't . . . Thank you so much for being here today,' I finally manage. 'I genuinely think it made a difference.'

'Oh no, we're not taking any of the credit for this,' Angela says. 'This was all on you guys.'

'And there I was just about to ask if you could come back again next weekend,' Dad says.

She smiles warmly. 'I'm flattered, but I think the *Dying Days* production team would have something to say about it if we're not back on set on Monday.'

She and Alasdair spend a bit longer chatting to our delighted players before they thank us again for our hospitality and are escorted back to their waiting car. Levi does try to persuade them to come to The Fox, but they've both got friends to catch up with while they're on this side of the Atlantic, which is probably just as well because when we arrive at the pub it's already mobbed.

Ben calls me while I'm queuing at the bar. 'Wow, it's loud there,' he says when I answer.

'There's quite the party kicking off,' I explain.

'And so there should be. I've just seen the score on your website. You must be buzzing.'

'We all are. It was such a brilliant afternoon.'

'Hopefully the first of many. Please pass my congratulations on to all the others. I'd love to be having a celebratory drink with you. I'll actually be in Hamcott in a couple of hours, so I could always drop in to The Fox for last orders, if that felt okay to you.'

Just the thought of it makes my heart race. It's nearly six weeks since we've been in the same room as each other. I know we've been talking more lately, but I don't know whether seeing him in person will upset me or give me closure – and I'm not sure I want to find out with the whole of Crawford United watching.

'How long are you down for?' I ask.

'I've got my grandparents' anniversary lunch tomorrow, then I'll head back in the afternoon.' Sensing the vibe, he says, 'We can meet for breakfast tomorrow morning, if that would be easier. But I would really love to see you.'

'Breakfast sounds good,' I tell him, even though my insides have turned to jelly.

He promises to have a full English ready at his place at ten thirty.

47

My heart pounds in my chest as I stand on his doorstep, finger on the buzzer. Memories of all the great times we had here tug at my heartstrings. Cake night, snuggling up on the sofa, that first kiss out in the swimming pool – I was so damn happy. Maybe agreeing to meet at his place was an error.

I tell myself it's just breakfast, just the Whitehouse, just a guy I used to love. He might even feel like a stranger after not seeing him for so long.

But no matter how many times I repeat 'it's going to be fine' in my head, I'm unprepared for the thunderbolt that shakes me to the core when he opens the door and I'm finally faced with that oh-so-familiar smile. I almost feel like turning and bolting as I realise I'm not even close to being over him. I shouldn't have come. It's too heart-wrenching.

He leans forward as if to kiss me, then checks himself and steps aside to let me in.

'Come on through,' he says. 'Breakfast's nearly ready.'

I take a deep breath, will myself to be strong and follow him into the kitchen.

Our first words to each other, while he's making egg tortillas to wrap our breakfast burritos in, are polite and stilted – the traffic on my journey over, where his family are going for lunch later; we even talk about the weather, which has suddenly turned autumnal. He asks if I want him to turn the heating up at the same time as I admit I might not take my coat off yet. It makes us laugh, breaking the ice despite reminding me how often we used to share similar thoughts.

I think we've both relaxed a bit more by the time we've got plates of food in front of us, and while we're eating he asks me about my dad's party, the win at Ashbridge and whether Dad managed to keep his cool in front of his hero, Frowley.

'He was fine once I'd talked him out of asking Alasdair to sign one of his books,' I admit. 'He even came round to thinking it should actually be him getting all the players to sign a Crawford shirt for Alasdair. So he's going to sort that out this week and get it posted to him.'

'What was Angela like?' Ben asks.

'Unexpectedly normal. I could imagine having a pint with her at The Fox. But at the same time there's something enigmatic about her – you know that thing you can't quite put your finger on that just makes everyone warm to her.'

A bit like you, I find myself thinking.

'A bit like me,' he says, grinning.

I wonder if he guesses why this makes my cheeks flush.

'But what happened at your match yesterday?' I ask, quickly changing the subject. 'I saw on *Top Goals* that you came off at half-time. You didn't hurt yourself, did you?'

'Not at all, it's just a thing the new coach likes to do. I think it's designed to stop me from getting too big for my boots.'

'Is it working?' I ask.

'Of course not. I know my value. I tell you what though – your boys at Crawford don't know how lucky they are having Cassie as their coach. This guy might be more experienced, but I reckon he must have had to deal with some tough love in his childhood and now the rest of us are getting a taste of it. But annoyingly we just have to suck it up because he's getting the results, so Millford aren't about to get rid of him.'

'Well I'll pass the compliment on to Cassie anyway. She'll be happy to hear it.'

'So what else is new at the club?' Ben asks. 'Does Barbour still bring Barbour Junior to watch you play?'

'He does. But Nathan insists on supporting Millford as well as Crawford after you gave him that ball. He says he'll only pick a favourite when Crawford reaches the Premier League – which he's adamant should happen just in time for his fifteenth birthday, when he thinks he'll be old enough to make the right decision. I don't think he's calculated this would mean us getting eight promotions in twelve years.' I wince at the thought of it. 'No one has the heart to tell him he might be nearer fifty.'

'Nothing wrong with aiming high. It's one of the things I really miss about Crawford – there's something so refreshing about having everything to play for as opposed to just trying to cling on to what you've already achieved.'

'I've never thought of it like that. But you're right – the only way is up when you come from such humble beginnings.'

'I miss seeing you there every week too,' he says, and time seems to stand still as our eyes lock. I miss him too, my God do I miss him. But our circumstances haven't changed. Even the thought of leaving here today makes me acutely aware of how hard it would be to have to say goodbye to him every Sunday.

'We could try being friends,' I suggest. 'Maybe catch up over a drink when you're down here, keep in touch with the occasional text.'

It's heartbreaking seeing how this seems to deflate him. He shakes it off though. 'If it's friends or nothing, I'd rather take friends.'

Suddenly unsure what else to say to each other, I thank him for breakfast and tell him I should probably get going. 'I'm meeting Phoebs after,' I explain. I thought I might need the distraction after seeing Ben.

He smiles and says, 'Yeah, and I've got my lunch to get ready for. Nan will give me grief if I turn up late or look too scruffy.'

'Tell her I said hello.' I thread my arms back into my jacket sleeves. 'And to your parents.'

'Of course, and likewise to Mike and Cassie.' There's a pause, then he adds, 'It was really good to see you again, Lily.'

'You too.' I try not to sound as flustered as I feel as I turn towards the door.

He follows me to see me out, and when I fumble with the lock, he quickly comes to my rescue, his hand brushing against mine as he reaches across to release the catch for me. I freeze. I can hear him breathing right behind me. It would be so easy to turn round and step into his arms. But I don't.

A tear threatens to escape as I stand there, wishing things could be different, then I pull myself together. 'Good luck with the rest of the season,' I tell him as I step out into the fresh air. I don't look over my shoulder as I walk back down the driveway. I don't want to see the look I know will be on his face.

48

We exchange a few texts over the following week and although it comes with a bit of heartache I do find myself looking forward to hearing from him. I know the pain will fade eventually and until then I've got Crawford United to keep me from really dwelling on it.

He wishes me luck on the morning of our next away game. Kidstow came twelfth in last year's table, so they should be easier to beat than Ashbridge, and we'll just gloss over the fact that we lost games to teams lower down in the league before that. That was when we were still finding our feet – today there's a new-found confidence on the coach journey to the match.

There's an inevitable rise in pressure too – not quite an expectation for the lads to repeat last week's success, but now we've had a taste of triumph I think everyone is aware it will feel doubly disappointing if we don't win.

We won't have the home advantage this week, but Kidstow is only half an hour away, so we're still expecting a lot of fan support. I wish that included Alasdair and

Angela. While it might have been the yoga or the new payroll plan that lifted team morale last Saturday, I still believe their presence helped spur the team on. This time, we're on our own.

Or so I think. Unbeknown to Dad, Cassie and I, Barbour has ordered fifty cardboard masks of Angela's face from Amazon and handed them out to everyone sitting around him, with the result that there are now somewhere in the region of fifty Angelas cheering on the team at today's game. I'm moved by the effort he's gone to and it gives me some more great photos for our website, especially when I capture a shot of them all throwing their arms up in unison as, for the first time in our very short history, Crawford scores a goal within the first twenty minutes.

This time it's Jamie who slips the ball past the keeper, although it's more by accident than design – it bounces off his head without him knowing too much about it. But it's still a goal and that's all that matters.

When we score again just fifteen minutes later, the Angelas are on their feet. Remarkably, they do seem to be having an effect. Going into the locker room two–nil up at half-time is such an invigorating feeling, not that Cassie is about to let the team get complacent. After she's praised them, she reminds them we're not out of the woods yet. 'There's still a lot of time left on that clock so your concentration and commitment are more critical than ever.'

Having decided to stick to her calming yoga plan, she leads them through the warrior poses and their variations, then makes sure everyone is properly hydrated before they return to battle.

At fifty-nine minutes Kidstow pull a goal back and I try to convince myself it's just a setback. But our rivals take full advantage of the resulting dip in mood and fire in an equaliser with just eight minutes remaining. Just like that, our lead slips away.

Our fans double down on their efforts to galvanise our players, belting out the Crawford team song over and over. And with mere seconds to go, Craig finally breaks through the Kidstow defenders, which has all of us on our feet, screaming at him to go all the way.

As he powers up the pitch I'm sure he's going to make it. But within metres of the goal, a sliding tackle sends him flying, arms and legs windmilling as he's literally propelled into the air. When he comes back down to the ground with a thump, I think every single fan winces as if bracing themselves for the fall, and there's a palpable gasp as he tumbles head over heels until the momentum finally runs out and he comes to a halt.

It's mere seconds but it feels like forever before he rolls on to his back and his body starts shaking. For a split second I'm terrified he's hit his head and is having a seizure, but I quickly realise that – be it from the shock, the realisation he's not hurt or the referee pointing to the penalty spot – Craig is trembling with laughter.

There's no protest from the opposition about the referee's decision. Their defender has left a two-metre skid mark in the grass, and Craig would deserve an Oscar if he'd pulled off a dive that jaw-dropping. Thomas pulls him to his feet, checks he's okay, then insists Craig takes the penalty as he's the one who forced the error.

Craig takes his time pulling his socks up, pushing his hair off his face and shaking the tension out of his arms.

The suspense is unbearable. We just need him to whip the ball into the top corner like we've practised at training and Crawford will snatch another victory.

But instead he ambles up to the penalty spot with a casualness that has me praying Cassie's yoga hasn't made him too zen, and in a moment that almost gives four thousand fans heart failure, he chooses to rely on wrongfooting the keeper and virtually dribbles the ball into the net.

It's bold, risky and unquestionably arrogant – not that I'd expect anything less from Craig – but thankfully it works and the crowd erupts all over again. Angela masks go flying into the air and sail down on to the pitch as the referee blows the final whistle. Our players run to the front of the stands, shaking their fists in the air and roaring along with the jubilant fans.

Had Craig missed, I think we all would have felt like he'd thrown the game away – and I imagine there'd have been some choice words from his teammates and some scathing comments on Instagram. But now? Now everyone's calling him bold rather than reckless and ignoring how very wrong it could have gone.

On the drive back to Hamcott, Dad confirms that for the first time this season, Crawford is no longer at the very bottom of the league table, and Thomas reminds everyone how honoured he is to be their team captain. I hope Olly's ready for another busy night at The Fox – today's result definitely calls for a party.

It turns out to be the first of many. Our victory over Kidstow marks the beginning of a winning streak that lasts for a record-breaking sixteen weeks and propels

Crawford right to the top of the league. Much to everyone's surprise, relief and delight, our rocky start to the season is forgotten. Every home match is a sell-out and the word 'miracle' is bandied about in the press. By the time we face Oakhampton for the second time we're feeling unbeatable.

Angela's legacy lives on, with many fans considering her to be our lucky charm and proudly wearing the Angela badges we now sell in our new online shop. Dad even starts hosting *Dying Days* evenings round our house on Sundays, with a couple of our players popping round to watch the latest episode each week, along with two or three of the fans who've applied to join us via the invite on our website. There's a pre-show prediction of who 'done it' and a ticket to the next Crawford fixture awarded to any fan who guesses correctly.

By far the best episode is the one where a model Crawford United phoenix makes a cameo on Inspector Marlowe's desk. I wonder if the producers notice or if Angela just slips it into a few scenes then quietly packs it away again before they realise.

By this point Ben and I have got into the habit of talking daily, sometimes on the phone, sometimes by text. He loves hearing about all of Crawford's successes, but admits the atmosphere in the Millford camp is increasingly tense. He hasn't been back to Hamcott for months because the new coach is still springing random team meetings on the squad on Sundays. He tells the players it's to keep them on their toes, but Ben reckons he's just on a power trip, because he still benches Ben periodically for no apparent reason and seems to have it in for at least half the team.

We also talk about Phoebs, who's started getting some party bookings off the back of Dad's fiftieth, and Cassie, who has finally set a date for her wedding. Ben tells me his nan is still trying her hardest to marry off Bailey – and that it might even happen one day if his relationship with Jasper keeps going from strength to strength.

Our conversations are back to being easy and funny, so I enjoy hearing from him every day. Of course there are occasional moments when I feel sad that things didn't work out differently, but I just remind myself to be grateful that we've managed to reach a point where he can still be in my life in some small way.

Phoebs worries it's stopping me from moving on, as I've shown no interest in dating anyone else.

'You must meet more men through your job than any other woman. Isn't there anyone you're even tempted by?' she asks. 'One of the other team's coaches, a manager, a little fling with a rival player? You could choose a different one every week if you don't want anything serious.'

My excuse is that this would hardly demonstrate loyalty to Crawford United, but the truth is, I can't yet imagine anything living up to the connection I felt with Ben. Nor do I feel ready to go through the pain of yet another romance not working out.

Ben and I mostly stay off the topic of our love lives. From time to time, he asks if I've started seeing anyone new, but it's always a very short conversation. I haven't. And I don't want to know if he has either. It's very much a case of ignorance is bliss.

Only once, around Christmas, does he ask if I could see us ever getting back together, and I understand why he says it. We get on so well, we always make each other laugh and sometimes it does still feel like we're perfect for each other. But I remind him things are good as they are. I'm happy and there are no complications.

'But if I was there?' he persists. 'If we could see each other more? You always said the biggest barrier was me being so far away.'

After talking to him so often, I'm comfortable enough to reply honestly. 'It was – and it still is. If our circumstances were different, I'd probably be the one suggesting we start over, but we can't live our lives by what-ifs.'

He drops it then, until the last week of January, when he's teasing me about my hangover on the day after Crawford's sixteenth win. It's just after midday and I'm not out of bed yet, thanks to another epic night at The Fox.

'What you need is a big bowl of chips and a foot massage in front of the telly,' he says.

'I'll call my masseuse and see if she's free.'

'I could offer you my services.'

'If only your arms were that long.' I sigh. 'I guess I'll have to make do with paracetamol.'

'What if I told you I was a lot nearer than you think?'

'Then I'd assume I'm still asleep and I'm just dreaming this conversation. I didn't think your coach let you pop down to Hamcott for the day any more.'

'He doesn't.' But then there's a pause and I hear him take a deep breath before he continues. 'But what if I told you I've quit?'

My first instinct is to laugh. 'You can't just quit Millford. What about your career?'

'You know I've not been happy there for a while now. So when the January transfer window opened, I started thinking about what *would* make me happy – and what came up most often, if I'm honest, was you. So I told them I was leaving and now . . . I'm here.'

My heart beats a little faster as I scramble upright. 'Here in Hamcott? But that's insanity. There isn't anywhere for you to play here.'

He's hardly going to join Crawford United for less than a hundred quid a week. And then I realise what's going on and flop back against the pillows, feeling foolish that I nearly fell for it. 'Oh my God, you are *such* a wind-up. You really had me going for a moment there.'

'It's not a wind-up,' he says, sounding affronted. 'Look out of your window. I really am here.'

'Nice try. You're not going to get me out from under my duvet that easily.'

I'm laughing again now, but when he stays silent on the other end of the phone, a sliver of doubt starts creeping in. I shuffle to the edge of the bed, pull my duvet round me like a giant cloak and pad across the room to the window, figuring it's high time I got up and faced the world anyway, so I might as well humour him.

My heart nearly stops when I see him in the street down below, smiling cautiously up at me. I stare at him wide-eyed, my mouth falling open. He looks as gorgeous as always and I'm unsettled by the way it gives me butterflies, even after all this time.

'Hi,' he says, still talking into the phone. 'I hope you don't mind me showing up unannounced like this.'

When I've recovered from the shock, I quickly rake my

fingers through my hair, wishing I'd brushed it. 'I thought you were joking.' He didn't even hint at this in any of our recent conversations. 'How long are you back for? Is it just until you find a new team to play for?'

It floors me again when he says, 'Maybe forever?'

And that's when I notice what he's wearing under his open jacket. 'Wait a minute . . . is that . . . is that a *Fulham* strip?' I ask, incredulously. I push the window open and lean out for a better look.

His smile gets even wider. He shrugs his jacket off, turns around and points at his back, where his name is printed above the number twelve. Spinning back round, he explains, 'They needed a new striker after De Freitas got nabbed by Chelsea. I had my transfer request signed before anyone else could get in there.'

'But that's absolutely incredible, Ben. Of all the clubs. You must be over the moon.'

He smooths the front of his shirt. 'Proudest moment of my career. I never even dreamed I'd have the opportunity to play for my own team.'

'I can't imagine how thrilled you must be. I'm so happy for you. Especially given the way Millford was going.'

'It had changed a lot since I started out there. There was a time when I thought I'd never want to leave that club, but I have a feeling I'm not about to regret it.' He hesitates for a moment. 'So I was wondering, now I'm going to be around a bit more . . . did you really mean it, all those times when you said there might be a chance for us if I didn't live two hundred miles away?'

And it's my turn to hesitate. Because although I've wished for this so many times, and seeing him is clearly doing funny things to my insides, wouldn't the sensible thing be not to upset the equilibrium now we've got ourselves to such a good place with each other?

But the part of me that still carries a torch for him argues that just because it unravelled the first time round, doesn't mean it would end in tears if we did try again. And if he's living just up the road . . .

As I look at him standing there, hope written all over his face, for the first time in a long time I stop trying to bury all the feelings I've worked so hard to suppress. I allow myself to picture us back together, to remember how we laughed, how much joy he brought into my life and how wonderful it felt to fall in love. And suddenly there's nothing I want more than to be back in his arms and have all of those things in my life again.

'I'm coming down,' I tell him, my hands trembling as I shrug myself out of my duvet. Then I race down the stairs, fling the front door open, and it feels like there are fireworks exploding all around me when I see him standing right in front of me on my doorstep.

'Nice pyjamas,' he says, his eyes sparkling.

'Nice football shirt,' I reply, excitement flooding through my veins.

'And if I'm not mistaken, it looks like you might be over your hangover.'

He's right – all traces have vanished. I nod my head. 'Never felt better.'

He takes a step nearer, his eyes not leaving mine. 'So what do you reckon? Do you think we could pick up where we left off now I'm going to be back in Redmarsh?'

'I think I could get used to the idea,' I tell him, a smile spreading across my face.

'Then I guess this is me officially asking you to be my girlfriend again,' he says, his grin widening to match mine.

And as I step into his arms, my body melting against his as I turn my face up to kiss him, I reply happily, 'I guess this is me saying yes.'

Epilogue

I like to think that Ben, who's playing Fulham's last match of the season not too many miles away at Craven Cottage, can hear the cheering that rings out round the Redmarsh stadium when the ref blows the whistle on Crawford United's final game. We've known for some weeks that none of the other teams could catch us at the top of the league table, but that doesn't stop the crowd from going bananas.

There's clapping and whooping as Craig comes tearing towards the dugout with the rest of the team in hot pursuit. We flood out onto the grass to meet them, along with all the reserve players, to give everyone bear hugs and high fives. Then, as if by some unspoken understanding, the players gather round to scoop Dad, Cassie and I up into the air above their heads, and I can't stop laughing as the cheers from the stands get even louder – I think it's fair to say we're all having the time of our lives.

Once we've been safely deposited back on the ground, our wonderful team turn and applaud the opposition, making their way back across the pitch to shake their hands and wish them luck for the following season. Although they've missed out on a promotion, they've still finished in the top five so their future looks promising.

But for us, to end the season with a win in front of a four-thousand-strong home crowd, a step up into the league above and enough money in the bank to know the club is guaranteed to survive – and not just survive, but flourish – I can't even describe how incredible it feels. There's such a jumble of emotions – glee, wonder, delight, disbelief. It's overwhelming and extraordinary and I think we all shed a few happy tears.

If I thought I couldn't be any happier, that's proven wrong when Ben walks into The Fox some hours later, his grin as wide as ever. His hair's still wet from the shower and he's wearing a purple cotton sweater, which he tells me he's been saving especially for this evening.

'Congratulations, babe,' he says, sweeping me into an embrace that makes my dad do an exaggerated eye roll. By now he's used to our public displays of affection, but he still pretends he doesn't like it.

'Well done, Mike,' Ben says, holding his hand out to shake Dad's. Then he turns to kiss Cassie on the cheek. 'Looks like you didn't need my help after all,' he says. 'You absolutely smashed it.'

The party is in full flow around us. Our lads will have a few weeks off after tonight, so they're planning to really go for it. And Ben and I have another reason to celebrate – as I spend so much time at the Whitehouse now anyway, he's asked me to move in with him. We've been waiting till he starts his summer break from Fulham so we'll have plenty of time for packing and unpacking boxes. We're even going to order some coloured bed linen, and a shoe rack for the hallway.

It's going to feel quite strange not seeing the players for our usual three-times-a-week meet-ups, but during our conversations about renewing their contracts, not one of them showed any desire to leave Crawford United, so it won't be long before we're all back together. Even Craig, who always seemed to have one eye on a bigger prize, is excited about the challenges being in the new league will bring.

I see a different person in him now to the one who first joined the club. Where there used to be imperiousness, there's now just pride and team spirit. Ben and I have even joined him and Phoebs for a couple of those double dates we once talked about, now I finally understand what she sees in him. She's even calling him her boyfriend these days, after almost a year of one-night stands.

The atmosphere in The Fox is buzzing. It's clear everyone is so proud of what we've achieved together. I lose count of all the kind words, handshakes and back slaps from fans and players alike, and I don't think I'm the only one whose cheeks start aching from the non-stop smiling.

When Olly finally rings the bell for last orders, everyone turns and raises their glass for one last time to me, Dad and Cassie, and three cheers ring out round the pub. I like to think we deserve it – it's been a helluva ride. Then in a final heart-warming moment of the season, as I look round the room at our newfound family, Craig thumps his fist on his chest and kicks off a chorus of 'We're Crawford till we die!'

Acknowledgements

Heartfelt thanks to my ever-patient editor Rachel Hart for your continued belief in me and for your much-needed help in getting this over the finish line. I couldn't have done it without your guidance and encouragement, and your endless enthusiasm will always be greatly appreciated.

Special thanks also to assistant editor Raphaella Demetris, copy editors Helena Newton and Vicknesh Sarveswaran and proofreader Penelope Isaac for helping to knock the manuscript into shape, to my agent Meg Davis for your ongoing support, to designer Ellie Game for a gorgeous cover and to cover illustrator Petra Braun for capturing the characters so perfectly. Thank you also to Maddie Dunne-Kirby for your marketing wizardry.

And a big thank you for the very welcome contributions from everyone else at Avon: Amanda Percival, Emily Gerbner, Jean-Marie Kelly, Sophia Wilhelm, Helen Huthwaite, Sarah Bauer, Amy Baxter, Elisha Lundin and Ella Young. I know I'm very lucky to have such a wonderful team behind me.

Last but not least, thanks to my friend and AFC Wimbledon fan Caron Smith for sharing with me the history of the club that inspired this story.

If you enjoyed *Playing the Field*,
then don't miss this funny, feel-good and
oh-so-steamy read . . .

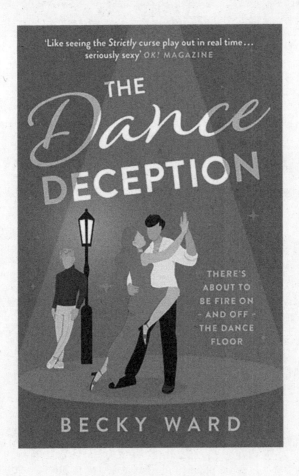

Available now!